Reviewers praise Pam Durban and *The Laughing Place*

"A quiet, richly detailed narrative. . . . Durban's graceful prose and her command of her material enable her to summon up the emotional and physical landscape of Annie Vess's world with a loving particularity that is all the author's own." —Greg Johnson, *Chicago Tribune*

"Ambitious and evocative . . . deeply satisfying, richly textured." —*Christian Science Monitor*

"A deeply felt, remarkably poised work of fiction. . . . A sparkling debut novel, beautifully written and uncommonly wise." —*New York Newsday*

"A robust sense of humor and wealth of small-town observation round out this fine novel about the workings and failings of family." —*The Seattle Times*

"Durban . . . has written a serious novel here, but she has also told her story with good grace and humor." —Valerie Sayers, *The Washington Post Book World*

"Captivating." —*The State* (Columbia, SC)

"Excellent. . . . Through an exceptionally intelligent narrator and prose that is lavish yet precise, Durban creates an absorbing, persuasive story. . . ." —*Cleveland Plain Dealer*

"Beautifully written, wonderfully wise." —*Charlotte Observer*

"A knockout of a first novel—and an impressive piece of work by any standard." —*Atlanta Journal Constitution*

The Laughing Place

Pam Durban

Picador USA
New York

Library of Congress Cataloging-in-Publication Data

Durban, Pam.
    The laughing place / Pam Durban.
        p.   cm.
    ISBN 0-312-13110-0
    1. Family—South Carolina—Fiction.   I. Title.
    [PS3554.U668L38   1995]
    813'.54—dc20
                                                        95-15229
                                                        CIP

First published in the United States by Charles Scribner's Sons

First Picador USA Edition: July 1995
10 9 8 7 6 5 4 3 2 1

This is for Frank, who always believed.

The author would like to thank the following groups and individuals for their support during the years this book was being written:

Fred Busch, sustaining friend. Special thanks.

The members of the Mrs. Giles Whiting Foundation for their generosity in awarding me a Whiting Writer's Award.

Gail Hochman and Barbara Grossman for their patience and encouragement.

My father, who taught me to search title records, and my mother, for her reference skills.

Rick Brown and Liza Nelson for the use of their farm, and Liza for her support and encouragement.

James and Eve Davis; Miranda Hapgood; Deb and Edith Wylder, for their friendship.

Randy Harber for his calm and resourceful solutions to many computer problems.

Dr. Virginia Spencer Carr, chair of the English department at Georgia State University, for her generosity in granting me leaves of absence.

To live in this world
you must be able
to do three things:
to love what is mortal;
to hold it

against your bones knowing
your own life depends on it;
and when the time comes to let it go,
to let it go.
—Mary Oliver, *"In Blackwater Woods"*

T he Laughing Place was nothing but an old brown shack perched up on stilts on the Keowee River side of the bottomland between the Isaqueena and the Keowee rivers, but to hear my father talk, that place stood near the heart of the world. Papa was a lawyer. He never could allow a fact, a place, an event to rest until he'd turned it around and around and commented on every facet and implication of its existence, then snapped it into place in some larger puzzle of space and time and history that he carried in his head. It was as if he wanted to give us a sense of where we lived that was so deep and wide and old, we would never be lost. And so, the Laughing Place was not allowed to be just a shack at the end of a sandy road wide enough for one car to pass, that wound through a forest of sweet gum, scrub oak, and pine. My father taught us how to find that place as though we were navigators, by the stars. In his words, Vaucluse County, South Carolina, which lies on the fall line, one hundred miles inland from the coast, became the shore of the ancient, eastern ocean which had rolled back centuries ago and left its mark on the wind that sounds like surf as it blows through the tops of the pines, and in the air that we breathed, full of old ocean salt.

My father bought the Laughing Place—ten acres and the house—in the winter of 1946, a month after he came home from the war, and on the day he bought it, so the story goes, my mother and father drove out there together and named it after that secret spot where Br'er Rabbit goes to laugh to himself about the foolish old world and all its busyness. In those days many of Mother and Papa's friends owned hunting and fishing camps like the Laughing Place. I remember being hauled to barbecues and fish fries at places like theirs all over Vaucluse County, and in my memory those shacks and cabins all lie at the end of the same sandy road.

Our shack had a steep tin roof and a rickety screen porch across the front, and a sign like a camp sign—dark brown wood and yellow letters that spelled out THE LAUGHING PLACE—hanging from two rusty chains under the porch eaves. The Keowee River ran close to the house, just beyond a line of tulip poplars, and on a summer night you could stand on the back steps and never quite place the steady hurrying *shush* you heard as the sound of the river or the wind in the leaves or your own blood pressing against your eardrums. In summer the woods filled up with whippoorwills and owls, and moonlight spattered down through the leaves, leaving a puzzle of silver and shadows on the ground. In fall, when the last leaves held to the trees along the riverbank, you might catch a rippling glimpse of leaves on water, a rich reflection like red and orange paisley cloth. In winter a slow silver curve of river gleamed through the bare trees.

Every year in early spring the land around the Laughing Place flooded, and we drove out from our house in town to see it. Drove until the road disappeared and there before us stretched a shining field of water where the rows of cotton and soybeans and corn had stood. When the flood rose there was only water and sky: water below and sky above, the sky reflected in the water, and the light from the water rising into the sky. And though it appeared to be still—a shallow silver tray of water held up to the sky—in fact, the water moved. In order to catch its motion, it was necessary to look at something fixed, at tree trunks or blades of new corn, then down, to what pulled and eddied around them.

A week later the water had vanished and left the fields soaked and webbed with dingy, brown foam. Scraps of cloth clung to the

[2]

skeletons of last year's cotton plants, and the fields steamed. From underneath the Laughing Place we raked out sticks, cans, boots, dead fish, a tangle of small branches. Once we found the carcass of a bat with a snarling face, its outspread wings tangled in fishing line as though it had been snared in mid-swoop. Above our heads, grappled by ropes to the undersides of the floor joists, hung a red canoe with battered gunwales. Every year my father tested the knots and exclaimed over that canoe, as though he could care for it again, having found it unmoved by this year's flood; because what my father loved best were the things that did not change.

In photographs of that place, there are always dogs sprawled underneath the house or lying in the faded sun with their heads lifted, their eyes half-closed, and their tongues hanging out. Dogs standing beside men in hunting jackets and boots, men whose shotguns are broken open over their arms, who smile at the dogs, at the heaps of ducks at their feet. In the background of these photographs, black men wait—cooks and dog-handlers dressed in overalls and long-john shirts and caps, standing quietly in the midst of a blur of dogs. My brother Davis went there as a Boy Scout and came back with a paper sack full of the Cherokee arrowheads and bits of pottery that sprouted in the fields after the spring floods receded. He stayed there alone for a few weeks the summer he came home from Vietnam, until one morning Papa got in the car without a word to Mother or me and went out and brought him back to town. Once, a black man who had worked for my father during duck hunting season, escaped from a chain gang, broke a window in the house and hid under a bed until the bloodhounds tracked him there.

Seen up close, my memories of the Laughing Place look random, a mosaic of oddly shaped pieces of old, cloudy glass. Summer or winter, the air in the house stayed cool; it smelled of pipe smoke and old fires, and it gusted out like a cloud when the front door was opened. I remember a single jar of instant coffee that sat for years in an open cupboard above the sink, among a jumble of mismatched dishes and heavy, white cups with chipped rims. The hot-water faucet in the kitchen sink was missing a handle; in its place someone had rigged a pair of pliers. A braided rug with a charred fringe lay on the stone hearth in front of the fireplace. I remember how it was to wake up there in the winter, your whole face numb with cold, and to hear the roar and snap of a fire in the living room.

Those are the pieces of my memories, a child's memories. When I was older, we stopped going there. But seen from a distance, the impressions fill in and collect around my father's dreams and plans for the Laughing Place, until the picture becomes, at last, the grand one my father wished for. In one old photograph he stands on the front steps, his arms spread wide in welcome, the way he dreamed he might have welcomed us there after the world blew up and forced us back together again: Papa, Mother, Davis, and me, a family of shocked survivors with Papa leading us back toward sanity, reason, a restored life.

During World War II, my father led a platoon of infantry against the Japanese in the Pacific. A picture taken in New Guinea by one of his men shows him at the head of a jungle trail carrying a full pack, a rifle in his hand, already half turned away from the photographer, impatient to get on with it. It shows him tall, thin-faced, resolute, a young soldier wearing wire-rimmed glasses and a helmet, whose eyes show no traces yet of the scornful amusement that came to rest in them after the world became a private trove of error laid out for his judgment.

As a soldier, he read maps and pointed the way. He read the terrain and moved his people across it quietly. After the disaster that he imagined would one day destroy the world, he would move us, calling on all of his military training, safely across the dangerous country the world had become, to the Laughing Place, which miraculously had been spared. There, he would remember all he had ever known about survival. He would study the arc of the sun and pace off the garden plot and forage for seeds. He would fish and hunt and drive the wild animals and the panicked human beings away. He would insulate the house with corn shucks and haul wood and keep the pump oiled and primed. He would keep our morale high as he'd done for his men in the Pacific, making sure they changed their socks every day in the jungle, kept their heads down, their rifles loaded and ready as the landing craft approached the beach.

Even when the world righted itself, we would not know or care. We would have discovered that we were happy there with Papa at the Laughing Place; we would be so grateful we would never try to leave again. It was his favorite story, a story of family and home and permanent loyalties. And because I loved him, because I believed him, I believed that what he wanted, what he hoped for, was good.

The Lower New Ground

Mother called at dawn that day. I felt the sound first, something urgent invading my sleep, a drilling deep inside the walls of the house. *Phone's ringing.* It drifted into place among the other facts my senses brought me. *It's dark. Cold. I am curled up, warm. But the bottom of the bed is cold. If I straighten out, my feet will touch cold sheets. Phone's ringing. Phone. In the kitchen. The phone on the kitchen wall is ringing.* I grabbed my bathrobe from the foot of the bed and started down the hall. Four steps and twist the thermostat to rouse the furnace. Three more, then one long step across the bar of light the night-light threw, and I had made it again from night to morning.

As I lifted the receiver toward my ear, a voice spilled from it. "Have I reached Annie Vess?"

Mother's voice, and something was wrong. She'd said my name, and we were past the need for names. Names, greetings, small talk, all these are fine for people who carry on conversations with beginnings and ends. But what Mother and I were having was one long conversation, and we'd been having it since I married Matthew and left home. Days, weeks, months were only pauses—short, breath-catching silences—in this long rush of talk. Who would interrupt such a conversation to say, "By the way, this is your daughter speaking."? It would take a person of very little faith to do such a thing.

"This is your mother calling," she said, as though she regretted having to call herself that name. Her voice seemed to start down in South Carolina and climb all the way to Pennsylvania, losing force with every mile, and when I heard it I stopped trying to push my arm through the sleeve of my bathrobe and stood very still. "Mother?" I said. "You sound tired. Can't you sleep?" It was dark in the kitchen, dark in the house, dark and cold. I could see my breath in the air.

Every night I shut down this house, I pulled shades, drew curtains, latched shutters from the inside so that I could open them one by one and let the light in slowly, when I was ready for morning to come. I lifted one slat of the wooden blind that covered the window beside the phone and looked outside. The sun skimmed the fresh snow at a low angle, it glittered red and green. From this house that Matthew had found for us—an old house made of whitewashed fieldstone that stood on a hilltop—it was possible to see for miles in any direction. "Wait until you see this view," he'd said. "You'll think you're flying." And he'd been right. To see from that hill was to see not the pieces and corners that you glimpse from the road as you drive through a place: a run of fence, the corner of a field, a roof or a window of a house. From our hill, you saw the logic of fences and the spread of fields around houses and barns. To see from that hill was to see the order of things, the way the pieces drew together into something whole.

A thread of white smoke twisted up from the chimney of my closest neighbor's house. It was morning. And cold. The walls breathed it, the floors breathed it. I felt the cold, hard against the bones of my feet. Fieldstone houses are damp and they are cold. I tried to tell Matthew that when we first moved here, but it was summer then, Matthew wanted this house, and once Matthew wanted something, nothing on earth could stop him from going after it.

"Mother?" I said, "are you there?" I covered one foot with the other and fumbled on the shelf over the stove for the box of kitchen matches. I lit one, but as I waited for her to speak, I held it still. And it seemed at that moment that the world had suddenly stopped the way it will during an eclipse, and that in this still, silent world, the only signs of life were the sound of Mother's breathing and the small, ragged sound of the match flame. It burned without wavering and I felt its heat on my face.

"Annie," she said quietly, "I think John's gone."

So. I touched the match to the front burner and watched the blue flame sprout and run around the rim before I set the teakettle down over it. I yanked the shutters open. All around me, gray shapes turned into jars of rice and beans and pasta, the calendar on the refrigerator: my kitchen, my house in Pennsylvania, Monday morning, February 25, 1980. I lifted the pencil that hung by a string beside the calendar and x-ed out the square that set this day apart from other days. It always made me feel that I'd accomplished something, crossing off the day like that, even when I did it first thing in the morning. "Now where, Mother?" I said impatiently, to show her whose side I was going to take, because my mother is like a queen to whom one always brings a gift, a show of loyalty, especially when the subject is Papa. Sometimes Papa called her "Queenie" to mock her. "Queenie??" sounding through the house, searching her out, its pitch composed of equal parts deference and challenge, anger and love.

I draped the phone cord over one shoulder, opened the refrigerator, and slipped a slice of bread out of the wrapper. This is what it will be then, I thought, as my head cleared of sleep. Another long distance breakfast with Mother. I would eat my toast and drink my tea in a kitchen in a house far from Timmons, South Carolina, where Mother sat at the pine plank table in her own kitchen in the house on Wyman Street. As the early light slanted through the pines along the back of the lot and laid a track of morning across the backyard lawn, we would dissect Papa's motives, one more time. The foolish stubbornness that had taken him again, swearing that this time would be the last, to Columbia or to Greenville to try and stop the Corps of Engineers from damming the Isaqueena and Keowee rivers and turning half of Vaucluse County into Lake Charles B. Hartley, Jr.

No doubt, this morning he'd gone out the back door carrying the split-open leather book satchel—his briefcase for twenty years— stuffed full of revised Environmental Impact Statements and petitions for redress of grievances signed by the latest group of landowners he'd enlisted to oppose the lake. He'd kept the satchel for the same reasons that he fought the lake: They were both matters of principle to him. Everything was. And principles were not something you picked up and laid down as it suited you. No, a person's principles held in every area of life, high to low. Principles organized a person's life and made it count for something. So he kept the briefcase because a person held onto things as long as they were useful, no matter how they looked, and he fought the lake because a person ought to keep what belonged to him. And so, through seven years of legal maneuvering, Papa had not given up. He was not known in courts all over the state as a lawyer who gave up. That much was certain. Knowing who he was, how could I not know where he'd gone, or why? Columbia or Greenville, that was where he'd gone. That was where he'd been going for the past seven years. That was why my mother had called.

Out into the morning he went, across the sagging latticework porch that opened off the kitchen. He kicked through the litter of empty Field Trial dog-food sacks there, passed the warped shelves stacked with plastic boxes full of rusted screws and nails and cracked rubber washers. Over one of these shelves he'd hung a map of St. Helena Sound, a mariner's chart, which showed the branchings and windings of the tidal creeks and rivers in that part of the world, the depth of the waterways, the location of shoals and buoys. Here he might pause and study this map, rummage in a box, pick out a rusty screw or nail or washer and contemplate it for a moment with his fingers, then slip it into his pants pocket. He grew up in this house and we moved there after his mother died when I was ten, moved into the clutter that already existed, and started adding our own to it, layer over layer. Now it would take an archaeologist to make sense of that house, someone with an eye trained for piecing the whole pot together out of the shard, the fragment.

The screen door slammed, the steps creaked and bowed. Next door, across the privet hedge in Colonel Stark's backyard, Napoleon and Josephine, the last pointers that Papa and the colonel had raised and trained together, stirred in their run at the sound of his footsteps on the back stairs. "Hello, boys and girls," he called to them, and Napoleon—that idiot—groveled and grinned and peed on himself, trembling with adoration, while Josephine stood calmly and watched Papa drive away, her golden brown eyes never wavering.

"Annie," Mother said, and I heard panic pushing up beneath her voice, searching for an opening, "I looked at him from the door. He's lying so still. Something's wrong. I don't think he's breathing."

I looked at my hand—there was a slice of wheat bread in it— and I almost laughed when I saw it. We were safe. If this were real, I would be doing something more important than standing in the kitchen of a house in Pennsylvania on a winter morning, holding a slice of wheat bread in my hand, while Mother told me that my father had stopped breathing. "Not breathing? What are you talking about?" I said, and I dropped the slice of bread into the trash. I felt the words go out of my mouth, thin and insubstantial. Light—snow-brilliant, clear light—poured in through shutters, not to be kept out, and in this light I saw dust on the slats. I swiped at one and wiped the dust on my bathrobe. I will clean this before I go to work today, I thought. As soon as I get off the phone.

"I'm trying to tell you about John, Annie," she said. "It's bad." Her voice was firm but it was hollow, a voice in a dream in which familiar people speak but their voices are not their voices and their words are the words of strangers. Calm that way, and absolutely wrong. I covered one ear and leaned against the wall. And then, because we were being so calm and dream-reasonable, I said, "Well, now, Mother, are you sure?"

"Don't leave," she said sharply. Then quietly, "Now that you're here, I'm going to go see."

"I'm right here," I said. "Where would I go?" But my lips felt numb and it seemed like miles to the floor. The phone clattered onto the table, then the sound of her footsteps moved off down the hall past the photographs that lined the wall there: Papa in his dress white uniform, Mother in a blur of tulle, ducking as they ran beneath a line of bright, drawn swords held by other young, smiling officers on their wedding day. Me with my arms around Matthew's neck while he holds a glass of champagne over our heads on our wedding day in the living room of that house. My brother, Davis, becoming an Eagle Scout. Grandmother Vess and Grandmother Holt as girls in their high button shoes and wide brimmed hats, their ankles primly crossed. Then the end of the hall and the stairs.

Now, I am not the sort of person who panics easily. In fact, people seem to think of me as being steady and strong and able to bear up under things. Hadn't Matthew counted on it when things got rough? Hadn't Mother said so at the start of every phone call during the seven years that Papa fought the Corps of Engineers? "You are my strength," she would say.

"Mother," I'd say. "What's up?"

"I cannot stand one more day of this." People pestered her, she said. Strangers felt free to stop her *on the street* or in the beauty parlor and deliver their opinions about my father and Save Our Two Rivers, that fight-to-the-death, never-surrender, God-on-our-side group of angry landowners he'd organized to keep the Corps from taking their property and sinking it under twenty feet of water. He had fought them, too; he'd slowed them down at every turn until they were almost three years behind schedule before they even began clearing land for the lake. Every front-page picture in the *Courier-Tribune* of Papa making an angry speech, every report of his latest lost appeal moved my mother closer to the condominium she'd buy for herself down at Hilton Head and the life she'd lead there, a lonely life, but noble in its loneliness, the life of an exiled queen waiting for her country to right itself and welcome her back. Let him take care of himself for awhile and see how he liked it. "Shoot," she'd say, "he can't even boil water."

During those years, it had been exhilarating to sit in my house and look out onto the Arizona desert or the Pennsylvania hills—wherever Matthew and I lived at the time—and to talk to Mother back in South Carolina, to tug her down to earth again out of the thin atmosphere of outrage into which she'd soared. It had nothing and everything to do with my life, and from these places—as close as her voice and as far as the miles between us—these places on the frontiers of distance and intimacy, I could afford to be compassionate. The trick was to find the best angle, the doubt closest to Mother's heart.

"Now, let's just think for a minute, Mother," I'd say. "Who do you know at Hilton Head?"

"Well, nobody," she'd answer, already impatient with me. "But shoot, if you can play bridge, you can always find friends. I tried to tell you that when you went away to school, but you wouldn't listen to me, of course."

"How would you go about finding friends?" I'd ask.

Much exasperated sighing. "Oh, for heaven's sake. People in this part of the world still go to church, you know. There are senior citizens centers everywhere."

"That's true," I said. "They do, and there are."

In the silence that had followed my answer, we both let those visions settle. Mother at the Ladies' Altar Guild, smoothing down the linen altar cloths and filling Christmas baskets for the poor. Mother at the senior citizens center, spunking up the ladies and gents over the tuna casserole. Finally, she sighed. "Oh, well," she said. "I've held on for this long, I might as well hold on a little longer."

"I think you'll be happier in the long run," I'd say. "You've got to think about the long run when this will all be over."

"I guess you're right. I guess I'd just dry up and blow away without his foolishness to contend with. The long run it is."

I could say that then because I believed in long runs, in a life that stretched out, like the rays of the sun, in all directions. As far as you cared to travel, life would open to reveal new possibilities; it would carry you as far as you wanted to go. Or rather, I should say that Matthew and I believed those things, or, more truthfully, Matthew believed, and I believed Matthew.

Beneath the floor there was a click, a whir of gears. The furnace grumbled and warm air rose from the heater vent nearest the stove. *This cannot happen*, I thought. She will find Papa and in two hours I will be at work at Westinghouse Learning Systems. I will flash my ID badge to the guard at the desk and let myself be carried by the crowd down the curving concrete tunnels that led into the underground honeycomb of cubicles and to my desk, where I wrote multiple-choice questions for the learning programs Westinghouse sold. I had worked there for a year on a full-time, temporary basis while Matthew made his way through the graduate program in philosophy at the University of Pittsburgh, one course at a time, and worked as a carpenter framing houses when the weather was good. Lately I had gotten very good at my job, very fast. Third World countries. Consumer economics. Language arts. In a few hours' time I could skim any subject and distill it into five sparkling and lucid questions, which went into booklets with bright covers and were sold in learning units to high schools all over the country.

That fall I had become the wonder of my division with my record-setting pace and my green eyeshade, the kind gamblers wear, that I wore pulled low to filter the glare of the fluorescent lighting. Everyone around me believed that the eyeshade was my way of announcing my individuality the way other people did by decorating their cubicles with posters of Rocky Mountain meadows in full bloom, or by wearing bright socks. They were wrong. I did not care about individuality then. What was individuality? Something light as milkweed silk that protected you from nothing. Something discarded and left behind, like shed skin, for others to hold and remember. Something, then, that caused pain. Better to promise nothing, want nothing, to work, and then close each day like a box and put it away.

And when I left work that afternoon, while I paused at the front door to button my coat, pull on my hat and gloves, and feel my existence slowly gather inside me, drawn down to a point that was as quiet and clear as a star hanging suspended in the cold sky of my body, someone would surely squeeze my elbow or put her hand on my shoulder. "Take care," she would say. "Be strong." Because Matthew was gone. He was dead, is what I mean. And taking care is what I thought I had been doing with my job, my friends, the orderliness and equilibrium of my life. Down the tunnel at eight, up the tunnel at five, with work in between—a wide and empty field of work. Then home to the stone house behind the door I had painted sky blue, the color the old black people in the Low

Country of South Carolina used to paint their doors and windowsills and thresholds, the color a spirit will not cross.

Almost a year ago, it had been evening when Mother called. A Thursday evening in April. April 12. The Sunday before, Matthew had left for Cheraw to help his parents on the farm that had been in the Settles family for four generations. No matter where we lived, Matthew would make his way home sometime during the year. His pilgrimage, we called it, his migration—to turn the garden spot, paint a shed, or help with the cane syrup making or the butchering, to spread the big skirts under the pecan trees and gather the nuts. That Thursday, I had just finished washing my supper dishes and stacking them in the dish drainer next to the sink. The front of my shirt was wet with dishwater and chilly against my skin. I leaned against the sink and looked out of the window at the last light that sloped across the field below our hill. The field was newly plowed and steaming. Flocks of red-winged blackbirds wheeled from furrow to furrow, and a brown dog bumbled over the dark clods, his tongue hanging happily out. I was watching all that when the phone rang.

"Cheraw?" I said to my mother's voice. "What in the world are you doing in Cheraw?"

"Annie," she said, "I have to tell you about Matthew. It's bad news, honey. In fact, it's very bad." Her voice had a terrible force behind it, a blunt tenderness that could not be refused or run from. And it just kept coming, pushing the truth toward me as though truth were the greatest kindness, the essential thing, like water or food or air. While the dog crossed the field, the blackbirds rose and wheeled in clouds from furrow to furrow. That afternoon, she said, Matthew and his father had been clearing underbrush in the lower new ground. Matthew drove the tractor with the bush hog attached. He drove the tractor and mowed the field, and then he looked back over his shoulder, which is something he knew better than to do. Matthew had grown up on a tractor. He knew how a bush hog upset a tractor's balance, and he knew that you had to stay alert to avoid slopes and uneven ground.

But he looked back and he ran up onto a stump, Mother said. The tractor turned over on top of him. We had been married for twelve years, since we were both twenty. We had no children. It wasn't time for children yet. We had each other and we had the whole world that kept opening in front of us as far ahead as we looked.

"Annie," Mother said that night, as though she were trying to slip a message through a closing door, "he never knew what happened and he didn't suffer, it was so sudden." Cremations are sudden, too. We waited—the Settleses and Mother and Papa and Davis and I—in a white chapel in Columbia that had an altar but no cross—while organ music played softly from speakers mounted high on the back walls. Outside, a man moved a sprinkler on the bright green lawn. Three feet to the right, then over to the left. He stepped back, satisfied that the new fan of water the sprinkler threw overlapped the old one just so. I saw the water fall and sparkle on the grass in the sun, but I could not hear it fall. Someone came through the door and handed me a plain, white cardboard box. It was light, and when I took it in my hands, I knew what had happened to Matthew. Annihilation happened, oblivion happened. A bomb went off in my head, a soundless rush of light that rose and blew things to pieces and left the pieces drifting there, suspended in the chaos of their breakup. And that is the day when I felt the power of death move over me. The power to empty, to take everything from you and leave the world intact and unchanged, just to show you that the place where you'd lived so confidently—as though it were the whole world—was in fact so minute a fragment of this larger world that its destruction caused not even a wince, a shudder, or a pause. Since that day, I had been a citizen of this larger, more indifferent world, and once I knew how small I was, I let myself be light as well. After all, it did not matter where I lived or how I passed my time or with whom, and I tried to live as if I were weightless, drifting the way all weightless things will do.

The teakettle shrieked and sent up a jet of steam, so I yanked it off the burner. I sat down on the floor and pulled my feet in close to my body and tried to pull my nightgown down to cover them. Be strong. Outside the kitchen window, the sun was so bright on the snow it made the pointed shadow of the big hemlock beside the kitchen door look crisp, as though it had been snipped from the pure, transparent darkness of a photographic negative.

When I heard Mother's footsteps coming back, I felt like laughing. Her step was quick; it was light, not heavy. Always I had been able to gauge Mother's moods by the sound of her heels on the wide pine floors. This was the way she walked when she was late, hurrying for her purse or keys. And now she was coming to tell me that there'd been a mistake, because it was not possible that Papa was dead anymore than it had once seemed possible that Matthew would ever die or, as it must have seemed impossible to Papa, that the Corps of Engineers would build a dam and flood half the county.

She picked up the phone. "Annie," she said with a terrible, clipped briskness, and then her voice collapsed and a high, strangled sound came out. "Please," she said, "not this."

Then we were both talking. I do not remember what I said. Words came out of my mouth and tried to form questions, but I garbled them all, and Mother's answer was his name, over and over. "John?" she said, tentatively. "*John.*" Angrily.

"Have you looked in the living room, Mother?" I asked. It was a dark room, and there was a wing chair with its back turned to the door, where a person could sit and not be seen. My father liked to sit there in the dark and listen to his old 78 records of Benny Goodman's orchestra, or "You Were There" with Edward R. Murrow. He could hunch down so far in his chair that, from the door, you might believe the room was empty except for the voice of FDR recalling the day of infamy, or the reporter's voice crumbling as the dirigible Hindenburg burst into flames above his head.

Finally I got control of myself, though I trembled so hard I thought I might drop the phone. "Mother," I said, "now listen to me. Are you listening? Go next door. Go to the colonel's and call Doctor Mac. Wait there until he comes. Do you hear me? I'll call you there in five minutes, starting right now." The clock on the kitchen wall read 6:15.

"Doctor Mac?" she said. "You think I should call Doctor Mac?"

"Yes. Yes, call him, Mother, go call him right now." I realized then that we were shouting, as though we called to each other across a crack that had opened in the earth while we slept.

"All right," she said, then slowly, bearing down as though she were writing it on the notepad beside the phone and underlining each word, "Call Doctor Mac."

"Mother," I said. "Listen to me." But the line was empty.

For some reason known only to herself, Mother insisted on riding in the front seat of the limousine with Deke Taylor, one of the Taylor brothers who ran the funeral home. It's just like Mother to do something like that, something so resolutely private it makes everyone a stranger to her motives. After Papa's services, while everyone milled around on the gravel drive outside All Saints Episcopal Church and sorted themselves into cars for the ride to the cemetery, my brother Davis or I would take her by the wrist or the hand or sleeve and steer her toward the back door of the Lincoln. But every time we reached for her, she looked at our hands as though they were some strange, new form of life. Then she'd pry our fingers loose as patiently as if they were sandspurs caught on the sleeve of her jacket, and head for the front door again. Meanwhile, Deke Taylor stood back near the church steps palming a cigarette and frowning at a delegation of anxious-looking robins advancing across the church lawn. And not a word was spoken during all of this, except when Davis bent close to her and said, "Mother, please, everyone's watching." Which wasn't true. In fact, everyone was making a point of not watching.

Now, Mother is big like a draft horse is big: wide through the hips and face and legs, not fine-boned like the Vesses with their high cheekbones and long, thin noses. She strains the seams of whatever she wears. Her hand is broad, blunt, heavy through the knuckles, and when that hand touches you, you know what's meant by it, though it is her eyes that hold you as much as her hands. They are a deep, clear brown with a force within them, a store of something about to be said, that holds you to her words until she is ready to let you go. Finally she took each of us by a wrist and shook them. "Stop snatching at me," she said, and she yanked her short, black jacket down over her hips and adjusted the pin on the jacket's lapel. The pin was a garnet, broad and flat as a mirror and mounted in gold filigree, that my father had given her on the day

I was born. "I'm fine," she said. She looked at us as though we were children again, and really I suppose we were, grabbing at her that way, pretending to be in charge so we could hear her take charge and set things right. Then she climbed into the front seat beside Deke Taylor.

My father would have loved the day of his funeral. Weather was one of his pleasures. When we'd left the church it had been low, February weather with a frosted gray grain running through the air, coloring the morning twilight gray. But as we drove around the courthouse square and out Main Street toward the cemetery, the sky lifted and turned a high, clear blue with clouds like brush strokes of cold vapor streaked across it. Mare's-tail clouds, my father called them. Ice clouds. Each morning Papa got up before the rest of us to eye and smell and feel the morning. He thumped the glass of the barometer that his mother had mounted on the wall beside the back door and watched the needle shift. At the breakfast table, he predicted fair or foul or changing. Of course, for him, the day's weather was not a straightforward case of temperature and barometric pressure and cloud forms and wind speed. For him, the weather was like an enormous script that wrote a mysterious story. Once, I'd seen signs and wonders in the sky, too. No matter where I'd lived, I could walk out under it and feel that everyone I loved was out there somewhere, sheltering under the same sky. But that feeling had died with Matthew. And now my father had slipped out, too. I could search the world and never find him again under this, or any, sky. Perhaps, I thought, it had lifted and cleared to let him pass.

Deke Taylor drove the gray limousine slowly around the circular drive and stopped beside the blue tent, the crowd, the flowers. Mother and Davis and I walked toward the tent with our arms around each other. I watched our feet move over the thin, brown grass and felt the sky above us, pale and emptied now as we moved through the air toward the crowd and the line of metal chairs facing all the flowers. Father Reid stood with his hands folded over his Bible, a small, solemn smile on his face, his white hair combed back to show his fine forehead.

As Deke Taylor steered us to our places in the first row of

chairs, the crowd shifted to let us through. Everyone in town was there, it seemed. All those people who stood around the tent and spilled over across the road, a wall of people holding back eternity into which we'd come to deliver my father. The entire Timmons city council was there, and the members of the old human relations council my father had helped to organize during civil rights days. Senator Charles B. Hartley, Jr., was there, too, and he had ordered the grave blanket of yellow roses that covered my father's casket. He bent and spoke to my mother as we walked by, and she patted his arm and nodded. Across the narrow aisle that separated the rows of chairs, I saw the colonel and my cousin, Melody, and her fiancé, Canady Reeves. The colonel leaned on his cane with both hands and stared at the silver vault, the casket, and the flowers as though they were his enemies. Mel sat up straight in her chair. She looked like visiting royalty in her sunglasses and her wide-brimmed navy hat. As we sat down, she reached up under her sunglasses with a Kleenex to dab at her eyes. Mel had loved my father. When her mother, Charlotte, died when Mel was eighteen, and Big Tom, my mother's brother, her father, moved to Houston, Mel stayed in Timmons. She wanted a whole family, she said, and we were the closest thing to it she could find.

When he caught me staring, Canady nodded, his mouth crimped down in sympathy. For once, he didn't wink, and I nodded back and tried not to look at him again. But he hovered there at the corner of my eye saying, Look, now look again. Isn't there more you want to see? Have you gotten enough of this lazy, bandit's smile; the thick, black hair; the way I fold my arms across my expensive suit and don't leave a crease?

My father never could stand you, I thought, but I felt all stirred up inside anyway, as if bits and pieces of feeling were blowing around like loose leaves blown into turmoil by a gust of wind.

Father Reid began to speak about winter. I matched my palm to Mother's palm, folded my fingers through hers, held on tight as he spoke of the death of plants, the dying of the light, and the waning of the spirit that often accompanies these short, dead days. And then, like a man who has come to a familiar brink, he paused and gathered himself and jumped, gliding on a smooth current of words out of this dead season and over into spring. I thought he looked relieved at the smooth crossing, the soft landing, the way he found himself once again, safe on familiar ground. He held up his Bible and shook it gently. "For we have assurances that spring will come," he said, as he looked at Mother over the top of his half-moon reading glasses. "I am the resurrection and the life," he said. He looked almost cheerful when he said it. Merry is the word that comes to mind, as if he felt it was his duty to be more upbeat than the rest of us, more buoyant, to show that it could be done.

I held one of Mother's hands while Davis held the other, and watched the light come and go. I listened to Father Reid's words because I knew he was trying to bring comfort with his story of the earth that had opened to receive my father as it had opened to take in the dead before John Vess or John Vess's parents or their parents were born. "And yet," he said, "it is this same earth that each year brings forth flowers and leaf buds and new, green grass. How can this be?" he asked, looking brightly at me, and I felt as if I might stand up and answer him. I thought of the box of Matthew's ashes placed in my hands, how light I'd felt since, how small. "Maybe it isn't," I wanted to say. "Maybe you're wrong."

He opened his Bible and the gold-edged pages flashed. "I'd like to read one of John Vess's favorite scriptures," he said. Mother looked up in surprise, then rested her cheek on one hand, squinting at him the way she did when she was trying to figure someone out. "The Lord is my light and my salvation. Whom shall I fear? The Lord is the stronghold of my life; of whom shall I be afraid?" A pause. "We believe this," he said, "and yet, we come to dust. Dust to dust. The way of all flesh." Mother looked down again with a private smile on her face. And yet, and yet. He closed his eyes, squeezed them shut. Imagine with him, he asked, that down in that earth in the place of death, shut away and out of reach of all speech or sight or human grasp, life gathered itself again, and it would rise, opening toward the light, the ever-returning light. Only with the eyes of faith, he said, can we see this.

I looked around then, but there was no earth to be seen, only flowers and the silver casket resting on the undertaker's incorruptible bright-green carpet, and Papa hadn't been to church in at least ten years. He had no favorite scriptures. So those were greenhouse words that Reverend Reed spoke, freed like the greenhouse flowers around us, the sprays of gladioli and mums with their fluttering pastel ribbons, from the season's truths and dangers. What was real was the coffin and Mother's warmth next to me, her profile as thick and solid as an old Toltec warrior's. And the way the wind trifled with Davis's bright hair, and the beauty of his hands that were long and bony and narrow like our father's hands, clasped between his knees.

When Father Reid invited us to join him in prayer, I bowed my head like everyone else, but I didn't pray or think of spring. I studied the way my fingers interlaced with Mother's, and I began to search for something about Papa that I might hold onto to remind myself that his life had branched and grown fuller with each year he'd lived until he came to that hour between midnight and dawn when his heart, so Dr. Mac said, just stopped cold.

I tried to remember my father smiling, expansive, generous in the seven years before his death, but all I could remember was the last Christmas Day we would spend together and the silence while we waited for Papa to begin his Christmas talk, a meditation on the year just past, written in pencil on legal pads in his tall, violent handwriting that sometimes tore the paper. Something you put up with and waited for at the same time. Actually what he told were stories, intricate stories, woven together in such a way that Davis's promotions at the bank in St. Louis where he worked were connected somehow to all the bridge tournaments Mother had won that year and to my travels with Matthew, which had all been connected for the last seven years with Papa's fight with the Corps of Engineers. Somehow the connections all held and brought us each year to this moment, to this table where our lives, for the time, shared a common force, a common purpose.

But that year Papa had sat with his head bowed, no paper in front of him. "Ladies," he said finally. "Son." He pronounced our names the way he sometimes said the names of the accused in court: slowly, clearly, and with knowing malice, as though even their names were evidence against them. Papa wore an ascot (an ascot?) of navy-blue polka dots. There were patches of white stubble on his cheeks where his razor had missed. He folded his hands over his stretched-out cardigan sweater and stared over our heads the way I'd seen him do in court, his eyes moving quickly over some private landscape in the air where the facts of the case were arranged in ways that only he appreciated.

"Does anyone assembled at this table know what they do up there in Rabun Gap, Georgia, where people still have some guts left?" Vess guts, very important. Vess courage. I had almost forgotten that part of the story. All Vesses down through time have been extravagantly, recklessly, brave, beginning with the first Vesses who came up from the coast, following the rivers inland and upland, traveling blind and called by something they'd never seen with their own eyes nor felt under their own feet. Something which they would recognize when they found it by the smell of the air, the look of the place that spoke to the heart through the eyes: home. In the Low Country, they left behind the other branch of the family, those not destined to be heroes, whose history would be only the dreary drone, the repetitive catalog, the endless minutiae of merchants, ship's chandlers, mumbling in their narrow shop beside the spools of anchor rope that spoke of depths they could never plumb, oceans they would never cross. They were not heroes, that much is clear; they were the outfitters of heroes.

At the other end of the table, Mother sat perfectly still with her head cocked to one side as though she were waiting for a sound to repeat so that she could identify it. I listened, too; I looked. When Matthew died, the coroner said that the injury to his head was so subtle they'd needed X rays to locate the fracture in his skull that had killed him. That Christmas Day, I felt as if I were looking for a fracture. The fracture was there but it was impossible to locate; it was a web of fractures, really—hairline cracks that had weakened the whole vessel so that a tap in the right spot would reduce it to powder.

Papa looked at me, then at Davis; when he came to Mother, he waited, and she stared back at him strongly. What passed between them I had not seen before. He stared at her as if he wanted to take her in his hands and break her, and she stared back as if she were taunting him, just out of reach. Finally she sighed, "What's that, John?" she said, without enthusiasm, as if this were a long, rehearsed scene of which she'd grown tired.

"When the government comes in there trying to push them around, they take matters into their own hands, by God," he said. "That's what they do. When the federal government tried to close off access to the Chattooga River, why, they just went in there and set fire to the woods." He looked among us as though he were opening doors, looking into familiar rooms, finding each one empty. "They'd rather destroy it, you see, then give it up that way. They say no more and they say it in a language even the damn government understands." *Smack.* He struck the table so hard with his palm that the goblets jumped and water splashed onto the tablecloth, Grandmother Vess's silver chimed, the flames of the tall, white tapers in their silver candlesticks staggered, recovered, burned steady again. Davis chewed and swallowed quickly, as if he were afraid someone might catch him at it and stop him.

Of course, Mother could not have let this go by. She looked at Papa as though she were seeing God or a pygmy for the first time. Color spread up from her throat and made red blotches on her face, and she seemed to swell. Her people's courage, Holt courage, is different from Vess courage; it is of the earth, not of the mountain-top or the judge's bench, as Mother was fond of reminding us. It is the kind of courage that working people, Bibb Mills people from Covington, Georgia, must have. It is the courage to do what must be done and to get up the next day and do it again. It is more volatile, too, this courage, Mother likes to say with a definite nod, a dangerous look, drawn up to her full height, her coppery hair blazing. It is flammable as fat wood that bursts all at once into flame. "Well," she said, "that is just plain pointless, if you ask me, John, cutting off your nose to spite your face like that."

You can always count on Mother to lay it out the way she sees it. That is the help she brings. She went back to Pennsylvania with me after Matthew died and she stayed for a month, helping me to sort out his things. She guided me through each day with the same kind of forceful tenderness with which she'd told me he was dead, as though she were seeing me through an illness whose course she knew, and knew when I must keep moving and when it was safe to rest. In her hands, Matthew's possessions took on a clarity that I might have missed on my own. Of course, I thought, that must be given away, that should be kept. But Papa just smiled at her and the smile soured on his mouth. "Maybe so, Louise," he said. "Maybe so."

Then there was an awful stillness. Davis's fork made no sound against his plate, and the candle flames burned clear and steady while Papa looked at each of us, and one by one we looked away.

Once, when I was a child, not long after we moved into Grandmother Vess's house, a hurricane veered inland from the coast and swooped down onto Timmons. Papa herded us into the basement and for hours we sat there, wedged in between shelves of canned tomatoes and beans and pickled peaches, while the wind rose outside, the big pines around the house moaned and broke with a boom like cannons firing, and the rushing, tearing sound of wind was everywhere. Rain streamed down the small, ground-level windows and their frames hummed in the wind. The weather stripping under the door buzzed, and I felt the house give when a strong gust of wind leaned against it. Then it subsided, and then it stopped dead still, and Papa said we were in the eye of the storm. The other side, he said, would be worse. The eye of the storm. I imagined us adrift in a small boat, crossing a swirling cloud of gas and dust. We had gone so far into this crossing that we had lost sight of either side, yet he knew the way. He kept one hand on Davis's shoulder and one on mine, while Mother sat behind him on a peach crate with her head resting against his back, humming "Begin the Beguine" over and over.

We sat there through an hour of quiet while the sun came out and shone through the basement windows, and outside, birds began to sing. We begged to go out, but Papa wasn't fooled. The storm had conspired with its sudden quiet to lull us into complacency, but he was wise to this trick, his was the insider's knowledge of the danger below the calm that might have lured us out, and so he made us wait until the other side broke over us and all the storm had passed. The air, when we finally came up from the basement, was clear as a mirror and everything shone: the downed pine limbs with their gleaming needles, the split golden-yellow hearts of pine, the grass, everything gleamed. But even now, what I remember most clearly of that afternoon is not the rushing, tearing sounds of the wind, or the crashing of limbs, or even the gleam of the world when we came up into it again, but the absolute stillness, the quiet of the lull, while we waited for the other side of the storm to break against us.

Finally, Mother threw her napkin onto the table. "Why can't you count your blessings, John?" she said. "It could be worse, you know. They could be building something nuclear. We've got a lot of those around here now. There's that Savannah River place down at Aiken. They say they'll never clean up that mess. There's Barnwell where they're going to dump all that radioactive garbage. And how about Keowee-Toxaway? Think about those places and be grateful. This is only a lake, for God's sake." Her cheeks were red, as though she'd scrubbed them with a coarse washcloth. "I guess I'm just too dumb to be anything but thankful for what I've got," she said. "I guess that comes from growing up without having everything handed to me on a silver platter."

I looked at Davis, Davis looked at me. I thought he shook his head. *Don't do it.* Of the two of us, I'm the one who would always speak up to Papa. Davis, though he is a year younger than I, has always been about a century wiser when it comes to self-preservation. Once he'd left Timmons to go to college, he only came back for holidays sometimes, and once for the summer, the year he returned from his tour of duty in Vietnam. For three months before he got the job at the bank in St. Louis, he lay up in his room all day reading news magazines. Or he would tinker half the night with a red Harley-Davidson he'd bought in California after his discharge from the army and driven across the country. That summer, he lived in the house asking nothing but food and a place to sleep, like one of those children who have been raised by wolves and must be introduced, gently, to the fundamentals of human contact—touch first, then trust, and only later speech and desire.

But I couldn't stop myself. "Well, it seems to me," I said, "that regardless of what happened up in Rabun Gap, you've made your try here, Papa, and it was a good one, it was the best one you could make, and now it's time to go on. What I mean is, don't you think that it's time for a different kind of courage, Papa?" I asked. He chuckled, indulging me the way you might indulge a child's long, pointless story. "Well," I said, going on without conviction, "you talk a lot about courage, but aren't there other ways to be brave than falling on your sword or burning up what's left of this place?"

"Amen," Mother said, so quietly I might have been the only one who heard. Then she had more to say. "I like that," she said, narrowing her eyes at me as though she were appraising something. "*Falling on your sword*, that's very good." She reached over and patted my arm and looked at him defiantly. *There.* Her eyes shone, and the old hungry look was in them. "Listen to your daughter, John," she pointed her fork at him. "Change is what keeps you young."

"That's not what I meant," I said, and I looked down at my plate.

Then the willed patience was back in his voice. "I know you wouldn't be so quick to say that if you really understood, Annie," he said. "I know that things have been hard for you here these last few years. You can't be expected to really dig in and come to a clear understanding of the history and implications of this thing."

An answer came to me then, and just like that the rage was back, quick as a flame that burns instantly blue, taking me by surprise. After Matthew died, when the numbness left me, it would happen this way. Stalled in traffic, detained in the lunch line at work, or waiting for a long-distance call to connect, without warning the rage would come up in me, sudden and sharp, a blade of anger in the middle of my body. I'd thought I was done with that, and spoke without thinking. "Understand?" I said, in a way that made Mother's eyes widen in alarm. "What exactly is it you want me to understand, Papa?"

He gave me a startled, twisted look and Mother said, "Why, John, look at you, you didn't get any dressing." She stood up suddenly and took his plate and served up a scoop of dressing from the dish on the sideboard. She pressed a little depression in the top with the back of the spoon and filled it with giblet gravy. Then she set the plate down in front of him and waited, with a hand resting on his shoulder until he picked up his fork like a dutiful child and began to eat. We all began to eat again.

But the rage did not subside. It kept on chattering and dancing, blurting out its story. Let me tell you, Papa, it said, what I understand. Let me tell you how I am no longer opaque the way people seem to be, about how I have become transparent, how I extract the sadness from whatever I see and suck it in through my pores, the marrow of my bones, up the hollow shafts of my hair. I watched my father; I will remember that moment as long as I live. The thin, winter light came in over his shoulders. It shone around him, it seemed to shine through him, it shone on the silver white of his hair, his fierce, beaked face, the military set of his shoulders. In that light he looked brittle, as though all yielding had been burned out of him to expose a hard, bitter substance, glassy and friable as mica, of which he was made.

That is when Davis bolted. He slapped down his napkin. "Excuse me," he said. "I'm going to do some work now. Mother, thank you for dinner. Annie, John." He bowed to each of us, holding his tie against his chest to keep the tip from dragging in the gravy boat. If my father noticed that Davis had called him by his first name, he gave no sign. If Papa had jumped up and ordered him back, Davis would have kept right on walking. Davis has never been one who could put up for long, he says, with all that family bullshit, and there is something in my brother that has given up backward looks. He is a soldier crossing enemy territory, his senses trained on the ground where his next step will fall, the way out of danger.

So Davis left, but Papa went on with his story. The story of the lake, the lies, the sellouts and betrayals that Mother and I stayed to hear. He was like one of the archaeologists from the University of South Carolina who'd come down to the bed of the lake, to the site of the Cherokee village, trying to uncover some artifact important enough to stop the lake. All day they would brush at the sand

and the clay with brushes so fine and small it would break your heart to see them; by dark they would have uncovered the rim of a broken pot.

Everywhere, everywhere, all the time, all over this country, he said, the federal government is watching, like a giant eye that never closes. Searching out wild and intractable places, looking for whatever moves to unpredictable rhythms. In Vaucluse County, this eye spotted the Keowee and the Isaqueena Rivers and the land between the two rivers—twenty miles of rich bottomland planted in fields of millet and sorghum and beans and corn, with peach orchards and pecan groves and a few small places, like Little Awando, standing on the margins of the land out of reach of the flood. Because the rivers flooded every spring, that was their crime, that was what caught the attention of the giant eye, and that was the genesis (if it could be dignified with that name) of Lake Charles B. Hartley, Jr. The Flood Control Act of 1966, sponsored by none other than our illustrious Senator Hartley, and the Army Corps of Engineers was summoned to discipline the river's whims, and after that it was all eminent domain and treachery, arrogance and sorrow.

This story was about revised Environmental Impact Statements, the rights of the upper and lower riparians, and the trickery that had subverted those rights. Papa numbered all the pieces until he came to the oxygen—the last, best hope, evil in its simplicity. An aeration study he'd commissioned had shown that damming the Isaqueena and the Keowee to create Lake Charles B. Hartley, Jr., would deprive the streams and rivers below the lake of oxygen. For a long time, he'd believed the oxygen would save them. Now, he picked through the wreckage of that hope until it failed him again, with an old man's fastidiousness, an old man's rancor at the failure of the past to keep its promises. "And when they finished with us, they tossed us a bone," he said, and I knew the story was about to end. His faith was gone; what was left were the powdery ridges and the lower sandy miles, land good for nothing except what thrives on nothing. For sandspurs, broom sedge, scrub oak, and twisted yellow pine. For kudzu, blackberry vine, and jasmine. Land so poor a copperhead would have to carry lunch to crawl across it.

But not everyone was suffering. Oh, no. Some thrived. Southland

Timber Company loved the good pine land the county had turned into. They were buying it up as fast as it came on the market. Acres of hot, glaring, sandy flats, perfect for growing pines for the pulp mills down in Charleston. And right here in Timmons, every n'er-do-well in town had found his calling at last. They'd all opened real estate offices and they were putting up developments with names like Whippoorwill Cove and Panorama Shores faster than the poor have children. Our own Canady Reeves among them. You could hear them any day of the week now, shouting their good fortune to one another across the courthouse square, shaking hands and closing deals in the First Commercial Bank, hitching up their pants as they paid the check at the Steakhouse, and giving the toothpick dispenser an extra tap just to show they were prospering. Before long, Papa said, mark his words, every jackleg developer would be running for public office.

I twirled the stem of my water glass and watched his face, taking it in. Now came the part of the story where he named what had been lost. Breezy Hill and Chimebell Church Road. All the houses along those roads had been pushed into their foundations and bulldozed over. Storm Branch and Indian Ground. Big Branch and Little Branch. Mt. Figuration and Welcome Traveller churches. Givens, Huttoes, and Grady's Ponds, and Yonces Mill. Gone. And the Laughing Place. They had come with a bulldozer one day and pushed it over, too, he'd watched it fall into itself like a house of cards. How many times had we heard that story? "They're even moving the cemeteries, Annie," he said. "Or rather, I should say, they have moved the graves with legible headstones or the graves of those who had relatives to claim them. Those without either will be fifty feet underwater soon."

Finally I could not stand it anymore, this silent listening. "Papa," I began, "it's a terrible time, I know." And then I stopped. I'd wanted to say more. I'd wanted to say that maybe people could give one another something more than laments and ruined maps. I'd wanted to say that what we might give as well were our stories about how we'd come through terrible times, or our maps that showed the paths we'd cut across this wilderness of trouble. But I wasn't strong enough to say it all then. He gripped my wrist because he had more to tell. What I'd said might have been a pebble tossed into a river. His talk flowed over me and on, and then we were sitting on cold metal chairs under the bright blue tent while Reverend Reid spoke the words that committed Papa's body to the earth and left his spirit to wade and wander through the universe until it found a home that was unspoiled enough to give it peace, rest, ease. Everyone around me said, "Amen," but I did not because I had not prayed.

Ballast

Davis went back to St. Louis, and for two weeks the house stayed crammed with funeral flowers. They tipped over in corners, shed their petals and leaves onto the dining room sideboard. Every mirror, upstairs or down, reflected ferns dried to brown powder and yellow mums that curled in on themselves and gladioli collapsing against their stalks. Mother and I stepped around them, squeezed past them, and tracked brown fern dust all over the house. By the end of the second week, only the fragrance of gardenias lingered, though the fragile white flowers had been the first to die. By day the smell of gardenias hid in the curtains and carpet threads, but at night it slipped free and filled the house. One night I woke up suddenly, and it seemed that even the moonlight that fell in broad white stripes across the floor of my bedroom smelled of that sweet, white flower, a blossom unfolding petal by petal, filling the air with its fragrance until I imagined that the house floated in it and that from the windows Mother's face and mine looked out, mouthing "Help," waiting for rescue.

The next morning, before Mother was awake, I gathered up the dead flowers and carried them out to the garbage cans in the backyard, behind the stand of bamboo that Papa had planted years earlier to screen the cans from sight. I made two trips, but on the third, as I was carrying out the last load, I noticed the weather and felt afraid. Overnight, it seemed, spring was coming, a warm current smuggled in on the underside of the cool March air. I could see my breath, and it was too cold to be out in a nightgown, but the tips of the hickory branches closest to the sky had swelled and turned pearly green, and the air had a silty smell. The winter in which my father had died was ending. I hurried back inside and followed the sound of the vacuum cleaner into the dining room. Mother was dressed for work—tennis shoes, a tired navy wraparound skirt, an Icelandic sweater broken through at the elbows—vacuuming up the last of the brown flower dust off of the ancient red Oriental carpet, and on the table there were stacks of heavy, cream notecards, two fountain pens and bottles of black ink, a roll of stamps, and a list of names. "Time to do our thank-you notes," she yelled over the roar of the upright. Then she shut it off and dragged it out of the room back to the hall closet.

This house was built to confound heat, long before the coming of central air, as if the heat were alive and had to be outwitted. It sat back from the street on a shady lot, and a deep porch wrapped around the front and sides of the first story. Double screen doors closed across the front door, which was recessed, too, making a pocket of air between the two doors to trap the heat before it could slip inside. Old photographs of the house in its prime show a sunny, welcoming place surrounded by trellises and arbors and young camellias. But over the years, as the camellias grew into trees that crowded up under the eaves of the porch, and bamboo invaded the front yard, the house took on a secretive, hulking look, as though it had burrowed deeper into the lot and was crouched there, hiding.

Inside there were high ceilings and narrow windows that my grandmother opened at night to let in what cool air there was to be let in, and closed during the day to keep it there. Still, the heat slipped past all these baffles, and the house soaked it up like a wick. Every summer for seventy years, it steeped in heat and humidity that softened the finish on tables and chairs and turned the paint sticky on cabinets and woodwork. The heat even crept into the dining room china closet, and mold ran up the mended cracks in dinner plates and china cups. Upstairs, on summer nights, an attic fan thundered constantly, though on the hottest night it only dragged heavy curtains of hot air through every upstairs room. Even now, after ten years of central air conditioning and paint and dry wall and Mother's potpourris—rose petals, cloves, and orange peel set out in bowls in every room—the house still breathed out what it had breathed in all those years. Candle wax and pine, furniture polish and spice and bacon, and underneath it all a moldy, swamp smell—cloudy, lush, and edged with rot.

Of all the rooms in that big, dim house, the dining room was the dimmest, the coolest, the only place to be on a hot, still day. My grandmother had hung the sheer curtains behind the tired, wine-velvet drapes. It was she who drew them across the window at the end of the room, where they blurred and softened the light, and they had never been drawn back since. The long, oval, mahogany table with its twelve chairs occupied most of the room, and in the center of the table sat a silver bowl full of wax fruit and two glass candlesticks hung with crystals in which there were always two white candles. On the matching sideboard under the gilt-framed mirror, there was a silver service on a silver tray, and to each side of the mirror, portraits of Great-great-grandmother and -grandfather Vess. To each side of the portraits hung old-fashioned wall sconces that threw sour, yellow fans of light up the cracked, plaster walls. Since the funeral, without talking about it, we'd eaten all our meals here, sitting in our usual places across the table from each other, with Papa's coffee-stained place mat still at his place at the head of the table.

That day, I sat down in my chair on one side of the table and looked at the list. Time to do our thank-you notes. Catherine (Mrs. Buck) Henderson—pot of yellow mums, squash casserole. Miss Ruth Ashley—camellias, crab bisque. Eulalie and Jenny Hanks—dish garden, pineapple upside-down cake. Thelma Reece—gladiolus spray, ham. Four pages of names, single spaced. I hadn't written a thank-you note in years, not since Matthew and I had gotten married. Thank-you notes were part of the old world of obligation that Matthew and I were leaving behind. I had not even written any notes after

Matthew died. In one of those talks you have about everything you believe and want and hope for, Matthew and I had both decided that when we died we wanted no funerals, no flowers. We would leave this world, we promised one another, as simply as we'd come into it. Right after he died I held onto that promise, and I insisted. And so he'd been cremated, and what flowers and food there had been—sent by relatives and old country neighbors of the Settleses who could not imagine a death without flowers or grasp the logistics of sending flowers all the way to Pennsylvania—had gone to the Settleses' house in Cheraw. And Matthew's mother had written what notes there were to write.

As she pulled her chair up to the head of the table and put on her half-moon reading glasses and filled her pen and picked up the list, I watched Mother for clues. Finding none, I said, "I don't know how to do this, Mother," I said. "How do I start?"

"Have you forgotten how to write a letter?" she said, already writing. "You just thank people for what they did for us," she said, "and you tell them how highly Daddy thought of them."

So that was all there was to it. It was a relief to find something that simple. I picked up the first piece of paper and filled my pen. I looked at the first name on the list. Miss Ruth Ashley. Camellias. Mother's head was bent, she wrote swiftly, tipping her head back and forth as she wrote, admiring her work. Miss Ruth Ashley. I closed my eyes, reached back. There was the smell of lavender cologne; a thin, severe woman with brown hair; a fat chihuahua with bulging eyes; a small, neat greenhouse where my father and Miss Ruth Ashley worked at hybridizing camellias. They slipped one stem into another, wound the stems tightly, wrapped them in plastic and burlap, and set them on a shelf close to the glass. They treated one another with an elaborate and stylized formality, calling each other Miss Ashley, Mr. Vess. And once, when the wrapping came off and the graft had taken, the shoot grew into a new camellia, clear white with bold red streaks running through the petals. Mr. John Vess, they named it. That is what Miss Ruth Ashley had sent. A bowl of them, floating in water. "Dear Miss Ashley," I wrote. "You may not remember me as the child who tagged along with my father on those

Saturday mornings when he came to your greenhouse to work, but I remember those mornings well and fondly. My father always said that you knew more about camellias than anyone in the state."

Whenever I looked up, it seemed that the eyes of my great-great-grandparents watched from their portraits that hung on the wall to either side of the gilt-framed mirror above the sideboard. *What are you writing?* they seemed to ask, craning and peering suspiciously. Seddell Palmer Vess watched—a seasick expression on his long, bony face, a palmetto cockade pinned to his tri-cornered hat, a sailing ship in the background. Elizabeth Hardee Vess watched ("Har-DEE," as it is pronounced in the South Carolina Low Country from which they came), mildly aggrieved at what she saw. It was the same look of mild and haughty disapproval that had traveled down the generations and lodged in my grandmother Vess's eyes, and in my father's and in my own if I surprised my reflection in a mirror. A look that said that whatever they were watching was less than it should have been, but what could you expect, people being who they were?

Now, I know that people like to claim that the eyes in their family portraits follow them around the room. It gives you a way to lift your history above the ordinary and touch it with glints of supernatural power. But in this case, it was literally true. The eyes of Seddell and Elizabeth Vess seemed to look everywhere because their portraits had been painted by a clumsy painter who had no sense of perspective or proportion. Their eyes had been painted on either side of their heads, like the eyes of insects or fish, and so they seemed to be looking at once in all directions. But the distortions did not end with their faces. Elizabeth Hardee Vess's fingers looked eerily long, spindled on the head of a brown and white spaniel as though she were screwing the head onto the dog's body. In the background of her portrait, if the space behind her can be called that (everything in these paintings exists on the same plane—so small as to be almost incomprehensible as human figures), three children play in front of a dark forest wall. In the air above Seddell Vess's right shoulder, as deserted and ghostly as the Ancient Mariner's ship, sails the ship that brought him and his family from England.

The effect is dreamlike and modern, as though the painter had distorted his subjects deliberately in order to make a point about alienation and distance.

As it turned out, the painter had been no colonial prodigy, only a man with no experience at portrait painting, desperate to feed his family, whose knowledge of perspective stopped at the foreground. These had been his first portraits, and though he struggled half a year with the paintings, he was never paid a penny for his work. The portraits, however, had been passed down reverently, their oddness triumphed over, turned to proof finally of the Vesses' standing in the colony, while the story of the painter cheated out of his money grew into a fable about the admirable rectitude of these early Vesses.

I had laughed about them all my life—their warped, spooky figures and the fantastic stories that had grown up to dignify these distortions—but as I looked at them and wrote the thank-you notes, it seemed that I saw something else about them. I saw that beneath that warped surface of which so much had been made in this family, so much fun and so much snobbish boasting, they were people once, they were mortals. They might have once sat grieving on a day just like this one for the two children they lost during their first year in the New World. I have seen their children's graves down near Beaufort: two girls, Elizabeth and Amelia, who died within a week of each other in the autumn of 1798. They might have stood beside their daughters' graves and felt their mortality as a truth for the first time in their lives. Because mortality is not something you can know until it touches you, until you see that it's not something that happens to you, it's something you are. And knowing that is like being let in on a secret about everyone else in the world as well.

The best notes, I read to Mother. "Dear Fanny and Charles," I wrote one day. "We thank you for the beautiful pot of mums you sent to the house and for the ham. My father always spoke highly of you both and valued your friendship. He especially enjoyed coming out to your place every year for pecans. He always said that your trees grew the sweetest pecans in the county." As I wrote that, I remembered: They were long, smooth pecans, their shells a light and creamy brown, and they almost always slipped from the shell whole. As she listened, Mother capped her pen and folded her hands on the table, her chin high, her eyes bright and moving, as though she were watching Fannie and Charles Gregorie on their farm on the Stamp Creek Road, the collapsing equipment sheds, the shaggy pony standing in grass up to his withers, the mean rooster we dodged as we crossed the yard toward the sheds, and the long, vaulted aisles of the pecan grove. "Oh, honey," she said when I'd finished, "that's just beautiful."

And then she'd read one to me. "Dear Sara, Thank you so much for the beautiful spray of glads that you sent for John's funeral. I think about what good friends we all were. Remember the times we went square dancing together on Saturday nights? I was looking through some pictures the other day and I saw us in those funny skirts and cowgirl blouses. They were a sight, weren't they? And didn't the men look handsome in their spangled shirts? It's hard to believe that John and DeLeon are both gone now and that we must go on without them."

"You did go dancing, didn't you?" I said.

"Almost every Saturday night. Do you remember that?"

"I remember how pretty you looked in that red taffeta skirt with all the sequins on it. I thought you looked like a gypsy. And I remember sitting on the floor with Davis back in you-all's room eating popcorn and watching Jackie Gleason on TV while Penny sat in a straight-backed chair in the middle of the doorway. She looked so grim, I always thought you'd told her not to let us out of that room."

"You remember all that?"

"Right now I do."

With each note I felt calmer, clearer. The world might be all flux and whirl, but I had found a place that was still, and in this place I knew who I was and who I had been. Because home is the place where things come back to you, I thought. I wrote my father's name, connected it with other names, conjured his presence in the room, kept him close a while longer, the way he had always been.

By the end of the week, we'd written 150 thank-you notes; I

kept a tally on one of Mother's bridge scorepads. And then, three weeks to the day after Papa's funeral, I took the last batch down to the post office. When the door to the metal mailbox clanked shut and I heard the envelopes hit and scatter in the bottom, I felt the way I'd felt standing on the top step at home holding the last load of flowers from my father's funeral. Just exactly like some timid animal, I thought, caught out in the open and panicking, looking for the closest cover. It made me so angry to feel that way that I drove the long way home, all the way around the bypass and back. I even made myself turn onto a road I didn't know and find my way home from there, just for practice. Still, after I'd gotten home and eased Mother's car into the space in the garage, where it just fits between the stacks of cast-off chairs and towers of old, clay flower-pots that have accumulated over the years, and started for the house, I felt that same sense. What now? What next? And silence where an answer should have been.

Luckily Mother had the answer, as she seemed to have the answers to so many questions I hadn't even asked. When I got back from the post office, she was waiting on the back porch. "Good, you're back," she said as I started up the steps.

The back porch used to be a sleeping porch, screened above and latticed below, where my father and his brother, Stovall, had slept in hot weather. It was, my father always said, a wonderful place to sleep: cool, open, out under the stars. They had slept there the night before Stovall left for Europe during World War II, where he was killed on a parachute jump into France. My father had slept there the night before his wedding. Since we'd lived in the house, it had been Papa's porch, strictly his. There he'd collected every-thing that Mother banished from the house: dog things and hunting things, oily things and boyhood things. Sometimes he still slept there on hot, summer nights or on cool nights when only he and Mother knew the reason, on a narrow army surplus bed with the army blanket tucked in tight. Coming in from a date, I would some-times find him stretched out there with all his clothes on, his hands behind his head, looking out into the night sky. "Hello, Champ," he'd say. "Papa," I'd answer, and hurry on into the kitchen, anxious to allow him (and myself) the dignity of pretending that his being there was the most natural thing in the world. It was the last place I'd imagined him alive on the morning Mother had called, and all his things were still there: the map and the dog-food sacks, the rusted lengths of chain and the bed stripped of its sheets and blankets now, with the mattress rolled up and tied with string, still showing the rusted marks of the mesh that had supported it.

"Come help me get these old birds out of here," she said as she unlatched the screen door and swung it open. She slipped off the Vess diamond, the gold wedding band, and pocketed them. Without looking, she felt for the key that hung from a nail by a piece of jute twine on one of the uprights and lifted the lid of the freezer chest that sat against the back wall. A cloud of cold steam rose from inside the chest, smelling faintly of blood, and she stepped back, fanning it away from her face.

Down in the basement, a larger freezer held vegetables and meat and ice cream, but this one was Papa's, and it was full of the birds he hunted every fall. Ten years worth of frozen dove and quail. Now she wanted to get rid of them.

"Why throw them out, Mother?" I said, keeping my voice calm. "They're frozen, they'll keep."

She looked at me as though I were being willfully, stubbornly dense. "Because I never liked them anyway," she said. "And I need this freezer for other things."

"What things?" I bit my lip as soon as the words left my mouth. The question defeated her. I had forgotten that too, the way you go forward again after you lose someone you love, moving carefully, your hands out in front of you. Balance is all. Momentum. And if someone stops you, says, "Look down," you see where you are and you fall.

"Well, I just might like to freeze some fruit this summer," she said, her chin trembling, her eyes full of warnings.

"I'll get a garbage bag," I said.

It is comforting to think that death makes you meek and gentle, that it breaks and humbles you. It changes you, all right. It makes you fierce, it makes you itch to avenge yourself on the person who has done this. But where is he? Come back here, coward, you say. All right, I thought, as I rummaged in the pantry for the box of garbage bags, this is revenge, I understand revenge. After Matthew died I sat down one night to fold his jackets that I was going to give to the Salvation Army. Instead I found a ripped seam on the sleeve of one jacket and I worked it open with my finger. The thread gave, the sleeve fell open, a miracle of ease. I got out my scissors and began to cut the threads that held Matthew's jackets together, but scissors were too clumsy and the work went too fast. So I got out my seam ripper and began to rip the thread out stitch by stitch. I ripped pockets, collars. It's amazing how intricately clothing is put together. When I was done with the jackets, I started on his pants, then his shirts. I worked most of the night, and when I was done, Matthew's clothes were laid out around the chair like hides, and I felt drained and peaceful, not angry any longer. If he came back, I thought, he would have nothing to wear.

Mother came up from the freezer with frost on the arms of her sweater and a freezer bag in each hand. She held them up and shook them. Inside, the frozen birds—icy feathers, claws, beaks, and pale, scaly-lidded eyes—shifted in their nests of frost. Without a word, she held them out to me, her mouth grim. "Look at this," she said. "He didn't know any more about freezing things than a man in the moon," she said as she dropped two frozen birds into the garbage bag that I held open at my feet. Then she stood on tiptoe again and plunged back into the freezer chest.

"These birds aren't plucked, Mother," I said, and I heard my own twelve-year-old voice speaking to her, protecting my father, accusing her of neglect.

"Well, don't blame me," she said from inside the freezer chest. "I just put my foot down finally. I told him, 'I'm not going to pick those things for you any longer, John, or clean fish, either one. You want to bring dead animals into this house, you're responsible for them.' " She came up then with frost on her hair, holding an armful of freezer bags stacked on top of one another. "You know what John's biggest problem was?" she said, steadying the bags close to her chest.

"What, Mother?" I said, though she wasn't talking to me, not to me personally. She was talking to someone listening, to an ear down which she could pour her grievances until they filled up head and heart. And I felt a sudden loss of altitude inside, the way I'd always felt, taken aside by each of them and loaded up with their disappointments with each other. Had I ever imagined them happy? Of all the bewildering things that had happened since my father died, this was the worst, the way her memories of him were hard, not soft, as if what she had to keep telling herself was how impossible he was.

"His mother babied him until the day she died," she said, her eyes clouded with fury, her mouth stubborn and sharp as a turtle's beak. She was working furiously now, throwing the frozen birds into the bag so hard they clattered like stones. The bag was cold against my legs and already the birds had begun to thaw. The frost had melted inside some of the bags, leaving the birds looking puckered and dull. "Do you know what she told me just before she died? She said, 'John's a good boy. He always loved his mother best.' Can you imagine? Well, after she died I broke the news to him. 'Time to grow up, John,' " she nodded sharply, stabbing with her chin and dumping an armful into the bag I was holding. The whole mess landed on my foot and I felt tears come up in my eyes. Seeing them, Mother's tone softened. "You see, he thought he could do anything he wanted and everyone would love him for it," she said, holding up a freezer bag by the corner. Then she looked at what was in her arms and her face was the face of someone on a ledge who finally looks down. "Oh," she said in a thin voice, and I saw that in the bag she was holding, the one from the bottom of the freezer, the birds lay together, smooth and white, not a feather on them. She smoothed out the bag on top as tenderly as if she were stroking a baby's head. "Of course, I did it for him for years. It didn't ever occur to me that I didn't have to until women's lib came along."

"Oh, Mother, really," I said. "Women's lib. When did you give a hoot about women's lib?" It was the wrong thing to say, of course; her version of things means more to her than any fact. Her eyes went flat as nail heads. I cannot look at my mother when she is angry. It seems dangerous to do it, like staring too long at a wild animal. You might provoke it to spring. And now there were no men to step between us. No Papa to gentle her down, say, "Easy, Queenie, easy, let it go." No Matthew to touch my shoulder, say, "Let's go for a walk." Just me and Mother, who watched me that way while I watched the frost in the bags of doves melt. "Well, whose side are you on, anyway?" she asked at last.

It was a relief to have it put so simply. I set down my garbage bag and, remembering the way she'd been with me about Matthew, the swift mercy of fact, I took the bag of doves out of her hand. "Give me that, Mother," I said. "The argument's over."

"Is that right?" she said. And she sat down all of a sudden on the folding metal chair next to the freezer—a chair like the chairs set in rows under the Taylor Brothers' tent at Papa's funeral, only this one was all rust—and folded forward as though something had deflated inside her, and rested her elbows on her knees and covered her face with her hands. Her shoulders began to shake. "Go on, Mother, get it out," I said. "I'm here." Because it is more frightening to remember love than bitterness or anger, I know. But remember it you do, you will. Love and bitterness, all mixed up together, waiting for you everywhere you turn. And when it comes, you have to go with it. Because grief rises like a tide and like a tide it falls, but unlike the tide, no one can chart its cycles, and to survive you must let each wave carry you and allow it to set you down. Else you exhaust yourself in struggling against its power, because the power of grief is the same as the power of love. It comes from the same source, and you can drown there if you fight it.

I knelt down beside her and put my hand on her arm. I wanted to say something tender and steadying, but the wave caught me, too, and I wrapped my arms around her knees and laid my head in her lap and let go. She kept her hand on my hair and cried. And I cried, too, the kind of crying you do when you feel a hard core of sadness down inside of you and you believe that if you could only cry deeply enough, you might dissolve it once and for all. I cried until I thought I'd touched the bottom of the sadness. That's the relief of crying like that: You think you've reached down deep enough, that you've scooped out the last of it. It fills back up again, of course, the way a hole dug in the sand at the beach fills again with ocean water, but for the moment you think you've gotten it all.

"Such a waste," Mother said, wiping her cheeks with the palms of both hands. "My mother used to say that wasting food was a sin."

I wiped my own eyes and got up from my knees. At that moment things seemed very clear. She needed me, I needed her, we needed each other. We could help each other through this time and other times as well. We knew each other all the way back.

"They're probably all freezer-burned by now, Mother," I said. "They'd be tasteless, you know? Your mother would understand that, don't you think?"

"She might have. We'll never know that now, will we?" She braced her hands on her knees and pushed herself up, and went back over to the freezer, one hand on the small of her back as though it ached. She waved away the steam and stared down into the empty freezer. "All those little bones," she said. "Those things were the dickens to eat, anyway," and she shuddered. Her eyes were red-rimmed when she looked my way again. "Lord," she said, "just let me hold onto my faculties long enough to take care of my own affairs before I die and not leave things for my children to clean up after me." She slammed the lid on the freezer, locked it, hung the key back on the nail on the upright behind the chest. Then she reached around behind the freezer and pulled the plug.

"Your mother did that, didn't she?" I said. "I remember your telling me that you went to see her just before she died and she was doing something with your father's letters."

"Burning them. She burned them all in a hatbox out in the driveway, and when I said, 'Mother, what on earth are you doing?' she said, 'Louise, I'm getting rid of these letters that your father wrote to me over the years. Nobody has any business reading them when I'm gone.'

" 'Oh, fiddle, Mother,' I said. 'You'll live to be a hundred.' She died the next week. She knew she was going to die, I'm convinced of it, and she was a very considerate person, Mother was."

•   •   •

And then the notes and the food and the freezer were done. Every evening after supper we wandered into the den off the kitchen. When my father was a boy in this house, it had been the cook's room, and in those days, he said, the room had been meager and stark. A single bed with an iron bedstead, painted white. A rag rug on a dark floor and curtains held up with string. A rocking chair. Coal burning in the fireplace grate. Now it was a retreat, a refuge, paneled in pine, with shutters over the windows. The clock from Grandfather Vess's office sat on the wide, pine mantel above the fireplace like a small, steepled church made of mahogany and glass, measuring off the hours with a slow, steady clucking. In this room every night after supper, Mother put on her sewing glasses and went back to work on the Carolina Gamecock pillow she was cross-stitching in shades of red and black for Canady, who was a big Gamecock fan. I should go back to Pennsylvania, I thought, but something had happened to time, and it seemed that we moved through the days like swimmers in thick liquid.

Sometimes, I would close my eyes, and let the clock's sound carry me back to the store on Main Street that Grandfather Vess had tended all his life. On the first floor there were tools and bicycles, carousels of nails and screws, burlap sacks of animal feed, pulleys and lawn mowers and spools of rope and chain. The second floor held stoneware crocks, pots and pans, pressure cookers, and canning jars. The walls of the third floor were lined with glass shelves jammed with porcelain figurines: English ladies in powdered wigs and scalloped blue dresses, and crystal vases, and teapots. Tables in the center of the upper floor room were covered with lace cloths and laid with china and crystal and silver. It was as if as you went up the wide wooden steps that led from the lower to the upper floors, you climbed from coarse earth into an airier world until, at the top, with a skylight pouring down light that set fire to the crystal and danced in the silver, you might have found your way to heaven where God's banquet table waited.

Sitting quietly in the den while the strutting Gamecock formed out of the repetitions of Mother's needle, I listened to the March rain and the clock and the sound of Mother's needle as it poked through the canvas, and I imagined a circle slowly woven around me again, filled with familiar people, places, and things, all connected somehow and safe. Not even the dead would leave there finally and forever. No wonder people take vows and live in cloisters all their lives. In a cloister there is a wall around the world, and within its confines you know your place. Remember Gulliver on the shore, tied down by thousands of Lilliputian ropes? The picture books all show him waking up terrified, fighting his tethers. But if I could draw, I would show him rejoicing, after the terrors of the ocean, to find himself pinned so tightly to the earth again.

When my supervisor called from Westinghouse Learning Systems a month after Papa's funeral to find out when they could expect me to come back to work, I was halfway out of the chair before the phone rang, as though I'd heard the phone the split second before it rang. The truth is, I had just gotten up to get a glass of water. Still, I might have sensed the vibration of the phone the instant before it rang. After all, my mother's family, Bibb Mills people for two generations back, were famous Georgia clairvoyants and mediums who'd been written up in several books about the paranormal. One was a Rosicrucian and an astrologer who'd drawn up natal charts on the children as they'd arrived, starry blueprints of our destinies. My mother's own mother was born with the caul over her head and her eyes squinched shut as tightly as a kitten's, which is supposed to give a person special gifts. For three days, as the story went, she lay in this birth darkness, cared for by an old black woman who prayed over her and lifted her up every day, an offering to the universe. All her life, it's true, though she'd often been poor, my grandmother had seemed blessed and guided. She went where she wanted to go, did as she pleased. When she died, the church could not hold all the mourners.

I caught the phone on its first ring. When I heard Ed's voice, I cupped my hand around the receiver, though Mother was across the kitchen in the den, and explained in a low voice that Mother still needed me. It was all terribly complicated, I said, there were legal difficulties, a tangle of finances still to be unraveled. None of that was true. I stood on tiptoe and looked at Mother sewing in the den. Glasses pulled halfway down her nose, the pillow in her lap, she frowned at the TV. She needed no one. And my father had left nothing to chance or to anyone's whim.

What he had left was a wide, well-marked path for Owen Gandy, the lawyer, to follow. The trail began in the safety deposit box down at the First Commercial Bank of Timmons, where there were keys, each labeled with a numbered tag, and life insurance policies and savings passbooks, also numbered. In case we might be confused by the numbers, there was a note: "See top right-hand drawer in home office. Red spiral-bound notebook." There, each number matched a description of the article and instructions, also numbered 1, 2, 3, in Papa's tall, broad handwriting. There had been nothing for anyone to do but to follow this trail and take what Papa had left us: $75,000 each went to me and Davis; the rest, of course, went to Mother.

Ed cleared his throat. "Well, I guess we'll have to start looking for someone to take your place. Temporarily, of course," he said. "We hope you'll be coming back to us."

"Maybe you'd better go on and do that," I said. "Just temporarily." After I hung up I sat down in the absurd little chair that was part of the absurd little fifties blond-wood telephone table, the kind with an attached seat and curving lines that somehow goes with the word housewife and its aprons and casseroles and club meetings. At one time it sat on the dark, wood floor next to the peeling radiator, against the faded pink wallpaper in the hall. What was it doing here? I knew that too. One of Mother's fizzled crusades to modernize this house. But Papa liked it the way it was, the way it had always been. The house, and Papa, always won. No matter how many of what she called her "touches" she put into it, the house went on being all dark varnish and heavy drapes and blackened silver frames on the photographs that lined the wall in this dark, narrow hall.

I sat there listening, and it seemed as if I heard my blood rushing through my veins. I thought of what I had wanted to say to Davis before he left for St. Louis, when he'd refused to take anything of my father's home with him and insisted that I drop him off at the Delta baggage claim area in front of the terminal without even coming inside to say good-bye. Don't you know, Davis, I'd wanted to say, that we must hold onto things? Because death is so empty, so light and full of space and endless, that the smallest object or memory is weight, ballast, a dot on a map that marks your place. Without it you might become weightless like ash, and blow away. And then I said something to myself out loud, the way you say to yourself the heart-stopping thing that you meant to say the moment before, only you didn't have the nerve. "Ed," I said, "you need to find somebody else to work for you because I am going home." And I felt as though I had just surprised myself sneaking back into my body, the way I used to sneak back into this house as a teenager at dawn after wandering around the county half the night, drinking from a bottle of Old Mr. Boston gin and looking for a way to lose myself.

Thank You, Miss Jenny Hanks

I meant to unpack and find places for my things, but whenever I touched any of the boxes I'd brought down from Pennsylvania and stacked around the walls of my bedroom in Mother's house, I got so tired I had to lie down and sleep. No, sleep is wrong, sleep is too shallow a word for what I did. It misses the pleasure of it, the depth, the delicious sense of being pulled below some bright surface, submerged in a dim, deep place where the current moved slow and warm and I drifted with it. Before long, sleep was my element; I luxuriated there like some underwater creature rolling in an ocean of sleep, and when I was not in it, I climbed hours as though they were walls that kept me from this place that I longed to dive into. I had never waited for Matthew more impatiently than I waited for my mother to leave for work at the tax assessor's office every morning. Then I could climb the stairs to my room and shut the door behind me, lie down, and sleep.

My room. It was just the way I'd left it when I went away to college fourteen years earlier. The Land of a Million Flowers, I'd named it, because of the wallpaper on the ceiling. Bachelor's buttons, daisies, poppies, roses, so many they were uncountable; single flowers on stems—not plants or bouquets—they floated overhead, all caught in the same current, drifting in the same direction. The wide, pine floor sloped so that a marble dropped on one side of the room rolled to the other, and the doors on the chifforobe in the corner had to be tied shut with string against this tilt.

But if everything was still inside the house, outside the world rolled on. Now the pine tree that grew just outside the window was almost engulfed in wisteria. For years I had watched the vines, sinewy as muscles, climb the trunk and coil around every limb, until, when the wisteria bloomed, the brown, scaly bark and green needles of the pine disappeared entirely in a cloud of lavender blossoms. Inside this room that looked out on but did not join this growth and plunder, I would crawl under the green chenille spread on my spool bed that had come over from England with the Vesses. The joints on the old bed snapped, the horsehair mattress rustled, the ropes that supported the mattress creaked. As a child I had let myself be carried into sleep by those sounds and imagined I was on a sailing ship setting out for a new country. And now, with those million flowers floating above me and the sigh of the central air-conditioning muffling other sound, I'd let go and sink down to the place where there was no Matthew and no Papa to lose, no life that demanded choices or permitted dreams, only the current of sleep that I drifted in.

Some days I slept straight through Mother's lunch hour. The sound of pots and pans banging down in the kitchen, the smell of something green cooking, the voices of Mother and my cousin, Melody Givens, would float up the stairs and land on my sleep like water-striders on the surface far above me, talking, talking endlessly about Mel's wedding. Since I'd come home, I'd heard of almost nothing but that wedding. Soon, in July, Mel and Canady would be married on a boat on Lake Charles B. Hartley, Jr., in sight of the played-out stretch of shoreline that Canady had transformed into two hundred acres of fairways and tennis courts and high-priced homes. Everyone in town predicted great things for the two of them. With Mel at his side, with her degree in interior design, her *flair*, how could they fail? The name had been Mel's idea, and I have to admit there *was* something inspired about it. Planter's Landing. That name bundled up the grandest images of South Carolina's lost past and offered them to anyone who could write a big enough check. The age of the planters. Sea island cotton stacked on wharves in the sun. Carriages traveling down avenues of live oaks, and the broad backs of slaves bent to satisfy every whim.

The challenge, Mother said, was to make this wedding a dignified occasion. After all, she had confided in me, a wedding on a pontoon boat on a lake the color of tomato soup, so raw and new the red-clay mud hasn't settled to the bottom yet—she "had to say it, but please don't breathe a word of this to Mel"—it simply lacked class. But Mother and Mel were up to it. With Mel's flair and Mother's will, they would pull it off. On the day of the wedding, the boat would look as respectable as the sanctuary of All Saints Episcopal Church. "Let's go with the peach with ivy accents," Mother's voice would say. "That will make a lovely table." Mel's voice would answer, light as a chime: "Aunt Louise, what would I do without you?" And just for a second, as I floated up through layers of sleep, I'd think it was my wedding she was planning.

Matthew and I were married in this house, in the living room in December, in front of the fireplace. I remember waxed wood and polished silver and smilax behind every picture frame and mirror. I remember potted palms and a fire roaring up the chimney. Mother had had fresh orchids shipped down from Columbia. They floated in bowls on tables around the room. Earth, air, fire, and water— the elements had come to bless my wedding, too. As Mother and Melody talked, I would open my eyes slowly, watch the light drift up and down the walls, and the mass of wisteria blossoms lift and fall in the breeze, the bees in them. All this I could see but not hear; it was peaceful and I would sleep again. When I'd wake, the house would be quiet, and by the slant of the sun coming through the bedroom window, I would know that it was late afternoon.

If I managed to pull myself out of bed and wander downstairs when Mother came home for lunch, she would start cleaning. Maybe it was my tangled hair, my old blue terry-cloth bathrobe worn thin on the seat that drove her wild. More likely, it was the *contrast* between me and her kitchen, that oasis of sunny yellow formica and blond wood and bright, blue Mexican tiles—her one victory over this dark old house—that affronted her. But whatever the reason, whatever the offense, the sight of me drinking coffee in her kitchen at noon sent Mother into a cleaning rage. Sometimes she sharpened all the pencils on the telephone table in the hall—there must have been a dozen—with the pencil sharpener mounted on the doorjamb in the pantry, then shoved them back into the drawer. Or she forced stray sheets of paper back into the memo-pad holder beside the phone, swept the newspapers off the kitchen table, sponged down the counters, snatched the burner grates off the stove, and swiped at the drip plates, while I measured coffee into the Mr. Coffee machine. "Good morning, Mrs. Vanderbilt. I trust you slept well," she'd say, dropping a curtsy as she hurried by on the way to the sink.

But I felt so *serene*, as though I were in a bubble that nothing could penetrate. Even her words, sharp as they were, glanced off and fell harmlessly onto the shiny, no-wax floor. "Good morning," I'd answer as if I hadn't seen her grimly pursed lips, her anxious forehead, or heard her heels rapping angrily on the linoleum. What else could I say? *Mother, I'm frightened. I came home all this way and now I can't wake up and I'm scared?* Even to think of talking about fear to Mother was painful because I knew what would happen. I'd tried it once. "It's funny, you know, Mother," I said, one evening after supper as we cleaned up the kitchen together. Something cozy and intimate about the feel of warm, soapy water on my wrists and Mother standing next to me with the dishcloth ready, drying the plates and cups and silverware I handed to her, tricked me out of my wariness. "I had all these plans when I came back here," I said. And it was true. I'd come home full of plans, brimming with plans, miles of plans. I would take my place in the life of this town where I had grown up. I would find a job, a place of my own to live. I would resurrect old friendships. Maybe I would run for a seat on the city council or the county commission. On the drive down from Pennsylvania, I'd seen the life I would lead here so vividly, had felt it so keenly it seemed to be in place, waiting for me. All I needed to do was to walk into it.

"But, now, I can't seem to wake up. It's the strangest thing."

She'd set down the plate she was drying then with a decisive *clink* onto the drain board, pulled out a kitchen chair, and patted the cushion. "Sit down," she said. "Those can wait." As she pulled a notepad and pen out of her purse, I did what I was told. Each page of the notepad showed a smiling, snaggletoothed cat holding onto the strings of a flock of bright balloons. "Hang in there," it read. Then she sat down next to me, pulled the Tiffany lampshade down low over the table, clicked out her pen, and, tipping her head to one side, began to write out a shopping list. "1. Get out of the house every day," she wrote. "2. Set yourself a daily task and finish it." On and on she went, numbering down the page while I folded my arms, crossed my legs, slid lower in the chair, folding myself up the way I used to do, tightly, tightly, the way you'd fold a piece of paper around a secret message or a treasure. When she'd filled one page and was about to turn to another, she looked up at me. Without a word she drew an X clear across the page she'd just filled, tore the sheet off of the notepad, and threw it in the trash.

After that, we did not talk again about my plans or fears. Instead Mother left articles from magazines or newspapers or church bulletins lying around where I could find them. She tried to be casual about it, but Mother cannot hide her feelings, which, in a funny way, is why you can trust her. When she believes she is being most opaque, she is most transparent.

For one thing, she ripped the articles so violently they had to be mended with tape. And the subjects! "Coming Back from Depression." "A Modern Woman's Guide to Peace in This Changing World." "When a Spouse Dies." Sometimes, just reading their titles made me weep, and when I was done I read the articles. I read them all, and I tried to read between the lines what Mother was trying to tell me. They were like the talks Mother and I tried to have about Papa or Matthew—full of the same misplaced, infuriating advice, the same tenacious, uncomprehending tenderness. Some, such as "When a Spouse Dies," I read carefully. Mostly it was full of phrases like "Life belongs to the living" and "Time heals all wounds," but at the end of the article was a numbered list of suggestions. "Take your time." "Go easy on yourself for awhile." "Stay in touch with close friends." Beside these were Mother's red check marks, smudged and faint. When I saw them, I thought of Mother, studious as a schoolgirl, ticking off the progress of her grief, and how we were spies on the edges of each other's lives, leaving messages in a code to which neither of us held the key.

And then one day in late April, after I'd been home for close to a month, as I sat at the kitchen table at noon drinking my first cup of coffee and looking through the paper for the second time, Mother hustled around behind me and stopped. I kept reading. It was the Wednesday paper and there was a lot to read. I was working my way through the small type of the Public Records section and the lists of land transfers, marriage licenses, divorce decrees, when she sighed and gave her dust rag a pop, then lifted my braid off of my back and wagged it. "You know, a pageboy would look so attractive on you," she said. I set my coffee cup down and drew my braid slowly out of her hands while the hair prickled up along my arms and up the back of my neck, because it occurred to me that I was the clutter, the waste that must not be allowed to settle like a film of grime over the house. Mother was about to begin dusting and straightening me.

"I like my hair the way it is," I said.

But it was too late. After that, the sleeping was ruined. When I slept I no longer sank. Instead I bobbed on a surface that wouldn't let me through. Or worse, I sank into a shallow trough of sleep and dreamed. I dreamed that I stood at the edge of the field up on the farm in Cheraw while Matthew passed by on the tractor, so close I could see his shoulder blades through his sweat-soaked T-shirt, and the sweat that dripped from his nose and chin, the tensed muscles in his forearms standing out as he fought to hold the wheel of the tractor steady. So close. As I watched, he turned and looked back over his shoulder and I called to him, "Turn around, watch where you're going. Watch out." But in the dream he was alive and dead at the same time—in the dream I knew this—and so he could not hear me, though he waved and smiled as though he'd seen me.

Now, I suppose that we're always preparing ourselves for the next thing that's going to happen to us. Somewhere inside us there must be a place where fate or destiny or luck or grace incubates and slowly forms words to name the next step. Like a gyroscope that rights itself or a compass needle that swings back to true north, no matter which direction you point it.

I like to think that this is why I noticed the newspaper one Friday morning in early May. As soon as I saw it, I knew that it had been left there for me to find. Mother *always* folded the paper and stuck it into the magazine rack next to the loveseat in the den. But that morning the paper lay on the kitchen table, open to the "Lifestyle" section. The new Mrs. J. C. Pruitt smiled up brilliantly from the center of the page, her bridal train swirled around her feet. On the same page, down in one corner, there was a photo of the Jaycettes presenting the Stamp Creek rescue squad with the Jaws of Life, a kind of giant forceps used for freeing people from wrecked cars, though anyone living with my mother would naturally learn to appreciate the subtler meaning of that name.

I picked up the paper and held it closer to my face. What was the clue today? Was she making a point about my driving? That was certainly a possibility. When we rode anywhere together in my car, she kept one hand braced on the dashboard while her foot pressed an imaginary brake to the floor. More likely there was something in the Jaycettes' faces she wanted me to see. They were all girls I'd known in high school, grown into women who got up in the morning, put on their flats and wraparound skirts and round-collared blouses and pearls, and went at their lives with energy and purpose. They seemed so sure of themselves, so competent, like my cousin Melody, and self-assurance—poised, feminine self-confidence—was certainly a persistent theme around our house. Even the way they faced the camera showed an awareness of their bodies as something to be presented with an eye toward good taste and the feelings of others. The heavier ones turned sideways and held their heads high, the thinner ones faced the camera with confident smiles. Some of them I'd known in high school. A few had been friends. We'd written letters from college and gotten together over Christmas vacation our freshman year. But as I studied the faces of Marybeth Ashley Long and Nancy Lowry Pruitt, I realized that I knew not one person here any longer.

Still thinking about those faces, I turned the page to the classi-
fied ads. Of course, I thought when I saw them, Mother wouldn't
leave the paper open to the *exact* page. That would have been too
obvious. The ads were a relief to find, as when vague aches and
pains erupt finally into full-blown sickness. On the classifieds page,
in the middle of the Employment Opportunities section, a neat, red
box was drawn around an ad for something called a "Gal Friday"
wanted by Foster, Graves, Lovett and Crouch, Attorneys at Law.
When I saw it I stopped *breathing*, and a desperate feeling came over
me, as if something in the back of my head were scrambling to get
away over loose rock. Mother had drawn a fat, red exclamation
point in the margin beside the ad and flicked double red dashes
under the words *mature* and *educated*, qualities the four attorneys
desired in this gal. She would act as their receptionist, the ad went
on, and she must be "cheerful," "attractive" (Mother had underlined
this word *three* times), possess "an outgoing personality" and "a good
telephone voice." Oh-*ho*, I could hear her say, fumbling in her purse
for her red pen. This suits Annie to a tee.

I read the ad again, then I put the paper down and set a coffee
cup and saucer over it. She wanted me to get a job. I didn't want
a job, not yet anyway. I had some money, quite a lot of money, it
seemed to me—$75,000 that my father had left me. There was
something that needed doing, but it wasn't a job, exactly. It had to
do with getting my bearings again, with knowing where I was before
I could decide where I was going. Besides, I *knew* Chuck Foster,
Lonnie Graves, Toy Lovett, and Marvin Crouch. I went to high
school with them, and any woman who'd work for those men has
to be desperate, crazy, nymphomaniac, or a lucky combination of
the three. I'd even been out with Lonnie Graves once right after I
came home. He was divorced for the second time, he said when he
called—divorced and ready to boogie. "Hey, I'm free, white, and
twenty-one," he said. "How about you?"

I hadn't heard anyone say that since high school. "Sure, Lonnie," I
laughed. "Why not?"

Why not, indeed. *Why?* is the better, the tougher question.
Why did I go, knowing Lonnie as I did? Remembering his face

peeking around the doorway into the girls' locker room after high
school gym class? I have asked myself the same question too many
times to count, and I have tried on too many flattering answers.
Curiosity, I have said. Recklessness. Tolerance. Compassion. All
flimsy self-deceptions. The true answer is simple and I will write it in
colors stark and bold: need. The universal catalyst. If the medieval
alchemists had ever discovered a way to distill the essence of need
in their retorts, they would have found a substance potent enough
to turn smoke into pure gold.

Well, that is enough said about Lonnie and me, except to say
that during the evening we spent drinking beer at the Steakhouse, I
learned a lot about him. He still wore his khaki pants short and his
Weejuns (with the original pennies intact) without socks. He went to
every Carolina home game with his old fraternity brothers. They sat
in the same stadium seats, Row G on the thirty-yard line, and drank
their tall Buds from the cooler they'd carried to every game since the
winning season of 1968. He knew all the verses to "She Got the
Goldmine, I got the Shaft." He could name the winners of the Masters
Golf Tournament for the past twenty years, and he had strong opinions about women. And knowing these opinions, I could guess at
the definitions of the words they'd chosen to describe their Gal
Friday. "Mature" meant stacked. And an "educated" woman was
one who could measure coffee, keep their lunch orders straight, and
take coherent telephone messages with the digits in the right order.

The depressing thing was that Mother knew them, too. In Timmons
all important gossip winds up on Mother's desk at the tax assessor's
office, where she sorts it, highlights the juicy parts, and sends it out
again through the proper channels—namely her bridge club—to do
its work in the world. Around here, you half expect gossip to come
packaged with a little slip, like the sheets used to come from the
Piedmont Mills plant: "inspected by #4, Louise Vess." Of course,
she knew about Lonnie. She'd kept up with all of them and their
divorces. Toy went to Mexico to divorce his second wife; his first
one had divorced him by publication from Atlanta so she'd never
have to see him again. She knew about their secretaries, too. They
always managed to hire a varsity cheerleader or the homecoming

queen fresh out of high school, but she never lasted more than a month or two before her father or her boyfriend made her quit. Sometimes there were ugly scenes at their offices.

Mother knew all this. She knows things before they happen, and yet she'd forget all she knew if she could just get me out of the house and doing something productive again. Productive on her terms, that is. "Foster, Graves, Lovett and Crouch," I imagined myself breathing into the receiver, my good telephone voice a husky whisper. I tore out the ad and half the page with it, stuffed it into the trash can under the sink with the ad and her hopeful red marks and slashes showing, and left the cabinet door ajar. That way, Mother would be sure to find it. Then I walked, I did not run, to the back door and onto the back steps, letting the screen door slam behind me.

Mother had wasted no time. In the month it had taken me to pack up my things in Pennsylvania and come south, she'd torn Papa's sleeping porch off the back of the house. In its place she was building a patio. It would have a low, brick wall and a fountain, railroad ties and hostas, hanging baskets of fuscias, and bricks laid in an elaborate herringbone pattern. When it was done, Mother's patio would look exactly like the patio in the pictures she'd cut out of *Southern Living* and stuck to the refrigerator with a rainbow magnet that arched above the words *Today is the First Day of the Rest of Your Life*. I say Mother was building, because the workmen she'd hired wouldn't dare lay trowel to cement without sending someone to knock on the back door and call her to come out. Looking over the tops of her glasses as though she suspected she might be walking into an ambush, and with her mouth set as though she'd already been cheated, she'd approve the consistency of the concrete they'd mixed. So now the steps led down to sacks of concrete and piles of new latticework and a fountain still in its crate, a little barefoot girl holding her skirts out and looking down shyly.

The breeze felt good in my hair, the sun on my face. I shut my eyes and stood there with my hands clasped on top of my head, letting the wind sweep my head clear of the good telephone voice of Lonnie Graves's gal Friday and of the memory of his face beneath the vivid green of his Masters golf cap. When his face wasn't bright with talk, it had sagged into misery, and once, in a lull in the talk, I had looked up to find him staring at me with such pure, stricken sadness in his eyes, it was as if all the sadness of his life had swum to the surface. Poor Lonnie. He'd been as miserable and needy as I was, only his way of disguising it had been through talk, while mine had been to smile and nod and shred the label on my beer bottle and never once interrupt or offer any opinions of my own. When he brought me home, I was out of that car before it had rolled to a complete stop. "Thanks for the ride," I said.

"My pleasure," he said. He was out of the driveway before I'd unlocked the front door.

So Mother had torn the back porch off the house, and the colonel, our next-door neighbor since forever, was gone, gone for good. Mother said it was the saddest thing. His daughter and son-in-law, Ethel and Charles, came up from Summerville and put him in the car along with a suitcase and a few cardboard boxes and Mary's portrait, the one that shows her in her green, velvet gown and DAR sash and that had always hung over the sofa on the living room wall. Mother said he fought Ethel and Charles for that picture; he wouldn't leave without it. She said he walked to the car carrying that portrait, with his back just as straight as a rod and he never looked back. Not even in the car. Not even when they drove away. She said she waved and waved and called his name, called good-bye after them, but he never turned around to look at her or the house where he'd lived half his adult life.

Mother said that when Willie Mae quit, that was the final straw. For a long time since Mary died, it had seemed that the colonel was supported by a net that was held by many hands. Hands at the courthouse, the doctor's office, Mother's hands and Willie Mae's hands, worn smooth and dry from a lifetime of sliding hot irons over starched shirts, lifting frying pans off the stove, sinking dishes into hot water. Sure, the colonel wandered, but people all over town knew to bring him home or to call Willie Mae to drive his car down and pick him up. Sometimes he knocked on Mother's back door at three in the morning, dressed and ready to be driven to the doctor's office for his weekly appointment. Mother took this in stride. "He's just old and forgetful," she said. "No crime in that." He left the burners lit on the electric stove in his kitchen until Mother and Willie Mae came up with the idea of unplugging the stove right after supper, before Willie Mae left for the night.

Then, one Friday evening in April, Willie Mae's son, Jerome, called Mother and said that his mother wouldn't be coming back to work on Monday morning. Now, Willie Mae was almost as old as the colonel; she'd worked for him and Mary for close to thirty-five years, and she'd nursed Mary through her long, final illness. Then she was gone and it was discovered that the net that held the colonel was fragile. Like any net, its strength was the strength of something whole and connected: When Willie Mae's strand broke, the net unraveled and he fell through.

"Well, Willie Mae has a right to some ease in her old age, too," I said to Mother.

"Of course she does," Mother said. "But she could have at least given notice. It was her son that put her up to it. Once he got elected to city council, he couldn't stand the thought of his mother working as a maid."

So Willie Mae and the colonel were gone now, too. Mother and I aired the house once a week and fed the two old pointers, Napolean and Josephine, the last of the line of bird dogs that the colonel and my father had raised and trained together. Beyond the privet hedge that separated our two yards, Josephine lay on the grass in the sun with her head up and her eyes closed, sniffing the late morning smells: hot pine straw and green grass and jasmine.

I whistled, called her name. She opened her eyes and looked at me, and her tail wagged once before she went back to her dozing. Jingo's Little Josephine, my father had named her. It could almost have been a song, like the names of the rivers, the Isaqueena and the Keowee—all things with music to their names. For three years running, she'd been field trial champion of South Carolina. I saw her work once when I was a teenager, and even now, in my mind, it exists as one of those still moments in which you believe you're seeing a clear picture of something important about life. I remember standing in a field while the sun set and a cold November wind clipped across the broom sedge, and my father held Jo on a short leash. She shifted from paw to paw and watched him for the signal, trembling as though a current of electricity were running through her. He steadied her, bent and spoke to her. She looked up at him with a look of almost human understanding and he unsnapped the leash and signaled with his hand. And then she was gone, flashing back and forth, and then, as though she'd simply flowed from one shape into another, Josephine snapped into a perfect point. From her crisp, curled paw and outstretched nose to the stiff tip of her tail, she made an arrow that flew straight toward the birds that were her heart's desire. Josephine, they said, would hold point forever if my father had asked it of her—as long as the birds flew, so immersed in it that she didn't notice the rising or setting of the sun or a shotgun fired at close range. Such was her faithfulness, my father had said, such was the steady desire of her pointer's heart. If the Lord himself had gotten pick of the litter, Papa used to brag, he would have chosen Josephine.

Just then Napoleon raced around the side of the house and charged at Jo. When she didn't open her eyes, he stuck his butt up in the air and yapped at her. Without opening her eyes she showed him her teeth, which sent him into a gale of hysterical barking. "Goddamn it," I could almost hear the colonel say, "if I had a gun handy, I'd shoot that dog and put everybody out of their misery."

I had to laugh. For some reason it made me happy that the colonel had never had a gun handy, that Napoleon was alive, though he'd never gotten it through his thick skull what it meant to be a hunting dog. He wouldn't honor another dog's point or work a field in anything but dizzy circles before he'd light out for God knows where and turn up two fields away, cheerfully flushing covey after covey of quail, yapping with hysterical joy, and leaping through the grass with his ears sailing straight out from his head like wings. He'd forgotten what he was supposed to do, or he'd never had a clue. And yet here he was, alive on this May morning, as dumb and slaphappy as ever with his swampy back, his oversize lumpy skull, his china eye. Surely, I thought, his existence was a sign of goodness, of spaciousness, of a flaw in the tight weave of the world through which mistakes slipped, of a force that had nothing to do with perfection or the siring and training of champions or the jaws of life and their relentless grinding.

The sun felt heavy, like a weight on my head and shoulders, and for the first time in weeks I felt myself getting sleepy. Next door, at the Hanks's house, the back door slammed and Miss Jenny Hanks came slowly down the steps as if she were carrying a sack of pain on her back. She held onto the metal railing with both hands and looked around anxiously, as if she expected the steps to be yanked out from under her at any moment. I waited until she'd reached the bottom of the steps, so as not to frighten her, and then, as I always did if we happened to be outdoors at the same time, I spoke to her. I thought we might at least speak, since we saw each other every day. "Morning, Miss Jenny," I said, and, as she always did, she looked up incensed as if I'd yelled an obscenity at her. She shook her head, frowning, muttering, then she hurried across the yard toward the grape arbor in the far corner. When she got there, she sat down heavily in the white, metal glider under the arbor, folded her hands in her lap, and nodded once, "So there." She wore pink terry-cloth house slippers, an old brown sweater buttoned up to the neck over her faded, pink housedress. Half a dozen bobby pins held back her thin brown hair. She began to push herself back and forth, chin high, staring straight ahead as though she'd promised to watch for someone who'd walked away a long time ago.

Miss Jenny was not a person you'd ever see out in her own front yard. In her youth—which is what people around here like to call your past, in order to flavor your life story with a dose of loss and decline—she and her husband had been called to the Baptist mission field in Brazil. When he disappeared along the Amazon (headhunters, some said, though others said he'd run off with a woman and had been seen slipping into the jungle behind a village in the country's interior), she came home to her mother and vowed never to go out the front door of her house again until the Taylor Brothers carried her through it and loaded her into their hearse.

Still, just about this time every morning and again in the afternoon,
she'd come out to sit in the glider and push it back and forth for a
few minutes, though it never seemed to give her any satisfaction or
pleasure to be there.

Ever since I'd come home it had puzzled me to see her there, but
that morning, as I watched her push the glider stubbornly, grimly, as
if she had a certain number of pushes to complete before she could go
back indoors, it came to me why she was there. It was because of
Eulalie, her mother, whose clean white tennis shoes hung drying on
the backyard clothesline. Eulalie, the undaunted. Still busy at eighty-
seven, she directed the Keowee District Girl Scout Council, walked a
mile a day out at the new Civic Center track, washed her tennis shoes
three times a week, and wrote weekly letters to the *Courier-Tribune*
condemning the destruction of historic buildings, oaks, attitudes, and
ways of life. "Now, Jenny," she'd said before she'd left for her morning errands, clapping her hands in her brisk, Scout leader's way,
"for goodness sakes go out and get some fresh air. Scoot."

And Miss Jenny was doing just that, carrying out the letter of
her mother's law. She was out in the fresh air, the bright, spring
air, under the grape arbor where the bright, spring-green leaves
waved above her head as wide and new as baby hands and bunches
of tiny, green grapes rounded beneath the leaves. But she never
looked up, not once. She wouldn't give her mother the satisfaction.
She would destroy her own life just to keep it out of her mother's
brisk hands. After a short time had passed, she stood up suddenly
as if an alarm had gone off in her head, climbed the back steps,
and disappeared inside the house, letting the screen door slam behind her. I have seen Jenny's picture in one of the colonel's photo
albums. Once she was beautiful, with a long, slender neck and dark,
eager eyes. Now she was an old woman with a vein of defiance that
ran through her like a taproot, and drew up enough bitter water to
keep her alive in her mother's house. Back in the arbor the glider
continued to swing and creak for the longest time, as if Miss Jenny had
left her angry ghost behind to carry out the spirit of her mother's law.

When the swing finally stopped, sunlight filtered down again
through the grape leaves and dappled the swing and the ground

below where Miss Jenny's feet had scuffed two grooves in the bare dirt. It's not often that a person is granted two visions on the same morning, one of the past and Josephine's glory—the more hopeful one it seems to me—the other of her own future. But that is what happened. I saw that I could live here forever, beating Mother back from my life, sure of what I wouldn't do and didn't want; I could know everything there was to know about what I wouldn't do and nothing about what I could do, did want, wanted, until there was only one answer to every question and that answer was no. And in the end I would be an angry ghost, flitting around Mother's house, rattling the windows, knocking over furniture, and smashing glasses when her back was turned.

At the bottom of the steps, I saw Mother's patio. The workmen had left a radio on when they'd gone for lunch. It played a sad country song about drinking in a bar to keep from going home to an empty house. There was a shovel stuck in a pile of sand, string and stakes marking off the shape of Mother's new brick wall. Move on, they seemed to shout. Stand aside, make room.

Now I saw the mistake I'd made, coming back here: I'd dreamed the wrong dream, the dream of rest, pause, ease, the dream with too much stillness in it. The way I see it, there is something in the world, a force as restless as air or roots or the stuff that holds the whole branching shape and fruit and seed within the small circumference of a seed. Something that has to grow, to change, to move on. And it seems to me that this force is in us, too; it carries us like a wave. But if we stop, we become obstacles; it climbs over us and goes on. If you've ever watched kudzu take over an abandoned house, you'll know what I'm talking about. One summer the vines poke through window frames, crawl under doors, climb walls and porch posts, and start over the roof, waving their tendrils in the air. The next year the place is no longer a house but a green mound in the middle of a field with an old, bleached tree skeleton standing beside it to show that this was once a dwelling place.

People are always saying to me: "Now, Annie, be reasonable. Don't go to such extremes over everything." I don't know what that means anymore, extremes, going to extremes. It seems to me that everything *is* extremes—everything that matters anyway—because everything is in its own small or large way a choice between life or death, and we have to decide where we'll stand and then work as though our lives depend on it. And if we find ourselves with nothing but what's fallen down around our heads, then we'd better start looking at what's left and stop wasting so much time wishing it weren't so, or looking for a place to hide or a place to run where things are going to be better. "Thank you, Miss Jenny," I said to myself.

Next door there was a quick movement behind the back screen door, then the door itself, closing.

You Are Here

That night, in the den off the kitchen, with the steady *cluck* of Grandfather Vess's clock and the *creak, creak, creak* of Miss Jenny's glider in my ears and the sight of Miss Jenny herself under the new spring leaves shimmering at the edge of my vision, I told Mother what I had decided. She came in all wilted from her day at the tax assessor's office. I handed her her drink, let her look through the mail, then we moved into the den. I let her settle into one of the two recliners aimed at the TV while I took the other, let her tip back and kick up the footrest, push off each shoe with the toe of the other foot, and loosen the bow on her blouse. She took a swig of her drink with her usual groans and wheezes, sighs and grimaces, as though she were shrugging off a harness, feeling the delicious lightening and unbending of everything that had been cramped and pinched and weighed down all day. Then I said, "Mother, I have something to tell you that you're going to want to hear."

"Let me guess," she said. "You're going to tell Mel that you'd love to be a bridesmaid?"

"No," I said. "It's not that. She was just being kind, Mother, you know that. It's too late to be asking anybody to be a bridesmaid now, and besides, I'd feel funny about celebrating out on that lake after the way Papa felt about it and all."

"Well, for heaven's sake, life goes on," she said, punching through the TV channels with the remote control, looking for the news.

"Yes," I said, "I know it does, with you or without you." And I sat back, rolled my glass between my palms. On one side of the glass was a picture of a hunter behind a bird dog on point, his rifle up at his shoulder, ready. "Actually, I have a project in mind," I said.

"Oh?" she said, elaborately casual, drawing it out exactly as she does when she wants someone to go on and hand over the latest gossip. I'd picked the right word this time. A project, with its overtones of energy, plans, direction, will, progress.

"I need to start somewhere," I said. "I need to get to work. I don't know what I'm doing yet, exactly, but I'm going to start by cleaning out Papa's study. I'll start tomorrow, if that's all right with you."

"Papa's room?" she cried, gripping the arms of the recliner wild-eyed, as if I'd just told her a thief was in there, plundering it. For a moment it looked as if she might jump up and run back there as she'd done so often in the past, running to answer my father's call: "*Queenie*, come here, I need you." Then she caught herself, sank back in the chair, and changed channels. The announcer said something about Israel, then President Carter appeared on the screen, smiling and waving from the door of Air Force One. "Fine with me," she said, with a wave of her hand. "As long as you throw out more than you keep."

In the morning I tied up my hair, drove out to the Winn-Dixie, and brought home a carload of cardboard boxes. My father's study in the back corner of the house underneath the stairs had been his mother's room when he was a boy, the place where she'd kept her household records and written her notes and letters—her "correspondence," she called it—sitting in the chair in front of her lady's desk with her ankles crossed, her back so straight it never touched the back of the chair. When we moved in, Mother took it over as her sewing room, and when she stopped sewing and Papa started Save Our Two Rivers, he moved in there.

It was his room, and it still smelled of cherry pipe tobacco and typewriter ribbon ink and dust. Each morning I would step into that room and close my eyes, and in the quiet, I would feel my father's presence and the power of his convictions as though these were rolled up in the maps and the Environmental Impact Statements and stored in the loose-leaf notebooks that he'd filled with pages of evidence in the case he was building against the lake. Evidence piled onto the sagging pine-board shelves that he never got around to painting, or lined out on the map that he'd thumbtacked to the wall next to the desk. The map was made of four aerial maps joined at the corners to show the whole of the county as it used to look before the Corps of Engineers made a big hole of the middle of it and filled the hole with water.

It showed Vaucluse County when the Isaqueena and the Keowee curved like the two arms of a wishbone around the land between the rivers, when the clusters of towns and communities— Little Awando, Stamp Creek, Twelve Mile—held together the way constellations are on a map of the sky. Timmons was at the center, the hub of a wheel of roads named for their destinations: to the north, White's Mill; to the south, Sinking Springs; Bean Blossom to the east, and Town Grove to the west. Over the years, as the land was bought up and vacated and cleared, my father had taken a marker filled with indelible black ink and drawn the outline of the lake over these places, x-ing out names like Little Awando and the Laughing Place as he went. In places, he'd corrected himself, whiting out a section of line and redrawing it two inches to the right. That's how careful he'd been. For years, whenever Matthew and I came home, my father would take us to this room and show us the progress of the black line that was slowly encircling the middle of the county.

For years I'd watched the line inch around the center of the county, but I was impatient with his mapmaking then. It had seemed a waste, another way for my father to drag out his suffering over the

lake's coming to Vaucluse County, and I was impatient with suffering. Matthew and I lived in Arizona, we lived in Louisiana, then
we lived in Pennsylvania. We wanted to throw out maps, to go
where we wanted to go until we came to the place we were meant
to be, as though who we were supposed to be lay waiting out there
somewhere, always just in front of us, and all we needed to do was
to catch up with it. Now I thought I saw what my father had been
trying to do, redrawing his map. He'd been trying to find the X that
marked his spot, to keep it in sight no matter how it changed, to
track it through the wilderness until it came to rest again.

I knew what I'd wanted to feel as I pulled my father's notebooks and
Environmental Impact Statements down from the shelves, pulled the
maps and charts out of the pigeonholes in the desk and looked at
them again, at his underlinings and exclamation points and notes
in the margins, the red arrows flying between contradictions, eva-
sions, lies. I'd wanted to feel sad for my father and awed again—
the way I'd felt when he was alive—at his tenacity, the will that
had kept him going and fighting the lake long past the time when
there was no fight to be fought, long after the whole thing was old
news, an embarrassment. After people crossed the street downtown
or remembered errands and ducked into stores to avoid him and his
briefcase full of papers, his face full of bad news.
　　I knew what I'd expected to feel, but as I lifted down maps and
shook papers out of manila folders into the cardboard box at my
feet, all I could think about was how much life those papers had
cost him and everyone around him. Already the pages of the reports
were yellowing, but the harm that they'd done seemed permanent.
I thought of the weeks and months of tirades and last chances that
I'd felt even at a distance, like an earthquake sending out its shock
along fault lines that ran under the ground wherever I lived. I
thought of the end, when he'd roamed around the county with this
new petition, that new hope, a new suit to file in the circuit court
of appeals. I thought of all this and I remembered Mother's face,
the famished, frightened look that had come over it when I'd told
her I was going to clean out Papa's study, as if she still had to swear

allegiance to protect what had gone on in this room for so long. And what I felt then was anger, cold and clear in the middle of my brain, at what he'd put her through, put us all through with his pride and his stubbornness that wouldn't allow him to let go, to give up, to rest.

One week, two, and the shelves were bare, though I left the map tacked up on the wall so that it would go on being my father's room for awhile longer. In the back of the closet there, I found the sign from the Laughing Place, and I hung it over the desk on two strong hooks. Davis had made it one year in high school woodshop out of a heavy slab of pine board stained dark brown. Into this board he'd carved THE LAUGHING PLACE in letters that looked like crossed sticks, like the letters on a camp sign. For fifteen years that sign had hung under the eaves of the house, and on the day that the Corps of Engineers brought in their bulldozers to knock the house down, Papa had made them wait until he'd climbed up and taken it down. Then he brought it here where it stayed in the closet until I took it out that morning and hung it on the wall. And I thought my father might have found it funny too, my hanging that sign over the empty desk and shelves beside the map that told the only story he wanted to tell at the end of his life—the story of how he'd failed to save Vaucluse County. Funny, I mean, in the way he found things funny toward the end of his life. As though everything were a joke, a trick, and nothing could be believed or trusted. The sign belonged here now, I thought, with the faded wallpaper and the dusty shelves, roped off, preserved, a room in a historic house, the scene of some great failure.

On the kitchen table early one morning in mid-May, I found a note underneath two pots of yellow mums. "Please take these out to Papa's grave, *today*, this morning, as soon as you get up," it read. "I drove through there yesterday on the way home from work and the headstone looks so shiny. The mums will soften it some. Love, Me."

I decided to walk to the cemetery. It wasn't far. Three blocks to the courthouse square, then four blocks out Main Street to the cemetery, through the old part of town, past houses like ours in various stages of collapse or restoration. Houses where old ladies lived behind triple locks and closed shutters, their front steps rotting, camellias crowding against the front-porch screens next door to houses painted yellow with white trim, with hostas lining their front walks and American flags flying from their porches.

I walked along, savoring the morning the way you will appreciate something when you know it cannot last. It was the middle of May, summer was coming, and the time for walking would soon be over until fall. Already there was a pearly cast to the sky, and the azaleas had faded in the yards of the houses I walked past. Around here, the season can swing from delicate to brutal almost overnight. One week it's all azaleas, jasmine, lime green leaves against a bright blue sky; the next week flowers turn brown and drop, the sky turns white, glaring, the heat moves in to stay, a thick, white wall of heat that you walk into everyday. Any day now, thunderheads would pile up in the sky: fat cloud boulders stacked on top of one another. Up and up they would rise, and in the afternoon they would darken. Around four, the clouds would open and pour down heavy sheets of rain that soaked but did not cool, then pour down light again— thick, steamy slabs of light—while the trees dripped and the gutters trickled and the wet pavement glared with metallic light. While around and over and through it all, the wax and wane, the buzz and snap of cicadas ran like the song of the heat, playing long past midnight.

Down on the courthouse square, sprinklers whirled on the courthouse lawn; the heavy chain that marked off the lawn was freshly painted dark green. Timmons is a pretty town right out of the Old South, with the courthouse and its Corinthian columns, the cupola with the four clocks lifted above the magnolias and the canopy of live oaks, some of them so frail and brittle it takes steel cables to grapple the limbs to the trunks. The buildings on the square have all held on to their tall, old-fashioned second-story windows, while down on the street many of the storefronts are vacant, for lease, for sale.

As usual on a day in late spring, the parking places around the square were lined with cars with out-of-state license tags. U.S. Highway

25 runs through the middle of town; it's marked on maps as a Heritage Trail, and travelers still leave I-20 and follow it into Timmons. Cars with Ohio or Michigan tags drive slow, slower, their windows full of amazed faces, then whip into parking spaces and the people tumble out. "Can you believe this? Is this for real?" their expressions ask as they snap pictures of each other in front of the courthouse or next to the statue of the Confederate soldier, as they read the historical markers on the front lawn, bounce on the lowest branches of the oaks, or bury their faces in magnolia blooms. Actually, it is real. Sherman spared Timmons, one of the courthouse markers says, even though it lay directly in his path from Savannah to Columbia, because he'd gone to West Point with a man from Timmons whose character he had always admired. Which is the only human feeling I have ever heard Sherman credited with: the humility to recognize the moral superiority of his classmate from South Carolina. So he tore up the railroad tracks that led toward Columbia and burned the cotton bales waiting on the railroad siding, but he left the town standing. People think that's a wonderful story about Sherman and how he spared the town; my father always said so. It confirmed for him that right wins out, that character is something tangible, forceful, convincing.

From the second-story window of my father's law office, his name still shone in the morning sun, an arch of gilt letters: JOHN VESS, ATTORNEY AT LAW. Down below, my reflection, a thin woman in sunglasses carrying a pot of yellow mums under each arm, traveled with me across the plate-glass windows of Faye's Bandbox, the Steakhouse, the Courier-Tribune office, and the Western Auto store that had once been my Grandfather Vess's hardware store. That morning it seemed as if I lived in a deep, layered place and knew the strata, top to bottom, bottom to top.

It had been right to come back here, I thought as I walked. And though I spoke to Faye and to the old men on the benches that lined the walk leading to the courthouse, and though everyone spoke to me and said how pretty the flowers were and wasn't it getting hot early this year, no one asked where I was going. They all knew that I was on my way to the cemetery. The men who laid out Timmons planned it this way, a lesson set into the bricks of the sidewalk. If you started at the courthouse and walked north up Main Street, and made no sudden swerves or reckless decisions about where you were headed, you'd naturally arrive four blocks later at the cemetery gates, as if this were the only journey: To finish your business on the courthouse square, walk quietly out to the cemetery, and lie down.

It was a busy morning in the cemetery, though there was no funeral in progress or prepared for. No crowd around a bright, blue tent, and no tent with its rows of chairs waiting for the mourners to fill them. But cars lined the oval driveway, and everywhere people pulled weeds and raked, laid wreaths, and set jars of flowers in front of headstones. I recognized a few of Mother's friends in their straw hats and gardening gloves, on their hands and knees in their family plots. Shading their eyes with their hands, they waved in my direction and I waved back. No wonder Mother had sent me here this morning. Her social antennae, exquisitely tuned, had caught the vibration: Today the cemetery will be full of your friends. She had to make a good showing, too. I set the mums down on the gravel in front of the headstone. It was new and shiny and wide as the headboard of a double bed, and it carried Papa's name:

JOHN SEDDELL VESS
DECEMBER 12, 1918–FEBRUARY 25, 1980

and my mother's, one dash from reaching its own conclusion:

LOUISE HOLT VESS
AUGUST 16, 1921–

I set the flowers down, one below each of their names. Now, Mother, I thought. Rest easy. When your friends ride around the cemetery slowly, slowly, so as not to miss anything, they will smile to find that, in death as in life, Louise was taking good care of John.

I sat down on the wrought-iron bench that Papa had placed in the Vess plot in memory of his mother. "At rest," her headstone read, and my father's echoed it: "At rest." His brother Stovall's headstone was there, too, a plain military slab, though Stovall's body was far from this place, in France, where he had died: STOVALL VESS. CORP. U.S. ARMY 3RD ARMORED DIV. KILLED IN ACTION, APRIL 3, 1941, REIMS, FRANCE. AT REST.

As I sat there, I remembered how my father had liked to sing as he went through the routines of his life. I remembered one song, an old hymn called "Bringing In the Sheaves." He was not a religious man; this might have been the only hymn he knew in its entirety, but he sang that song as he shaved in the bathroom in the morning, and he sang it from the cellar where he kept his woodworking tools: "Bringing in the sheaves, bringing in the sheaves/We shall come rejoicing, bringing in the sheaves." He had a clear, rich voice with a touch of tremolo to it, and he sang the words slowly, as though he were handling each word.

As a child hearing that song floating up from the cellar, I had pictured a procession at harvest time, and the laborers, stooped under bundles of golden hay, singing in my father's voice. I pictured it that way until I was old enough to know that the wheat had been cut down, that it was death that was being sung about. And yet even when I knew this, when my father sang that song I would see the earliest picture of the harvest, but darkened, as though it were happening in the early evening instead of in the morning sun.

And maybe that is the beauty, the purpose of an old hymn such as this, and why you must sing it all your life in order to make it your own. Sing it with the earliest faith, that the wheat is immortal and harvested without hurt or pain, and while that faith fills with the scythe's cut, the idea of autumn, and the fall of the stalks against the ground. Sing it until when you sing of the harvest, you are singing of this darkness, too. And yet if you sing it long enough, and faithfully, you come to see that though the song has filled with darkness, it is not itself darkened, that what you are singing about is large enough to hold all darkness and still remain a harvest: a triumph and a mystery. But when I tried to remember exactly when my father had stopped singing that song, I found that I could not.

·   ·   ·

Just then a maroon Lincoln Town Car drove slowly around the circular drive and stopped. Pug Simmons, the editor of the *Courier-Tribune*, got out of the driver's side, walked around back of the car, and opened the passenger door, and out stepped Miss Leola Fenton. Miss Leola Fenton! I felt myself crouch, ready to run. But she'd seen me already; no doubt, she'd taken note of everyone here. Now she shaded her eyes and pointed at me, smiling, a tall old lady with perfect posture, a hooked nose, and valiant eyes. County genealogist, president of the Wade Hampton chapter of the United Daughters of the Confederacy, she was also a columnist for the *Courier-Tribune*. Her weekly column, "Over the Coffeecups," was the first thing I turned to in the Wednesday paper. It was a combination of high-minded gossip column and sermon, full of stories about the services at the First Baptist Church, the comings and goings of the people she called "Timmonsites," news of who had visited whom that week, expressions of sympathy for the sick, or the grieving and good wishes for the recently married or recovering. She wore her bright, white hair pulled back into a bun on the nape of her neck. This morning she was dressed in a navy blue suit and a white blouse buttoned to the neck and ruffled down the front. And she wore gloves. White, cotton gloves, short and buttoned at the wrists with tiny pearl buttons—the kind of gloves little girls used to wear to church. Pug carried a long, white florist's box tied with gold cord. He looked funny carrying it, like a bear with a crewcut and round glasses, clumsily handling something man-made.

As they walked closer, I stood up. "Good morning, Pug. Good morning, Miss Leola," I said.

"Annie?" Pug squinted. "Annie Vess? Well, I'll be doggone." He came through the gate with his hand out and I moved to shake it. "I heard you were back in town."

"Pug," I said, "good to see you." Then I hugged him, hugged him hard, box and all. We had been friends in high school, good friends. I'd forgotten that until now.

"Yes, well, good *morning*, Annie Vess," Miss Leola said, inclining herself my way as she looked from the roses to me and back to the roses again. She had a low, throaty voice, broad and cultured-sounding, and long, horsey teeth that showed when she smiled.

"Good Morning, Miss Leola," I said. "You're all dressed up today."

She frowned slightly. "Well, I should hope so," she said. "I see that you've already been hard at work this morning." She raised her wild, white eyebrows and nodded toward the graves of the four Confederate soldiers who'd died in the Battle of Timmons. A rusty iron fence surrounded this plot, which was half hidden under a cedar tree. Usually the grass there was knee-high, but today it was freshly mowed, and on each grave stood a single red rose in a bud vase tied with a red ribbon.

"What are you all doing here?"

"Shame on you," she said. "What is today?"

"Monday, May 12?" Pug cleared his throat and looked up at the sky.

"Why, it's Confederate Memorial Day!" she said. "Mr. Simmons and I are here to lay these floral tributes on our graves."

"It's a tradition," Pug added, and he shrugged. "We do it every year."

I was suddenly conscious of my sleeveless dress and open-toed shoes; the way my hair must look, scattered all over my shoulders; my sunglasses; my legs, bare of stockings. "I'm sorry," I said, "I've been away." Confederate Memorial Day. Of course. That would explain the wreath of red roses on the Confederate statue down on the square, and the courthouse flags flying at half-mast, the freshly mowed grass around the four soldiers' headstones.

Of course, I knew that story. Growing up here you learn that the only real story is a history, that nothing is real until it has been connected to what went before and what came after. There are no fragments here. I suppose there's strength to be drawn from that, and I think that if I had to start over again I would study history; I would train myself to see the great patterns.

A ragtag end of a Union scouting party had sneaked off from Sherman's main column and was on its way to loot the town. Around a bend out on the Prosperity Road, they galloped into a group of Confederate militia from Timmons that had been organized to stand in Sherman's way, galloped into and through each other and could hardly load and fire their rifles before they were past each other and gone, leaving behind four dead Rebels. As children we were loaded onto buses on this day and driven to the cemetery in our white dresses and suits. I remembered holding my flowers, yellow sweetheart roses cut from our yard and stuck through a doily, their stems wrapped in a damp paper towel. I remembered the smell of roses and tea olive and the warm, sticky air of the bus, close and sweet. We'd stepped up one by one to place our nosegays on the four graves, and when we'd finished and the graves were piled high with flowers, we'd sung a chorus of "Dixie." I didn't quite know what it meant except that it was sad; it made our teachers more insistent than usual on order and silence and best behavior.

"Weren't you living up north somewhere when you lost your husband in a tragic accident?"

"I was living in Pennsylvania, yes ma'am, when my husband was killed."

"Well, we're certainly grateful to have one of our own returned to us from life's troubled waters."

"Yes, ma'am," I said. "Thank you. I appreciate that." But I could feel myself growing suspicious. Did Miss Leola really not remember where I'd been and what happened to Matthew, or when I'd come back to Timmons? I doubted it. More than likely, the engine of my car had not cooled from the trip down from Pennsylvania before she knew that I was home. The week I got home, Miss Leola had welcomed me back in "Over the Coffeecups." She'd spoken of troubled waters there, too. What a beautiful idea, I thought then. The waters of life might be troubled but here was a cove, a harbor, still water. I had cut out the column and put it in the drawer of my bedside table, and sometimes late at night I took it out and read it again just to hear a voice giving thanks, welcoming me back, as though I'd been expected, and missed.

But this was not a conversation in any ordinary sense of the word, an exchange of views. No. This was a test to find out if my thinking about myself conformed with the general consensus about it, and to judge if I understood the duties and obligations that went along with the place that I'd been assigned.

"Well, you poor thing," she said, patting my hand between both of her own. "Widowed so young."

The Laughing Place

Sit down, Miss Vess, I thought. The results of your aptitude test are in. It looks like you're particularly suited for two roles: poor thing and widow. Both of them high callings. Best of luck with your career. Your bed jacket is in the mail, wear it in fragile health. Like that poor girl, Betsy Lane Neil, whose picture rests in the glass case in the Vaucluse County Museum in the courthouse basement, surrounded by her collection of miniature glass vases. There she sits propped up in bed in her satin bed jacket, smiling her tired, sweet smile, and the story of her life fits, single spaced, onto a three-by-five index card that leans against her photograph. "Betsy Lane Neil," it says, "traveled the world in the service of God. At the young age of twenty-five, she was taken ill and came home, where she went to bed with a tired heart. She was much loved, and before she died at the age of twenty-seven, people sent her these curios from all over the world to brighten her last days."

"Thank you, Miss Leola," I said, "but I'm doing all right."

"Of course you are," she said, "of course you are." She squeezed my hand, looked at me sadly. I had said the right thing, the brave thing, though everyone knew it was an act. She squeezed my hand again and wagged it, and two thin, silver bracelets jingled on her arm. Their sound brought back to me something I hadn't thought about in years. *Home is the place where things come back to you.* I almost laughed out loud, remembering that feeling that had come over me after Papa's funeral, while Mother and I wrote those thank-you notes, cleaned out his freezer. The trouble is that what comes back to you is not always what you'd choose to remember.

Miss Leola always wore the same white gloves and bracelets. She may have even worn the same *suit* (like my father, she would have kept her clothes for years) the day she came to my South Carolina history class during my senior year in high school to talk about her great-grandfather, Manse Jolly, the famous South Carolina Yankee-killer. During the war, Manse had fought with McGowan's South Carolinians in every big battle from Manassas to Atlanta, and he'd surrendered with them at Appomattox. But something happened to Manse during those four years of war. Shell shock or battle fatigue, we'd call it now, but he developed such a hatred for Northerners that when the war ended, he couldn't stop killing. Carpetbaggers, soldiers walking north toward home, it made no difference to Manse Jolly. If he found out they were Yankees, he killed them.

Manse was a barber by trade, she'd said. He'd offer to shave and barber these Yankees, and then he'd slit their throats. She said there were bodies buried all over the Jolly homeplace out near Little Awando. "He'd kill one," she said, "dump the body down the well . . . Kill another, dump that one down the well." Her hands in those clean, white gloves danced death in the air. "And when his sister tried to put a stop to the killing, he killed her, too, and disappeared out west where he became an Indian fighter. He was finally killed himself at Sand Creek by the savage Sioux Indians."

That was when I raised my hand. My father might have *written* this country's military history, so jealous and possessive was his interest in it. Any deviation from the truth he took as a personal slight, and I had cut my teeth on his history lessons; I was John Vess's daughter, his ally, co-defender of the truth of the past.

"Excuse me," I said, "but Sand Creek was where Colonel Chivington rode into Black Kettle's village at dawn and massacred the *Cheyenne*. It was a treacherous thing to do." Behind me a few boys snickered, but I went on. "They were betrayed by the same government that had promised them protection," I said. "They'd been given an American flag and told that if they flew it above the village, they would not be harmed." Of course, my father would have told it to Davis and me this way, a massacre, an appalling betrayal. Treachery, betrayal, he saw it everywhere, slinking through history, disguised in each century's events. I stood beside my desk and waited.

Miss Leola stared at me with a bright, fixed light in her eyes: "And what is your name?" As she spoke, she capped and uncapped her ancient, tortoiseshell fountain pen.

She knew, of course she knew, who I was. The question was meant to draw me out into the open, but I went willingly. "Annie Vess," I said, trembling.

She tapped the cap back onto her pen with one blow of her palm. "John and Louise Vess are your parents?" she said.

"Yes, ma'am."

"Well, John and Louise Vess never raised a child to defy his elders," she said.

"No, ma'am," I said, "I did it myself." I grabbed my books and ran, not waiting for the bell. I had done it, I had done it—my heart pounded for blocks—I had stood up to Miss Leola Fenton. I walked the long way home from school, and as I walked I blew my rage into a high, purifying flame, and by its light I imagined that I saw the death and the meanness in everything, the current that flowed just below the surface of all the graciousness, the bowing, smiling, kissing, and cooing, the whispery sweetness, the way black river water swirls under the bridges down in the Low Country, waiting to suck you down. By the light of this rage, I *saw*, and warmed by its heat, I made a vow. I would leave Timmons and that death forever. The wisteria vine strangling the pine outside my bedroom window, Miss Leola Fenton and her murdering relatives, my own smothering family. I thought I could walk out on those stories, not carry them with me or live by them, or even remember them after a while.

If Miss Leola remembered that day, she gave no sign. All had been forgiven long ago. It had become an anecdote from her teaching days, or it had never mattered much to begin with. Certainly it could not possibly have carried the weight of personal and malevolent intention I'd seen in it then. Now my father was dead and the Jolly homeplace with its weight of bodies was twenty feet underwater. As for me, the rude girl, I had come back to a place I'd promised myself to leave forever.

"Don't you favor your daddy, though?" she said.

"People say that, yes, ma'am."

"Well, bless your heart," she said, leaning forward from the waist and whispering, as though this were our secret. "Your daddy was a dear, sweet soul."

No, he wasn't, I almost said. I looked down at the step in the granite curb where I stood. "VESS," it said, the cuneiform letters chiseled so deep into the stone that two hundred years from now, people would still be able to find where the Vesses are buried. I felt heavier all of a sudden, as though my bones had grown heavier and were pulling on me from the inside. It had come to this again, as I'd known it would. In Pennsylvania nobody would ever walk up to you on the street and start talking about anybody's *soul*. But here it's as if everybody carries around a complete set of everyone else's X rays. And these are not ordinary X rays that show the craft of your bones, the shape and status of your organs. No, these are privileged X rays. Hold them up to the light and there is your soul, every scab and thin spot, every shriveled, dead patch, and every fertile spot where virtue or love has taken root—all there so that anyone can look, nod, and say, "Well, no wonder she's like that."

It was as though I had never been away, or had conveniently forgotten everything that came flooding back over me now, the way the heat swamps you when you first walk into it out of an air-conditioned house. My trouble is that I confuse the way I want things to be with the way they are. And I forget, how easily I forget. For years, no sooner was I out of Timmons before a remarkable transformation began to take place in my mind's eye and in my heart. No sooner had I merged into the traffic on I-20 or climbed above the clouds over the Columbia airport than Timmons began to wash itself and mellow, to exist in a soft, blue spring twilight. And yet when I'm here, I feel as though I've been caught and shut up inside a box, a hot, windowless, stifling place where nothing comes in and nothing goes out, where the questions already have answers and all conclusions are foregone. Where the responsibility of the individual is to slip in as quietly as possible, take a seat, and pick up the card on which her lines are written, then to speak these lines and no others, for the rest of her life. And as usual, once I was inside the box, I saw only two possible ways to escape: I could kick a hole in the box (and break my foot trying) or go underground, leaving a cutout or a doll of myself up above to smile and voice the right opinions.

"Yes, ma'am," I said, and Miss Leola smiled at me tenderly while Pug checked his watch, looking out through the cemetery gates. "Where is that photographer of mine?" he said. "I hope he didn't forget about this, doggone it."

"Mr. Simmons," Miss Leola sniffed, then squared her shoulders, "it is a sad truth of the modern world, but if you rely on young people these days, quite often you'll find yourself waiting at the station long after the train has come and gone."

"Let's hope not, Miss Leola," Pug said. "This man is usually extremely reliable."

Just then a blue Mustang flashed through the cemetery gates, circled the drive, and stopped behind Pug's Lincoln. A man got out and leaned on the roof of the car and looked over at us. "Well, Pug, I made it with seconds to spare," he said. He was tall and thin with a high, wide forehead and golden-brown eyes, and he wore a white shirt with the sleeves rolled up. His face was startling: gaunt and sad and bony, as though it had been put together all wrong out of pieces that did not fit, and somehow had come out right and kind and alive.

"Welcome, sir," Miss Leola said warily, sizing him up.

"This is Legree Black, Miss Leola," Pug said. "He's our local bug man and sometime photographer. Mr. Black, Miss Leola Fenton." The tall man nodded and I watched him again. I know you, I thought, where have I heard your name before? "Bug man?" Miss Leola said, her hand at her throat, drawing back as if she were about to be handed a plate of something bad to smell.

"I'm a biologist with the state, Miss Leola," he said, gravely polite. His voice was nice; it came from some place deep in his chest. "I work for DHEC." He pronounced it "Dee-heck," and he spoke slowly, as if words were something to be treated with care.

"Oh," she patted her chest rapidly, "of course. Insects, bugs. And good morning to you, sir. Are you one of the Blacks from Little Sandy?"

"No ma'am," he said. "I'm from Honea Path. That's upstate a ways."

"Well, we won't hold that against you," she said, and we all laughed.

"Annie Vess," Pug said, "Legree Black."

"What relation are you to John Vess?" he asked, nodding toward my father's headstone. He had a quick, canny way of looking with his oddly slanted eyes, like the eyes in a Modigliani painting, as though he hoped to catch you off guard, to surprise the truth out of you.

"He was my father," I said.

"Well, how about that?" he said. He spoke as if we had all the time in the world. He and Pug exchanged looks. "I took his picture once." That's where I had seen that name before. "Photo by Legree Black," stamped on the back of that photograph of my father down in the lake bed, the one my mother had bullied Pug into giving her after they ran it in the paper, the one she'd stuck away somewhere and tried to forget, or thrown away, she hated it so. "It's ugly," she'd said. "It shows your father in the worst possible light."

So he'd been there that day, the day they bulldozed the Laughing Place and my father disbanded Save Our Two Rivers, when he stopped believing in goodness, and started looking for revenge. Legree had taken the photograph of my father straddling the bull-dozer tracks beside the Keowee River, his hands balled and shoved deep into the pockets of his hunting jacket, his eyes cold, his mouth a grim line. Now *there* was my father's soul, the one he had made for himself and taken with him out of this world. There was nothing dear or sweet about it. It was made of iron and winter weather and rage, and it howled when it spoke: Never surrender. Never yield. Betrayal is everywhere, in every loss. And this man had seen that in my father, had waited for the moment when Papa's face had settled into its truest lines. Then he'd opened the shutter and let in the light and made a picture of my father's darkness. Legree Black folded his arms on the roof of the car, his chin propped on his fist. "Morning, Annie," he said, and he smiled. He said "morning," but there was night in it too; he said "morning" as if it meant something between us, a reminder of the night before, a promise of the night to come.

I felt something answer inside me, something like the Edisto River the way I'd seen it once—dark, slow, deep, flooding the cypress swamps down near its mouth. "Morning," I said back to him, trying to color it the same shade as his word. And he smiled again. Light seemed to strike his face all at once, and then it was gone.

"Shall we?" Miss Leola asked brightly as she drew a sheet of ivory notepaper out of her purse, straightened her back, and began. "On this day," she read in a strong voice, as though she were speaking to an audience in a big hall, "we gather once again to remember those who have gone on before us with brave spirits fighting for their country and for what they believed to be right. We place these tributes in honor of their memory and in faithfulness to their loyal hearts." When she looked up, there were tears in her eyes.

Pug stepped to her side and squeezed her elbow. "That was lovely, Miss Leola," he said. "As always. Now let's get some pictures."

The time had come for me to go. I had no business here, but I could not go. As they maneuvered again for photographs, I watched Legree. He wasn't in any hurry. He seemed to have hours to wait until Miss Leola had found the right spot. Under the leaning cedar? He obliged and waited while she smoothed down her skirt and adjusted her hat and pulled her gloves up at the wrists. Then he pointed the camera toward her. "Sorry," he said, lowering the camera, "not enough light there, Miss Fenton. We'll have to try for another spot." As if he hadn't known that all along, I thought.

"Well, how about over here next to the gate with the head-stones behind me? We've done that one before, though, haven't we, Mr. Simmons?"

"We have indeed," Pug said.

"Let's give it a try," Legree said.

"Miss Leola," I heard Pug say as I walked away, back toward the Vess plot, "how long have we been bringing you here?"

"A good twenty years at least."

"And what shall we tell the readers this year is the reason you come back here year after year?"

"Oh, Mr. Simmons, let's just say it's an old habit that can't be broken. Nor would I want to, I might add," she said. "I certainly wouldn't want to."

In the Vess plot, I sat on the bench and pushed my heels through the gravel. *An old habit that can't be broken,* she'd said. *You are here*. Is there anyone in the world who's not looking for a place where habits can grow long roots, down from the head or up from the hands and straight on to the heart? Looking back through the cemetery gates, I could see the columns on the front of the court-house through the trees. This used to be the edge of town; beyond the cemetery, the soybean and cotton fields began. Now, through a break in the trees where the power lines ran, I saw underbrush piled up in heaps, the marks of heavy equipment. This would have pleased my father, I thought, to be buried here, next to the Confederate dead, where he could see betrayal and treachery sprout all around him, proving that he'd been right. My father, who never got the chance to make his peace or find a new answer when the old one gave out on him.

Then the picture taking was done, and Legree was coming my way. He had a loose, loping walk, a way of covering ground that looked as though it could carry him a long way. Camera slung over his shoulder, fingers pushed down into the front pocket of his jeans, he walked toward me, and he didn't pretend to be doing anything else. "Hello," he said, when he got close, and I waved back. He looked at Papa's headstone, then back at me, and I watched for mockery on his face, in his eyes, but I didn't find any.

"Mind if I sit down?" he said.

"Please."

It was a short bench, but still, I thought, he sat too close, his leg almost touching mine. There was nothing pushy about it, but I felt crowded, feeling his body beside me, feeling it move as he bent over to pick up a smooth, white piece of gravel and run his thumb over it as though sensing the curve. His clothes smelled clean, cedary, as if they'd just been taken out of storage.

When the silence got too long, I said, "I just can't seem to stay away from cemeteries." I hated the bright, chirpy tone in my voice, but I couldn't seem to stop it. "I come here from time to time just to get my bearings," I said. "It's the only place I know of where things hold still long enough for you to get a grip on them."

"Well, now, that's for sure," he said. He gave me a curious, sideways look with his long, flat eyes as he set the camera down on the bench between us and spun the rock away with a flick of his wrist. "You're from here, I take it?" he said. He slouched forward with his knees spread, his hands clasped loosely between them, moving his old, soft-looking workboots back and forth in the gravel. Loose, that's exactly what he was. He looked as though he were at home in his own body. Nothing like Matthew. Matthew had always chafed against his as though it held him back. He'd moved quickly, impatiently, in bursts of anger, bursts of joy. There was nothing halfway about Matthew. There was nothing easy about him or the way I loved him or he loved me. After he died I promised myself that there would be no one else, not then, not ever, unless I loved him the way I had loved Matthew. I didn't realize, though, until now, with Legree sitting so close, how faithfully I'd kept that promise. How I'd held back, as if Matthew were nearby, watching, listening, as if I could even now betray the life we'd had together or turn a corner and find him, waiting.

"I'm from here," I said. "But I've been away for a long time. After my father died, I came back here—I don't know, it seemed like the right thing to do at the time. It was because it was one of the last places I really knew. You know, like you'd do if you were lost? Something my father taught me, I guess. He used to take my brother and me out in the woods around the Laughing Place and leave us there to find our way back to the house. I mean, he didn't just leave us, he spent a lot of time before he ever did that, teaching us how to find our way around the woods. And he never went far away. I think he was always there, watching us to see that we went the right way. Anyway, it was something like that that brought me back here."

He squinted up into the sun so that fine, white lines ran out from his eyes. In profile his face looked bony, almost grim. "I know that one," he said. "I asked to be transferred out of Columbia after my divorce, and the state sent me here." He looked at me quickly out of the corner of his eye. "That was three years ago. For about two and a half of those three years, I felt like I was stumbling around without a clue."

"I guess I'm not that far along yet," I said, and I concentrated on making two straight grooves with my heels through the gravel.

"No?" he said. "Well, it comes."

"I'm ready."

He pushed both hands back through his hair. It was thick, reddish-brown, and his fingers were very long and quick-looking, but his hands were covered with scratches.

I pointed to them. "What do you do to scratch your hands up that way?"

He turned them over front to back and studied them. "Oh, I travel around the state testing water and making trouble for people who want to dump their sewage in it. Things like that. Right now I work with the turtle project down at Kiawah Island."

"I've been away," I said. "I don't know much about that."

He laughed, dropped his hands to his knees. "You've missed a lot."

"I can see that," I said. And I laughed, too.

"It's really something," he said. "I just got back from down there. They're nesting right now. I've worked with the turtles for four years, and every year I'm amazed all over again. See, these loggerhead turtles, in the spring they swim halfway around the world to get to the beach where they were born and lay their eggs.

"My job during nesting season is to sit on the beach all night and wait for them. That's my favorite part of the job, I think, sitting out on the beach and watching the waves, waiting for that first glimpse of one of their shells." He made the shape of a mound in the air, smoothing the sides as he talked. "One minute, all you see are the waves. The next minute, it's like a small mountain rise up out of the water. And it's one of those big, old queen turtles coming in through the breakers and onto the beach. I mean big, too. Some of these old ladies weigh two hundred, two hundred and fifty pounds. They drag themselves up onto the beach and row through the sand until something tells them to stop and make a nest. Then they dig and dig with their flippers. They dig for hours sometimes, until they've dug a hole that's deep enough to satisfy them, and they drop their eggs in that hole. Hundreds of them, little leathery eggs about that big, about the size of Ping-Pong balls. And when they've laid their eggs and covered the nest, they turn around and drag themselves back into the water and they're gone for another year. Then we go out there and mark the nests, put down sections of wire over them, and weight the corners so the coons can't dig them up."

"Why do they need you?" I asked.

"Well, that beach—all the barrier island beaches, really—are so built up now. And the turtles are very wary when they're coming up to lay their eggs. If something startles them, a light or a loud noise, they'll turn around and go back into the ocean without laying their eggs and no one knows what happens to them then. Also, we run interference for the turtles once they hatch. As soon as they're born, the hatchling turtles move toward light. Ideally, they hatch when the moon's full or almost and then they'll head for the track of the moon on the water. But if somebody turns on a flood light on a house behind the beach, they'll go toward that and they'll crawl up in the dunes and die, or the coons will get them, or the gulls. So when they're hatching, we go house to house and ask people to keep their outside lights off at night; if the turtles hatch during the day, we carry them into the water to keep the gulls from getting them." He held up his hands as though he'd decided something about them. "But to answer your question," he said, "I scratch my hands cutting wire to go over the nests," he said.

"You should wear gloves," I said. How prissy, I thought, and bit my lip. What I mean is, your hands are beat up and graceful, drawing turtle shells in the air.

"Listen," he said, still holding up his hands, squinting between the fingers, "what do you do with yourself?" He dropped them into his lap. "Are you married?" he said, and looked directly into my eyes as if he might surprise the answer out of me. His eyes had layers to them, like the dark, clear water of a pond.

I swallowed, and my mouth felt dry. I felt confused by his bluntness, as though I'd suddenly found myself in an unfamiliar place where I didn't speak the language. But I made myself say it, I wanted it to be plain and true. "My husband was killed a year ago last month," I said. "He was bush-hogging a field and not looking where he was going, and the tractor turned over on him. At his parent's farm, up near Cheraw. His name was Matthew."

He wiped his hands down the legs of his jeans, but he didn't look away. Right then, a hot breeze sprang up and raced around and around the hill. It whipped the limbs of the cedar tree and blew up a dust devil that glittered with sharp flecks of mica. It whipped my hair all over my face and into my eyes so I couldn't see Legree, but when I'd brushed it all back again and held it with one hand, he was still there. His face was not blank or stunned or already easing out the door, as the faces of other men had done when they'd learned about Matthew. Instead it was as if someone had sprung a question on him, one that would take time and care to answer, one that could be answered just the same. He ducked his head. "All right," he said to himself as he picked at a thumbnail. "I've never lost anyone close. I don't know how a person survives that. I can't figure it, can you? Some people get knocked down and they get up. Some people stay down. Why is that? I'm sorry," he said. "But I'm glad you got up."

"I think I might have made it up onto my knees," I said, and at that moment I knew it was true. "At least that far." It was an absolutely ridiculous thing to say.

"Knees are fine," he said. "Knees are good. I spend a lot of time on my knees, too."

"That's good," I said. And then we just sat there smiling at each other.

"Young people, oh, young people." From outside the fence that surrounded the Confederate graves, Miss Leola flapped her white gloves at us. She and Pug stood in the shade of the tall cedar beside the broken iron gate. "Thank you, Mr. Black, for your patience and perseverance. Annie Vess, good day. Do, please, tell your mother hello for me."

Legree slapped his knees and stood up. "Me, too," he said. "I told somebody I'd meet them for lunch."

Lunch? From the way he said it, I knew that the someone was a woman.

"I have an appointment, too," I said, and I stood up, checked the watch I wasn't wearing.

"Listen," he said, and he touched my wrist, touched the bone there as though he knew the exact spot he wanted to touch. "Could I see you sometime?"

"I was going to ask you the same thing," I said. "I'd like that very much. I'll give you my number, you give me yours."

"I'll get it from information," he said, slapping his pockets. "I don't have a pen on me just now, but I think I can remember your name. My number is 647-6391."

"I have a pen," I said.

"I'll get it from information," he said, and something stubborn happened to his eyes and mouth, something willful.

"All right," I said, "It's under John Vess, on Wyman Street." He looked puzzled, shook his head. "I live with my mother," I said. "She's a widow, too." Why did I say that? I thought. Because I have to know. Does he scare easily?

He faltered, but he didn't spook. "Well, now," he said. He ducked his head and made a big show of picking up the camera from the seat between us, brushing it off, testing the give on the film advance lever.

"It's all right," I said, "that's kind of a joke." I wanted to poke him, shake him. Laugh with me, Legree. That's the best joke I've told on myself since I came back here. Isn't it amazing that, without knowing quite how you got there, you realize you're beyond the place you used to be? Someone reminds you *you are here*, and you turn and look back and see how far you've traveled. So laugh, Legree.

Honea Path

On Saturday morning, before full light, there came a knock on the back door. It wasn't a loud or an urgent knock. Just *knock, knock,* then a pause and two more knocks. Persistent. As if whoever had knocked and waited would keep on knocking until someone opened the door. Workmen, I thought, and I had my bathrobe on and was halfway down the stairs before I remembered that it was Saturday, and no one here worked on Saturday, not even for my mother.

Mother would have been horrified to learn that I'd gone on down the stairs. As I passed through the kitchen, I could almost hear her frantic whisper: "Come back here, have you lost your mind? Get back in bed, call the police." I hadn't been home a month before she'd had the phone company come out and install a telephone next to my bed, just in case. And just in case, she'd personally written in the numbers on the emergency numbers sticker and pasted it to the receiver where it glowed a sickly green all night long. All I had to do was call the police, whisper my danger, and wait for help.

I opened the door, and there on the front porch, holding our quart of milk and a bunch of pussy willow branches wrapped in green florist's paper, was Legree. Over his shoulder the gray in the sky had been stirred with gold. He held out the milk first, then the pussy willows. "For you and for you," he said. "I had to run down to the coast. I got back late last night and got your messages." In the half-dark, his white shirt glowed and his face was like a place where erosion had done its work.

As soon as I saw him, I knew I'd been fooling myself. Since Monday, the day we'd met in the cemetery, I'd called and left three messages on his answering machine. After the third one, I'd gotten strict with myself. You are being a fool, I said. If the man wanted to see you, he would call. That was just a little dance you both did for your own reasons up there in the cemetery. And I'd put him out of my mind as neatly as though I'd crossed his name off a list. Or so I'd thought. But now that he was here, I saw that I hadn't x-ed him out at all. What I'd done was lose the list. And when I found it again and saw his name, it all came back. Oh, yeah, that's what I wanted.

"These are beautiful," I whispered.

He checked his watch. "Listen," he whispered back. "Did I wake you? What time do you get up?" Then he tapped his watch and held it to his ear, frowning.

"That depends," I said, "on what kind of day it looks like it's going to be. What time is it, anyway?"

"I see," he said, in the way he'd said "morning" in the cemetery that day. "It's six-thirty," he whispered, "and I've come to ask if you'd like to go somewhere with me today."

I held the door open. "I think I would," I said.

"Why are we whispering?" he said.

I pointed to the ceiling. "Mother."

"I'll take my chances," he said, louder this time.

"Me, too," I said. "Come in." As he brushed past me, I thought I smelled ocean air, salt marsh. A man in this house early in the morning, a man's body, so close. A man's smell, the kind of smell I used to love about Matthew, so rich and warm you wanted to put your hand, your face, your whole body against skin that smelled like that. Just inside the door he stopped, and he studied a pussy willow bud with one finger. "They had all these flowers out at Kroger's, but

I brought you these because I thought you might be a person who liked pussy willows. You sure do look nice holding them."

The buds felt downy-soft and tender against my cheek, like a cat's paw when it barely touches you. "I think I must be a person who likes pussy willows," I said. "Thank you." He smiled then, that wide, slow smile that forgives his face its errors, that is like a river broadening, catching the sun.

As I dressed, I heard him helping himself to coffee in the kitchen, and when I came down again, I found him in the dining room studying the portraits of the Vesses. "Who are the old folks?" he said.

"My great-great-grandparents."

"Your looks must come from the other side of the family," he said. And then he sat down at the dining room table where he'd put his coffee cup and saucer, as though he belonged here. I liked having him in my house so early in the morning. His presence shook things up, rearranged them, and gave them different possibilities. I liked the way the pussy willows looked when I put them in a deep, blue vase and set them on the dining room table between the silver candlesticks with their perpetual white candles. I liked the way he moved into the kitchen with me and the way he sat at the table, scooped up the eggs I'd made for us, and spread them onto his toast. And the quick, sharp way he looked up and stopped chewing to listen when I talked. When he'd mopped up the last of the eggs and finished off the toast, he said, "I thought I'd go up and see my folks today. They live up the country a ways, and I thought you might like to go. They're old," he added. "I go and see them as often as I can."

It was the way he said those two things, about their being old and going to see them often, the matter-of-factness of it, that did it for me. "Well, I guess the sort of person who likes pussy willows would be the sort of person who might like to go with you to see your parents," I said.

He looked surprised, then pleased. He folded his hands on the table in front of me. "Well," he said in his thoughtful way, as though everything deserves listening to, contemplating. "I guess you might say that, yes. I guess that might have entered into it."

I left Mother a note: "Gone off for the day. Don't wait supper."

As we drove north toward Honea Path, the land rose and dried and reddened and cracked; the sky grew white, as though it had been bleached. *The white skies of Carolina*, Matthew used to say. To him, they symbolized all that was oppressive and numbing here. It wasn't even June yet, and in the pastures beside the highway, the grass looked sparse and thin. The cattle standing in the narrow washes of shade under the trees were bony, as if no matter how much thin, brown grass they ate, they wouldn't get any fatter.

By the time we turned off the four-lane highway an hour later, I knew plenty about Legree. I knew about his parents. "Well, they're old," he'd said. "I forget every time how old they are. I was what they call around here a change-of-life baby. And my father's sick. He's got emphysema from breathing cotton dust in the goddamn Piedmont Mills for forty years. Or at least that's what I've tried to tell him, but he never listens to me. He just sits there with his oxygen mask over his face when it gets really bad, taking little sips of oxygen like that's all he's entitled to. Won't say a word against the company. Some people came around once trying to collect information about the workers in that plant who'd gotten sick like he had. They were going to try and bring a class action suit against the company and get some compensation, but he had Mama send them away. He wouldn't even talk to them. Do you know that when he retired, they gave him a watch? A goddamn Timex watch like the ones you buy at the drugstore, and this little nothing pension, and he keeps that watch in a box on the mantle in the living room like it was the Congressional Medal of Honor or something."

"And Mama," he said. He laughed. "She's just like Daddy. She still works at Regency Textiles—that's the other big mill around here—sewing the button plackets on shirts. Takes what they give her, never complains. Every Christmas, instead of a bonus or even a turkey for Christ's sake, they give them each a bolt of cloth. She's got a chest full of them in there. Never throws a thing away. I swear."

Up ahead I could see a brick church with wide steps and a steeple. It was set in a treeless yard covered with white gravel and with a cemetery spread on three sides. Abruptly Legree swerved over into the church parking lot, killed the engine, and scrunched down into his seat so suddenly that I looked around to see what he was hiding from. *Mt. Hebron Baptist. Rev. J. B. Cathcart, Pastor. Sunday School 9* A.M. *Services 10:30* A.M. *Wednesday evening Bible study 7:30* P.M. *Register now for Vacation Bible School. All welcome,* read a portable sign out near the highway. The heat rolled into the car like a big flag unfurling. He wiped his hands down his thighs and took a deep breath, worked his shoulders. "So Mount Hebron's gone modern," he said, nodding at the sign. "I always stop here and get my bearings," he said, then he braced his hands on his knees and rolled his head, worked his shoulders.

"We could have some long talks on that subject," I said.

"I hope we will," he said.

"Me, too."

He stared out through the windshield, wiping at the dust on the dashboard with his free hand. "This is, as they say, my home church. I always have to stop here to psych myself up. I have to remind myself that it's going to be the way it is, not the way I'd like it to be. What are you looking at?" he asked. "Do you always take everything so seriously? You look at things so seriously, like you're trying to get their number, size them up."

"You have to," I said. "That way, there's less chance that something's going to sneak up and surprise you."

"You mean that, don't you."

"I do."

He reached under the seat, pulled two cans of Colt .45 Malt Liquor out of a paper bag, and offered me one. I had to laugh. "Colt .45," I said. "We used to get drunk on that in high school."

"Me, too," he said, as he pulled back the tab and dropped it onto the floor. Then he took a deep swallow and shook his head. "God, that's awful stuff," he said. That's why I have to drink it here. To show myself that the Baptists haven't got me too much under lock and key. You'll forgive me?" he said. "You're not Baptist, are you?"

"I'll forgive you," I said, "if you'll forgive me for taking every-thing so seriously."

"Done," he said, and he slid down in the seat until his head rested on the back. "Well, then, let me tell you about Brother." His mother's brother, Legree said, and never called anything but that. He'd been kicked in the head by a mule when he was six and sent to the State Hospital in Columbia when he was fifteen. "Then Mama started grieving," Legree said. Something touched me about that word, grieving. There was something old and unashamed about it that belonged here, with him, in this place. "She grieved for two years, and Brother kept walking away from the hospital. Finally she and Daddy went down to Columbia and brought Brother home. He's lived with us ever since I can remember. I used to be ashamed to bring people here because of Brother." He took a big sip of beer and wiped his chin.

"What changed your mind?"

"It wasn't my mind that changed," he said. "I got older. Things happened to me. I wasn't so ashamed of Brother anymore." He shook his head as though he'd just come up from underwater, then he tossed his beer can over his shoulder out the window. It landed with a clink in the gravel of the parking lot. "Legree," I said. "What are you doing!"

"That's another thing you need to know about me. I'm a redneck—I like to drink beer and throw my beer cans out into church parking lots." He draped himself over the steering wheel and started the car. Then he flung it into gear and floored the accelerator, and we fishtailed back onto the narrow blacktop road.

The road we were on had no center line, and kudzu lapped at the edges. The sun came through the windshield and caught him full in the face. In its hard light he looked undernourished and bony, like this place with its pale sky and spent fields. As a child, he might have been pigeon-chested, milk-blue, his collar bones and ribs showing. He might have grown up into a man who stumbles drunk along the shoulder of the highway late on a cold night, with his shirt flapping open, no shoes on his feet, no house in sight. But he had turned into another kind of man instead. "Well, what happened to you, Legree?" I asked.

"What do you mean, what happened to me?" He gave me a sharp, sideways look.

"How come you aren't working at Regency Textiles or Piedmont Mills? How come you're a biologist with the state instead?"

He laughed. "I never really thought about it," he said. "When it was time to go, I went. Lots of people didn't. And my parents didn't try and stop me, not once. I think that's why I come back here as much as I do now, because they never once tried to convince me that I ought to stay and do what they'd done. And me being an only child, too. It's a real tribute to them that they could do that, and that's what makes me so angry when my father just sits there and breathes his oxygen and takes his pills and never questions how he got to be that way. That's what got me interested in biology, in a way, because I wanted to understand what had happened to him and to be able to explain it to him so that he'd understand. But it's gone way beyond that now, of course. You sure got me going with those questions," he said.

"Good," I said. "I'm glad." I slid down into the seat with my knees against the dash, stuck my hand out the window, and pushed against the air that pushed back against it. I was feeling unaccountably happy to be going on this morning with this man wherever he was taking me, happy to listen to him tell how he grew from that milk-blue child into this man.

"Now what about you?"

Just then, a persimmon tree flashed by, across a ditch on the edge of the field. Then two more. Tall, skinny trees with deeply furrowed bark, flowering now, a blur of white flowers. "Not much to say," I said quickly. *Too much to say*, I should have said, and if I start telling you, I may not be able to stop myself. Everything will speed up until I'm going too fast, and if I go too fast and think too much about Matthew, I may finally remember the one thing I loved most about him, the thing I cannot live without. And then where will I be?

"Fair enough, I guess," he said, frowning. As we drove in silence, I thought of Matthew and me driving from Chapel Hill to Cheraw for the first time to introduce me to his family. I remembered how eagerly I went, how I wanted to know everything about him, to see every place that had mattered to him, to walk on the ground where he'd grown up, to sleep in his house.

It was Thanksgiving and we were headed for Cheraw to have dinner with his family. We'd promised to bring something, but we had no money, no food. We lived on a high, ragged edge where whatever we had—rent money, food money, clothes—was scavenged or borrowed or somehow miraculously appeared at the last minute. People trusted Matthew, and he trusted them back. He had an open face, friendly and strong, and when he talked, people believed him. Matthew said not to worry. We would start for Cheraw, he said, and something would turn up.

It was a low, cold day, the sky like a bowl of gray overturned, and we'd driven for miles down long stretches of highway through bleak, lost country—like this country except that it was winter then. We took a back road to Cheraw past sandy fields and patches of scrub oak and pine, and chimneys to mark where houses had once stood. And suddenly, there beside the road was a persimmon tree, holding up branches bare of leaves and crowded with globes of coral-colored fruit. And the ground beneath this tree was also covered with fruit, as ripe as it would ever be. Without a word Matthew backed up and set the parking brake. Without a word we filled a basket with fruit, then sat down on the cold ground together and divided a persimmon, its inside's clear amber, candy-sweet. And though we never said a word, we both knew that we were going to be married and that our lives would be full of grace. Matthew told his parents while I baked the fruit into a loaf of sweet bread sprinkled with pecans from the Settleses' trees—a loaf so heavy and rich and sweet, not a slice was left by the end of that Thanksgiving Day. And now I was thinking about that time again. I had promised myself I would not do that. Why had I come with Legree on this trip where persimmon trees appeared beside the road with no warning? Why hadn't I stayed at home, where there were no persimmon trees?

The car slowed to turn. "Are you all right?" Legree asked. "Are you crying?"

"No," I said. "I'm sorry. Let's go on."

"We're there," he said, and we turned up a rutted driveway almost hidden in the spreading shade of a tremendous live oak. Its roots showed in the eroded ditch bank, and we drove around behind an unpainted house, weathered deep brown. A face appeared, then disappeared in a window that was lined with pots of bright-red geraniums. "Those are Brother's flowers," Legree said as he set the parking brake. "That's what he does every year. They have to be red geraniums, nothing else, set in that same window. And that person you saw was Mama," he said. "She's now in the kitchen starting dinner. I swear." He got out and stretched, then looked around with his hands on his hips.

An old brown hound with a chewed-up ear rose and stretched underneath a chinaberry tree whose trunk was covered in welts from the dog's chain. "Hello, Samson," Legree called, and the dog settled back into a pit in the clay under the tree and thumped its heavy tail twice on the ground. A big man in short overalls and unlaced workboots stood by a leaning shed filled with cages behind the chinaberry tree. He was squinting at the car and holding a halter in both hands as if he were trying to pull it apart. "There's Brother, with his pigeons," Legree said.

When Brother saw Legree, he dropped the halter and loped toward the car, his mouth working, a fierce frown knotting his face—a moon of a face under a thin fringe of hair, unguarded and fragile, the vulnerable face of a child. His smile, when it finally came, was almost painful to see, too bright and too hopeful. As he came closer, I saw that his face was caved in around a faint but unmistakable hoof mark in the middle, as if someone had taken the features and crimped them around the hoof mark, then pushed the whole arrangement in. "Hey, Brother," Legree said, "come say hello to me," and he crossed quickly to where the big man stood frowning at the ground. Legree lifted Brother's chin and looked at him. He put his arms around Brother, and the big man laid his head on his shoulder and sighed and patted Legree on the back with hands as flat and wide as paddles. "Gree," he said. "Gree," and he closed his eyes.

Legree turned Brother around and held him by both arms, and Brother stared at me with eyes that might once have been brown but had paled to a shallow, splintered gold. "This is Annie," he said. "She's a friend of mine." Brother frowned and turned away.

His hands worked furiously at each other as if they were covered with something sticky. Legree took him by the nape of the neck and turned him to face me. "No, Brother," he said. "Say hello. You know how to do that."

"Hello, Brother," I said. He stretched his neck toward me like a goose. His eyes popped and his fingers worked at each other, then cautiously one hand inched out until it touched mine; it rested there for a moment, damp and cool and heavy. Then he nodded quickly, drew back his neck and hand, and looked at Legree. "That's good," Legree said. "That's good, Brother." Brother wandered off again toward the shed. He picked up the halter and studied its junctures, keeping a suspicious eye on us.

Beside the back door a twisted pear tree grew, its trunk ringed with borer holes and a few flowering branches held up like blossoming sleeves on skinny arms. At its foot was a millstone sunk into the ground. From there, several steps led up onto the rickety wood porch where half a dozen gaunt cats sunned themselves among old coffee cans that spilled over with thrift, and washtubs full of tomato seedlings. Legree went up the steps on tiptoe. He pressed his face against the screen door and called, "Anybody home?"

"Oh, Lord," a woman's voice said from inside. "Look who's here. And me up to my elbows in flour."

I found myself enjoying this immensely, watching Legree come home, listening to him talk to his mother. It had the well worn feel of a much-rehearsed, much-performed scene from a play, and yet there was such pleasure in his face as he stepped to the side of the door, pressed himself against the house, and put his finger to his lips. I stepped aside, too, off of the millstone and around the edge of the porch just as a woman came to the screen door, wiping her hands on her apron. "Legree, son," she called. "Where are you now? Don't tease me like that."

One, two, three. Then he stepped into sight, and she was out the door and holding him with her wrists, her hands all covered with flour. She held him away from her and looked at his face. "Oh, son," she said, "it's just so good to see you. Why didn't you tell us you were coming?"

"I like surprises," he said, "but my friend here doesn't." She was a tall, thin woman, angular as a prow, her thin, dark hair pulled back severely into a bun. But when he turned her around by the shoulders to meet me, I saw where Legree had gotten his eyes, a brown so deep and still it looked as though the peace in them went all the way down.

"This is Annie," he said, and her hands went up to her hair.

"You don't need to go to any trouble for me," I said. When she hugged me, I smelled frying grease and sweet soap. "I'm happy to meet you," she said. She watched Legree while she said it, as if she couldn't keep her eyes off of him, as if she counted on him to tell her whether what she'd done was right.

"And I'm happy to meet you," I said. "I'm happy to be here."

"Daddy's lying down," she said, "He'll be up directly. You all come in the kitchen if you can stand the mess."

Inside, the kitchen was extraordinarily clean, the floor freshly mopped, and the table in the middle of the room covered with a blue-checkered oilcloth. The chrome gleamed on the stove and the tinfoil under the burners looked new. Even the old, brown space heater that stood at one end of the room and the stovepipe that led from the back of the heater through a hole in the ceiling had been polished. I imagined Legree growing up under that care in these rooms, thought of his carefulness, the patience in his hands and voice, and I felt as though I knew something about him that I hadn't known before I'd walked into this place and seen his mother's eyes.

When everything was ready, and the platter of fried chicken and bowls of rice, gravy, and lima beans had been laid out on the table, Brother came in. He washed his hands and ducked his whole head under the sink faucet, dried his hair on a thin, white towel that hung from a drawer pull, and seated himself. Legree disappeared into the back of the house. In a few minutes he came back leading his father, a frail old man with something of the narrow-eyed, smiling dimness of a Chinese sage about him. He also wheeled an oxygen tank attached by tubes to his father's nose. Mr. Black looked soft as old cloth—much worn and washed and folded, then put away and taken out and worn again. When he shook my hand, I was surprised at the hardness of his palm, the strength of his grip. But after he said grace, pausing between each word to breathe, he couldn't speak. Breathing seemed to take all of his strength.

Of course, they asked about me. What I did and how long I'd lived in Timmons, and did I think it was going to be as hot as they said it was supposed to be this summer. But it was Legree they were hungry for. They treated him like the crown prince or the prodigal son returned to nothing but welcome. Before Brother took anything from a plate or a bowl, he passed it to Legree, and whenever Legree spoke, Brother stopped chewing and listened, frowning hard. Legree's mother hovered behind his chair with the tea pitcher and the platter of chicken, ready to fill up any empty spot that appeared on his plate. His father looked up and smiled and squinted as though the sun were in his eyes every time Legree spoke.

And I watched and listened and wondered about Legree. He basked in the attention the way those skinny cats basked in the sun on the back porch, but there was nothing arrogant or lazy in that basking. He seemed to take it seriously that these people loved him so. I imagined him growing up here, growing up alongside Brother who did not grow, among everything else that did not change so much as it repeated itself, daily, yearly, round and round. What force had come up in him that had carried him out and away!

As he talked to his mother about the turtles, her fork moved slowly. "How many do you figure'll hatch out cafe this time, son?" she asked.

He shrugged. "No way to tell," he said. "Depends on how many nests the coons or the people get into."

"People?" she said, laying her fork down in surprise.

"Right. People steal turtle eggs, too. You know what for?"

"What?"

"Pastry," he said.

"You don't mean it."

"*Pastry*," he said again, shaking his head. "Turtle eggs are supposed to make great pastry."

"Lord, have mercy," his mother said, looking at him proudly. "It takes all kinds to make this world, doesn't it?"

"It does," he said. And as I watched and listened, I wondered if it might be possible that I was hearing and seeing the source of his patience, of the kindness and care he took, here among the people who loved him, who counted on him to see and hear and be so much for them.

Over the banana pudding, his father finally spoke again. "Got your work done on that island, did you say, son?" His hands shook when he picked up his glass of tea. That's why she'd filled it only halfway, I thought, so he wouldn't spill it.

"Not yet," Legree said. It was the shortest answer he'd given all day, and he didn't look up from his plate. There was something closed and tight about his face, the way he'd looked earlier in the Baptist church parking lot.

"Well, when it's finished, then what?"

"Then I take a vacation," he said as he squashed grains of rice into the gravy with the back of his fork.

"Well, now, son, you don't want to go doing anything that'll make them question how steady a worker you are," he said, still smiling that wise man's distant smile.

Something seemed to go out of Legree then, and he put both arms on the table on either side of his plate. "No, sir," he said, "I won't." And he reached over and squeezed his father's arm where it lay on the table.

After I'd done my share of washing dishes, I went into the living room to wait for Legree. On top of the heater, I found a photograph of Legree in a gold frame. There he stood, skinny and solemn, in a pool in front of a wall painted with a landscape of rivers and hills. The day of his baptism, no doubt. A man stood beside him, one hand on Legree's shoulder, the other raised. I should not be doing this, I thought. Poking into your life, seeing who you were once and matching it with who you are now. But already I knew it was too late. Even now, I thought, if I never saw you again, I would know what I had lost. It happens too fast, how people come to matter."

By the time the dishes were washed and put up and the counter scrubbed and the floor swept, it was close to four—past time for his father's afternoon nap. But the rest of us went out onto the back porch. Legree's mother sat in a straight-backed chair from the kitchen, a damp dishtowel spread out on her lap to dry while the scrawny cats wove themselves in and out of her legs. "All right, Brother," she called. "We're ready." This was, Legree had said on the way here, telling me what would happen, the eternal and unchanging end of every summer afternoon. Brother walking solemnly toward his pigeon cote, looking down at the ground. Brother coming back around the corner of the cote with three pigeons, soft brown and speckled like eggs, nestling in his arms. Brother standing beside the porch and handing his pigeons up to Legree's mother, who took them from him and looked at their eyes, opened their beaks, lifted their wings while Brother watched her, his small, close-set eyes moving anxiously from her face to the pigeon and back to her face. "The tumblers today, Brother," she said. "Well, this one looks fine to me," she said. "And this one, too."

"Watch this, now," Legree said. He squatted down on the porch beside his mother's chair. "You won't believe it." And then Brother crouched, and then he sprang, throwing both pigeons up into the air. And there he stayed, with his hands flung up, balanced on one foot like a statue of a man reaching after what he has just set free, a man who has just felt a lightness rise up through his own heavy body, and has let it shape him, and hold him, in this posture of flight. The pigeons rolled end over end through the air, flashing brown and white, then landed in small puffs of dust one behind the other, and walked around, clucking. Brother let his arms fall and smiled at us—that dazzling, trusting smile—and then he began to run, the waddling run of a woodchuck, toward where the pigeons walked on the ground like ordinary pigeons. He scooped them up and cuddled them close to his chest, talking to them in a low, urgent voice.

"Who in the world taught them that?" I asked. "Brother?"

Legree and his mother looked at one another and laughed. "Those are parlor tumbler pigeons," she said, as Brother disappeared again around the edge of the leaning shed. "Nobody taught them. They just do that, that's what they're bred for."

"If that's all they can do, that's enough," I said. "I've never seen anything like it."

After Legree's mother had gone back inside, he said, "Let's go for a walk."

"Let's do that," I said, and up close his eyes looked like brown river water with the sun going down into it, picking out flecks of gold. He got a red blanket out of the trunk of the car and we walked past the shed with its cages of cooing pigeons and onto a dirt track that was grown up in plume grass and broom sedge. It led away from the back of the house until all we could see were the gables of the roof. Then we struck out across a patchy little field covered thinly with grass, and soon the house dropped from sight.

We walked until the field we were crossing ended at a hickory grove so thick the ground beneath the trees was bare and it was already night inside. He held the blanket to his chest and stared into the grove as though he were trying to decide something. "Let's stop here for awhile," I said, touching his back. When he turned, there was a fierceness to his face that I hadn't seen before, and as he spread the blanket at the edge of the woods, his arms trembled.

We lay down apart from each other. It was nice just to lie there and feel the flattened weeds and grass softening the hard rocks of the field under my back. Currents of cool air moved over my arms and legs and face like little eddies of water moving, smelling of heat and grass and the damper, loamy smell of the hickory grove. The sun came at a low slant through the grasses, drifted through spider webs and dust, and the sound of cicadas rose and fell, rose and fell, like a pulse waxing and waning, and it seemed as if the whole field were alive with sound and heat and insects that moved in small galaxies against the light. My shirt stuck to my rib cage and I could see Legree's ribs, too, and I imagined putting my mouth on them, kissing them, running my fingers along each one. Be careful, something warned me, and I put my arm up over my eyes. There was only a bright darkness under my eyelids, and the sounds of the field, the rustlings and rattlings and brushings and scurryings, and the feel of Legree's body there so close, still separate from mine. And for the moment, that was enough.

I felt him before I saw him, felt the sun blocked out, and then Legree kissed me and I kissed him and drew him down, held him and felt his ribs, ran my hands down his back, over his face, every place that I had wanted to touch. We took a long time undressing each other, and when he finally lowered his body onto mine I was surprised at how heavy he felt. He was a skinny man but he was solid—that was the wonderful secret of his body, and I gasped to learn that secret. I closed my eyes and kissed him again and again, kissed him long and kissed him sweet, though Matthew's angry spirit flew up like a red mist in the dark behind my eyes.

When he entered me, he was looking at my face. "Hey," he said softly, "you know why I brought you those pussy willows?" He propped himself on his elbows and brushed the hair back from my face.

"Legree," I said, "don't talk, not now," and with my hips and hands I eased him deeper.

"There's plenty of time," he said, and those words made me feel cold and scared. "No there isn't, don't you know that?" I almost said, but he bent down and whispered in my ear. "It's because I'd been thinking about you all week, how soft you'd be right here. So soft And I was right." And then he moved, and I rose to meet him, moved around him like a wide, slow mouth, and he said, "Oh," softly, "oh," as though he'd just discovered something.

And then I felt myself open in front of him, and I was crying out for everything I'd forgotten that was coming back to me again, running through his body and into mine and back to him, like color washing through me, deep blue with a gold center. And we swam toward that center until there was no place else to go except into the color that ran all through my body in broad veins of gold.

Afterward, we lay still, holding each other. Over his shoulder I watched a spider weave a web between two tall spikes of grass. It wove with such precision, all its legs moving at once, plucking and drawing and joining threads of the web, and I felt as if I could have woven the same fine junctures with my hands. Because I could feel my body, every inch of it where it was pressed against him, it was as though my body had been returned to me; I loved to feel it move, feel the air touching it, feel the sun and his hands. In the car going back to Timmons, it took only the feel of the weave of his shirt and the skin beneath it against my cheek to bring the sensation back to me.

"You know what?" I said later, as we drove through the dark, back toward Timmons.

"What?"

"I'd go back there anytime just to see Brother and those pigeons," I said. "Or to sleep with you in that field."

"Is that what you'd go for?" He brushed my cheek with the back of his free hand, then turned the palm for me to lean against. "Well, I'd go to that field with you any day of the year. Any day."

"Do you ever think you'd go back there to live?"

"No," he said. "That place played itself out years ago. That's one reason everybody went to work in the mills. There's nothing for me there but them." I had not talked with anyone like this since Matthew died. Easy and open, like friends.

We sat in the driveway in front of the house that was lit up like a freighter on a reef, and kissed for a long time. "Why'd your mother leave so many lights on?" he said. "It's awfully bright around here." His mouth was on my neck, up under my hair. "How about you come to my place for awhile? Come on," he said. I leaned my head against the back of the seat and stroked his back, felt his lips brush my neck, brush down toward my breasts. Warmth rose in my body, as though it were rushing up toward the surface. *Be careful*, a voice said inside me. Remember Matthew, remember what you lost. I sat up. "I couldn't do that," I said. "Mother'd have the police out after me."

"All right," he said, and he started the engine. "I wouldn't let them in, but if that's what you want, all right."

"I know," I said. "Look, give me time, Legree. You said there was plenty of time, remember?" I touched his mouth, and it was full and soft, but he pulled away and draped his arms over the steering wheel, gunning the engine. "Did I say that?" he said.

Mother was gone, but I found a note on the kitchen table. "Where have you *been*?" it read. "I've been waiting for you all day. Mel and

I had to run out to the mall to see about a mistake in her bridal registry in the linen department at Belk's. When I come back, I want to hear all about your day. Love, Me."

I mixed myself a bourbon and water and carried the drink down to Mother's patio and turned on the fountain. The little girl held her umbrella over her head and water showered off her umbrella and back into the fountain pool at her feet. She held her skirt out with one hand and looked into the water, a secretive smile on her face, and I had to admit that Mother had been right about this. It was peaceful here. I sat down on the white wrought-iron bench that faced the fountain. The evening was so soft and fine, the light violet-gray and fading. A last current of light flowed through the tops of the pines along the back of the lot and set their needles gleaming. I took off my shoes, leaned back, and looked up at the sky where the stars were beginning to show. In front of the house, kids ran up and down the sidewalks, their voices bright and far away.

I thought of Legree's face, his hands on my body. Something in me leaned toward him the way you'd lean out of an open window on a beautiful day. Something had begun between us up there in Honea Path. Honea Path. It might have been the name of the path we'd taken from his house out into the field. I would have to ask him how the real place had gotten that name. Who had named it Honea Path, the little faded town we'd driven through on the way back to Timmons, with its single traffic light and its war memorial, its drugstore and department store showing sun-faded, pastel dresses in the window?

That is when I felt the sadness coming. I'd learned to smell it, the way you can smell rain in the air. Time to go back inside. I hurried through the house and up to my room. I opened the closet and touched the box that held Matthew's ashes, up on the top shelf where I'd put it when I first came home, then I went to the window and looked down. When I saw that I'd left the fountain on, I lay down on my bed and I let the sadness come. It wasn't the bad, swamping sadness or the sharp, tearing kind. The time for those was over. It was another kind of sadness now—quieter but broader, the sadness of finding the world different than Matthew and I had agreed it had to be, finding myself changed to live in it while he stayed behind, dead, finished. Dead, when what I'd wanted was for us to change together, to lie in bed at night and laugh, looking back on who we'd been. "What *kids* we were then," I'd wanted us to say to one another, and forgive our younger selves their foolish hopes. But Matthew would never change now, and every change in me carried me farther from him.

The Known World

My mother and father were great party goers and party givers. When I was growing up, a month didn't pass when they weren't planning to go to a party or to throw one of their own, as though the year had a cycle of parties as well as seasons through which it moved.

My parents' parties polished ordinary days and made them into celebrations. On the opening day of dove season, they gave their annual buffet supper, and before the Clemson–South Carolina football game, they always hosted a tailgate picnic in the parking lot outside the stadium. There were Christmas parties and New Year's Eve parties and Easter egg hunts for the children, and sometimes there were parties for no reason at all except that my parents liked to be with their friends, eating, drinking, playing cards. Each fall, they gave an oyster roast. Papa hired Herbert Jenkins to drive down to the coast and bring back a load of oysters, iced down in the back of his pickup. He dug a pit in the backyard and fitted a grate into the pit, and on the day of the party he tended the slow-burning fire under the grate where the oysters roasted. He shoveled them himself onto the wooden plank tables lined up under the porte cochere, then he circulated through the crowd of guests, passing out advice along with the stubby knives we used for prying open the shells.

There were people in town who swore they wouldn't want to live through a year in which they weren't invited to a Vess oyster roast. Before one of their big parties at the house, the downstairs gleamed with silver and waxed furniture and polished floors, and the upstairs was steamy from bath water and sweet with perfume and aftershave. There were earrings and necklaces scattered all over the top of Mother's dressing table because my mother owned special jewelry—even some diamonds. Before a party she would take them out and lay them on her dress, hold them up to her neck as she sat in her slip in front of the mirror, admiring herself in her jewelry. She smelled wonderful just before a party, and her smell was not one odor but a complex blend of soap, cream, perfume, new clothes. Carefully she removed the cellophane wrapper from a new package of stockings and unfolded them from around the cardboard, then she ran her hand all the way down into the foot of one of her new stockings, spread her hand, and inspected the stocking all over for runs. Holding a bunch of long, crimped hairpins in her mouth, she sat in front of her mirror and turned her head from side to side, studying her face or profile as she pinned up her deep chestnut hair in a roll at the nape of her neck. Her shoulders beneath the straps of her slip were thick and freckled.

Now Mother was giving a party again. The year had moved on; already the season of my father's death was ending because even grief lifts, changes color and hue. When I heard it, I let out my breath as if I'd been holding it and hadn't known why. "Just a little prenuptial celebration for Mel and Canady," she said. "Just something to christen the new patio. Ask that boy, if you want to," she said.

"His name is Legree," I said. "And I do want to."

By the time Legree and I got to the party, they were all back on the patio behind the house, their voices mixing with the music, a syrup of strings and a man's voice singing about yesterday when he was young. In the dark alongside the house, I took Legree's hand and kissed him because I'd felt him hesitate, and I wanted to take him in, to include him the way he'd done for me that day when we'd gone to Honea Path. We walked around the side of the house and out into the light of dozens of white candles flickering in brass holders on Mother's white wrought-iron table. Mother sat in front of the fountain and she stopped in midsentence, set her wineglass down with a clink, slapped the arms of her chair, stood up, and came toward us with open arms.

"Here we are," she said. "Here's my baby girl." She wore a floaty, pink caftan and a ribbon of the same color in her hair, with the bow tied over one ear. I hugged her close and kissed her cheek. She smelled of bourbon, and she felt electric, as though a charge were running through her, something coiled and wild. She held me by the wrists and studied me, smiling in a sly way, as though she could sense on me the weight and smell of Legree's body.

"Mother," I said, "this is Legree Black." Her attention swung to him like a lighthouse beam. She held his hand between both of her own and narrowed her eyes and gave him one of her long, soulful stares, nodding the whole time. A warning bell went off deep inside my head, and the happiness I'd felt since I left to pick up Legree began to shrivel around the edges. She'd had too much to drink, and the sly, crocked glimmer in her eyes made me want to bolt and run, dragging Legree with me, away from what was bound to come. Because when Mother drinks she imagines that she becomes the kind of person she admires most: a free spirit and a shrewd judge of character. I say that she imagines it because when she drinks, things get all snarled up. Love turns to rage, rage to sadness. Cloudbursts of hunger, anger, pain, love pass over you and pass on, leaving you soaked and bewildered. Through it all runs a vein of exaltation, as though she'd just discovered something glorious or sad about life that she couldn't quite find the words to name it. As though she were on the verge of a great revelation.

"And I'm very happy to finally lay eyes on the person who took my daughter off traipsing around the countryside at the crack of dawn."

"Yes, ma'am," he said. I felt a flash of shame, as though she'd slapped me. Why is it, I thought, that Mother can always make what I do sound dirty or foolish? *That boy, Traipsing around the countryside.*

"Mrs. Vess," he said, "I'm very pleased to meet you." She held onto his hand and searched his face until she was satisfied with what she saw there. "You look great tonight," he said nervously. Bless you, I thought, bless you. Then she nodded once, patted his hand, and let it go.

We were ushered into the circle of little flickering candles, where Mel and Canady sat on the chaise lounge. Mel had one sleek leg folded under her, and a white sandal dangled off the other foot whose toenails were painted the exact shade of coral as her dress. Her hand with the Reeves diamond—all two and a half carats of it that Canady had had specially set for her down in Atlanta—rested against Canady's shoulder. And under that hand was Canady. As usual, when I saw him, my heart gave a big thump. It was Matthew all over again. Not his looks, exactly, but their effect. Matthew would never have worn $300 alligator tassel slip-on shoes polished to a mirror shine, or a green golf shirt, or that expensive watch on the alligator band. Matthew hadn't been indolent or spoiled, but my God, there he was, all sleek and dark with a lazy smile. Granted, Matthew's smile had been sweet while Canady's was more like light glancing off of broken glass, but even so, taken all together, Canady was more like Matthew than anyone I'd ever seen. "How's it going, Annie?" he said. He detached himself from Mel long enough to stand up, and he winked at me as usual, as though we shared a secret, which in a way we did.

Not long after he and Mel announced their engagement, they were staying at the house one weekend, Canady in Davis's room, Mel in the spare bedroom next to mine. I was home without Matthew. I'd gotten up early to go to the bathroom and found Canady standing outside the door to Mel's bedroom with a beer in one hand and his other hand on the doorknob, buck naked except for a Carolina Gamecock cap pulled down low on his forehead. I must have made a sound, because when he saw me, he put his finger to his lips and winked and grinned, a little drunk, and then something seemed to dawn on him; a sly, drowsy look had come over his face. He turned loose of Mel's doorknob and turned to face me, just as relaxed, took a sip of beer, and watched me watch him over the rim of the can. I looked, too. I took a good, long look. I'd always wondered about his body, and now I could see for myself. He had a body that guides your eyes from one pleasure to the next, and after I had finished following them all the way down, I looked up again, saw that he was just about to take a step my way—and knew that I was about to let him. At the last possible second, when the next moment would have sent me toward him, or brought him toward me, I held up my hand and shook my head. He laughed to himself, winked, drained his beer, and tiptoed into Mel's room, shutting the door behind him without a sound. Now, whenever he saw me, he winked, and in his look I saw the same question: Come or go? Your room or Mel's?

"It's going OK, Canady," I said. "And this is Legree Black."

"Charmed," Legree said. I had never heard that tone in his voice before. It reminded me of the way that Baptist church up near his home had looked, hard and square and blinding white in the sun.

"Likewise," he said, looking away from Legree as though he were bored. Then he sat down next to Mel again, and I took everybody's drink orders and went to the kitchen to fix them.

When I came back, Mother was standing behind Mel, stroking her hair. "Mel's dress arrived today," she said, "and I have to tell you . . ."

"Aunt Louise, please." Mel sat up straight and moved her head out under Mother's fingers. "That's a secret. You know that."

"Oh, all right, all right. But aren't they just the handsomest couple?" Mother beamed on them as though they were something on display. "I'll go get the snacks now," she said.

"Oh now, Aunt Louise, stop," Mel said to Mother's back as Legree and I sat down on the wrought-iron loveseat across the table from Canady and Mel. "Annie," Mel said. "That teal blue is a good color on you. You must be a summer." I thanked her, but under Mel and Canady's stares I was conscious of Legree's rough face and scratched hands, the knobby look of his elbows and his too-short tie, the roughness that Canady had buffed away until he was all shine and polish and smooth, fine angles. Why had Legree worn that short-sleeved shirt? Why had he been churlish with Canady? We might have been immigrants, peasants with dark, anxious faces who'd walked a long way to reach this place only to be hauled up in front of the lord and lady of the estate. As Legree sipped his drink, I could feel him watching Mel the way men always do, as if they're absorbing her through their pores.

Mel had dark eyes and bright, blond hair, and she wore it pulled smooth and drawn into a chignon at the nape of her long neck. She was tall and knew how to arrange herself on any piece of furniture. In the candlelight, with the moonflowers blooming on the trellis behind her, she looked like a heavy drop of gold poured from a golden pitcher. These looks stopped beauty pageant judges in their tracks. She had been Miss Sun Fun, Miss Vaucluse County, Miss Rural Electrification, and first runner-up in the Miss South Carolina Pageant. Men always looked at her as though they were dreaming, except for Canady who looked at her as if he'd only gotten what he deserved.

"Here we are now." Mother came down the steps that led from the kitchen to the patio, holding the tray of cheese and crackers to one side and looking at each step. At the bottom of the steps she paused in astonishment. "Will you just please *look* at my moonflowers?" she said. "Will you all please look at my moonflowers?" This time she stamped her foot and pointed to the trellis where the moonflowers bloomed like soft faces pressed against the dark. "Now, will somebody please tell me how they do that?" she said. "What makes them bloom at night?"

"Something in the DNA," Legree answered. He didn't know that was purely a rhetorical question.

"They are miraculous flowers," I said, to keep him from getting any deeper. "No doubt about it."

"Annie has such a way with words," Mother said. And she glowed at me with an intensity just this side of rage. Mother swung toward Legree, hugging one knee. "And what do you do, Mr. Black?" she said.

"I work for the DHEC," he said. "I'm with the loggerhead turtle project down at Kiawah. And I take photographs now and then for the paper."

Mother sipped her drink and looked at him through her eyelashes. "Did you know that I'm an amateur photographer myself?" she said. Mel and Canady snuggled on the glider. Mel had slipped off her sandals and curled her legs up under her. She leaned against Canady as though she were exhausted, as though she'd traveled a long, hard road to get to his shoulder where she could rest at last.

"Is that right, Mrs. Vess?" Legree said. He pressed his fingertips together and looked down through them, frowning. Bless you, I thought, bless your goodness and your patience, your refusal to be surprised at what people will do.

"Oh yes, indeed," she said, giving him her burning look, that liquory passion she turns on people like a skewer. Forgive her, Legree, I said to myself. I wish I could say that she's not herself these days, but the truth is she *is* herself—more herself than ever— since my father died.

He seemed not to notice. "Well, what do you photograph?" he asked. There is a stillness about him when he listens, a seriousness, a kind of respect, as though he knows the difference between who people hope to be and who they are, and why they have to keep talking, trying to match one with the other.

"Well," she said, brushing an invisible something from her lap, "I tend to gravitate toward the beautiful things in life. You might say I'm a seeker after beauty in God's creation."

"I didn't know you took pictures, Aunt Louise," Mel said. I felt my face getting hot and that familiar sick feeling starting in the pit of my stomach. "Neither did I," I said.

"Oh, yes," she breathed, glaring at me.

Legree was having a hypnotic effect on her. Under the spell of his attentiveness, she spun out the incredible story of her search for beauty while I watched the ice cubes melt in my drink. For the first time I felt how lonely she must be now without my father. I tried to remember Mother with a camera in her hands, but all I could see was Mother hunched over a Brownie box camera, pointing it at us as we sat on the benches at Middleton Place Gardens with the azaleas blooming behind us while my father gestured angrily, "Louise, damn it, hold the camera straight!" But Legree was a photographer. All right, she was a photographer, too. She was whatever she needed to be to keep him listening. Sometimes I think that there must be this eternal heat-sensitive needle in the middle of women's bodies that swings east, west, north, south, toward the slightest warmth. I thought of myself with Matthew in Louisiana, sewing, cooking, and canning while Matthew worked the rigs, then soaking and bleaching the grease out of his clothes at night. And in Pennsylvania, finally, while Matthew went to school, I waited, and I thought it was Matthew I was waiting for to find himself and find me, too.

"In any case," she said—and her voice wavered, lost conviction—"I try and look for the beauty in things. I try and see the good in things." When she was finished, her face looked haggard. She stared at me angrily, as if she expected me to challenge her.

"You always have, Mother," I said, in order that the silence wouldn't be so deep around her. "You've always done that."

"Yes, ma'am," Legree said. "I can certainly see that you have the knack for it." I took his hand and squeezed it. Mother lifted her head. She looked at me gratefully, as though I'd saved her from drowning. From inside the kitchen, the stove timer pinged. "Rice is done," Mel said.

"Mother," I said, "come inside with me and let's get this supper going, why don't we?"

You would have thought we were giving a state dinner. The dining room table shone with the Vess silver that Mother and I had spent the morning polishing, using rags for the handles and Q-tips for the detail work, the curlicues, and such. Two big serving spoons with a flowery V engraved on each handle were laid out at Mother's place, and the Vess candlesticks stood on either side of a crystal vase full of pale yellow spider mums. Enormous starched linen napkins lay on the best Vess linen tablecloth. And all of this—candles and silver and the three brilliant tiers of the crystal chandelier—was reflected in the mirror above the sideboard, while Elizabeth Hardee Vess and Seddell Palmer Vess looked down out of the gloomy world of their portraits, keeping an eye on the silver and on Mel's wedding gifts. Toaster ovens and soufflé dishes, sets of glasses and mixing bowls—

they were all displayed on shelves covered with white paper and set up on concrete blocks against the wall at the end of the room. Every afternoon now, our driveway filled up with idling Buicks and Pontiacs, Oldsmobiles and Cadillacs. Mother's friends ran in with their wedding gifts wrapped in silver foil, tied with silver ribbon. At the door, I felt Legree hesitate, and I took his arm.

"Louise, you've outdone yourself," Canady said as he pulled out Mel's chair. Mother dimpled and curtsied on her way to the kitchen, threw a flirtatious look back over her shoulder as she pushed through the swinging door. Only the presiding male deity could have called Mother Louise and gotten away with it. It suggested a bond between them, "a meeting of the minds," as she would say, that flattered her. "Canady and I are just so simpatico," she'd said that morning as we polished the silver, holding up two fingers pressed tightly together to show how close they were. Well, Canady was simpatico with any woman. He is the original shape-shifter, but knowing this about him in no way makes him less dangerous.

When we were all seated, Mother came back through the door holding the casserole in the silver chafing dish out in front of her. It bubbled on top, cheesy and golden brown. "Ta-da," she said. "Shrimp casserole, a special Vess family recipe from the Low Country. We have Annie to thank for this," she said, setting the dish down onto a trivet in the middle of the table.

Canady leaned over and made a big show of passing his face back and forth through the steam, smelling it, then he winked at me. "Annie is a woman of many talents," he said. Beside me, Legree stiffened and made a noise in his throat, a low growl.

"And broccoli," Mother said, coming back in from the kitchen, setting down another bowl. "And salad, and good old biscuits." She set down a basket of biscuits buttoned into a linen warmer with a scalloped edge and fine, open-work embroidery. Beside it was one of her famous salads in the wooden bowl, topped with thin rounds of red onion and slices of avocado and sprinkled with Parmesan cheese.

"Canady," Mother said as she sat down and shook out her napkin, "would you bless us, please?"

"No problem," he said, moving his shoulders as though he were limbering up for a workout.

I took Legree's hand and held it in my own, high up on my thigh.

"Sanctify, Oh Lord, we beseech you," he began, "a portion of this food for our use." I squinched my eyes shut and tried to listen to the words, but Canady's voice kept getting between me and thankfulness. A prayer or a cost analysis, it all sounds the same in Canady's mouth, and so it's hard to feel the proper respect.

When we were all served, Mel said, "So, Legree, where do you come from?"

I felt Legree startle beside me. "Up near Honea Path," he said, and he planted his elbows on the table and pointed with his fork up toward the chandelier, chewing as he talked and looking at Mother and Mel and Canady one after the other, as though he expected them to make something of it. Any objections? that look said. Any complaints? He's doing this deliberately, I thought, deliberately being sullen and rude.

"And your parents," Mother said, "are they still living?" She was nonplussed by surliness—who wouldn't be, living in this family?

"Yes, ma'am," he said, and he seemed to have recovered himself. He swallowed and lowered his fork. "My father is retired from Piedmont Mills up there and my mother works at Regency Textiles."

"Interesting," Mel murmured, taking a teeny bite of shrimp casserole from the tip of her fork.

"Well, Mr. Black," Mother said, "has Annie told you that my family worked for the Bibb Mills for lo these many years?" The way she said it, the way she sat and touched her napkin to the corners of her mouth before she began to speak, suggested that they might have owned the Bibb Mills.

"No, ma'am," Legree said in the same tone of voice I had heard when he'd answered his father's warning about being a steady worker: resigned, but holding his own thoughts in reserve.

Well, the talk went on like that, with Mother stepping in whenever she had to in order to keep it from sagging. I talked a little about cleaning out Papa's study. I tried to make it sound funny.

Legree talked about the turtles and what he did to try and save them, and Mel said it was so sad what happened to them. Then Mel told about the progress of their new house out at Planter's Landing. "I guess I've about got every contractor in Vaucluse County mad at me," she said. "But it has to be perfect, and I know what I'm doing even if they don't." She'd made them tear out the chair molding in the dining room three times. As she spoke, Canady kneaded her shoulder and looked at her as though it reflected well on him to have a wife with such expensive tastes. From there the talk widened into a general survey of Canady's success at Planter's Landing: Phase One construction finished now, all the Class A lakeside homesites sold, and the homes in the upper-300 range sold, too. The golf course just about completed, condominium construction under way. Legree made that growling sound again low in his throat, and I pressed my leg against his under the table, and he pressed back.

"Have I ever told you all the story of how I started Planter's Landing?" Canady asked.

"Why, no, Canady," Mother answered. "But I wish you would."

Canady went into the kitchen and came back with a bottle of wine. Without asking Mother if she minded, he opened it and poured us each a glass. Then he settled back into his chair, pushed back from the table, and swirling the wine in his glass, he began. "Picture this," he said. The scene is the kitchen of his apartment in Columbia. Canady and some of his old fraternity brothers from Sigma Nu, who'd gone with him into the MBA program at USC, are sitting around his kitchen table, ready to play the last hand of a high-stakes poker game that has gone on all night. It is dawn now; light seeps in around the edges of the blinds and sifts over the collection of wallets, checkbooks, gold cuff links, and highball glasses where cigarette butts float in half an inch of JD Black Label. They are all a little wired, a little haggard, beard stubble on their faces, their shoes kicked off. The stereo has been playing the same Ray Charles record for over an hour.

Now a lot is riding on this hand because Canady has been

winning, winning big all night. Two car titles, several IOUs, and the deed to a beach house at Isle of Palms are stacked neatly in a pile on the table in front of him, and now they're playing the last hand. Sudden death, winner take all. "All or nothing, boys," Canady says as he draws. "Let's see what you got." Then he lays his cards down crisply—one, two, three, four, five, a royal flush—and looks around the table at the faces of his brothers, all slack now, all showing in their expressions various combinations of shock, terror, confusion, nausea, and shame as they throw their cards down in disgust and defeat. And he asks himself, Can I do this to them? And the answer comes back: No. No, he says to himself. They've been my brothers for too long. They've loaned him money, bailed him out of jail, even rescued his car from the police impoundment lot one spring break when they'd all gone down to Ocean Drive. The black Corvette he used to drive. Never has forgotten that. Drove it down to the beach and got into an argument with the owner of a motel who wouldn't rent him a room for the weekend, so he drove it over the man's shrubbery on the way out of the parking lot. Hadn't been on the beach five minutes before there was an all-points bulletin out for him and that car. Hadn't been on the beach ten minutes before they picked him up and threw him in jail. Hard to miss a black Corvette with a red leather interior and Canady at the wheel, tearing down the main drag at Ocean Drive at ninety miles an hour. He couldn't forget what they'd done for him then, these brothers of his now watching him with slack, dazed faces, waiting for the ax to fall.

Then he thinks that what he needs most is money. Capital. He thinks about being married to Mel. (He doesn't say this, but I see his eyes when he talks about this money he has to make. Maybe he thinks about Mel and the six children she wants to have, her expensive tastes, the talk he has had with her father, Big Tom.) He has been turning an idea over in his mind for awhile now. An idea about the lake and the money to be made there and how to make it. He knows contracting. He worked for his brother in Baton Rouge building condos in the summers all through college. Why not me? he thinks. Why not me instead of somebody else? And he pulls the deed to the beach house closer. He picks it up, and Tom Little's face goes gray. "Now wait a minute, Tom, my man, hear me out before you have a coronary," he says. "All of y'all, hear me out."

He has in mind a little venture, and he proceeds to sketch it out for them. A luxury real estate development on the northern shore of Lake Charles B. Hartley, Jr. Strictly first-class. A Jack Nicklaus golf course and country club. Maybe some condos on the golf course. *Beaucoup* expensive houses—some of them in the quarter- to half-million-dollar range. He's done some marketing research and found out that he could be on to a sure thing. Nobody spends money like retired executives looking for cushy digs in a warm climate. They like water and they like golf. They like their amenities. Look at Hilton Head. He knows where to get ahold of some land right where the shore of the lake will be. What he needs is start-up capital, seed money. That's where *they* come into the picture. He holds up their deeds and car titles. "Comprende?" he says.

Well, they just about fall all over each other agreeing to whatever Canady wants. Walter Boatright, Jr.'s father is a banker in Walterboro now, but forty years ago, at the Citadel, he'd played fast and loose with his own daddy's money in the weeklong poker games that went on in his room. Walter will go home and call him right now about arranging a loan. As soon as he gets his MBA, Rob Pope is headed back to Orangeburg to take over his father's NAPA Auto Parts distributorship, the biggest one in the Southeast. He's good for it. And so it goes. They all give Canady checks, big ones, and he gives them back their property. By the time it's full light outside and people are stirring in the other apartments, and cars are starting up in the parking lot outside, Planter's Landing has been born— Canady Reeves, President and CEO. "That was my nest egg," he says. "I knew from that moment on that the foundation of my empire would be real estate."

Now, throughout the telling of this story, Mel has been staring at him, ever more dazzled and excited. Who wouldn't be? I feel it myself, the heat and light coming off of Canady's success. And to think of yourself married to him, entitled to that—the power arcing, crackling from him to you. Canady makes a little signal to Mel with his hand; he tips his head ever so slightly toward the door. She stands up, then he does. He stretches, yawns. "We're going out to get a pack of cigarettes," he says, and arms around each other's waists, they go out the door leaving a curtain of perfume and expensive aftershave and desire shimmering in the air.

After they'd gone, the only sounds in the room were forks scraping, chairs creaking, the sigh of the central air-conditioning. There were Mel's plate and Canady's plate, their napkins thrown onto the tablecloth. I pressed my leg against Legree's and he made that growling sound again deep in his throat.

"Well, goodness," Mother said, fiddling with her pearls. "End of story. I guess they didn't want any cobbler."

"I guess not," I said. No wonder pride is the deadliest sin. We all die of it eventually, telling these stories in which we appear larger than life to ourselves.

I drove Legree home and I stayed as long as I could. He lived in an apartment over the old carriage house behind Thorpe's Hill, one of the antebellum houses that Sherman spared. Nobody lived in the big house, a real white-columned wonder at the end of a lane lined with magnolias. It's on all the postcards, and as regularly as Pug Simmons runs the picture and story about Miss Leola in the cemetery on Confederate Memorial Day every June, he also runs a front-page picture in the *Courier-Tribune* of a beautiful young woman in front of Thorpe's Hall. For the past three years it's been Mel—in crinolines and a big picture hat, holding a magnolia blossom and standing on the veranda—welcoming visitors to South Carolina Heritage Days. At Christmastime the Jaycettes decorate the house with smilax and a Christmas tree lit with real candles for their Carolina Christmas open house. Legree lived there and kept an eye on the place when he was in town.

"I want you to come in," he said when we pulled up to his place. Not "Will you come in?" or "Why don't you come in?" but "I want you to come in," and a hand on my arm. Inside it was peaceful, spare. It was like being inside a seashell, cool and light and clean. There were a few pictures on the wall and a rocking chair with a rush seat. The sofa was covered in deep blue cotton and a big fern hung in the side window. It was simple here, and quiet, light-years from the house on Wyman Street and all its complications.

"That story was one of the damnedest things I've heard in a long, long time," he said when we were settled on the couch with beers. "Is it true?"

"Who knows? He believes it, and for Canady, that's enough. He is what you might call a supremely confident human being." I slid over closer to him. "So where do you think they went to get that pack of cigarettes?"

He slipped his arms over me. "Her apartment would be my guess. I bet they've bought several packs of cigarettes by now."

And then we were in the bedroom and he was stripping the white spread off of his bed in one smooth motion, and we lay down there on the cool sheets.

Afterward, we lay looking up at the seabird mobile over his bed, watching the cranes and pelicans and gulls turn in the breeze from the open window. I rolled over and grabbed one of his earlobes with my teeth. "Did you know that you growled like this at Mel and Canady twice tonight?" I asked. The streetlight behind the hickory tree cast a speckled cape of shadows across the bed.

He laughed once, low in this throat. "Being around money does that to me," he said. His eyes were closed and he brushed his fingers around my back in slow circles.

"Money?" I said. "Whose money?"

"Your family's money. Your cousin and her handsome fiancé's money. Everybody in the world's money but mine. I guess you have money, too," he said, and he sounded so miserable about it that I had to kiss his throat, his face, his eyes. "My ex-wife had money," he said. "She never let me forget it, either."

And it occurred to me then how strange he was to me. Sex fools you, the way it carries you close in to a person and makes you believe that you know more than you do. "My family used to have money," I said. "Which, around here, is even better than having it now. You know, the lost wealth, the good family ruined. And me. I have $75,000 that my father left me. At first that seemed like a lot of money, but now I see that it'd be gone in a year or two if I tried to live on it. So how much is that worth, really? Besides, don't let my mother fool you with all that stuff about the Bibb Mills. Her brother worked in the weave room for thirty years. Her father started off as a spooler, then he went on to repair looms for the rest of his life. And Mother worked there in the summers sweeping lint."

"Well, she seems like a great lady to me," he said.

"I'll be sure to tell her that," I said. "She works hard at it. She'll be so pleased."

Instantly he was on top of me, pinning my arms down, straddling me. "Don't you dare," he said, coming down to kiss me while I rose up to kiss him. "Don't you dare."

It was almost three when I left. Just as I was about to start down the stairs, he grabbed my arm. "Look here," he said. "I'm going down to Kiawah for a few weeks. I'm leaving tomorrow. I wouldn't have told you if you hadn't wanted to stay with me."

"What would you have done, disappeared?"

He shrugged, "Probably." The porch light was behind him; I couldn't see his face.

"Jesus, Legree."

"I want to tell you something," he said. "You took me into your family tonight and I appreciate that. I want to tell you something that you need to know. The day my divorce from Janice was final, the hour it was done, I got in the car and I drove straight up to the Joyce Kilmer Forest, and I parked the car and hiked back as far as I could go—no tent, no food, no nothing. I stayed there for three days. Didn't even register with the ranger or any of that stuff. Nobody knew where I was. Nobody. I can do that, too—I can come and go, just like you like to do."

"Look," I said, "let's not complicate things. Let's not put pressure on something so new." I started to kiss him but he pulled back.

"I'm not making a claim on you," he said as I started down the stairs. "But I do have to matter."

"You do matter to me."

"Those are words, Annie. I mean matter in some way other than being useful."

"The way we make love, is that just useful to me? Is that the feeling you get?"

He leaned over the porch railing, "No, it isn't," he said. "It isn't at all. I just want you to know straight out, right here from the start, how things are with me."

To help them sleep, some people make lists or count blessings, sheep, stars in the sky. I made maps. I'd start from where I was and move out from there, placing people and things, moving in all directions until I had made a map of my world with all the people and the places that mattered to me, anchored in time and space. As I drifted off to sleep, I made up this map. Legree was there close to the center, his weight that was always surprising as he laid his body down onto mine. And there was Brother in his moment of flight, and Papa's office window above the courthouse square with his name still lettered in gold on the glass. And there was Mother. Mother's new patio and flowers. Even her darkness, even her drinking were as familiar to me as the sight of my own face in the mirror. And there was Planter's Landing, just north of the Laughing Place, where Canady was king. It was the known world and I had come home. I went to sleep with that world gathered around me, thinking, I understand now. This is how you live. Ruin and rescue, rescue and ruin.

$1, Love, and Affection

In the morning Canady's story hung on in my mind—the story itself, not the way he'd told it, leaning back in his chair with his hands clasped behind his head as though he were soaking up rays from a sun that shone only on him. Now that story had passed through the night and come up plainer, stripped of its boastfulness. Now it was a story about how Canady came into some money and bought some land. And it occurred to me as I lay there, watching the morning light sift through the wisteria vine and spread across the foot of my bed, that I could do what my father would have done had he heard Canady's story.

My father said listen, but don't believe everything you hear. "Keep your own counsel," he said. Listen to the words, and beneath the words, for the hope or fear or trouble—whatever drives people to take a circumstance or a fact and invent around it a story that makes that fact seem to mean something. That's what it was all about, my father said. People make up stories to prove to themselves that they matter. That is why you had to be careful, you had to pay attention to the stories people told about themselves, because they were trying to tell you that they counted for something. So you listened, he said, then you looked into the facts. Where had Canady gotten that land?

I got up right then and walked down to the courthouse, but the heat had gotten up before me. Ninety-five degrees at nine A.M., the clock on the First Commercial Bank of Timmons read, and a hazelike smoke from a long-smoldering fire hung between the trees and filled up the gaps between buildings.

Inside the tall, double front doors of the courthouse, I stopped, out of habit, to let my eyes adjust to the dim light, in the spot where so many people had stopped for so long. Their feet had worn two foot-size dips in the marble. And when my eyes adjusted I saw what everyone had seen who had come through those doors for the last seventy-five years: marble underfoot and lights high up on a peeling ceiling, a bust of Wade Hampton on a pedestal, and then the marble steps lined with fancy, scrolled iron railings that began on either end of the foyer. They curved up and around until they met and formed a long mezzanine on the floor above, centered with the rosewood doors that led into the main courtroom.

After the noise and busyness of the other offices I'd passed— the sheriff's office with its crackling radios and ringing phones, the tax assessor's office where I heard Mother's voice in one of the back rooms—the Clerk of Courts office seemed serene. It had more tall, curved windows and dark wood, more leather and brass and oak than any other room in the courthouse. Papa said the Clerk of Courts office looked so dignified because it was the most important room in the courthouse, the place where you found the history of the county told in marriage licenses, divorce decrees, birth certificates, maps, and deeds. In a glass case over in one corner lay the muster rolls of the Confederate regiment that was raised here, along with their battle flag and a saber with a faded yellow tassel. Eugene Vess, my great-grandfather, had been among them, and his name was written there in brown ink on paper that looked as gray and fragile as the layers of a dirt dauber's nest. My father came here almost every day of his adult life. Sometimes he came on business; other times he came just to browse through the title books, to rest his mind against the orderly progression of ownership, the stories these books told about the make-over of land into property. For him, the title books were a kind of Bible with many books of Genesis.

At the desk closest to the door, Becky Loudermilk, the head clerk, still sat as she had for thirty-five years, stamping documents and answering questions and directing visitors. Her face, though it was old now, still held to a calm, purposeful expression; her eyes were clear, her gray hair parted on the side and clipped with a tortoiseshell barrette, her white blouse freshly ironed. Just before my father died, word got out that the county council came back from the annual convention of the Local Government Association down at Hilton Head with plans to computerize the records here like other clerk's offices around the state were doing, plans that Miss Becky, with my father's help, squelched.

"People ask, 'What would be lost?' " my father wrote in letters to the *Courier-Tribune* that were signed by him and Becky Loudermilk. "By computerizing the county records, by consigning all the old books and maps to the basement?" Even here, he could not keep the contempt from his voice, as though to ask that question were a sign of profound and willful ignorance. "Texture," he wrote (answering for these imaginary questioners since they would not answer for themselves), "the mark of the human hand, the look of a nineteenth-century notary seal drawn by hand, of real ink on old paper. In our increasingly mass-produced, featureless, and hurried world, these qualities are not to be given up lightly." Mother sent me all the letters. "There go a few more friends," she wrote in letters of her own that she wrapped around the clippings. In the end the county council backed down; my father had won. Because he'd been *right*, he wrote to me in a letter of his own. "You can see that in this case, justice was done. Yours, Papa." Reading those letters and the clippings they contained, I was glad to be so far away. Away from my father and the righteousness that his causes took on. Away from my mother who refused to see righteousness in anything. Away from the quarrel of their life, free of them both. I got these letters in Arizona and I walked out into the desert glare, the heat, gladly, just because it was so far from home. Now, according to Mother, the word around the courthouse was that the county council had resigned itself to waiting until Miss Becky died before they even used the word *computer* around that office again.

As I came through the door, she looked up from her stamping. "Miss Vess," she said. "Anything I can help you with?" she asked, obviously pleased. Other people in the courthouse spooked or ducked when they heard the name Vess, but Becky Loudermilk beamed, and I was grateful for that.

"No, thank you, Miss Loudermilk," I said. "I know my way around, I think."

"Help yourself, then," she said, as though she were welcoming me to a feast.

I had spent the summer between my sophomore and junior years of college—just after the lake trouble began, just before I met Matthew—here in this room, working for my father. Papa's secretary, Thelma Radford, had taught me how to search a title, and I did it day in and day out. I could have searched a title blindfolded. Today, as usual, the room was full of lawyers and realtors paging through title books and writing on legal pads at the long, oak tables in the center of the room, or turning the wide, crackling pages of the county maps. Today, as usual, as though I'd never been away, we nodded and spoke like old friends picking up conversations we'd laid down the day before. "Morning, Annie. Mother doing all right these days?"

"Doing fine, thank you, Mr. Gandy. Mrs. Glover, good to see you."

"And you, Annie."

"Miss Vess, I was telling your mother the other day that I wish you'd come go to work for us."

"Thank you, Mr. Poteet. She told me, and I'm thinking about it."

You started with the index books, Thelma Radford said. Their red leather spines were each printed with a gold letter and a span of dates: A/1946–1968, B/1946–1968, and so on through the alphabet. And on another shelf another row of books, a time closer to the present: A/1968–, B/1968–. "When you own a piece of property," Thelma's voice said, "you own *title* to that property." She'd underlined the word with her voice, a habit she'd picked up from my father. "These titles are indexed alphabetically and chronologically, by grantor and grantee. Do you know what those words mean?"

"Yes," I said. "The grantee is the buyer and the grantor is the seller."

"Very good."

Thelma Radford's voice was breathy, wispy, like the chiffon scarves she wore, the pink lipstick, the sleeveless blouses, and high heels. Wispy and delicate, small, a doll's voice not made to speak about serious things, and yet she did. Before she and her husband, Buck, moved to town, she'd taught third grade out in the county. When she went to work for my father, she learned fast; in two years she knew as much as he did about property law, so he said.

I had learned quickly, too, Thelma said. "A quick study," she called me. I'd learned quickly, and I hadn't forgotten. Now I walked between the narrow rows of tall metal shelves, until I came to the corner nearest the window that looked onto the courthouse lawn. I read the spines on the index books, until I came to *R/1968–. R* for Reeves. Inside, there were lined pages—one column of names per page—all written in Becky Loudermilk's handwriting with a broad-nibbed pen and blue-black ink. It looked as though she'd filled her pen from the same ink bottle year after year and entered the details of flux and change in the same careful hand. But in the column of names on the *Re-* page, there was no Canady Reeves, Grantee. No Canady Reeves, Grantor, either. No Canady Reeves anywhere to be found. My father would not have been surprised, I thought, as I slipped the book back into its place on the shelf. Canady had made up the whole thing to impress us, which it had. He'd told it to himself so often he believed it. Papa said that happened a lot with people. They wanted to believe something was true so badly they talked themselves into it. Even Canady, the prince of confidence, had to make himself look larger than he really was. I thought of his eyes again as he'd talked about marrying Mel and the money he needed, and how my father had been right about people and their stories, as he'd been right about so many things.

It wasn't far from *R* to *V/1946–1968*, stamped on the red leather spine. The cover was red cloth, the end papers marbleized. In the corner of the first page, the bookplate read, "Made in the plants of E. F. Warner and Sons by skilled South Carolina craftsmen." It was the kind of gesture my father would have appreciated, speaking as it did of pride, tradition, continuity, the orderly handing down of valuable things.

Vale, Vance, Vanderhouse, then Vess, John. Three entries: one in 1946, one in 1960, the third in 1968, and the numbers of deed books listed neatly beside each one. I found the shelves that held the thicker books, with *Deeds* stamped in gold on the red leather spines. I pulled out the 1946 volume, balanced it on the ledge, and turned to the right page. There was the deed for the Laughing Place, bought from Herbert Gunter for $750 on the third day of January, 1946. In 1960, the year before Grandmother Vess's death, Papa bought her house in town—the house where we lived now—for "$500 and other considerations." The third deed had been registered in October of 1968. "All that piece and parcel of land lying and being in the County of Vaucluse and in the State of South Carolina, containing five hundred (500) acres more or less, bounded as follows, north by lands of Ella Gunter; east by lands of Herbert Williams; south by lands of John Vess; west by lands of Tyler Williams." For these 500 acres, he'd paid $3,000. There was his signature to make it true, the imperial J and V towering over the other letters, staking out the territory of the rest of his name. I read it once, then I went back and read it again. He'd bought the land adjoining ours, the land to the north of the Laughing Place and beyond, across the river. I tried to remember what I'd heard about that land, but the memory wasn't there, as if I'd lost a piece of something. Fear began to turn inside me like a revolving wheel. Ever since Matthew died, this had been happening. A room or a house or a scene from my life would pop into my mind, and I would have to find a place for it right away: year, date, city. If I couldn't, I would begin to panic.

In the *Grantor* index books I found my father's name. Two entries, both in 1977. The facts do not change, my father said. They are like a trail; every time you follow them, they lead to the same place. In March of 1977 he'd sold the Laughing Place to the

Army Corps of Engineers for $2,500. In April he'd sold the 500 acres to the Jo-Tel Corporation for "$1, love, and affection."

The Jo-Tel Corporation? The clerk at the front desk in the tax assessor's office said that Mother had left to go to lunch with Melody a few minutes earlier and she wouldn't be back until one. On the way back across the square, I looked up at the second-story window of what had been my father's office. It was an insurance office now, with blinds over the street-level windows, but the window on the upper floor was the same. JOHN VESS, ATTORNEY AT LAW written in gold. After Papa died, Mother and I went up there to dispose of the boxes of files, and that's when we found the chair. It was an old easy chair upholstered in dusty, green tapestry material, with a matching footstool pulled over close to the window that faced the courthouse lawn. An end table stood beside it, and we found a pipe in the ashtray there, a beautiful pipe that neither of us could remember having seen at home. It had a fine, straight, rosewood stem and a bowl carved into the angular face of an old sailor. As Mother had picked it up, she'd sucked in her breath, then crammed it down into a box of files and carried it out to the street. Now, remembering that chair and the pipe, I was aware of an uneasy feeling in the pit of my stomach that had been there since I'd read about that land. I thought of my father sitting in the window, smoking the pipe that no one had given him, looking out across Timmons. I imagined that he could see where no one else could see, all the way up to the Keowee River, to that land that he had bought and then sold for nothing.

Give Mother a straight stretch of road and an errand, and she drives as though she's been called to the scene of a disaster, where rescue cannot start until she arrives. Tensed, angled stiffly over the wheel, glaring at the road, she steers the Oldsmobile as if she were the driver of a skittish mule team pulling a wagon train over a fogbound pass high in the mountains. Only her eyes, her will, her hand on the reins keep the wagon from diving off the edge into oblivion. Today the crisis was about Mel's wedding. Mr. Greer, the carpenter who was building the ramp up which Mel would walk onto the bridal boat, had called Mother at work. If he didn't have the measurements by the time he closed that afternoon, he couldn't promise that he'd have it finished in time for the ceremony, which was exactly one week, two days, and five hours away. So Mother had taken the afternoon off. She'd found me walking home from the courthouse and now we were on our way to the lake.

Riding with Mother is like surviving the summer heat: You float and let yourself be carried. I laid my head back against the seat and let the heat come over me. I listened to the peeling sound the tires made on the hot asphalt and the patches of cicada noise that we passed through as we drove north out of Timmons and onto the Southland Timber Company land, where the small pines flashed by behind the haze of heat, row after row after long, straight row.

"Poor old soul," Mother said out of nowhere, and she slung the car into a turn.

"Who, Mother?"

"Oh, the colonel, honey," she said, and we fired back onto the straightaway. "Driving through here always makes me think of him. I'm just so upset about him, I don't know what to do." She waved at the rows of pines. The colonel and Miss Mary had owned this land once; his homeplace had been here, one of the oldest homeplaces in Vaucluse County. It was surrounded by close to a thousand acres of land, with five tenant farmers to work the fields of peanuts and soybeans and cotton. The colonel and Mary had lived there until Mary got sick with cancer, and it had been too far to the doctor in town, so they sold it all to Southland. They'd tried to move the house into town—a wide, low, wooden house with a porch that wrapped around three sides—but as it was being hoisted onto the bed of the house-moving truck, it had broken apart. "Too brittle," the house moving man had said. Those old heart-pine timbers had just dried out. You could almost count on that with these old houses. The picture of it from the front page of the *Courier-Tribune* was in a scrapbook somewhere. The house looked as if it had just sat down on itself, a pile of lumber with a roof on it. "End of an Era," the caption under the photograph read. After that, Mary and the colonel bought the lot next to my grandmother's house in town from her, and built a new house there.

"I know it," I said. "What about the colonel?"

"You didn't see the mail this morning, I guess."

From the significant sideways cut of her eyes, the way she bit her lip and lifted her chin and straightened her shoulders, I knew there was more to tell. Of course, she could not just come out and say what she had to say. Mother has the instincts of an actress. Every entrance an occasion, every occasion an opportunity for suspense, a sense of timing tuned to a perfect pitch of expectation. "And?" I said.

There was a letter in her purse, she said, pressing a Kleenex to her upper lip and forehead. It was from Ethel Gentry, the colonel's daughter. Find it for her, would I? As I dragged her tote bag across the seat and reached inside, I felt the old rising sickness in my throat. As long as we live, I will never be able to go into Mother's purse without feeling squeamish. I will always think of her purses as a kind of underworld below the bright world of her plans and clean linoleum and Sherwin-Williams paint cards—the dark into which those things sink, a chaos of broken compacts, spilled powder, unwrapped sticks of chewing gum, envelopes of BC Headache Powders, old lists, rubber bands, and partially sucked sour balls furred with Kleenex lint. As a teenager I became obsessed with the idea that touching Mother's purse was like touching her body, and for years nothing, not even the promise of money, could persuade me to go into her purse where some damp, gruesome reminder of her physical life might stick to my hands. Finally I found the letter, a single sheet of notebook paper folded three times, sweet and pink with powder. I unfolded it and read:

Dear Louise,
We had to put Daddy into the Pee Dee Nursing Home last Saturday evening. He got to wandering off so much, nobody could keep up with him. The doctor tells us that he's had a small stroke or possibly more than one and not to hope for any improvement or recovery at his age. He gets excellent care but comes and goes in his mind, and we never know from one time to the next whether he'll know us or he won't. He calls all the colored people there Willie Mae, and when they play along it seems to make things easier for him but when they don't he pitches a fit. Of course, not many of them do, so you can see, he has a time,

even there. As I've said, do what you want to with those dogs. Will be up soon to get some things for him and to talk about the house, etc.

Love,
Ethel

"My God, Mother," I said. I stuffed the letter back in her purse and zipped it shut.

"Do you think maybe he got wind that we're planning to put the house on the market?" She bit her lip and glared at the highway.

"Mother, no," I said. "Absolutely not."

"Well, I've sure been thinking about it. They say a terrific emotional shock can sometimes cause an old person to have a stroke. You remember old man Avery? The one who was getting ready to be on that radio program with your father and talk about all the things the Corps of Engineers had done to get his land away from him when he had a stroke and died right there on the spot?"

"I remember," I said. "But you can't think that way or you'll go crazy, Mother, really." But I knew how she felt. Finding yourself outside this place where someone you love has gone, finding yourself confused and small, you invent powers for yourself and give yourself a part to play—just to persuade yourself that they are still close by, in this world where you might have made a difference. You comb through conversations and minutes, searching for one that might have changed everything. If Matthew and I hadn't argued the morning he left. If I'd asked him to stay one more day until I'd made him understand why this time I would not move, I could not follow him, why I had gone as far as I meant to go. Because wherever we lived was the promised land, the place toward which we'd been headed all our lives. Arizona. Louisiana. Pennsylvania. For a year, sometimes two, we celebrated, then Matthew got restless again. If only I hadn't said, "Go to Cheraw, go on, we'll work it out when you get home." If I hadn't walked into the house without looking back or turning to wave or to watch his truck bump down the driveway and turn onto the highway. If only.

I stopped myself. At the end of this trail of ifs lay the last and more terrible one, the one that held the rest of our lives together and what they would never be: *if Matthew had lived.* And then the fear would come and I'd be lost in it, like being lost in a pitch-black ocean on a black night. "What did they tell him?" I asked quickly.

"As little as possible," she said. "I think they told him they were taking him to Summerville for a visit. He probably believes he's coming back home any day now, poor old soul."

"I hope so," I said. "Can you imagine how terrible it would be to know you were never coming back somewhere? It'd be like being told you were going to die. I'm going to go down and see him the first chance I get."

"Well, I'm not," she said. "I'd rather remember him the way he was."

"At least there's that," I said. But it wasn't enough. Thinking about Matthew had started it; my heart beat as though I'd been running. The colonel in a nursing home, just like that. It was the speed of it that was terrifying. One day, Matthew drove away. Two days later he was dead. My father lay down one night to sleep and by morning his life had ended. Three months ago the colonel had been at home, piddling around in his yard, working the dogs, being fussed at by Willie Mae for wandering off on a cold morning without his jacket. Now he was in a nursing home. He would never come back. This morning I had found a deed in an old deed book that did not fit with any story I had ever heard my father tell, and Mother and I were hurtling through the heat toward a lake that had been dry land a year ago. It was happening again. If we didn't slow down, we might break through some barrier between this world where we trusted that change was orderly and slow, and another world where the most terrible and permanent things could happen in an instant. Now we were out in the open fields again, soybean rows fired past like cross-ties on a railroad track. "Could you slow down a little, Mother?" I said. She eased up on the accelerator with an exasperated sigh. "I hope he doesn't have to be there for long. I think he would want to die soon. He was always terrified of being put in a home like that."

"Well, I know he did," she said, "but none of us knows, do we, what face death will show us, and that's the truth," she said, firming her mouth.

"Now, isn't that just like a doctor?" I said. The arrogance of doctors, that was always a good subject to rally around. "People recover from all kinds of things, even strokes, all the time. Aren't there lots of tests they have to do before they can say there's no hope for him?"

Mother shifted in her seat, her hands tightened on the wheel, and she stared ahead, harder. "They've done the tests," she said. Her voice was the same voice that had told me about Matthew and Papa, full of the hard mercy of the fact that had to be injected into you quickly, like medicine, full-strength, before you could water it down with too much hope.

"My God."

Now the road ran steadily down as though it were a stream hurrying toward the river where it used to end. Once this road had run down through peach orchards and vacant, spent fields into Little Awando and out again, and then through an emptying countryside. A few black churches with half a dozen houses close by. A crossroads and then the road to the Laughing Place—that unmarked sand track—had turned off of this road; we had driven this way to see the spring floods. Once when I drove out this road, I knew where I was going. Now Mother and I followed the road toward the river. We came up over a little rise and there was the lake, cloudy-coral like tomato soup, and the road ran down into it and disappeared. Now there was only water and the white heat haze blanketing the far shore, the silty smell of water heated by the sun, and the odor of fish and motorboat oil that rolled into the car when Mother and I pulled into the parking lot, the tires popping on the new white gravel there.

Already the place looked old and worn out. The shoreline dipped in deeply here and made a kind of cove, and a knuckly narrow spit of land—all clay and tall, skinny pines—stuck out into the water. There was a concrete picnic table there, set next to an oil-drum trash barrel already overflowing with soft-drink cans, fried chicken boxes, and disposable diapers. A few pickup trucks with boat trailers attached were parked in the faded grass around the edges of the parking lot.

You would have thought that Mother had just gotten to heaven. No sooner had the car crunched to a stop than she was out, binoculars around her neck, clipboard in hand. Then she began to stretch all the way up on her toes, and reached for the sky with her clipboard, eyes closed, inhaling deep lungfuls of air. "Lord, don't you wish you could bottle this air and take it home with you?" she asked, glaring at me, daring me to cross or contradict her. All that water, and it was still so hot you couldn't breathe out there, everything swaddled in haze, not even a breeze moving across the water. Right away, sweat began to trickle down my back, and the gnats found us and began to crawl along my hairline and into my eyes.

"No thanks," I said. "It's hot enough in town as it is. But you take some back if you need to, Mother."

Mother, let it go, put it down, I wanted to say. It's only me. But she could no more stop herself from insisting that it was beautiful here than I could keep myself from being frightened or Canady could stop boasting or Legree could stop being kind. The habit ran too deep. Papa must have brought her out here a dozen times that last year before he died to point out to her what they had lost. And every time, she refused to grieve—for herself and for him, too. Instead she opposed him with her enthusiasm. My mother should have been a diplomat or an architect, a designer of monumental buildings. Instead she married my father and had us, and like other women with large energies confined to narrow channels, she became vehement and fierce. Everything we did mattered too much; everything became a challenge, a fight, though I believe that she forgot long ago what it would have meant to win.

When she'd had her fill of the air, she marched down to the edge of the water and stood there staring out across the lake with her hands on her hips and her eyes narrowed. Off in the distance, almost lost in the haze, a boat passed, pulling two water-skiers. It made a small, persistent sound, like a power saw heard from far away. "Look at them go," she said, holding the binoculars to her eyes with one hand and waving the clipboard with the other, and they waved back. "Well, John Vess was wrong about one thing in his life, wasn't he?" she said as she let the binoculars hang again.

"He was wrong about a lot of things, Mother," I said. The lake was too remote, he'd said, there were no decent roads, no one would use it, and everyone would see that this was the biggest boondoggle ever foisted on the people of this state. But the truth was that Vaucluse County was thriving; as a prophet, my father had been a terrible failure. Every week the paper ran another front-page story about the lake. More than 500 people were expected to come to the official opening of the lake and dam the week before Mel's wedding, a Carolina Power Company executive was quoted as saying. And, of course, there was Canady and Planter's Landing. Just last week *The State* had sent a reporter down from Columbia to interview him, and they ran a front-page story in the Sunday business section about Mel and Canady and the fabulous success of Planter's Landing. "A total-concept development," the article had said. It was even integrated out there, Mel pointed out every chance she got. She had personally sold a home to the new black doctor in town, a beautiful Georgian home on one of the choicest lots right near the marina, and his boat, a cabin cruiser with a teak deck, was the biggest one on the lake.

"Well, I just hope that when I get to the promised land, somebody's thought to build me a nice, cool lake to paddle around in."

"I hope so too, Mother," I said. The thought of the elect paddling around in a celestial lake of light, bass fishing and water skiing as though they were on some eternal church picnic, made me smile.

Then she handed the binoculars to me. "Look over across there at Planter's Landing," she said. "Isn't Mel's house coming along?"

I trained the binoculars on the lake. There was a sailboat with a rainbow sail, becalmed out in the middle of the lake, and beyond it I saw the house rising out of the mud on the hill overlooking the lake, big as a castle—4,500 square feet with a master bedroom suite, live-in closets in every room, and a room with floor-to-ceiling shelves specially built to hold Canady's stereo equipment.

And then, as I looked at the houses and the lake in between, something happened. Call it the return of a sense of scale or perspective or proportion. Call it a revelation, a vision, a dream, but it was as if I could follow the road that ran under the water now, into Little Awando and out again and on to the Laughing Place and the river. And I saw Papa's map laid over the water, and that 500-acre crescent moon of land. Little Awando would have been just there where the sailboat floated, becalmed. And beyond that would have been the Laughing Place and beyond that, where Planter's Landing now stood, that would have been the 500 acres my father had bought and then sold. And as soon as I saw it, I knew why he had bought that land. When he first learned about the lake, he wanted to move us to a place out in the country that would not be touched. He would have bought up *all* the land in Vaucluse County and put us in the middle of it just to keep us from harm. But that is not what he did. He bought that land, then he sold it for nothing. That was the piece that would not fit.

"Let's get this show on the road," Mother said. I took the binoculars down from my eyes. She came up beside me and handed me the tape measure. I took it from her, handed her the binoculars, and started walking down what had been the road to Little Awando, into the water. I felt the surface of the road, bumpy asphalt, under my toes. The surface of the water was tepid, but just below the surface it was startlingly cold. I edged down the boat ramp, feeling with my toes for the drop-off. I knew from the articles I'd read in the paper that the water here could be unpredictable and dangerous. In one place the water might be two feet deep, then drop without warning to fifty. Though many hills had been cut down to make way for the lake, they hadn't disappeared entirely; the contours of the land remained underneath the water. Even the earthmovers had not entirely changed that. People would drown here, you could count on that. Somehow I knew that fact would have given Papa a kind of grim pleasure, the only sort of pleasure he'd allowed himself at the end of his life, the satisfaction of having everything confirm the worst for him. Then I was at the end of the boat ramp. The concrete stopped and I felt past its edge with my foot, felt nothing but a current flowing underneath. "That's it," I said. "That's as far as I can go."

"Now, be sure and measure right to that edge," she said. "This has to be just right. Mr. Greer is so picky about these things."

I turned around and looked back across the lake, then down at the tape. "Twelve feet, one and three-quarters inches," I said, and Mother began to write on her clipboard. Then I remembered something, one of those things that you miss because you tell yourself that nothing could be that simple, that obvious. Papa had sold that land to the Jo-Tel Corporation for one dollar. The Jo-Tel Corporation had turned around and made a killing selling that land to Canady and his partners at Planter's Landing. And who was the Jo-Tel Corporation? I almost laughed out loud. My father was a lawyer; he would know how to set up a dummy corporation or a blind trust. I thought of my father and mother together as I'd seen them often at tax time, with the checkbooks and bank statements and stacks of receipts spread out all over the dining room table. Papa called out figures and Mother worked the adding machine till the tape trailed out and spilled over the edge of the table and coiled on the floor. She used to tell me that a woman ought to be involved in the family finances the same as her husband so that she'd know what to do when he was gone. She'd had too many friends, she said, who'd lost their husbands and didn't know how to balance their own checkbooks.

They were in this together. No doubt it was risky, just this side of illegal, but Papa had seen his chance and he'd taken it in order that she might be safe, that we might all be safe. He'd done it, and then he'd gone right on fighting the lake from the same high ground on which he'd always stood.

The tape measure jerked in my hand. "Annie," Mother said, "come on out of there before you catch cold." She dropped the end of the tape in the water and I started to wind it back into the case. As I walked up out of the water smiling, I said, "Where'd you come up with a name like the Jo-Tel Corporation, Mother?"

She wrote on her clipboard, frowning. Then she stopped and she looked at me. Now, Mother can bluster, she can rant and rave, but she is a terrible liar. We looked at each other. "I don't know what you're talking about," she said. And the worst thing was, I believed her.

"The Jo-Tel Corporation? The people Papa sold that five hundred acres to? The Jo-Tel Corporation, that was you all, right? You and Papa?"

She shook her head again. "What five hundred acres?" she said, and she looked out across the lake warily, as though she were afraid it might rear up and break over her like a wave. "I think you'd better come on out of there, the sun's getting to you."

We didn't speak about it again all the way home. The sun was behind us now, and the car's shadow rippled and plunged ahead of us down the road. "I like that boy, Legree," she said out of nowhere. "He has substance, you can tell."

"You can, can't you?" I said, but it made me want to weep, the way his name felt as it came to rest against my heart, like a moment of cool air on a long, hot day.

"You ought to hold onto him."

"I'm going to try."

And then we didn't speak at all again until after the supper dishes had been dried and put away, the TV had been turned off after the eleven o'clock news, and we were going upstairs to bed. She was coming out of the upstairs bathroom and I was going in. In her pale blue satin pajamas, her hair all brushed up into a ribbon, white mules on her feet, she looked like some grand, severe movie star. She stopped with her hand on the bathroom doorknob and said, "This Jo-Tel Corporation, who'd you say the officers were?"

"I thought you might be able to tell me that."

"Well, I can't. Why don't you look it up?"

"Why don't you?"

"Because I don't want to know." She went inside her bedroom and shut the door behind her, and the light was still burning there when I went to sleep.

The March of Progress

I had three errands of my own to run that day: one for Mother, the other two for myself. It was exactly one week and four and a half hours before Mel's wedding, and this was the day the lake would officially open, the day the *Courier-Tribune* would publish the "March of Progress" edition, the day I would go to the Clerk of Courts office and find out for myself the names of the officers of the Jo-Tel Corporation.

Earlier that morning I'd gone into Papa's study and closed the door. I looked at the marks on the wall where the shelves had been that had held the Environmental Impact Statements, the maps and charts and folders full of notes and petitions. "Clean it down to the bare walls," Mother had said. Then she'd have the painters in to wake up those beige walls with some color. Who knows? She might even hire Mel to decorate in there, coordinate the drapes, buy a new armchair or love seat, make a guest room out of it for the grandchildren that Davis and I had better give her. A month earlier I would have said that's all in the future, far in the future. I'd believed it would take months to clean out my father's room. After all, a person's life is a deep thing: You can never really get to the bottom of it. That is the beauty of being an archivist, a sorter, and a preserver. You never finished, really; there was always more to discover.

Now it seemed that what was left of my father's life in this room was disappearing fast. Another week and it would be entirely gone. The week before, I'd put an ad in the paper and sold Papa's shotgun and hunting vest—the one with all the pockets for shells, the deeper pockets for birds—on the first day the ad appeared. Now, even the cardboard boxes into which I'd shaken all the papers and thrown the charts and Environmental Impact Statements, were gone. Several days earlier I'd carried the boxes out and stacked them along the curb. The garbage men had picked them up and slung them into the back of the truck, crushing them as efficiently as they crushed tin cans or cereal boxes, then moved on down the street. Yesterday I'd unscrewed the metal shelf runners and detached the brackets that had held the shelves; I'd tied the whole bundle together with rope and taken it down to the Goodwill. Now the desk, the sign from the Laughing Place, and the easy chair were all that remained of my father's life in this room. And the map, his revised, drawn-over map of Vaucluse County that I had revised myself. On the night of the day when Mother and I had gone out to the lake and measured for Mel's boat ramp, I'd drawn it in with a permanent black marker, that 500-acre crescent of land just beyond the Laughing Place where Planter's Landing now stood. The land my father had bought and sold. Sometimes at night when I couldn't sleep, I'd go into the study, snap on the light, and look at the map, hoping that in the dark the slice of land might have edged away from the Laughing Place. But it never moved of course; no matter how often I looked, the map told the same story.

That morning I sat down in front of Papa's desk and slid the curved cover up on its track. For years my father had rubbed soap on the runners, and the cover still slid easily, lightly, without a sound, a miracle of balance and care. The smell of pipe tobacco and cedar pencil wood lingered, but already Mother was laying claim to the desk. Her address book, covered in paisley cloth, was stored in one of the cubbyholes there along with four clipboards that held lists of chores for the wedding, bridge scorepads, a gold stamp-roll holder and several lined "Things to Do Today" pads. I took one of these out and made my own list.

The Laughing Place

Jo-Tel Officers
March of Progress Edition
Lake

It had its own kind of progress, a movement of one thing that led to another, as though what I'd find at one would lead me to the next and the next.

"Mercury Tops 100 for Fifth Straight Day," the *Courier-Tribune* headline had read in Monday's paper, and underneath, in smaller type: "95% Humidity Increases Heat Woes." But you didn't need the newspaper to tell you it was hot. At night the temperature only dropped a few degrees so that in the morning, as soon as the sun came up, it could start climbing the thermometer again. It was disease weather, cholera and typhoid and diphtheria weather. The kind of weather that stirs up grievances and saps your energy for taking care. Earlier that morning I'd taken a teacup down from a shelf in a kitchen cabinet and found mold growing up a mended crack in its side. Rather than wash it, I threw it into the garbage. It was one of Grandmother Vess's cups, too—bone china with pink roses on it, part of the set she'd left me. No wonder we can't make much progress down here, when for half the year most things are too much trouble.

On the courthouse square, people cranked down the awnings over their windows as if they'd forgotten that in this weather, shade is just a place for heat to collect. There were only a few people on the street, old black women mostly, carrying umbrellas and shopping bags, as they headed slowly for McCrory's dime store. Sparrows sat stunned on the sidewalk with their beaks open, and the sun multiplied in every piece of chrome and every window. But I was glad to be walking. I pushed through the heat as though I were fighting my way through underbrush.

I was waiting at the door when Becky Loudermilk arrived to open the Clerk of Courts office. At one minute till nine her heels squeaked up the hall. At thirty seconds till nine Miss Becky herself appeared, tall and thin in a seersucker suit with a straight skirt and a white blouse. Her straight, gray hair was pulled to one side with a barrette. She carried her keys in one hand, her lunch bag in the other, her eyes focused on the clock at the end of the hall, and as the hands of this clock clicked forward and locked onto the hour, she inserted her key into the lock, turned it with one sure motion, and swung the door open, kicking down the rubber stop as it swung inward. She snapped on the light, moved to her desk, and watered her dish garden from a pitcher filled with water that stood on the desk. Then she could speak. "Good morning, Miss Vess," she said. "You're out early this morning."

"Yes, ma'am," I said, and then I waited. The next word had to be hers. Miss Becky could be an ally, but she had to make the moves. I had seen her turn away impatient lawyers who were too important and busy to understand that this was her territory; it worked as she worked, slowly, deliberately, or it didn't work at all. Once, she'd stonewalled my father when he'd tried to push her around. It was the summer I worked for him, and I was with him one morning when he pushed through the door to the clerk's office and threw a piece of paper down on Miss Becky's desk. "Look this up for me, will you, Miss Becky?" he said. "I've got to be in court in half an hour." Then he stood there with his suit coat knocked back, his hands on the waist of his starched shirt, looking around impatiently.

"Take a chair, Mr. Vess," she said, nodding to a metal folding chair beside her desk. "I'll get to you as soon as I'm able." Then, while he sat there with his hands hanging down between his knees like an overgrown schoolboy, she'd proceeded to paint Liquid Paper over several lines on a typewritten page. First she took her glasses out of a needlepoint case in the wide middle drawer of the desk. For several minutes she untangled the silver chain from the stems, positioned them on her nose, and read the instructions on the bottle. Then she took off the glasses, polished each lens with a soft cloth, folded them, then unfolded them with an exasperated sound, and folded them again, being careful to keep the chain from tangling this time. Finally she inserted them back into the case and put the case into the drawer. Then she was ready to begin. Meticulously she dotted on the liquid, letter by letter, pausing between letters to dip the tiny brush back into the bottle and wipe off the excess liquid on the tip. It seemed to go on for hours, and when it was done, when the Liquid Paper had dried to her satisfaction—it took three minutes timed on her wristwatch—she rolled the paper into her typewriter. She retyped the two lines, addressed an envelope, folded the letter and put into the envelope, stamped it, and placed it on the top of the outgoing mail stack in the wire basket on the corner of her desk. Then she brushed the dried Liquid Paper crumbs that had fallen onto her desk into her hand, dusted them into the trash, and turned to my father. "Now," she said, "how may I help you?" My father never pushed her again, and since that day, I have known, too, how Miss Becky works—and how to work around her.

"Well, now," she said, folding her big, bony hands on the clean desktop. "What can I help you find this morning?"

"Information about a corporation."

"What sort of information?"

"The officers, that sort of thing."

"Yes, certainly. Information about corporate charters, et cetera, is located in the *Miscellaneous* books, alphabetically and by year. The *Miscellaneous* books are located along the west wall of the office. Please return them to their proper position on the shelf when you've finished."

This is the beauty, the safety of facts, I thought, as I skirted the map tables and walked toward the shelves on the west wall. They stay put, they do not change, you can lay them down and pick them up again, handle them at your own speed, in your own time, feed them to yourself in small bites like food after an illness— something plain, then something stronger. I was alone in the office and the sun slanted through the tall windows and onto the old, red bindings. I went to the west wall and found the *Miscellaneous* books for 1968. I found the book where the J's are listed, and paged through it until I came to the right page. There it was, officially stamped, officially sealed and notarized. The purpose of the Jo-Tel Corporation was to operate a land development company. There was a long, legal description of this purpose, full of *whereases* and *wherefores*, and at the end of the document the signatures of the officers appeared. "James Frampton Stark and Mary Boykin Stark, 145 Wyman Street, Timmons, S.C. Thelma Tuttle Radford, 851 Delray Drive, Timmons, S.C." The colonel and Mary, his wife, and Thelma Radford. I traced the raised ridges of the notary seal and looked at the colonel's signature and Miss Mary's and at Thelma's signature—that careful, grammar-school cursive. Papa had bought up all that land and then he had sold it to the colonel and Mary and Thelma, for nothing. The colonel and Mary I could understand, but what was Thelma Radford's name doing there? I took the book over to a window and looked at the signatures again in the strong sunlight, as if I could make myself believe that those names had been signed in special ink—the opposite of disappearing ink—that would allow you to write two stories at the same time: the official story and the one below it. Held up to the light, the ink would dissolve and the true story rise up.

From this window you could look across the square, over the spreading crowns of the oaks and into the second-story window of what had once been my father's office, where the gilt letters still spelled out his name. There was one last fact to find, and I knew where to find it. It would be in the *Grantor* title books for 1968, as straightforward, as neutral as all the rest. I didn't need Miss Becky's help to find this one. As I crossed the Clerk of Courts office, I kept my eyes on the green, ribbed-leather spines of the *Grantor* books. As long as I'd needed Miss Becky's help, it had been a public thing, but this was private, a free-fall without a net. I lifted down the *Grantor* title book for 1968, under the letter J, and paged through it slowly until I came to the month of December and read: on December 12, 1977, the Jo-Tel Corp. sold to Planter's Landing, Inc., for $500,000, the 510 acres that it had bought for $1. The purpose of Planter's Landing, Inc., so the *Miscellaneous* book told me—the one I hurried back across the office to find and pull down—was to develop the land on the northern shore of Lake Charles B. Hartley, Jr., as a luxury real estate development. There was the colonel's signature again, Mary's, and Thelma's. Seeing Thelma's handwriting again, it occurred to me what she was doing there. Of course, I thought. She was always there, a permanent witness to my father's transactions. I'd seen her signature on hundreds of documents. She'd *worked* for my father, hadn't she, for close to twenty years?

"Miss Vess," Becky Loudermilk's voice pursued me. As I passed her desk. "Miss Vess, are you all right?" But I pushed through the double glass doors of the office and out into the hall. Was she running after me? I thought I heard her come to the door, heard the rapid squeak of her shoes, but I didn't turn around, I kept walking. I would not go to Mother this time, Mother could not help me now. She knew less than I did, and to hear her talk, she knew as much, *more*, than she wanted to know. "What you don't know can't hurt you," she always said. Once, I'd believed her. I kept my hand on the cool wall and counted the squares of marble on the floor, then headed for the tall front doors of the courthouse.

Outside I had to stop and lean against a column on the courthouse porch until my heartbeat slowed. Then, I walked to the bench under the live oaks that faced the statue of the Confederate soldier and sat down there. I looked at the veins in the hands of the Confederate soldier who gripped his rifle. I looked up through the intricate and orderly universe of dark green, oak leaves and the cables that held the old limbs to the trunk, at the concrete that patched the holes in the trunk. *I know what to do, I thought. When you are lost, you sit down and get your bearings. You tell yourself whatever piece of truth you can stand at the moment, then you move on to the next.*

So Papa owned the Laughing Place—ten acres and that shack on the edge of the bottomland between the rivers. The ground flooded every spring, but the shack stood. Papa and his friends went out to hunt ducks and quail in the fall, and if his world had a center, this was it—the place around which the rest of the world arranged itself.

Fact: Just before the lake was announced, Papa bought 500 acres where the lakeshore would be. The timing is too precise to dismiss as simply a coincidence, a good business hunch, or anything else unintentional and lucky. He knew, he had to have known where the lake would go.

Fact: Almost as soon as he bought it, he sold it all for one dollar to the colonel and Mary and Thelma Radford, who turned around and sold it to Planter's Landing, Inc., for half a million dollars. And on that land that had changed hands so luckily, Planter's Landing stood today.

But why? Why had he done it? And where was the money? My mother didn't have it, that was for sure. My father's entire estate did not total half a million dollars. It had been a shock, I remembered, to Mother and me; it had even shocked Owen Gandy, the lawyer who executed Papa's will. "Sit down, sit down, Mrs. Vess, Miss Vess," he'd said without looking up from the documents spread out across his desk, after his secretary had shown us into his office that morning. I remembered the way he pulled out the middle drawer of his desk again and again, took out a different pen each time and, frowning, made a mark on one of the documents. The way he looked over the documents half a dozen times—top to bottom, bottom to top—as though he were searching for something he was sure was there, he just hadn't been able to find it yet. At last he'd taken off his glasses and leaned back in his chair. He looked at my mother for the first time since we'd come in. "Louise," he said, "I don't understand this, but there's just not that much money here." He'd seemed embarrassed by it, as though he were apologizing for not being able to find more. And I remembered the look on my mother's face: shock first, then a slow hardening, as if she'd gotten bad news that she'd been expecting. As if she'd given a lot of thought to what she would do when this moment came.

Across the street from the courthouse, I stopped to watch Faye Willard dressing mannequins in the front window of Faye's Bandbox. A pile of arms, legs, and torsos topped with smiling heads lay on the floor among brightly colored paper leaves. Faye held straight pins in her mouth and she moved quickly. She picked up a torso and pulled a gold sweater over its head and set it on a pair of legs already clothed in tweedy, brown slacks. She topped it with a head on which she set a plaid tam. Autumn already. In spite of this poisonous heat, autumn was coming. It gave me a funny feeling, as though something sharp as wire had just been twisted tight around my heart. I had to hurry.

I'd promised Mother that I'd go down to the *Courier-Tribune* office and get her a copy of the "March of Progress" edition as soon as it came out. Then she could read what Pug Simmons had written about my father, without having to come face-to-face with Pug. As feuds go, this one had not had long to grow, but its roots were as deep as the taproots of pines that can survive all but the longest droughts. Five years ago Mother decided that it was time for Pug to quit running articles about my father and Save our Two Rivers in the paper every week. Mother told Pug that it might help my father forget about the lake if he wasn't forced to read about himself in the paper twice a week and get all stirred up again every time he did. Pug said that Papa was a public figure and that he, Pug, had an obligation to report on public figures in his newspaper because that was what newspapers did. Mother badgered and pleaded and threatened—she might have even offered him money at one time. Papa hinted that she had, and I wouldn't put it past her. And still, Pug wouldn't give an inch.

Mother never forgave Pug. She'd *struck him off her list*, she said. And once you're struck from Mother's list, you can never crawl or claw or flatter your way back on. So when Pug called her not long after I ran into him in the cemetery, to say that he was working on an editorial piece about Papa for the "March of Progress" edition and how he deeply admired him and hoped she'd be happy with the job he'd done, she was just plain hostile. Politely, of course. She answered the phone, her back straightened. "Yes, Mr. Simmons. I'm fine, thank you." Then she listened. "I'm sure it will be satisfactory, Mr. Simmons," she said, and I swear I saw frost forming on the receiver and felt it chill my own insides. I'd heard that tone often enough. *Satisfactory*, said in this way, opens up before you a world of excellence in which you will never live. It means, of course, the best *you* can do, which is pathetically less than one might hope for or expect of a better class of human being.

"Well, Mother, good Lord," I said, after she'd hung up. "Maybe he's ready to bury the hatchet."

"Is that so?" she said. "Well, I'd like to bury the hatchet in his head."

Pug knew *that*, too. Make no mistake about it, he got the message. He grew up here, same as I did. He'd been born with that specially evolved sense of hearing that registers the pleasant word and its damning judgment, that hears both, and knows instantly which one is intended.

The glass front door of the *Courier-Tribune* office was propped open with a concrete block, and the sounds of a party drifted out into the hot air: music and laughter and loud, excited voices. A party. I put on my sunglasses and stepped inside. On the front counter, papers were stacked so high I could barely see over them, but I could stand behind them and look through the cracks. From there, I saw gray, metal desks pushed back against the wall, and in the center of the room a desk covered with a soaked and torn white paper tablecloth, empty and full champagne bottles, a plate of Triscuits and cheese, jars of dry-roasted peanuts. A radio played loud music, and milling around the desk in the open space, hugging each other and dancing, drinking champagne and eating peanuts from the jar, were a bunch of people who looked as though they'd been up all night. In the center of this circle, Pug Simmons shagged with a black woman with beads in her hair, spinning her out to the end of his reach, then pulling her back again, concentrating fiercely. Even Miss Leola Fenton sipped a cup of coffee and nibbled on a cracker, showing her big, horsey teeth when she smiled at Raymond Edwards, the sports editor.

"Could I pay someone for these papers, please?" I said. Mother would have been proud, I thought, at the way my voice turned a request into a command.

Everyone turned around, and Pug Simmons set down his glass and started for the counter, squinting as though it were a mile from there to here. His clothes looked as though they'd been slept in. His shirt was green like lettuce, with big rounds of sweat under each arm, the breast pocket ripped halfway off by a dozen ballpoint pens he carried there. His pants were smeared with ink. The stems of his glasses were tipped up on his head so the glasses rested at an angle

on his face, making his eyes look as though they were floating in
an aquarium. He looked the same as he'd looked in high school.
His face had been pudgier then, but he'd worn the same dark crew
cut; the same owly eyes looked out from behind the same thick
glasses. And the pens—God, I'd forgotten how everyone teased him
about the pens. I remembered his entry in the yearbook our senior
year: "William Pugmire ('Ballpoint') Simmons." And now he was
walking toward the front counter squinting, with his mouth hanging
open as if he couldn't believe his eyes, walking the way he'd always
walked, as though he knew just where he was going: to journalism
school at USC, then home to take over the paper. He'd been the
only boy in the history of Timmons High School who'd ever finished
Typing I *and* II. After school and every summer, he worked at the
paper. Our senior class took a field trip to the newspaper office and
Pug worked the linotype for us, like someone playing a machine
that was half guillotine, half iron pipe organ, his feet pumping the
pedals, his hands slamming the iron keys, the floor around him
littered with shiny, metal filings. Now here he was, arrived where
he'd always been going.

"Annie!" he said.

I took off my sunglasses. "You caught me."

"Come in, come in," he said, motioning me with his chin.
"Come in and have a glass of champagne with us. Hell, have two
or three." Everybody laughed.

Who am I? I thought. Mother's spy? Mother's feud was Mother's
business. If I spent my time keeping up with all her grudges and
disliking everyone she's ever had an argument with, pretty soon I'd
be like some floppy rag doll without a bone in her body. I'd be
stuffed with Mother's opinions, and whatever angry, hard chip of
myself I'd managed to hold onto. "Why not?" I said. "Why not?" I
followed him back to the desk where the refreshments were laid out
and I drank the glass of champagne he poured for me. We took
the bottle with us as we walked around the office and looked at
the awards the paper had won, framed and hanging on the walls—
first place in local news reporting, first place in sportswriting.
"This is Annie Vess," he said, every time he introduced me. "A

friend of the family." It sounded so nice I started to say it, too. "I'm Annie Vess, I'm a friend of the family," I said, and everybody smiled.

In what Pug called the back shop, we drank another glass of champagne, engulfed in the roar of the press. The room looked big as an airplane hangar, with long, slanted plywood tables lined up end to end down its length. A kind of metallic smoke hung in the air along with the smells of ink and electricity. Stretched across the width of the back wall there was what looked like a prehistoric roller coaster made of black iron with a river of paper running through it. Beside this machine, black teenage boys wearing headphones stood ready with ink-covered spatulas, and from time to time a tall, thin black man, who wore his headphones over a red beret, pulled a lever. The river of paper slowed and one of the boys ran forward and smeared ink across a roller. Under my feet the floor itself seemed to hum, and it was like standing on the deck of a ship during a storm with a wind of noise blowing right into your face, the kind of noise that makes you want to howl into it. Pug had to learn close to my ear and shout to be heard. "The belly of the beast," he shouted, and he began to bounce on the balls of his feet and wave his hands like a conductor in time to the beat of the press. At the end of the black, iron roller coaster, papers flew off and down a conveyor belt. As fast as they came, men and women grabbed them up. THE MARCH OF PROGRESS, THE MARCH OF PROGRESS, THE MARCH OF PROGRESS. Wide, tall, red letters, hurtled off the end of the line like a fire, spreading. I could feel the vibration of the press all through me. It seemed to be rising, toward some unbearable pitch that would make the whole building crumble and me along with it—me and everything I had just learned about my father, crumbled to dust. That would be a kind of progress, I thought, a progress my father might have wished for.

"Pug, telephone," the black woman with whom he'd been dancing came up and yelled in his ear. I followed him back. "Make yourself at home," he said. Out there, people were getting back to work. The tablecloths and peanuts were gone. The woman with whom Pug had been dancing lifted the side off of the typesetting machine and wound a roll of paper through the rollers there. Raymond Edwards was on the phone; Miss Leola was gone.

I poured myself another glass of champagne and sat down at an empty desk against the wall with the paper in front of me. THE MARCH OF PROGRESS. Below the words, an extraordinary photograph took up half the front page. It showed the dam and the lake and a boat that carried a waving family toward the far shore. The colors in the photograph were blurred and astonishingly wrong, the blue of the lake, the green of the shore, the golden hair of the family in the red boat cutting across this dream lake. I started to laugh. The typesetter turned around. I toasted her with my champagne glass and she turned back to her machine. It was, as Pug had written in his front-page editorial below that picture, a time to dream, and I was doing some fine dreaming. My head felt full of light as golden as the hair of the family in the boat. What good was a dream if it was about the way things really were? I hadn't lived for almost twelve years with Matthew Settles for nothing. At least I knew what dreams were all about.

OK now, easy, Annie, I thought, and I put down my glass. This is the tricky thing about drinking. It makes you feel as though you're about to break free of whatever has held you back from being the person you know you are, that everything is about to become very clear and definite. The trouble is that *what* becomes clear is never exactly what you'd imagine you'd find.

Look at the paper, I thought. *Just concentrate on the paper.*

The first section was filled with pictures of the lake and cutaway views of the dam, sliced through its layers like a cake. The writing in this section was about hydroelectric power: so many millions of cubic feet of water per day boosted into an astronomical number of kilowatts of power for home and industry. Praise to the power of the turbine and the floodgate, these pictures sang. Praise to the lake.

Further on, the industry and commerce section was filled with page after page of old, grainy photographs. Downtown Timmons in the twenties, a wide boulevard lined with trees just rounding into spring leaf and bloom. Aiken Simmons, Pug's father, holding up the first copy of the newspaper outside the original *Courier-Tribune* office, a white Victorian house with a cupola and a curved porch. Houses on deep shady lots and women in their flower gardens, their faces shaded by broad hat brims. Photographs of black people in their mule wagons in front of the icehouse or in the fields, picking cotton, stooped and dragging their long sacks along the rows. Then pictures of cotton gins gave way to pictures of the soybean processing plant, which changed again to Owens-Corning Fiberglass, and finally the industrial park out the Sinking Springs Road where the new industries had located: a microchip manufacturing plant, the Pepperidge Farm Outlet Store, the Burlington Mills Stock Outlet. "In this, too," Pug had written, "Vaucluse County has kept pace with the times." On one page there was an old map of Vaucluse County and Timmons, and beside it an aerial view of the present county that showed the lake, sprawled like a centipede up the center. There was a story about Senator Hartley and how the lake came to be situated in Vaucluse County. But when I looked at the map what I saw was my father's half-a-million dollar crescent of land fitted across the lake's northern shore like a puzzle piece snapped into place.

The next two pages were thick with photographs set as close as stamps on an envelope. "A Family Album," this section was called. It showed people in their gardens, on tractors, in stores and restaurants. There was Jake Estes cutting the ribbon across the door to the Steakhouse back in 1955. Miss Leola Fenton standing in the foundation of her homeplace out near the lake, pointing toward the room, the story said, where she had been born and where, years later, her mother had died. A picture of the church out at Sugar Hill being moved by truck out of the bed of the lake, with the deacons walking in front of it—a dozen ancient black men, some walking with canes and others supported on the arms of sons or daughters or wives. Melody riding in a convertible, holding roses in the crook of her arm, and waving. Her "homecoming parade," the caption read, after the Miss South Carolina pageant where she was named first runner-up. A grim-faced Aiken Simmons in front of the smoking rubble of the old *Courier-Tribune* office, which had burned to the ground one night in 1967 after he'd run an editorial calling for racial justice. The members of the Human Rights Commission, black and white, my father among them, which had been organized soon after the paper's office burned. Miss Hattie Lamar, teacher to two generations of Timmons's children. The Timmons City Council—Willie Mae's son, Jerome, among them—with their hands folded on the long, curved table in their meeting room. A large, black woman in a pale, print dress standing in front of a flowering quince tree with a bucket in her hand. "Beatrice Trimmer," the story read, "has lived on Bessie Creek for 27 years, and during that time she has been both witness and participant in many changes in the country and in her own family. She has lived through the lives and deaths of three husbands. During the civil rights movement, when she was almost 60, she joined the Freedom Rivers on their journey through the South. Over the years, six grandchildren have come to live with her, and she raised four of them to maturity and sent two of them off to college. And now, at 85, what does she see when she looks back across her life?

'The things that have come to me,' she says, 'were all meant to be. Not a one of them got left out.' She laughs and looks out across her chicken coops and garden. 'Not a one.' "

All those people, all those lives. There was a kind of genius, Pug's genius, the genius of someone who knew how things fit because *he* fit, in the way the pictures crowded together on the two pages, the way their stories collided and mixed and echoed one another. Much has been lost, those pictures seemed to say. Sometimes everything has been lost, but life moves forward by loss as well as by gain, by letting go and by holding on. This is the way it is. But what we have found on the other side of loss is also true, and it will carry us.

I turned the page and looked into my father's eyes. "Photograph by Legree Black," the credit line read, and I passed my hand over his name and imagined Legree looking at my father the way he'd looked at me sometimes, level and sober and holding me to the moment so I couldn't get away. But in this photograph, the last one ever made of him, my father looks into a private place and does not like what he sees. He stands in the bed of the lake, between a pair of bulldozer tracks, his boots caked with mud, his face grim, fists

jammed down into the pockets of his hunting jacket. Piles of up-
rooted trees smolder behind him. Anger smolders in his face. "Fool,"
his look says. "Don't you know? Life abandons, life betrays. Didn't
I teach you anything?"

The story beneath the photograph was about my father's life
and the history of his family in Timmons, and it was full of my
father's pride. It told how his branch of the Vess family had come
up from the Low Country to Timmons, how they had distinguished
themselves here. It spoke of my father's service in World War II,
how he'd founded Save Our Two Rivers and led them through seven
years, how he'd been its backbone and guiding spirit, and finally,
its only member.

Pug had written the story and an editorial, too.

"Perhaps only once or twice in our lives, it happens that we
must give ourselves totally to something or fail in our estimation of
our own courage. There are times when an individual conscience
and character is so aroused by what it sees as injustice, it can do
no more than be true to its own deepest convictions, regardless of
the opinions of friends, neighbors, family, or the community at
large. Such times require, and such people live by, the laws of a
personal ethic forged in the fire of conviction. Such a man was John
Vess, and we honor him, for the progress of this county is as much
the progress of the convictions of men like John Vess as any of our
more tangible industries and innovations."

I looked again at Papa's picture, at the line of his mouth. Yes,
such a man was John Vess, he was everything that Pug had said he
was. And he was another kind of man, too. Such a simple, such an
obvious thing to have discovered about your father: that he was not
what he'd seemed, that he was more, and much less, than the man
you'd counted on all your life. That his life had cracks in it, deep
unmendable cracks that divided who he was from who he'd intended
to be. That he'd lied and betrayed himself until the world filled with
betrayal like the lake filled with water. What kind of heart was wide
enough to hold all the contradictions? How could I accept all of
those things about him now that he was gone, when he would never
speak to me again or answer any of the questions that only he could

answer about the land he'd bought and sold. Or the questions about Thelma Radford, who drifted toward me now, a woman who knew things about my father that my mother didn't know, that none of us knew. And what do you do when even that other father, the fatherly voice in your head that answers your questions and gives good advice, refuses to speak any longer in words that you can believe or forgive? What then?

I must have made a noise, because everyone turned around. The black woman who sat at the typesetting machine got up and came toward me. And then Pug was there, waving her away. He looked down at the paper and then he had his hand under my elbow and he was helping me up. "Come on there, Annie," he said. "Let's go get some fresh air. You look a little peaked." He folded all my papers and stuck them under his arm. "I'm sorry," I started to say, but Pug guided me into the back shop, into that storm of noise, and out a door in the back wall, out into the sunshine and the heat of the loading dock. In the parking lot, people loaded stacks of newspapers into trucks and vans and station wagons. Next door, in a vacant lot, some hickory and pecan trees grew. In the tall grass I saw clumps of brown daffodils. No doubt a house had once stood there. "I'm sorry," I said again.

"Not to worry," Pug said. "Sit down, sit down."

Pug lost his balance and he sat down hard on the edge of the loading dock. Champagne sloshed out of the glass and onto one shoe. "Shit," he said, flipping champagne off his fingers. "Excuse my French. You all right?"

"Look here," I said. "That was a good editorial you wrote about my father. You touched on something about him, I think, but you didn't tell the whole story. How could you? You didn't know the whole story, I didn't know the whole story."

"Thank you, Annie," he said, "but do you think your mama'll approve?" He winced as though his shoes were too tight, and wiped his palms on his pants.

"Lord knows," I said, "but she'll sure let you know if she doesn't." And then we both laughed.

"Well, your mama's a great lady," Pug said, still wincing. "I value her opinion." And he leaned off the dock and looked around the corner of the building as if he expected her to jump out of the bushes at any minute and run at him, cursing as she came.

I didn't say anything because there was nothing to be said. If everyone agrees that my mother is a great lady, then that is who she is.

"You know," Pug said, "I really meant what I said about your daddy. He happens to be one of my personal heroes."

"He was one of mine, too."

"Past tense?"

"I don't know anymore, maybe so."

"Uh-oh," he said. And he braced his arms on the edge of the loading dock and put his head down, then knocked his heels against the front of the dock. In his silence I thought I heard listening, waiting, willingness.

It occurred to me then that Pug might be just the person to tell it to. After all, he'd been the one who'd taken the facts of my father's life and threaded them on that story line that made them seem to point in a certain direction. And he was a newspaperman, a journalist, someone used to sorting through things objectively and putting them into perspective. I felt the sweat trickle down my sides and back, and I took another sip of champagne. "Pug," I said, "what would you think if someone bought land out near the lake—quite a bit of land, actually, just where the shoreline would be—and then he sold that land to a dummy corporation for nothing, and they turned around and sold it to a developer for a lot of money, a whole lot of money?"

His eyebrows went up but he looked straight ahead, like a man staring out across the wide, gray ocean. "I'd say that that individual a. had friends in high places, and b. was trying to keep his name from being associated with these transactions."

"Well, who do you think the officers of this corporation were, the Jo-Tel Corporation, it was called?"

For a moment he studied his shoes. They were jogging shoes that had once been white but were covered now with ink spots, and he held them up side by side, frowned at the toes, then let them drop. He looked at me, his eyes clouded with fatigue and champagne, and he said quietly, "Annie, if you gave me a minute to think about it, I could probably name them all."

It was not the answer I'd hoped for. "But my father owned this land," I said.

"Well, didn't they all?" he said.

"Didn't they all *what*?"

"Didn't they all own something we wish they hadn't left us?" And he seemed to listen then to the building behind us, to the steady roar of the press. Then he raised his glass over his head and toasted the noise without looking back. "To the fathers, John and Aiken," he said, and he tipped back his head and tossed down the glass of champagne in one swallow. The courthouse clock struck eleven.

"I've got to get out to the lake," I said. I drained my glass, too, gathered up my papers, and jumped down from the dock, but my voice shook and my knees nearly gave way when I landed. "Mind if I take this?" I held up the champagne bottle.

"Help yourself, help yourself," Pug said, still caught in his reverie and staring up at the sky. It was white, blank as smoke. Who could read anything there?

As I walked up the sidewalk away from that place, I felt the champagne like a sour pool in my stomach, sending fumes into my head. I felt the sweat start down my ribs again. Mother was right about Pug; he had no respect for anything or anybody. He was callous and insensitive. The idea that my father's story differed only in its details from thousands of other stories just like it—that it was not a great, but an ordinary and familiar, tragedy—was as stifling to me as this low, bullying heat that all seemed trapped in town. Out at the lake, I thought, it will be cooler.

Senator Hartley's Lake

The Timmons High School Marching band played "Nothing Could Be Finer Than to Be in Carolina," as we stood on top of the dam in the sun, waiting for Senator Hartley to arrive. County government people and the Timmons City Council; Father Reid and Jake Estes, the mayor of Timmons. A TV crew had come down from Columbia for the occasion, and George Linker, the general assignment reporter, was there to cover the event for the *Courier-Tribune*. Children ran through the crowd holding up small American flags on sticks, waving and lashing them through the air, absorbed in the pleasures of motion. It looked as though everyone in town had come to hear Senator Hartley speak and to watch Mel break a bottle of champagne against the dam and officially open the lake.

The lake. When Papa used to take my brother Davis and me up to the bluff where you could see both rivers and the land between, he'd talked as though the beauty of that place were the purest, the most perfect kind of beauty on earth. And yet here was the lake, here was the dam. Below the white heat haze the lake water had a dark, restful look. On the shore, new green grass had sprung up everywhere, the trees were all leafed out. Even the dam was beautiful, looked at in a certain way. It had the still, eternal quality of monumental things. Never before, I thought, had you been able to see, really see, like this from anywhere in the county. Every view had been smothered in woods: pine and scrub oak above, catbrier and sparkleberry below, and the fields had been smothered, too, in soybeans and kudzu. Now there were vistas, open spaces. The wind swept over the surface of the lake and set it sparkling.

Just then the crowd shifted, and Senator Hartley walked through, surrounded by his security people. Pushed to the front of the crowd, the children waved their flags at him and he waved back. With his thick, white hair brushed back, and his open, big-featured face, he looked like a man handing out the gift of himself, sharing the wealth. His wife, Addy, walked beside him, dressed in yellow silk, her bright mouth smiling, vivid and energetic in spite of the heat, holding out both her hands to pull people in, to pull me in. "Annie, can you believe this heat?" she asked. I said I couldn't. "I always forget until I see you again how much you favor your father," she said, pressing my hands. "Charles, here's Annie Vess," she said. As I shook his hand I looked him in the eye, and when I did I realized that I had come here for this moment. If it's true that I favor my father the way Addy said I did, then when he saw me, Senator Hartley might see my father, his friend, and the guilt they shared. Every year they'd come to the big oyster roast at our house; my father and mother had both worked on his first election campaign, and when he'd left the Democratic party in the 1960s and become a Republican, my parents had switched parties too. But Charles Hartley's face did not change. I imagined I felt health, confidence, well-being emanating from him like some expensive aftershave. He looked like a man who's never made a mistake in his life. Only his voice changed, dropping into a lower, more intimate octave. "Well, Annie," he said, "good to see you, good to see you. The last time we met was under such sad circumstances." He looked over my head, searching the crowd. "And where is your dear mother today?"

"She didn't come, Senator Hartley," I said. "She said she wouldn't come out here today. You can understand that."

This was just like Mother, absolutely typical of her. After all the time she'd spent arguing with my father about what a great thing the lake was going to be—when to him it had been the worst catastrophe that had happened to Vaucluse County—you'd have thought she'd jump at the chance to come out here and be treated like a visiting queen by Charles Hartley; to watch Mel break a bottle of champagne on the dam; to celebrate what she'd told my father so many times she'd wished for: that this lake business would be over with so their lives could get back to normal. But when I'd asked her that morning if she wanted to come with me, she'd acted as if she and Papa had never spoken a harsh word to one another about the lake, as if I were the traitor. "No, thank you," she said. "I'll sit this one out." And I knew by the sound of her voice, by the look in her eyes, that she'd done it out of loyalty to my father. It was the same look that I'd seen on her face when she'd talked about the total strangers who'd once felt free to stop her on the street and let her know exactly what they thought of my father and his fight to keep the lake from coming into this county.

"Yes, of course," Senator Hartley said, and he patted my hand, finished with the conversation. "Well, please remember me to her, will you?" and before I could answer, he'd turned to the next person who waited to speak to him.

At two o'clock the speeches began. Someone from the Corps of Engineers spoke, then the head of Carolina Power Company, looking hot and earnest in his tan suit and his round, tortoiseshell glasses. Then Father Reid prayed and Senator Hartley began to speak while Addy stood beside him, smiling. He talked about how humble it made him feel to have this great symbol of progress named after him. "Y'all know I'm from around here," he said. "Little town called Eight Mile, doesn't even exist anymore; it's down at the bottom of this lake somewhere, along with the homeplace where my mother and daddy tried to raise me to speak the truth and to stand up for what's right." He said that he hoped in years to come that he would live up to the honor that the people of the great state of South Carolina had bestowed upon him, and that when they thought about the lake that carried his name, they would find no reason to wish that it had been named after another, more worthy man. "Now that's enough from a long-winded, ugly old man," he said. "Let's get on to the real attraction today." He clasped his hands as though he were praying, and he began to talk about Melody, reviewing the honors her beauty had won her. She'd been Miss Sun Fun, Miss Rural Electrification, Queen of the Hampton Watermelon Festival, the current Miss Vaucluse County, first runner-up at last year's Miss South Carolina Pageant. But he didn't look like someone who thought of himself as old or long-winded or ugly or humble; he looked like a man who was mightily pleased with himself, proud of his humility, a man who accepted every good thing as his due. And why shouldn't he look that way? I thought. He'd won; he was the victor here. They hadn't named this Lake John Vess. But no, it was impossible to see it that way anymore. Victory and defeat, winners and losers— those were my father's terms.

The band began "A Pretty Girl Is Like a Melody," the song Melody called her signature song, and everyone turned to watch Mel walk along the concrete path on Canady's arm, high-headed and swan-necked, smiling and nodding to people. She was dressed in a white linen suit, a jade-green blouse, and smart sling-back shoes, the perfect round of her head accentuated by the close fit of her golden hair, the perfect golden rounds of her earrings. In the crook of her arm, she carried a bundle of yellow roses. Canady wore a single yellow rosebud in the lapel of his jacket. Beside the speaker's stand, Mel stopped and held up her cheek for Charles Hartley to kiss, which he did to laughter and applause from the crowd. Then she handed her roses to an awestruck little girl and walked off toward the dam on the senator's arm.

Canady came over and stood in front of me, so close I could feel the warmth of his body and smell the expensive soap on his skin. He winked and then he waited, the way he always did, searching my eyes and my face as if he couldn't get enough, as though he were still waiting—the way we'd waited in the hall that night—for me to give him a sign that he should come into my room instead of Mel's. When I nodded he laughed and squeezed my arm and moved to stand beside me. As usual I felt stunned, as though I'd just encountered some kind of strange genius who'd shaken up my comfortable way of seeing. Canady's genius was to turn the question he asked every woman into *when*, not *if*, so that the only answer could be *not yet* instead of *no*. And yet, knowing this about him in no way protected you from him. In Canady's presence the clear and rational part of you shrank back, appalled at its cold primness, while the wild and passionate part bloomed and billowed toward him as though he were the man who had the power to name you a woman or something drier.

Once you've fallen into Canady's spell, it's hard to break free, but I tried. "Canady," I said, "I need to ask you something." If anybody knew, I thought, Canady knew about the sale of my father's land to the Jo-Tel Corporation, the sale of their land to Planter's Landing, Inc. It occurred to me that he might even know where the money was, that he might even have some of it himself.

"The answer is yes," he said, looking straight ahead to where a man helped Mel down onto a platform that hung suspended against the face of the dam.

"But I haven't asked you yet," I said.

Senator Hartley handed Mel a bottle of champagne. She said something to him and he laughed.

"Company policy," Canady said. "Whenever a good-looking woman asks me a question, the answer is yes."

You creep, I thought, but I said, "Well, maybe some other time, then, Canady."

Mel turned her head, closed her eyes, and smashed the bottle against the concrete, and everyone clapped while Senator Hartley helped her back up with the rest of us and recovered her roses for her. "You name it," he said, his eyes flicking around my face. "Stop by the clubhouse for a drink, why don't you? I'm there most nights."

"I didn't mean *that*," I said.

"Later, definitely," he said, "Now I have to go and get my bride." I did not like the way he said "bride." It sounded like the punch line of some joke that we'd shared, but as I said "Canady," he laughed to himself and went away, stroking his tie.

And then a rumbling began. It seemed to come from inside the dam itself. It shook the ground, and the face of the dam began to darken with water while everyone clapped and cheered and hundreds of balloons flew up and sailed off into the thick, white sky. As the balloons disappeared, people started down the sidewalk toward the parking lot.

Quickly, then, before they closed the gate to the platform where Mel had stood, I edged onto it and knelt to hold my hand flat against the dam so that water ran over it. The water poured over the lip and down the face of the dam until it hit the concrete sluices far below and churned there, a turmoil of water. It felt final somehow, the way it had felt to stay at the cemetery after everyone had left except Davis and Mother and me, while the Taylor Brothers' men loaded the flowers back into the hearse, pulled back the green carpet, and uncovered the pile of dirt that they'd shoveled out of my father's grave and the old, splintered planks on which the vault rested. That day, when I saw the hole in the ground, I understood in the way that I had not understood at the church or in the tent while Father Reid talked, that we were there to bury my father, to put him into the ground and walk away and never see him again. And now, with the water pouring over my hand, wetting the face of this dam for the first time, I knew all over again that he was gone forever.

A long, dusty line of cars drove bumper to bumper down the road from the dam to the visitor's center a mile away. I sipped a little from the bottle of warm champagne I'd brought from the newspaper office, and parked in the spot where the highway patrolman motioned me to go. The visitor's center was at the top of a hill. It was a hexagonal wooden building with tall windows on all sides and surrounded by azaleas, rhododendrons, small trees supported by wires, and squares of sodded grass.

Papa had brought Matthew and me here once, the winter before Matthew died, when there was nothing here but wooden stakes hammered into the ground, string marking off the shape of the building, and the lake bed at the foot of the hill. "Can you imagine," Papa had said, "can you comprehend the sheer, arrogant idiocy that conceived of this hill as the place to put the visitor's center?

Why, it's out here in the middle of nowhere. They'll have to spend more of the taxpayer's money just to build a road and run electrical lines. Can you comprehend the way these people's minds work?" Matthew said he couldn't. I kept quiet as they kicked clods of dirt, talking loudly. Matthew even yanked up a few marker stakes and snapped the string that ran between them, until my father stopped him and made him put them back. "There are lawful ways to go about this, son," he said. "There are still lawful ways and I will pursue them." And then my father and Matthew stood there, looking out over the muddy lake bed. Matthew put his hand on Papa's shoulder and pointed to something off in the distance. They looked like Lewis and Clark in that famous painting—two small figures standing on the edge of a deep, wooded gorge in a wilderness so dense it looks as if they could step off the edge of that gorge and walk on the tops of the trees all the way across the country. But the wilderness that my father and Matthew explored was a wilderness of ruin.

On the way back to Pennsylvania, I'd let Matthew talk about moving back to Timmons so that he could help my father fight the lake. I shouldn't have let him, but I did. I should have said, "No farther, Matthew, I won't move anywhere else," which is what had been growing in my mind to say to him for months. But I'd learned that if Matthew talked enough about what he wanted to do, he would not need to do it anymore. Without knowing exactly how it had happened, I'd stopped believing that Matthew meant what he said. I'd begun to count on the fact that his talk was neither map nor plan, that the words weren't connected to intentions. They were just words, and when he'd said enough of them, he would stop. So I rubbed portholes in the fogged-over window as we drove north and watched the gray fields and houses slide by—and let his words slide by until he'd said them all. Now I know that this was wrong, that I failed him with my silence. He needed me to stand up to him, to deflect his thought before it got lost in the pure, unbreathable air toward which it was aimed. Instead I let him talk. And now I was thinking about him again, letting him back into this world where he could come alive again and die. Because no matter what moment in our lives wandered into my mind, my thoughts always accelerated

from there and began to run straight toward the morning when he
left for Cheraw, the last time I saw him alive, when I didn't say,
"Don't go." The morning when I went back inside and shut the
door.

Mel stood at the door to the visitor's center, welcoming everyone. She'd changed into a long, off-the-shoulder gown that cascaded
down in frilly tiers of peach organza, the dress she'd worn for South
Carolina Heritage Days. "Welcome, welcome," she said as the crowd
moved past her. It was a relief to see her: the present, the future—
not the past, nothing that would hurtle forward and smash into its
own ruin the way thoughts of my father or Matthew would do. Just
Mel in the main room of the visitor's center surrounded by glass
cases full of arrowheads and pottery shards and copper rusted to lace,
old photographs of grist mills and peach orchards, dioramas and
maps. "Welcome, Annie," she said, and kissed me on the cheek.
"Isn't it wonderful?"

A crowd of children had gathered around a kind of animated
relief map that stood on a table in the center of the room. It showed
the lake and the dam and the land around the lake, the hills and
valleys. It showed the generators and pylons marching away over
the hills toward Columbia. The children took turns pushing the
button that made bright blue plastic water pour over the dam and
into the turbines, sending light running down the wires, lighting up
valleys and towns until it reached Columbia and set the skyline
glowing. Meanwhile, back in the lake, which was filled with the
same impossibly blue water, smiling fish jumped, families picnicked
on the shore, and families hiked up sunny trails accompanied by
bluebirds. When the kids moved on, I pushed the button three times
and watched the water flow, the lights travel down the wires. It was
as sunny a vision as my father's had been bleak, both of them drawn
too broadly to be true or useful. Each the story of some ideal so
pure you'd break your heart trying to live by it. Measured against
such visions, who would not fail?

Nearby I heard Mel's voice. She'd been waylaid by an old man
in overalls who wore a hearing-aid wire that traveled down from his
ear and disappeared into his breast pocket. He had small, brilliant

eyes and almost no teeth, and his voice sounded as though he were gargling. I went over and stood beside her, but she hardly knew I was there; she was listening, and when he was done, she touched his arm and answered him. Mel believed in what she called her "responsibility to the people of South Carolina" who had put her where she was. If I could stand beside her for awhile and listen, I thought, I might learn something valuable, something my father never taught us: how to live in this world in small, useful ways that touch other human beings.

The old man wandered off, and suddenly Mel grabbed my arm. "Annie," she whispered, "look who's here."

I felt my breath snag in my chest. Legree. He stood in front of a display case filled with Indian artifacts, with his back to us, his weight on one leg the way he always stood, like a crane, a hand down in his pocket and his head to one side as if he were listening. As I walked toward him he stared at me in the glass, his reflection mixing with the broken, blackened cooking pots. When I got close he turned around. "You're back," I said.

"Your mother told me you'd be here," he said. "I wanted to see you."

"I'm glad," I said. "I wanted to see you, too." Saying it, I knew it was true, and that it was dangerous to feel this way.

Legree looked right at home, leaning against the glass window that looked in on the Cherokee squatting around a fire, their tools and pottery and shell beads scattered around them. Legree could have been a Cherokee too, with his rough face and full mouth, his steadily watching eyes. "You look good," I said. "You look healthy, Legree. I imagined I could smell sun and water in his shirt and on his skin. He ran a finger down my arm from my shoulder to my wrist. "What happened to you?" he said. "You look a little frayed around the edges."

"Too much celebrating the 'March of Progress' down at the paper with Pug and the rest of them. Too much lake. Too much thinking about my father. Too much."

"You hungry?" he said.

It hadn't occurred to me until he asked. "I am."

"Let's go to the Steakhouse," he said. "I'll buy you something to eat."

"That would be wonderful," I said, and tears came into my eyes. So much of what was right between us had just happened again: good offered, good accepted. But it was too simple, and I no longer trusted that anything could be that simple, or that good.

"I Fall to Pieces"

I found a parking place on the square in front of the courthouse and the statue of the Confederate soldier under the oak. It was lit up by a strong spotlight, and as always in summer, the light was ringed with a fuzzy halo of humidity. The statue had been given to the city of Timmons in the thirties by the last Confederate widow in Vaucluse County, under the condition that it be kept lighted in perpetuity. A Confederate soldier advancing to the attack, his rifle ready. The spotlight brought the veins in his hands into relief and heightened the features of the boyish face under the little squared cap. Valor and heroic readiness, that's what I'd been taught to see in the statue's expression and what I'd always found there, until tonight. But now as I looked at the face of the young soldier, staring out from beneath the oak limbs, I thought I detected something new there: a look of doubt, of fear, a human look.

Papa would never have allowed such a thought. On summer nights, we'd walk down to the square, Davis and Papa and Mother and me, to sit on the benches under the oaks that had seemed as old then as now, and eat the ice-cream cones Papa had bought us. On these nights, Papa would study the statue in silence for awhile, and then he would say the same words: "Can't you just feel the thoughts going through his head?" I couldn't, but I never said so. Anyway, it didn't matter what we thought; Papa's story was the true one; we'd learned that long ago. So I'd knock my heels against the bench rungs, lick my cone, and watch the soldier's iron face while Papa talked. "He's just a boy a long way from home," he'd say. "He's never been in a fight before. Maybe he sees the enemy massing along that ridge line in the distance." Looking at that statue now, I saw none of those things. Instead I saw in his expression amazement and fear, the look of someone whose mortality has been made suddenly clear. Who understands for the first time that tomorrow for a soldier is never far enough away, nor tomorrow's possibility.

Papa was a soldier, I thought, as I locked my car door and started across the street toward the Steakhouse. He should have told us something real about that man. For four years Papa fought the Japanese in the jungles in the Pacific; he saw people die in ways unimaginable to us; other human beings had died by his hand or at his orders. He should have told us what he'd learned from all that instead of handing us these sentimental still lifes in which innocence survives the most horrifying experience: the boy by the campfire, the distant troops with banners richly snapping against the breeze.

I thought of the way my father spread his arms, grinned, shrugged. "How would I know about that?" he would ask. "I'm just a simple country boy." It drove my mother wild and I hated her for it, for backing Papa into corners, backing him down. Now I understood her rage. He should have taught us about what happens when you run out of reasons why you're blameless or fearless; when it's no longer the night before the battle but the day itself, and you leave the campfire and go into battle and kill another human being or watch him die; when you buy and sell in secret, and profit from the secrecy and make somebody else rich, too, but not your own family. He should have told us how it feels to lie about yourself and make everyone around you swear allegiance to that lie.

The Steakhouse is one of those places that had been added onto gradually and casually, without much thought: a room here, an alcove there, until it became a maze. It used to be that you had to wander through three dining rooms to get to the bar, until the owner, Jake Estes, gave up and cut a separate bar entrance door that opened onto the sidewalk. It was a heavy door made of dark, polished wood, and it opened into a large, dark room with a pine-paneled bar at one end and booths along one wall. A polished-wood dance floor occupied the middle of the room and overhead a mirrored ball revolved slowly, sending out spears of red, blue, and green light into the room's dark corners. Over the bar, the head of a buck had been mounted on the wall, and someone had long ago placed on its head a wide-brimmed, straw farmer's hat with a sweat-stained band.

Legree sat way back in the last booth, out of reach of the color thrown off by the mirrored ball. He sat far over against the wall, frowning and slowly turning the metal leaves of the jukebox mounted on the wall of the booth. Two beers and a plate of onion rings lay on the table in the front of him, and as I crossed the dance floor I could tell that he hadn't touched an onion ring or taken a sip of beer. That's how he was about so many things. He was in no hurry to eat, to drink, to talk, to make love. With him you felt time loosen, you felt sometimes that time might be doing something other than running out, that it might carry you toward something after all. Because Legree was a man who knew the value of waiting, of lingering over pleasure.

I slid into the booth across from him just as the low, slappy guitar began the intro to "Born on the Bayou."

"I ordered you a hamburger, lettuce, tomato, and mayonnaise. Right?" he asked.

"Right, thank you, you go on and eat," I said.

"I'll wait," he said. "And for your listening and dining pleasure, I've made a few selections on the jukebox. This is the first one."

The waitress came then with my hamburger. She set it down and lit the candle in the knobby red glass holder. "I like that boy," Mother said. "He has substance, you can tell." In the candlelight, I knew what she meant. The candle did good things to his face. Its light warmed the gauntness and filled in the hollows, and strength-ened the bones. It made his white shirt look clean and new. We smiled at each other across the light.

After he'd eaten a few onion rings, he wiped the salt and grease off his fingers with one of the stiff napkins from the dispenser against the wall. "These are by far the best onion rings I've ever tasted," he said.

"They're pretty good," I said.

"You know where to get better ones?" he said, keeping his head down.

"The restaurant in the pavilion down at Edisto Beach," I said. "The onions are always sweet, they use just the right amount of breading, and the oil's hot enough so they're never greasy."

"I stand corrected," he said, crunching into another one, tearing it with his teeth. "These are the best onion rings I've tasted in my limited experience."

"Well, don't take it personally, Legree, for God's sake. I like these onion rings, they're fine."

He circled the plate with his arms and drew it closer to him. "For saying that, you may not have any," he said, and he meant it—I knew he did. "So," he said, "our first turtle nest hatched out last evening. I must have carried two hundred tiny turtles down to the edge of the surf."

"In your hands?" I asked through a mouthful of bun. "Excuse me."

He reached over and touched my face with the tips of his fingers. "In buckets," he said. "I have to go back tonight. There'll probably be more nests hatching, full moon and all. I just came up to see how you were doing, to see you." He shook salt from his fingers and looked at me shrewdly.

"Tonight," I said, "that soon." *Tonight.* The word had a lonely sound, now that I knew I'd be spending it alone, with Mother. "I think of you down there at Kiawah," I said. "Now I'll think about you with buckets in both hands, carrying buckets of turtles down to the water."

He reached across, squeezed my hand, and I squeezed back. "You can't carry them all the way into the water," he said. "They have to crawl into the water themselves. The best we can figure, they have to actually cross some sand, feel it under them, and crawl through it before they get to the water or they get disoriented. If you just dump them into the water, they'll swim in circles until something comes along and eats them. So we take them down close to the water and let them find their own way from there, that's all we can do. They go for the light of the moon on the water."

"But not too much," I said. "I don't think about you too much."

"Ah," he said. "Why don't you slide on over here next to me and tell me what you've been up to?"

When I got there, I knew I'd been waiting for this. I laid my head against his shoulder and felt his shirt against my cheek, smelled its sun, and the warmth of his skin beneath it. He rubbed his cheek across the top of my head. It was always this way. We couldn't be together five minutes without touching one another. And for what? I thought. No matter how our bodies felt together, we'd fail each other soon enough. "They used your picture of my father in the 'March of Progress' edition of the paper," I said.

"Pug told me they might."

Maybe I could tell him about my father, I thought. Tell him everything, and let us sit together and sort it out, this man who carried turtles in buckets down to the water. Someone who did that would know what to do with what I'd learned about my father, and with what I was afraid to know. But even as I thought of telling him, I saw my father's face in that photograph, and the impossibility of it rose up inside me the way I imagined darkness rising from the bottom of the lake sometimes—rising and spreading, darkening the water from shore to shore. "It's an awful picture," I said. "It makes him look so grim."

It was as if whatever had come forward in Legree's face backed suddenly away and boarded up the door. He signaled to the woman behind the bar and pointed to his glass, and when he turned back, his mouth was set. "Well, that's the way he looked that day. I can't help that."

"I expect he did," I said.

Just then, "I Fall to Pieces" came on the jukebox. Patsy Cline's voice low and aching at the start, then rising, holding, a brave, blue sound. I laid my head back against his shoulder, and I let the music come over me, warm and true.

"This is a great song," he said. "One of the greatest."

"This was one of Matthew's favorite songs, too," I said.

He laughed then, once, and shrugged me off. He sipped from his beer and stared toward the door. Nobody can look as miserable as Legree. His skin seems to sink around his bones, and every error stands out, every bony angle.

"Is that why you loved him?" he said.

It was the tone more than the words that should have warned me, the tone and the way he peeled the label on his beer bottle into strips, and what had happened to his mouth.

"Other reasons, too," I said. "I had plenty of reasons to love him, if you want to know the truth. All of them bad ones, probably, but there you have it."

"That's what I'm here for," he said. "The truth." He took a sip of beer and wiped the foam from his upper lip.

I held my own bottle in both hands, and felt the air tighten the way it does before a storm, while Patsy Cline finished bravely telling about all the pieces she fell into each time she saw him again, and the song ended. Then Willie Nelson's guitar played the opening notes of "Blue Eyes Crying in the Rain." Legree watched me with a still and steady look. His eyes had many layers to them, like a cat's eyes, or the levels of sand seen through water. When he'd looked long enough, he said, "Look here, I have to go back soon. This is the last song I paid for. You going to dance with me before I go?"

We walked out onto the dance floor, while Willie Nelson sang and played the guitar as if each note and word were something marvelous he had just discovered. I draped my arms around Legree's neck and tried to move back close to his body. He smelled wonderful, like cloth that's been soaked and then dried in the sun, like the ground when it's opened in the spring, like sweat—not the sharp sweat of nervousness, but the rich smell of the sweat of hard work. He pressed me to him, fingers in the small of my back. Other times when we'd danced, this had been the best moment, the moment when I'd relax against him gladly. But now there was something wrong. His fingers, his body felt tense and angry, and the way he held me was not a wish or a desire but a challenge, a command. I tried to twist away, to lean back and see his face, look into his eyes, but he only gripped me tighter, pressed my head back firmly onto his shoulder, and held it there.

"Isn't that better?" he said into my ear.

"Much," I said, rubbing my cheek on his shoulder, smelling his skin, feeling the slow pull of letting go. I wrapped my arms more tightly around him and we danced. I kept my eyes closed tight and tried to move with the music and with Legree's body, to feel his body moving with mine, to feel us moving together that way—two people caught in the same current. But something was wrong. It wasn't working. Like a charm that fails. We didn't step on each other's feet; it was nothing that funny.

I felt fear begin in the pit of my stomach. I wasn't going deep enough, far enough, the way I'd once been able to do with Matthew, forgetting everything but the moment, forgetting myself. I wrapped my arms more tightly around him and tried to move closer to his body. I put my lips against the little V of sunburn in the neck of his shirt. But I knew that I was changed. I would never again be that woman who could disappear, dissolve into another. And he was not a man with wings. We were not going to fly anywhere. We were going to go by night, by day, over the ground, step-by-step. And then we were barely moving, shuffling our feet, and I had to get away. When I moved back, he held my head down on his shoulder. "Relax," he said.

"Stop it, let me go." Panic beat inside my chest like something with wings trapped in a room. "Let me go." Over his shoulder I saw two men in John Deere hats and dusty boots, leaning back in the booth on the other side of the dance floor, watching us.

He let me go so suddenly I almost fell.

Back in our booth, Legree tipped the beer bottle straight up, then sucked down the last of the beer. He set it down hard. "I wish I could do something to make this different," he said. "But it sure looks like I can't."

The way he said it, I knew that something had changed, as though he'd just been given a sign that he'd watched for. When I spoke, the sound seemed to come from far away. "What are you talking about?"

"Just tell me," he said, "what you were thinking about out there while we were dancing together." But before I could answer he said, "No," and held up his hand like a policeman stopping traffic. "No, I'll tell you. You were thinking about your husband." His hands gripped the edge of the table and something in his body seemed drawn up, coiled, as if it might strike at me across the table. "You were thinking about him and dancing with me."

I felt the moment, the question, held up like a globe made of glass. If it dropped—and lying would make it drop—it would break and there would be no putting it back together. "Yes," I said. "I was. But I was thinking about you, too. Things remind me of him, I can't help it." I felt it coming then, all that I might say about Matthew, a depth of grief I had not touched, that sense of being carried too fast toward somewhere I didn't want to go.

"Listen," he said, and the corners of his mouth tightened, and he crushed the leftover pieces of crust from the onion rings with the bottom of his beer bottle. "You and me and Matthew go a lot of places together, only he's dead and I'm alive."

The breath all went out of me then. "No," I said quickly, "that's not it."

"Well, what then?" he said, his voice gentler.

What I will always love about Legree and carry in my heart is the way he can say the most terrible things and then go on. It is this willingness that I will always love. I said, "You expect too much of me, Legree. You think I want to think about Matthew so much? But I was married to him for ten years. I can't just forget him like that."

"No," he said. "I wouldn't ask that of you, anyway."

"What then? What are you asking?"

"Be with me. At least let's make a start. I mean, Jesus Christ, are we having an affair, is that what we're doing? When we ride in the car, you check the rearview mirror constantly. When you're over at my place, you jump up ten times a night to look out the window.

Half the time I feel like I'm keeping you from going someplace you'd
rather be."

Why was he saying these things to me? I had to stop him.
"You've had your say," I said. "Now let me tell *you* something. I
could turn around tomorrow and you'd be gone in any one of a
thousand ways one person can leave another person. You could decide to take a swim in the ocean down at Kiawah and get caught
in the undertow and drown, because you didn't know how to look
at the water and see there was a current there, or you didn't know
how to swim out of a current once you were caught. I could find
out a year from now that you were really married all along. Or
maybe you just might decide someday that you didn't want me any
longer. Why should I count on you? Why should I?"

As I'd talked, his face had gotten sadder and sadder, but when
I was done he was angry again, ready to fight. "All that is true,"
he said. "It's also bullshit, by the way, but we'll save that for another
time. So what do you want? Sometimes I swear it looks to me like
you're trying to keep your virginity or some damn thing like that."

A sharp pain, like a stinger, went into me, and I wanted to
sting him back. "Fine," I said. "You know what I want? I want to
feel about you a way that I just don't feel."

Pain crossed his face and left behind the cleansed look of a
new understanding. I stood up then, but he was faster. He grabbed
my wrist and his eyes were tight with anger. "No," he said. "You
stay. Finish your beer, it's on me." He threw some bills onto the
table. He didn't even look at them, just yanked them out of the
pocket of his jeans and tossed them down. As soon as they landed,
I shoved them off onto the floor. The good old boys in their John
Deere hats and the waitress watched, their faces turned toward us
like moons floating in the smokey air, while the mirrored ball went
round and round above the dance floor, sending spears of light along
the ceiling.

Legree began to dump coins onto the table. Nickels, pennies,
quarters, they rolled and bounced, and when a quarter bounced into
my lap I knocked it onto the floor. Suddenly I was angrier than
before, angrier than I'd thought I'd ever be again. I picked up a

handful of coins and threw them at him. They bounced across the
dance floor and rolled in all directions toward the bar, but he just
smiled and kept unloading his pockets. I slid out and stood right in
front of him, and spoke so quietly no one but the two of us could
hear. "Why don't you go live with the turtles? Why don't you go
bury yourself in the sand somewhere where you don't have to put
up with any human beings? Why don't you swim away with them
or just go out and swim in circles for the rest of your life?"

He nodded, nodded and breathed, his body as tense as a shell
about to crack. "Thank you very much," he said. I almost giggled
at the formality of it. "I'm grateful to you, Annie," he said. "Really
grateful." A low bow, full of scorn, like Papa's.

"Why's that?" I said.

"For helping me to understand something. I used to sit around
and try to figure you out. What's she about? I'd think. How can I
help her? That sort of thing."

"Oh, Legree," I did not say, and suddenly I was afraid, as if
I'd found myself alone in an unfamiliar place. Then I remembered
the empty feel of my wrist after his hand was gone, the feel of his
body. I wanted him to stop talking, to sit with me quietly for awhile
and let this settle out and begin again at whatever we needed to
say, to sweep away what we'd said the way I'd swept the bills and
coins off the table and scattered them around our feet.

But he didn't stop. "Well, now I think I've finally got it figured
out. The problem is that I'm not good enough for you. The problem
is that I have been a fool not to see it." He spread his hand, fingers
wide, on his chest.

"No, Legree," I said. "Don't say that, it's not true. Other things
you've said have been true, but that's not."

He turned on me. "Yes, it is," he said fiercely. He smacked his
forehead. "It surely is. I don't have a goddamn dream that's big or
noble enough to lose so I can go around wounded all my life. I
don't despair of things grandly enough for you, I guess. I don't say
the right things about your father. I bully you about your husband.
But I'll tell you what," he said. "If you want someone to live down
here on earth with you, I'm your man," he said. "Or I *was* your

man, maybe, I don't know. Maybe I never was and never can be your man. And I *am* going to live with the turtles, by the way, in case you wake up some morning and wonder where I've gone."

I wanted to speak, to grab him, shake him, say that it wasn't true. But I knew from the way his words had struck, each one like the first cold rain against your skin, that what he'd said was true. "It's all right," I said. "We'd disappoint each other sooner or later. Better now than then, when it matters more."

"God," he said. He shook his head, then stabbed at me with his index finger. "That's what I mean," he said. "You just give up."

He crossed the dance floor in three long strides and yanked the door. It opened with a whoosh and let in a slab of glaring, afternoon light before it closed again. I sat back down in the booth. I sipped my beer and smoothed out my napkin. I moved the ashtray, the bottle of hot sauce, the salt and pepper shakers until their arrangement pleased me. I tried not to look at the coins and the bills all over the floor.

I sat through Dolly Parton and Emmylou Harris. I needed to be very quiet and still, to feel my way along the contours of this new place where I'd found myself. Everyone had gone back to their own news now. The John Deere men called for their checks and gathered up their papers. They stood at the cash register with toothpicks in their mouths and joked with the cashier as they paid their checks. *Virgin*, Legree had said. Turning the word around and around in my head, I felt relieved, as you might when you've waited a long time to know what's wrong with you, and somebody finally gives you the news. It's bad of course, this news, but you can face it because it's *there* at last, it's real. I wanted to laugh out loud with relief. Legree was right, and all along I'd missed it. Now Legree had named it for me. Now things were becoming clear, sorted and arranged around this new truth. I hadn't felt this sure since that time right after Papa's funeral when I'd known I was going to come back here. Virgin, he'd said. It would not be such a bad thing to be. Miss Annie Vess come home at last. A. Vess in the phone book. John and Louise Vess's daughter and Matthew Settles's widow. Matthew. A sound came up in my throat. I drank the last of my beer quickly and went outside. I was surprised to find it still light. Everything bleached and faded, the sidewalk empty. I felt heat from the concrete coming up through the soles of my shoes. Under the sheltering canopy of oaks the Confederate soldier looked into the distance, toward tomorrow.

John Vess's Own

By the time I got to the Pee Dee Nursing Home in Summerville, it was almost dark. The main building looked like the big house on a plantation. Fluted columns and climbing jasmine and white rockers on the wide veranda. But in the back, behind the big house, in two wings built of concrete block, were the rooms, the "guest rooms," the nurse at the front desk called them. She didn't want to let me in; visiting hours were over for the day. I said that the colonel's family had asked me to bring some things by that he'd been asking for. This photo album, a bag of apples. I held them up for her to see. She looked me over. Navy-blue skirt, white blouse, flats, my hair neatly braided. Miss Annie Vess visits a neighbor, an old friend, the last person who might tell me that my father was not the man I had begun to believe he was.

"Don't expect too much," the nurse said over her shoulder as she led me down a wide hall toward the colonel's room, her nylons swishing. Supper was over, and the smell of it lay in the hall: boiled cabbage and milk and something heavier, more discouraging. An old black woman, dressed in a bright pink housecoat with pearl snaps and slippers to match, her hair pulled into tiny, stiff, white plaits all over her head, maneuvered a walker up the hall, close to the wall. Over one arm, she carried a shiny, black patent-leather purse, and she looked straight ahead with a fierce, wary expression in her eyes. As we passed, the nurse swerved to pat her on the shoulder. "Going to get you your Baby Ruth, darling?" she stooped to shout into the woman's ear. The woman pressed herself against the wall, her walker held in front of her, staring straight ahead down the long, tiled hall. "Don't you be scared of me, now," the nurse said. "You know I love you."

Why, she's not frightened, I thought, not frightened at all, and she doesn't love you. She's waiting for you to finish talking and for us to go away. "Bless her heart," the nurse said, in a big, jolly voice that matched her bouncy, black hair and ice-blue eyeshadow, the rainbow on the pin of her starched white lapel. "Praise the Lord!" it read. "You can just set your watch by her." The nurse continued, "Every evening at six-thirty, she's got to go get her that Baby Ruth. We are such creatures of habit, aren't we?"

As we moved along the hall, the nurse stopped in every door. "How are you, Mr. Turner?" she said to an old man in a maroon plaid bathrobe who twisted his hands in his lap as he angrily watched television. He blew her a kiss, went back to his grievances. "That a boy," she said. "Well, Miz Lucille, what's happened to you? Let's just get you sitting up straight." An old lady with a pale fizz of hair sat slumped sideways in a wheelchair in front of the window at the back wall of her room. She wore a dirty white sweater covered with seed pearls and buttoned up to her throat. The room smelled strongly of stale urine. The nurse pulled her upright with one sharp tug, and the old lady cried out and held her hand against her cheek. She began to weep, a high, childish sound. "Oh, why can't you leave me alone?" she cried, wringing her hands. "Why can't you leave me alone?"

"Now, you know you don't mean that," the nurse said as she shook her hand free and walked out the door.

I wondered what it would be like to have your life, your habits, the failures of your body laid open like that to strangers who had power over you. To be vulnerable as a child again to anyone who came into your room. Where, I wondered, within such a life, could you stake out a small corner for yourself? I wished I had not come.

Mother was right, I thought. Better to remember the colonel the way he'd been than to see him here.

"Here we are." The nurse paused outside a closed door, knocked once, and opened the door before anyone could answer. The colonel was working a puzzle at a card table near the window, which looked out onto a tiny courtyard where someone had made a small, raised garden bed from railroad ties. In the lowering light I saw four tomato plants growing there, heavy with fruit and tied to stakes with strips cut from nylon stockings. A few bright zinnias bloomed around the borders of the bed. Beyond the flower bed there was a stretch of sparse grass and then the marsh began, a long field of grass with creeks winding through it. The tide was low, and a snowy egret picked its way along the shiny gray mud of a nearby creekbank. Watching the egret, I felt a tight sadness loosen inside me. A salt marsh is a place where the things of heaven and the things of earth trade color and light with one another, as if to show that the world is one long and unbroken expanse of kinship. Marsh grass is tinted all shades of earth—brown and tawny yellow and rust, yellow-green and gray-green edged in red. The tide pushes up the branching creeks and rivers, carrying the sky on its back. And sometimes out in the marsh a flash comes back at you as if from a signal mirror: *water, water, light,* and you look to see a curve of river where you thought there was only mud and grass. At least, I thought, there was this window and the marsh beyond the window. It would be good to live beside a marsh. Watching its changes and its constancies, a person might take heart.

The colonel was dressed in khaki workclothes, and cigarette smoke rose and curled around his head. On the bedside table, a portable radio tuned to an easy-listening station played softly. A shelf on the wall over the dresser held a line of books in green leather bindings—his Mark Twain collection—and field-trial trophies. On the wall nearest the door hung the oil portrait of Mary in a long, green velvet gown, her DAR ribbon across her chest, her hand resting lightly on the back of a chair upholstered in gold brocade—a chair from their living room on Wyman Street. I bit my lip and leaned against the doorjamb, holding the scrapbooks against my chest. He'd had a haircut, square across the back, and it exposed too much of his neck.

"How's that puzzle coming, hon?" the nurse asked.

He turned his head briefly, then looked back at the puzzle. *Good for you, Colonel,* I wanted to cheer. Don't answer. We are intruders here, after all.

"Someone to see you, Colonel Stark," she said, briskly this time.

"Send them in," he said, half turning in his chair. "Unless it's the padre again."

"Oh, now," she said. She gave me a significant look and rolled her eyes. "Call us if you need us," she said.

"Knock, knock," I said from the door. When he turned his smile was the uncomprehending smile one would give a stranger, and his face looked blank, loose.

I felt that sickening sensation of speed again, and the cruelty of the speed that had carried him here. My father's oldest friend. He'd stayed with Mother the morning Papa died, while Dr. Mac and then the Taylor Brothers came and went. Mother said he'd cooked for her that day, heated up a can of chicken noodle soup and brought it into the dining room and set it down in front of her. A bowl of soup and some stale saltines he'd found in the pantry. Ballast and anchor; kind friend. Then he'd grown too bewildered to take care of himself, and Willie Mae had quit after twenty years. There was no one to look after him, he'd had the strokes, and so, by the brutal logic of the times, he was here with his portrait, his trophies, his shoes that he polished every day—an old military man same as Papa—lined up on a square of newspaper beside his bed.

"You know me, Colonel," I said. "It's Annie Vess." I spoke forcefully, the way I'd learned you had to speak to him when he was lost in the wilderness of his confusion. As I crossed the small room, recognition seeped into his eyes. I put my arm around his shoulders, laid my cheek on the top of his head. He smelled old, like bedclothes and smoke and milk and medicine. Then I sat down in the chair across from him and held onto his hand. "Good to see you," he said, "good to see you. That nurse keeps sending the chaplain around to have a talk with me. Never had much use for that breed myself." He leaned toward me suddenly, and I saw what it means to be old. A skull behind a face. A radiance that shines out from somewhere deep inside the body. A far-seeing, old-animal look in the eyes. "Never get old, Miss Annie," he said. "There's no future in it." He laughed dryly to himself and rubbed his hands together. They made a whispery sound, like pieces of paper brushing against each other. Was it a joke they told among themselves, in the TV room, at the dinner table—a joke the nurses couldn't share, that set them apart, gave them the dignity of belonging to a group that they defined? "I'll remember that," I said, giving his hand a squeeze, then letting it go.

He braced his hands on his knees and leaned toward me. "And how is your mother?" he asked. He pronounced it "Muh-tha," in that senator's voice of his that rumbled and turned the words around as though it were rolling them in a dark oak churn.

"Mean as ever," I said.

He chuckled. "Willie Mae is looking after the dogs, I take it?"

I thought of the house closed up tight, for sale. Ethel and Mother and I had seen to that the last time Ethel was in town. Mother had hired a yardman to cut the grass and trim the hedge; every night at dusk, she turned on the lights in a different room. In the morning she turned them off. I fed the dogs, hosed out their runs, let them out to lie in the sun on the backyard grass. But I could not tell the colonel that. The truth had too many layers to it. Matthew thought it was easy, this walk between truth and lies. But he'd never sat with the colonel and seen his hands twist in his lap, seen his face eager to be told that something remained of what he'd left, that everything was not settled and decided. Let him keep his house I thought. The mimosa tree and the porchlight. The field trial trophies crowded onto the shelves in the den, the leftover supper biscuits wrapped in tinfoil and left on the stove until morning. To take from him that vision of permanence, of a place where nothing could be lost, would be cruel, useless. "Yes,' I said. "They're fine. Napoleon hasn't learned a thing; he's still dumb as a stick. They miss you, though."

He looked down at his hands where they lay folded in his lap.

Then he seemed to remember something, as though a voice had spoken inside his head, and he looked up at me sternly. "Young lady," he said, "have you given any more thought to starting your family?" It could have been my father speaking—the frown, the tone of voice his way of showing that he took seriously the obligation to guide me in the serious business of living that he'd accepted when he became my godfather thirty-two years ago.

I took his hand and patted it, though I felt my heart beating in my ears. "Not yet, Colonel," I said, looking at his polished shoes. *Please don't say it.*

"Well, what does your husband have to say about that?"

"My husband?" I said. "My husband, Matthew, died, Colonel. A year ago, April. You knew that."

He took this calmly. He nodded, frowned, slowly ground his cigarette out in the ashtray and studied it as the paper shredded and tobacco spilled out. Then he stood up. "Shall we go into the den?" he said. He half rose, then wavered and sat back down. His shoulders slumped and he looked around the room, bewildered.

"It's all right, Colonel," I said. "Listen, I brought these scrapbooks. I thought you might want to look at some pictures." Tell me that my father was not the man I have found him to be. I brought him his glasses and pulled another straight-backed chair next to his. I opened the album across our knees and handed him the magnifying glass I'd brought. We had done this many times right after my father died, before I went back to Pennsylvania and Willie Mae quit and his health failed and he came here. It had helped us both, it had steadied us. He turned the black paper pages slowly, smoothing down each one, running his finger over the faded pictures, the black paper corners. He studied the faces as carefully as though he were seeing them for the first time, and his lips moved as though he were reading the faces and bodies on the page. "That would be Mr. Lyle Barnett and Nero, the sire of our line," he said, pointing to a picture of a tall, skinny man in a cocked hat, holding a barrel-chested pointer. "Mr. Barnett lived, as I recall, out near Little Awando, and he kept the finest dogs around."

I turned a few more pages in silence while the colonel passed

the magnifying glass slowly across the pictures. Sometimes he chuckled to himself, sometimes he shook his head. At least, I thought, I
have no plan, just these images to guide me. He paused at the
photograph of my parents leaving the church after their wedding—
an officer's wedding—my father in his dress white uniform, my
mother holding up the hem of her wedding dress as the two of them
ran down the steps beneath a steep roof of drawn swords. The picture
had faded to that peculiar shade of creamy beige that makes it look
as though light shown from within their clothes. It might fade until
they became pure light, I thought, for it looked more radiant now
than I could remember. "August 25, 1940," someone had written
in white ink on the black page. Neither of us spoke as we looked
through the next pages: Davis becoming an Eagle Scout, my wedding. I tried to reach across and turn the page, but not before the
colonel passed the magnifying glass over the picture and Matthew's
smile rose up at me. I did not want to see Matthew with my garland
of daisies and ivy set carelessly on his head, raising his glass of
champagne, raising it to me—I had taken that picture—looking at
me with such tenderness in the kitchen of my parent's house while
sunlight slanted through the kitchen door, forever.

Then the photographs moved into the past again. Mother in
an old square-legged bathing suit and high heels, one hand behind
her head and her knee cocked in the cheesecake pose you see on
old calendars. Thelma Radford beside a tall camellia—small face and
blond marcelled hair—holding the collar of her black fur coat up
around her face. "There's the Laughing Place, Colonel," I said when
he'd turned to the next page. "Who are all those men?" Men in
hunting clothes, Papa and the colonel among them, a swirl of dogs
around their feet, a blur of leaves, and tall clouds above it all. I
watched the colonel out of the corner of my eye, ashamed of myself.
What was I doing? Trying to surprise him? But he was beyond the
reach of nuance or surprise. He bent low over the page as though he
were studying the tiny, intricate parts of some complicated machine.
"That's Buck Hinson, Charles Hartley, myself, your father, and Lyle
Barnett," he said, tapping the photograph with a fingernail that was
split and seamed and yellow. "Now, you know, Buck Hinson was a
fine man."

"Of course," I said, but I wasn't looking at Buck Hinson but at another part of the picture where Papa and Charles Hartley stood side-by-side on the bottom step of the Laughing Place, their shotguns cracked open over their arms.

"They were friends," I said. I thought of the blanket of yellow roses draped over Papa's casket, of Charles Hartley wiping his eyes at my father's funeral. Friends. The word bloomed into a new shape of meaning. "Friends in high places," Pug Simmons had said. Charles Hartley had told Papa where the shore of the lake would be. It would not have seemed anything more than talk among old friends, the insider's knowledge offered over the shrimp and highballs at a cocktail party. I pictured them there in their navy blazers and light blue shirts, their khaki slacks, their loafers polished to a high shine, dipping boiled shrimp in cocktail sauce. "Look here, John," Charles Hartley might have said, "somebody's going to make a lot of money if they're smart about getting hold of some land out where the new lake is going in." Of course. Because the public world, the world of work and money and elected office, is not the important world here. In fact, this world doesn't really *exist* except to support and sustain the real world of family connections and social obligation. In this real world, it would have been worse, much worse, *not* to have told my father about the lake. That would have seemed the greater betrayal. Because Pug Simmons and my mother both lived in this world, she felt justified in demanding that Pug stop printing articles about my father, and when Pug refused, she could write him off because it was the law of this private and more important world that he'd broken. Thus, the defiant, bewildered expressions on the faces of bank officials in small southern towns, indicted for making unsecured loans to their friends. What sort of man, their expressions say, would *not* loan money to a friend? And who would not tell an old friend how he might profit from some public act in order that the real world, the social and personal world, the world of loyalty and family, go on turning?

"Colonel," I said, and I put my hand on his arm, felt the starch in the sleeve. "I really need to ask you something. I hope you can help me."

He looked at me in alarm, as though I'd told him the building was on fire. Then it was as though his face had passed through a cloud. On the other side it was blank again. "Where did you say you went to school?"

I leaned toward him, held his eye. It was like looking into a room where someone was crouched in a corner. It was time to remind him of what he already knew. "Chapel Hill, Colonel," I said. "You knew that." I said it like someone guiding a blind man: *It's safe here. Now watch your step.*

He closed his eyes and I saw the thin skin molded over the eyeball, the veins on his eyelids like delicate purple shoots, then he shook his head exasperated. "You always were a curious young lady," he said.

I took his hand, folded it in my lap while he looked straight ahead out the window, where the dark gray of twilight was being rubbed into the grain of the light. Along the muddy bank of the tidal creek, the egret picked its way along, light against the darkening grass. Its head darted and it came up, holding something shiny in its bill. The bird tipped its head back and swallowed the creature. "Colonel, try to listen, this is important," I said. *Why?* I wanted to ask. *Why did you do it, buy that land from Papa for nothing, sell it for so much? Why? And where did the money go?* His head shook and his hand in my hand trembled slightly, as though a current of electricity ran in it. Is this what it means to be old? The current, your life, runs closer and closer to the surface until it breaks free of the skin finally and dissolves once again into air? And *why?* is too blunt, too wide a question. Like telling him that his house and the dogs were gone, a reality too dangerous to take in all at once, that would require the reorienting of everything in his life, and he was too old to pivot that fast. Best to break it down, the way you break down a complex task for a child, to keep her from being overwhelmed. And some cold center in my brain said you are young and he is old. Telling me this will not harm him, but not knowing it will harm me. Is this how Papa felt, I thought, all those years he fought the lake? This purpose so bright and clear, like a diamond in the middle of your brain, harder and brighter and clearer than anything else?

He sat with the photo album open on his lap. "Look at that

dickens," he said, nodding toward the egret. "Comes here every night just about this time."

"Colonel," I said. He inclined his head sideways toward me, as though we were sitting side by side in church. "That land Papa sold you and Mary and Thelma, that you all sold to Planter's Landing." He looked up in alarm and I could hear him breathing in and out; it sounded like cloth being pulled over a rough surface. On his face was the same angry look I'd seen at my father's funeral as he'd stared at the casket: as though he had a quarrel with that coffin and he intended to have his say. My voice shook, but I went on. "Did you need the money?" I said. "Is that why my father did it?"

He yanked his hand free of mine and paged backward through the album, while his mouth worked furiously. His head had begun to shake violently and his color was bad. What if he had another stroke? I thought. Or a heart attack? It happened all the time. And it would be my fault. "Colonel," I said. "Never mind, let's forget it." But he seemed to know exactly where he was going, because he stopped on the page where the pinup picture of my mother rested side-by-side with the picture of Thelma Radford next to the bright blooms of the camellia. He slapped his palm down on that page, over the picture of Thelma. "John Vess took care of his own," he said in a terrible voice, and he shoved the album at me, and brushed off his pants legs as though he'd found dirt there. Then he stared out the window again, his hands tightly folded, breathing harshly through his nose, his head nodding violently.

"All right, Colonel," I said. "All right, now." I felt a stillness settle inside me like a net settling through water. I thought of Thelma, standing in the crowd that lined the sidewalks in front of the courthouse as my father's funeral procession drove slowly around the square. I thought of Thelma weeping, her hands holding the collar of that black fur coat around her throat. And later, at the cemetery, Thelma had come into the tent and sat down behind us. Mother did not turn around, but as the smell of Jungle Gardenia perfume enveloped us—Thelma's perfume, a smell that had filled Papa's office and come home in the weave of his clothes—Mother sat up straighter, as though some subtle vibration had struck her in the back of the head. She half turned as though she were going to speak, then turned away and covered her eyes with one hand. For the first time that day, she sobbed, once, a terrible, dry sound.

"Excuse me," the colonel said. He stood up and bowed to me coldly. Then he was at the door. "*Willie Mae*", he called, and he stamped his foot. "*Willie Mae*, there's someone at the door." A nurse appeared in the doorway just as I slipped my hand through his arm. She had a froth of coppery hair, a sharp, country face. "Go back in your room, please, Mr. Stark," she said. "You know better than to yell in the halls."

"I'm a member of his family," I said, "I'll take care of this." The colonel looked up and down the hall and muttered to himself.

"There are rules here," the nurse said, her pale-blue eyes angry but uncertain now.

"Of course there are rules," I said, "and we are aware of them." Lessons from a patrician childhood, from that world where my father lived his life, betrayed us, died: how to use your manners coldly, tc remind the help of their places. "He's just overly tired," I said. "I'll take care of him. Please excuse us," and I shoved the door shut with my foot.

Then I led the colonel back to his bed. He was trembling all over and I sat him down on the bed, pulled off his shoes, swung his feet up onto the bed. He looked up at me from the pillow, but his eyes looked panicky, inward, as though he could see the inside of his own fear. "It's all right, Colonel," I said, trying to keep the panic out of my voice. What have you done? I thought. Who are you to have done this thing? "I'll stay until Willie Mae comes," I said.

I felt the tension leave his hand. "I would be most apprecia- tive," he said. He raised his hand once from the bedspread as though he were about to speak, then let it fall. He turned his head and looked out the window to where the egret stood, as pale as the last light that shone on the water.

I stayed until he was asleep, his hands folded on his chest. I covered him with a blanket and kissed his cheek, and he startled and brushed at his face as though a moth had grazed it. When he was deeply asleep and breathing evenly, I left the photo album on the table beside his bed. I hoped that when he woke, his memory that had failed him so often might have erased who had come there and why, and left only this photo album beside his bed, as though it had miraculously appeared or had always been there.

"Oh Promise Me"

Mel believed that she would have perfect weather on her wedding day, and so, during the rehearsal dinner, when the first heavy sheets of rain sluiced down the lakeside windows in the dining room at Planter's Landing, Mel didn't look up from her fruit compote. After the plates had been cleared away, while flashes of lightning lit up the sky and water, and heavy, thumping rolls of thunder shook the glass, Mel did not flinch or startle like everyone else, not once did she turn to look over her shoulder at the storm outside the window. Not once. Instead she watched from the bride's table as Canady passed from woman to woman, making the rounds. With Canady bending over them, they came alive: threw their heads back, shook out their hair, laughed with hands pressed to their throats. When he came to me, he winked. When I didn't wink back, he gave me a sorrowful look and kissed me on the forehead, squeezed my shoulder in sympathy, and passed on to the next woman. And when it was time to go home, Mel stood at the door and promised everyone a beautiful day tomorrow. She kissed them, tugged raincoats up onto their shoulders, and sent them splashing across the parking lot toward their cars through the downpour with umbrellas, newspapers, plastic bags, handkerchiefs held over their heads. "See you tomorrow," she called after them. "See you in the sunshine." And standing there beside her, I believed it would be sunny, too.

Mel and I stayed at Mother's that night. As Mother drove us home from Planter's Landing, the only sound in the car was the *thunk* of the windshield wipers and the *shush* of the tires and Mel's humming softly to herself a tune I didn't recognize. The lights of approaching cars fractured in the rainy glass, and the rain poured steadily, heavily, as though it might rain for the next two days. Mother leaned forward tensely over the wheel. In profile Mel's face looked as though she were watching something off in the distance, the way she'd watched Canady make the rounds at their rehearsal dinner. It was the look of a person who believes that if she watches long enough, she will understand what she sees and know how to manage it. I thought of photographs of Mel, the unbroken line of character they seem to trace. Pictures of Mel arranging flowers with Charlotte, her mother. Mel couldn't have been more than twelve, a gladiola poised to perfect the composition of flowers she had created. Mel in her majorette's outfit, her smile as brilliant as the light that flashed off her silver baton. Mel as high school May Queen. Mel with Canady after the Miss Sun Fun pageant at Myrtle Beach, her hand resting lightly, definitely on his arm. In all of these photographs she shows her enviable faith in her own capacities and destinations.

As long as I can remember, she's known how her house would look, from the color of the roof shingles down to the linoleum on the basement floor—and every floor and room between, in detail, as though her house were already built and furnished somewhere, and all she had to do was find her way to the right address and move in. For her twelfth birthday her mother gave her a Lane sweetheart chest, and over the years Mel has filled it with paint chips and carpet samples and linoleum tiles. There will be salmon-colored guest towels on the brass towel rods in the salmon and dusty-blue bathroom. Red poppies on the kitchen wallpaper. No yellow kitchens for Mel. It seems that all her life she has been collecting the parts, waiting to find the right place to put them together. And now that time was here. Sometimes it seemed as if Mel has been reincarnated as Mel over many lifetimes, each one similar to the other in all the essentials—practice lives that had given her time to smoothe out the kinks so she could get this one just right. She has always possessed the poise and grace of the practiced, the well rehearsed, the well prepared.

We stayed up late that night and watched Johnny Carson. Canady's best man and his friends who'd come to town for the wedding had taken him to Columbia, to the same topless club where they'd practically lived when they were fraternity brothers at USC, and where they still knew all the dancers by name. At home, Mother tipped the recliner back halfway so that she could see the TV and still work on Canady's Carolina Gamecock pillow. Mel spread out her manicure equipment on a towel on a TV tray in front of her and did her nails. I got out a deck of cards from the drawer in the coffee table in front of the sofa and laid out a game of solitaire while I watched Johnny Carson ogle Zsa Zsa Gabor. He gave the camera his droll, blank stare that made the studio audience laugh, while Zsa Zsa giggled and vamped and moved in her chair so that her skirt rode up her thighs. Johnny Carson reminded me of my father right then—the shrug, the boyish, wide-eyed stare, the arms spread in mock surrender: How should I know? I'm just a simple country boy.

Now and then, Mother looked at the TV and shook her head or shifted in disapproval in her chair. Or Mel looked up, waved her hand, blew on her nails, and stared at the set with a dreamy squint, as if she weren't seeing the TV at all, but through it and beyond. But mostly we were quiet together. On the mantle the pendulum on Grandaddy Vess's clock swung heavily, steadily.

Just after Papa's funeral, after the flowers and the food and the thank-you notes were done, Mother and I had sat in this room and I had felt my life gathered safely all around me. In this place, I had known who I was and where and why. Now I felt myself again on the threshold of one of those lives that might be possible to live here. In this life Canady doesn't show up for the wedding, and Mel comes to live with Mother and me, permanently. (How comforting that word is, *permanently*. How solid and settled and *relieved*.) She moves into Davis's room upstairs, puts in a canopy bed with a dust ruffle and decorates the room all in peaches and blues, with bold shocks of green to spark it up. ("Think of *dressing* the room," Mel says about decorating. "Think accessories.") Since there isn't much money to live on (my father having given most of it away to someone else), we all must work. In the world outside our house, Mel has given up the decorating business that has brought her to such grief and gotten a job at the Estée Lauder counter at Belk's out at the mall. Mother goes to the tax assessor's office. I go to work for the county agricultural extension service, carrying the news about easy-care fabrics and the serious business of home canning all over Vaucluse County. Before dark we are safely at home again, together. On the way, somebody would have stopped by the Piggly Wiggly for a loaf of bread, a dozen eggs to eat soft-boiled with toast and tea, because one of us would have a delicate stomach. And in this life there would no longer be any need to air our troubles, our losses or gains, out in the world. Men, marriages, children, ambition, longing, all those questions would be decided now. No need to move beyond this circle we had drawn to keep us safe, this place where everything is familiar, everything known, where nothing comes in and nothing leaves, this place of stillness and safety, this home. We would live here until the wisteria vine poked through the shutters, the front steps rotted and fell in, and such a forest grew up—bamboo, holly, cedar, pine, and oak—that from the street all that remained to see of the house was a dormer and one staring attic window. And when we were dead and the new owners cut this forest down, they would be surprised to find how close the house had stood to the street after all. And yet, even as I imagined it, I knew that none of these dreams of questions answered, of innocence preserved, were true or possible. That kind of dreaming was ruined for me.

In the morning—Mel's wedding day—I woke up early to the steady drip of rain off the eaves outside my window. Out in the wisteria vine in the rain, a bird sang a sweet and complicated song. It sounded like the name of the place where Legree had taken me that day we first made love in the field behind his house. Honea Path. Honea Path. I kicked off the sheet and went to the window to shoo the bird away. It was a mockingbird, perched on the wet wisteria vine, searching the morning with its bright, taunting eye. We stared at each other for a moment until it flipped its tail and flew away.

Then I heard a sound from downstairs, a radio voice talking in an easy, morning way, the slow clink of dishes being moved. I went downstairs quietly, Miss Annie in her nightgown, with her hair in one long braid down her back, the spirit of the house gliding down to find what was disturbing the household this early.

Mel stood in front of the open back door, barefooted, wearing the blue terry-cloth bathrobe with its seat worn thin that had hung on the back of the door in the upstairs bathroom for as long as I could remember. She stared out into the rainy dawn while the voice on the radio recited the prices of soybeans and sorghum and corn. Then I saw that she was eating from a plate stacked up high with pancakes.

"Good morning," I said, and moved to the cabinet where Mother kept the coffee. "I didn't mean to startle you."

She turned around and held up the plate of pancakes. "You didn't," she said. "I've been up since four. Last chance," she said, waving the fork in the air before she brought it down to spear a stack of cut-up pancakes. "Canady can't stand to see me eat a lot, and I love pancakes. Want some?"

"No thanks," I said. "Coffee's more my speed this early." I rummaged through the cabinet until I found the can of coffee, dipped some out of the can and into the basket of the Mr. Coffee machine.

"Suit yourself," she shrugged, and cut another wedge out of the stack. "They're good."

I groped around in the cabinet for a cup and saucer. Outside, the sky had turned to a marbleized gray crackled with pink, and Mel hummed to herself, ate pancakes, and watched the rain and the light coming up behind the rain.

"They say it's going to clear," I said.

"Oh, it'll stop," she said.

I moved for the light switch.

"Please don't do that," Mel said as she turned from the door, holding the plate of pancakes in front of her face with the fork poised to cut.

"I'm only going to turn on the light, Mel."

Her face flushed. "The bride's supposed to get what she wants on her wedding day, and I don't want the lights on, OK?"

"You're right," I said, and I dropped my hand from the switch. "I'd forgotten about that." Mel nodded, turned back to the door and the pancakes. It seemed ages since I'd been married. Matthew and I were married in the middle of December because that was a month in which nobody gets married, and we were not like anybody else. Matthew's uncle, a Baptist minister, married us in the living room of this house. It had been cold and gray and low outside, but Mother had filled the room with bowls of floating orchids and smilax behind all the picture frames. Afterward, we drove to Highlands, North Carolina, where we'd rented a cabin that straddled a fast stream high up in a cove. All night the strong sound of water came up through the floorboards. Nothing had seemed more perfect than that day and that night. Now I thought it was just this that had ruined Papa, the way he measured things against some perfect time and place so that they always came out lacking. Legree said it had ruined me, too.

Mel turned from the window with her empty plate. "You know what I want?" she said.

"What's that, Mel?"

"I want what Canady's got." She put the plate down on the drain board of the sink and shook a cigarette from a pack of Salems that lay on the counter. Squinting against the smoke, she looked older. "I've been going with him for all these years now, and I still couldn't tell you what that is, but I know that I want it," she said as she watched the cloud of cigarette smoke rise and break against the ceiling.

"I know what you mean," I said. I took a sip of coffee and I was struck again with how sensible Mel seems, even about the most unsensible things, how practical and matter-of-fact to say something like that. I thought of Canady circulating, Mel watching. She studied her cigarette, turned it in her fingers, and examined the glowing tip.

"I didn't know you smoked, Mel," I said.

"Oh, sometimes." I should have known. Mel can control anything, or thinks she can. "Legree coming?" she asked. "He didn't RSVP the invitation to the reception."

I looked down into my coffee. "We split up." Then quickly, before she could speak: "It was mutual," I said. "It wouldn't have worked out."

Instantly she put down her plate and pressed her hand to her heart, as though I'd just told her I'd been badly hurt or had a disease. "Oh, hon," she said. "Here I am, going on about the good things that are happening to me, and not even thinking about you."

"It was inevitable," I said, and I tried to sound ironic and resigned, but my voice shook. "He called me a virgin."

She drew herself up as if she'd been insulted, too. "Well, you just show him he's wrong," she said with a nod.

"How's that, Mel?"

She blushed. "You'll think of something," she said. She rinsed her plate in the sink and put it in the dishwasher.

"Don't listen to me, Mel, I'm just being cynical."

"Oh, hon," she said. She grabbed me by the elbows and held on. "You've got to stop that right this minute. It's not good for you to feel that way. It puts lines in your face and makes your mouth pull down." There were tears in her eyes. "Don't you give up," she said. "That's the secret, don't ever give up."

"Mel," I said, "do you have something old to wear today? Do you want Grandmother Vess's comb to wear in your hair?"

"Is it silver?" she said. I nodded. She stepped back and her face took on an expression of pity. "Silver is too pale for blondes, Annie," she said. "Blondes need gold."

As I poured myself another cup of coffee, I searched through my mind for what I knew about blondes. Did I know that blondes should not wear silver? I'm not a blonde, and yet I felt I should know about them, the way a decorator who never intends to work with primary colors must still know their force. There were rules, taboos of color and line and proportion—a world of knowledge as vast and arcane as that of an ancient religion—within this rich mystery of a universe, to which women must conform. Rules of taste and color and complementarity. *Especially* complementarity. Everything seen in relation to how it framed or accented you, how you blended, fit, harmonized. There were millions, billions of things to remember, and Mel knew them all. I imagine that Mel could hold a star next to her skin and throw it away if the color didn't flatter her. I felt my face getting hot, my palms getting clammy, the way they do when I'm asked a question for which I have no answer. "Well, I'm sorry Mel," I said. "I just forgot."

And then we both noticed the door. It was still raining outside, but now the rain fell in long, glistening strands lit up by the sun. "Look," Mel said. She threw open the screen door and stuck her head outside. The patio sparkled with water and light. "The devil's beating his wife behind the kitchen door," she said. She laughed, she clapped her hands, danced around the table, and hugged me. "See," she said. "See it's clearing. See what I mean about not giving up?"

By noon the house had changed. Mel was dressing in Mother's bedroom, her bridesmaids in Davis's room. Behind every door there was the rustle of tissue, the slipping of satin, the sound of excited voices. There were mirrors everywhere, leaned against walls and propped against bureaus. I avoided them because I didn't like the sight of myself peeking over someone's shoulder holding a slip or a dress or a hat—too dark, too serious, too quiet. Too virginal. "Cheers, Legree," I said once to my reflection, then went to dress in my room, slipped on the rose-colored silk dress with the tiny straps, the low-cut bodice and full skirt that flared out from the tight hips. It swung and curved around me lusciously, and I held it out and looked at it, felt it fall against my thighs.

I went down to Papa's study and shut the door. I hadn't been in there in over a week, and the air smelled settled, undisturbed. I sat in the chair in front of the closed cover of the rolltop desk and looked at the sign from the Laughing Place, the map of Vaucluse

County with my father's marks and my own drawn onto it. Then I gazed out the window to the leggy azaleas crowded in their beds mounded with pine straw. Looking down, I could see the tops of my breasts. It felt as though I shouldn't be here in that dress, as though I'd showed up for church in something shocking. But as quickly as that thought came, I squelched it. This was no church, and my father was no saint or priest. It used to be that when I looked at the map and the sign, even after I found out that he'd bought that land and sold it for nothing, I could always make it come out right. I could believe that he did it for us, his family, *for* us or *because* of us. But since I'd been down to Summerville to see the colonel, when I looked at the map now, all I could think about was Thelma Radford. Her mohair sweaters and tight skirts, the way she slid her desk drawer open with her fingertips as though she were protecting her nails. The contents of that drawer: hand lotion, perfume, emery board, compact, lipstick, and a comb made of abalone shell. The way she dabbed perfume in the crooks of her elbows and on her wrists, up under her hair. "Pulse points," she called them.

I heard Mother's footsteps coming down the hall—quick, sharp footsteps that signaled news. "Oh, my Lord," she said as she opened the door. She was dressed in her slip, and in her hand she held several makeup brushes. Her eyes were wide and pale, and a line of pink makeup showed along her jaw. "My Lord, I forgot about the car."

"Car?"

She stamped her foot, impatient. "I don't have time for your foolishness today. The Taylor Brothers' Lincoln," she said. "They're loaning it to me for Mellie to ride to the wedding in, and for the two of them to ride back into town after the reception."

"They're going to ride in a *funeral home* car?"

She made as if to slap me, then she put her hands on my shoulders and squeezed. "I don't have time for your foolishness today. We've got to go and get it right now. You've got to drive it over here for me."

The big gray Lincoln waited—washed and shining—under the porte cochere at the side of the Taylor Brothers' Funeral Home. The man who answered the door handed me the keys with a sympathetic look, as though every act were cause for consolation. I meant to go straight home, but when I got behind the wheel of that car, tilted the steering wheel until it was comfortable under my hands, and ran the smoked gray front windows up and down, I thought I would not go home, not just yet. I drove down the long drive that led to Legree's, between the rows of magnolias that lined the road. Down at the end of the drive, I saw his car; he was back. I would ask him to go for a ride with me in this car. Once I had him there, I would not let him go. We would drive until we found words to say to one another that would have eased even the saddest of hearts among the mourners who had ridden here. The front door of his apartment was closed and the curtain pulled across its window. A shrimp net hung over the porch railing. Under the shade of a mimosa tree beside the steps, his Mustang was parked beside a car I didn't recognize—a yellow Datsun Honeybee. Pink whisks of mimosa blossoms had settled on the hoods of both cars, as though they'd been parked there for awhile, overnight and maybe longer. I turned around in his driveway and switched on the radio. I wanted music, loud music; I wanted to see how fast the car would carry me, how far from here

I headed for the Bean Blossom Road. Driving, I felt the bulk of the car, its sealed and quiet weight. Once I was past the cemetery and outside of town, where the countryside opened up again into bean fields and cornfields and pecan groves, I opened it up, but even at eighty, at eighty-five, there was no sensation of speed. The world outside the smoked-glass windows whipped by, bean fields and cornfields, while inside the car the grief this car had carried, our own and everyone else's who had ever ridden in it, lingered in the upholstery—a faint, sweet smell like carnations. Once, in this car, I'd been taken to my father's funeral, still believing he was the person I'd believed in all my life. And it seemed that the odor of that foolish faith was trapped here, too. I pressed switches on the door panel and all four windows went down.

When I crossed Cateechee Creek, the speedometer ticked up toward ninety. Air whipped through the car, and I wanted to drive and drive until all the grief was gone, torn and pulled out of the

upholstery and left scattered and flattened like the grass beside the
road when the big car flew past. My hair stung as it whipped around
my face, but I kept both hands on the wheel and my eyes straight
ahead as the speedometer read ninety-five, then wavered upward:
ninety-seven, ninety-eight. Matthew would have loved this, I
thought. He would have sat beside me, cool and fierce. As I drove,
I saw the road opening and opening before me, and I started to
imagine how it would be just to drive straight across the county,
out through Town Grove, out of Vaucluse County. I wondered how
long it would take them to find me and what I would say when they
did. I thought that I might say that I had done it because it was
possible, because it seemed a way to live. It seemed to be a life like
the life Matthew and I had once imagined for ourselves.

Once, Matthew and I found ourselves in Kansas City, out of
cash and almost out of gas. We had a Conoco credit card, but we'd
been driving around for half an hour looking for a Conoco station,
while the needle on the gas gauge sank and finally settled on E—
and still we hadn't found one. I was on the edge of panic, and to
calm myself while we waited for a stoplight to change, I looked
around to size up where we were. Across the street I saw a restaurant
with a broad, steamed-up plate-glass window. Taped to the window
was a sign: "We Need a Waitress." And something eased in me. I
could simply cross the street, walk in through the door, and make
them hire me. By nightfall I would have money in my pocket again
and a meal for both of us, because nowhere on earth were you far
from home. Once you believed that the world spread a wide net of
luck, you knew you could not slip through.

At 100, the big car seemed to hunker down on the road. When
I saw the swamp coming up ahead of me, coming fast—tall, black
tree shapes reflected in dark water, and a wide, white concrete bridge
crossing it—I did as Matthew and I used to do a thousand years
before. I set that swamp as the last barrier standing between me and
the life I'd known was out there to find, if I just kept moving. If I
crossed that bridge, I told myself, I might just keep going. Matthew
and I would have done this, but Matthew was not here. I took my
foot off the accelerator, and the speedometer fell to seventy, then

fifty. Once I slowed, the spell was broken. I coasted across the bridge, pulled off the road onto the shoulder, and stopped. The still water was dark and cloudy as though smoke were trapped just under the surface, and water lilies bloomed in patches on the surface. On one fallen tree I counted six snakes stretched out in the sun. And I felt Matthew there, Matthew's presence so strongly that for a moment I closed my eyes, leaned my head back against the head rest, and tried to make it right to go on, the way we might have done had Matthew only lived. But back down the road, people were waiting for me, counting on me. Back down the road someone had stayed overnight at Legree's house, and my father had cheated on us all. I couldn't steal myself a life any more than I could live one that was handed to me. I made a U-turn in the road and started back for Timmons.

The boat that the men from Bowen's Marina had backed into our side yard earlier in the week (while Mother in shorts and an old straw gardening hat guided them with great sweeps of her arms, like someone guiding a passenger jet into its berth) had been a lumbering, gray pontoon boat, so battered and chipped and dented and scratched it looked as though it had never traveled easily over any water. It looked as if it had rammed every dock it had ever approached and scraped every submerged stump it had passed over. Back near the tiny outboard motor, one of the torpedolike pontoons carried a cluster of pock marks made by a shotgun blast, as though someone had stood back and fired, point-blank, into it. A boat with a corrugated roof held up by black, wrought-iron posts and a wrought-iron railing that ran all the way around it. The kind of boat made to carry a dozen people and their lawn chairs and beer coolers on a slow, trolling circuit around the lake. An unlucky boat, and I told Mother so. "Mother," I said, "my God, have you lost your mind? Getting married on this boat will jinx Mel for sure. Nothing happy has ever happened here."

She came around the bow just as I finished having my say, then she had hers. "Quiet, O ye of little faith," she said, aiming a finger at me. "It doth not yet appear what we shall be."

All week I held bolts of satin and spools of ribbon, ran to the store for pins, tape, and wire, and kept Mother and Mel supplied with Cokes and salads from the salad bar at the Steakhouse. What had been trailered out to the lake yesterday morning, slowly (and a man hired to stand guard until time for the wedding), with Mother and me following in the Oldsmobile, flashing the lights and blowing the horn if they drove too fast—what rode at anchor now—looked like a royal barge. Even in the smothering heat haze, it floated like a flower on the water, all of its unhappiness conquered. The florist had been out there working since daybreak, and now, at midafternoon, the roof was hidden under an enormous arrangement of magnolia leaves and ferns and pale peach lilies. Every inch of black wrought iron and gray metal had been draped and swagged with white satin, twined with lilies and pale yellow roses and ferns. On the boat itself, more white satin made a sanctuary where a candelabra stood (bolted to the deck), twined with greenery and flanked by two enormous arrangements of the lilies, roses, baby's breath, and ferns. I had seen the florist's bill: $2,000 worth of flowers. What money my father *had* left her, Mother was spending on this wedding as fast as she could tear the checks out of her checkbook, spending it as though she wanted to get rid of it all. She and Big Tom, her brother and Mel's father, had argued about it, but she'd insisted: She would pay for the flowers and the boat, the bridesmaids' luncheon. Money be damned. It was her money now, and it had bought her this. It was funny, too. Seeing the boat on the day of Mel's wedding, I couldn't remember it as the big, ugly hulk it had been. Even with my eyes closed I could not strip it down to what it had been; it had come too far.

Exactly at four o'clock, according to plan, Big Tom and Melody pulled into the parking lot in the Taylor Brothers' Lincoln. Mother tapped the crystal of her watch and smiled, then she led us onto the boat, walking forcefully with a rustle of green organza and taffeta. She looked exalted, like a big flag waving, and I followed her gladly, walking next to Canady's mother, Iris. Her dark hair was pulled back into a knot on the back of her neck, and her fingers and ears supported emeralds of an astonishing size and clarity. We followed Jewel Lee Glover, the soloist, and Father Reid and Canady's best man and Mel's two bridesmaids. We would be the only witnesses to the ceremony itself; afterward, we would get off the boat and the best man would take them across the lake to Planter's Landing, where a crowd of friends would be waiting to welcome Mel and Canady and take them up to the clubhouse for the reception. The rest of us would follow in our cars.

When everyone had taken their places, Jewel Lee Glover, resplendent as her name in peacock blue satin, sang "Oh Promise Me," a cappella. As she sang, I held onto Mother's hand and watched the ripples spread out around the boat, as though they were the promises Jewel Lee Glover sang about, spreading out and out to fill the whole lake with their motion. Next to me Mother nodded and stared across the lake, as though the song carried a message intended just for her. When it was over, she wiped her eyes one at a time and put her sunglasses on. Then the Wedding March began to play from a tape player behind the satin draperies, and Mel and Big Tom started down the concrete walk that led from the picnic shelter to the boat ramp. Mel wore a picture hat with miniature lilies on it, and her dress was fastened with tiny buttons on the sleeves and bodice, hundreds of buttons that she'd buttoned herself that morning, one by one. She walked up the ramp onto the bridal boat. For the first time since I'd known him, Canady looked scared. The back of his white jacket trembled as Mel walked up the ramp and onto the boat. She kissed her father and went to stand in front of Father Reid.

Then Father Reid opened his Bible and began to read, and his voice carried out across the water. During the part about how love is patient and kind, slow to anger, not puffed up, a speedboat circled the cove and the wake slapped our boat and set it rocking. While Canady and Melody made their vows to one another, Mother held my hand between both of her own, held it so hard it hurt. "Will you love, honor, and cherish till death do you part?" Reverend Reid asked them one by one, and they answered clearly: "I will, I will."

Then it was done. Father Reid spread his arms in blessing,

touched their heads, and Canady and Melody kissed, everyone hugged, Mother and Mel hugged and cried, and everyone but Mel and Canady went back down the ramp. While Mel blew us kisses, the best man pulled up the anchor and started the engine. Then the boat was moving, and the satin streamers trailed behind it in the wake as the boat gathered speed. The rest of us stood around the ramp and waved like maniacs. Mel waved back until they were far out in the lake, almost lost in the glare of the sun on the water. She waved and Mother waved back most furiously, as though she were trying to tell Mel something vital that she'd forgotten to say until now. Melody waved until Canady put both hands on her shoulders and turned her to look where they were going, toward Planter's Landing and their house on the hill above the lake, its windows flashing in the sun.

When they were gone, people wandered back toward their cars until only Mother and I were left. Matthew and I had done this once, said those words, believed them. "Till death do us part." It had seemed like two promises then: one that we made, one that was made to us—the promise of a long life ahead to finish what we'd begun that day. Mother stayed down near the water. Shading her eyes, she watched the boat cross the lake toward Planter's Landing, and when it moved into a pool of glare, she waved one last time and folded her arms. Her shoulders slumped, and she seemed to be looking for something in the gravel at her feet. Was she thinking, too, of promises made, promises broken? Of the beginning those promises must have seemed to her once and where they had led? It is dangerous to look back on promises when they are no longer part of the future, which you cannot know, but part of the past, which you can. Was she thinking, I wondered, of Thelma Radford? I felt the bitterness rising in me then, black and cold as the bottom of the lake, down there under Mel and Canady's boat down where the Laughing Place had been.

I walked down to her and slipped my arm around her waist. "Mother," I said, "it was beautiful, it was spectacular. Your talents are being wasted at the tax assessor's office."

She sniffed. "Humph. I do my share," she said, staring out

across the water. "I do what's needed. I always have and I always will. You better hurry up and give me a wedding to do. Now let's get over to that reception before anything goes wrong." And the look she gave me was as bleak as the gray of Mel's bridal boat before Mother had disguised it so well with flowers and satin.

719 Azalea Trail

Up near White's Mill, the Little Awando Road dead-ends into the Bean Blossom Road, and you have to choose: up to the right toward Planter's Landing, or down to the left toward town. One by one the line of cars turned right, following Mother's Oldsmobile. I was last in line, and I turned left toward town. After the wedding, when I was getting into my car, I'd noticed the papers lying on the backseat, two copies of the "March of Progress" edition of the *Courier-Tribune*. Already the newsprint had begun to yellow, but the family crossing the blue lake in their red speedboat looked as bright as ever, as if life had been good to them, as if the promises made to them had all been kept. Seeing the papers is what gave me the idea of where I needed to go. That and the way my mother had looked, all drooped and beaten and sad.

Down on the square, I parked on the yellow, no-parking stripes in front of the courthouse and snapped on the flashers. What I needed to know wouldn't take long to find. It was there in a title book in the Clerk of Courts office, waiting. Still, when I got back to my car, I found a ticket stuck under the windshield wiper on the driver's side. A twenty-five-dollar ticket. I was glad to see it there; it focused my anger the way a magnifying glass gathers and aims the heat of the sun. It felt good to tear it up into little pieces, to try and throw them as high as my father's name lettered in gold on the second-story window of the building where his office had been. Instead a breeze caught them and scattered them all over the courthouse lawn. Across the street on the sidewalk in front of the Steakhouse, a black woman pushing a baby in a stroller stared at me. The baby stared, too. When I looked back up at the courthouse, I saw people standing in the windows of the Clerk of Court's office, and I waved. At the Goodyear store down the block, the mechanics had come out of the bays and stood on the sidewalk, wiping their hands on oil-stained rags and talking to each other without turning their heads, as if they didn't want to miss anything. I waved to them, too, and they waved back, then I got back into the car and drove toward 719 Azalea Trail which is where Thelma Radford, grantee, had bought her house and lot—$100,000 worth of house and lot—in April of 1978.

Azalea Trail, Azalea Trail. As I drove down the street, I said the name aloud. It had a quiet, refined sound, like the street itself—a wide, quiet street with no one driving down it, no one outside in any of the smooth, clipped yards. Thelma had come a long way from that stiff, white box of a house over on Delray Drive where I used to go with my father to pick up the typing that she took home from his office. That place had been cramped and dim, its small front windows swaddled in dusty, blue velvet drapes and sheers; it had smelled of bacon and cigarette smoke and Jungle Gardenia perfume. In the dining room a large, round table made of dark, polished wood had stood on grotesque, clawed feet. The table was covered with a lace tablecloth and held a ruby glass bowl in the center filled with dusty wax fruit, but you could tell that no one ever ate there because the table was always messy with papers and adding machines and Thelma's typewriter. That house had filled up with hospital beds, oxygen tanks, and portable toilets during the five years that Buck had lain in the bedroom dying of heart failure after he retired from his foreman's job in the sewing room at the Piedmont plant. But this house of Thelma's had come up in the world. It stood at the top of a small hill, and it looked as though it had begun life as a long, brick boxcar of a ranch house, then came into some money, added columns and a wide front stoop, white rocking chairs on either side of the front door, hanging baskets of fuchsias that twirled slowly in the heavy air. There were azaleas planted near the front steps and thick beds of pine straw raked into neat islands around the trees. Clumps of pampas grass grew in the sloping front yard, and a white mailbox smothered with clematis vine stood down near the street.

No doubt, I thought as I turned into her driveway, Thelma has a yardman. It was so hot the tar on the street was soft, and as I turned off the street and into Thelma's driveway, the tires made a sucking, tearing sound. A new yellow Cadillac the color of butter was parked in the driveway, and as I walked up the driveway toward the path to the front steps, I looked inside at the fawn-colored leather upholstery, the white wicker litter basket with nothing in it.

The doorbell played an elaborate tune when I pressed the button. I caught myself grinning and thought, This will not do, to have Thelma peek out through the sheer curtains that covered the side-lights on either side of her front door and see me standing there in that dress (no wonder they were staring down on the courthouse square), adding up her front porch (nice rockers, fancy front door, expensive brass pineapple door knocker), holding a newspaper and grinning at nothing. What was I doing there? she might ask. And what would I answer? "Looking for my father"? I smoothed down my dress and tugged it higher over my breasts, tucked up my hair, listened to my heart thudding in my ears. How often and at what hours of the day or night had my father stood on this porch, glancing over his shoulder at the street, snugging himself a little closer to the house, or standing back casually, one hand in his pants pocket if a car went by. Perhaps he carried his split-open satchel of a briefcase. *Just bringing some paperwork by for my secretary. Just a simple country boy.* No, surely he would have had his own key, and it would have been to the back door, not the front. Wouldn't that be the way these things were done? But back door or front door, he had gone in, and surely he had left some mark on this house, and I intended to find it.

I was smiling again when the door opened. "Hello, Thelma,"

I said to the small, soft face with its round blue eyes and cupid's bow mouth. *Blink* went those blue, doll's eyes. *Blink.* She's let her hair go, I thought. Her hair that had once looked like spun platinum had turned brown. Age had creased and thickened her neck, and the gold chain there looked too tight. Her face was netted with lines, but she was still the daintiest woman I have ever known. Her eyelids were frosted blue; her lips, frosted pink. She was dressed in a pale-yellow velour jogging outfit and clean, white tennis shoes, and she looked soft, a pastel drawing beside Mother's portrait, which would have to be done on slashed canvas, with charcoal and red clay and splintered wood spilling out. Thelma had given us Cokes from the drink box in the back of Papa's office—so cold they were full of slushy ice on hot summer days—lifting the bottles out of the cooler by their necks and wrapping Kleenex around the bottom of the bottles so they wouldn't drip. The seams in her stockings were always straight, her heels high. In winter she wore pastel angora sweaters, in summer she wore crisp sleeveless blouses. I had watched her, studied her, trying to absorb from her the secrets of daintiness and tininess and grooming, secrets I could not learn from Mother.

"Goodness," she said, "it's Annie." She touched the gold chain around her neck. Her voice was still breathy and girlish. For a second an expression—fear? astonishment?—traveled over her face, and then it cooled into something harder, more watchful. "You're all dressed up," she said. "Your cousin's wedding was today, wasn't it?"

I opened my mouth to answer, and what came out was this: "Well, Thelma," I said, as I looked around her porch, "didn't Buck leave you well provided for?" Then we both stood there, with our mouths hanging open. She must have answered: "Yes, he did," or something like that, but her eyes changed, as though something in them had been thrown into reverse. She backed away from where I stood, stunned at the breathtaking bitchiness of what I'd just said. The pure, peach syrup–soaked, and saccharine viciousness of what had come out of my mouth. It had been just this way of speaking, of feeling, and of living that I'd spent years believing I'd shed like a snake's papery skin, scraped off and abandoned under some rotting log back in the swamp of manners I thought I'd left behind. "Here,"

I said, and I held out the paper. "I thought I'd bring you this. There's an article about my father in it."

"Why, thank you, Annie, but I have a copy," she said. Her mouth smiled, her voice smiled, but her eyes kept their distance and her arms stayed folded.

"You have a copy?" I said, and I felt tears start up the back of my eyes. I had not counted on this.

"Well, give it here," she said. Her eyes were still cool, but color rose in her face. "I'll send one to Cynthia Louise." She paged through it quickly. "There's that awful picture," she said. "Why won't somebody lay that thing to rest? It makes me so mad."

When Buck died, Thelma took two weeks off from work, and then she was back. So soon, everybody said, so loyal, so brave. Now she was angry that they'd mistreated my father, her boss for so many years, by printing that picture of him. Maybe the money, if he'd given it to her, had been a reward for a loyal employee. But if that had been the case, I thought, why hide the money? And Mother would not have made that sound, drawing herself up straight until her back had not touched the back of the Taylor Brothers' chair, if Thelma had been just a loyal employee coming into the tent to sit behind us at her boss's funeral.

Thelma shut the paper and dropped it onto the table in the entrance hall, next to the vase of flowers under the gilt-framed mirror there. I didn't feel like crying any longer once I saw that the flowers in the vase—extravagant speckled lilies and bird-of-paradise flowers—were fake. That Thelma had put on weight, that her backside sagged.

"Won't you come in and have a glass of tea on this hot day?" she said.

"Well, yes," I said. As I followed Thelma through the house, I noted details the way Grandmother Vess used to do, tallying up the right and the wrong way things had been done, and deciding on the basis of these scores what rung on the social ladder this person had managed to climb onto. Thelma, I was happy to see, had not gone far. No matter how much money my father had given her to spend, Thelma had bad taste. It was chilly, a few degrees cooler than comfortable. The house no longer smelled of cigarette smoke and bacon. Instead, a sweet smell like apples and cinnamon hung in the air; the carpet in the living room was pure white, and so thick it felt as if I might sink into it. The furniture there was all brocade and velvet, and velvet drapes, deeply swagged, hung from the windows, and were held back by gold cord that ended in fringed medallions. The kitchen was much like Mother's, down to the unglazed tiles on the countertop, the Tiffany lampshade pulled low over the kitchen table—the perfect table, I thought, for a frank talk between two soap opera heroines in which all the beans get spilled. One heroine (me) would knock on the door of the other (Thelma) and give her a sober and significant look that said, The time has come. I know everything you've done. And the two would sit down; they would not waste time.

I know about you and my father. I've come for some answers. Did you love him, Thelma? How long did it go on? Ten years? Fifteen? When did it start? How? How often did he come here, and how did you arrange your face, your life, so that it showed nothing all those years? And as I listened, I would be noble, magnanimous, wise and compassionate, while Thelma talked, on her face the grateful look of the accused sensing her chance for redemption, the cleansing chance to tell all, and be forgiven. When Buck died, John was so sweet to me. Brought me flowers and took me out to lunch and let me come in late, let me cry on his shoulder. Sometimes, you know, you just need to do that when you lose your husband.

I know.

"Won't you come into the solarium and I'll get us some tea," Thelma said, gesturing toward a sunny, glassed-in room off the kitchen, which was filled with white wicker chairs and trailing ferns. A white ceiling fan trimmed in brass filigree turned slowly overhead. I walked toward the room, feeling a malicious pleasure in the pretentiousness of that word solarium, the way she gestured, the well-rehearsed hostess. Papa would have seen how tacky this was. It was exactly like a picture out of Southern Living, right down to the polished cotton print on the chair pillows—trumpet vines and birds. Thelma didn't even have enough imagination to do her own room.

She couldn't have been *that* close to Papa, I thought. At least Mother could do that much. As Mrs. John Vess of Timmons, she'd learned the proper ways to speak and dress and keep up the house, how to send and reply to invitations. But Thelma had never had that chance. She never got to be Mrs. John Vess; she had to muddle along with her own tastes. She never got to be exalted by my father's greatness. I stopped myself then. If I went on thinking that way, I would start to understand Thelma, to sympathize with her. I sat down in one of the white wicker chairs that faced the small, bright-green square of backyard and waited for Thelma. On the edge of the birdbath outside the window, a coy, clay angel sat, its pudgy legs crossed. I felt tired and sad to be here, and I thought of the drive down from Pennsylvania, how endless it had seemed with the U-Haul bucking back against the car every time I hit a bump, and no one to drive but me. Is this what I had come home for? It was one of those moments in which everything becomes very clear, as though you'd been out wandering and come back into your body; not déjà vu exactly, because it's not the sensation that you've been here before that you feel, but a feeling of absolute locality, as though you'd gotten where you were going at last and everything that had been following you had caught up with you. As though this had been your destination all along.

When Thelma had set the plate of lemon cookies down onto the glass table between the chairs and handed me my glass of tea with a napkin wrapped around the bottom of the glass, when she'd snugged herself back into a chair and tucked her feet up under her on the cushion, she said, "So, how are you keeping busy these days, Annie?" She bit into a cookie with her front teeth and rounded her eyes at me. Of all the kinds of women in the world, Papa had said, the coquette was the one he could not abide. How could Papa possibly have come here, have cared for her? To imagine it, I would have to allow him a life completely unknown to me, alien to the life he'd claimed for himself and insisted everyone believe he lived.

"Oh, this and that," I said. "Sorting through Papa's things. Poking around the courthouse, that sort of thing." I watched her over the rim of the tea glass as I took another sip. Did I see shock, alarm on her face? I did not. She had a little mustache of powdered sugar from the cookies, which she delicately blotted away with a cocktail napkin.

"Well, how fascinating," she said. "Your daddy was so proud of you and your brother both." She smiled at me, a row of small teeth, very white and even. *Your daddy* sounded so chaste and formal at the same time, so platonic and friendly. If only she had called him "John," or even "he"—something more intimate. Look, Thelma, the soap opera daughter says to her father's mistress. Are those your real teeth? Why did you stop dying your hair? Where have you hidden my father?

I felt desperate, close to tears. I had to get deeper into the house, back to the private places. I asked to use the bathroom. "Down the hall," Thelma said, as she rose from her chair and picked up the plate of cookies and my glass. She seemed relieved. "You'll see it there on the right." I walked down the thickly carpeted hall, and when I got to what I was sure was the bedroom door, I nudged it open with my foot and peeked in, as though I might surprise my father's ghost sitting on the edge of the bed, putting on his shoes with that long, silver shoehorn that had disappeared one year from our house on Wyman Street and was never seen again. But there was only the smell of Jungle Gardenia and apple-cinnamon potpourri, a radio tuned to an easy-listening station, and a king-size bed covered with a yellow, quilted satin spread. On top of a tall shiny chest of drawers were some photographs of Buck and their daughter, Cynthia Louise.

In the bathroom across the hall, I closed the door, turned the lock, and leaned against the door because my knees felt weak. Here, everything was pink. The white carpet stopped at the bathroom door and the pink carpet began. It felt as though I might sink into it up to my ankles. The walls were pink and so was the shower curtain. Even the scale and the toilet-seat cover were carpeted in pink shag, and the Kleenex box on the back of the toilet tank was covered in white and cross-stitched with pink roses. I flushed the toilet and under cover of the noise, I opened the cabinet under the sink and looked inside. A pink toilet-bowl brush in its own pink plastic stand, a plunger, a pair of pink rubber gloves, and one can each of Drano and Comet set neatly on a folded piece of paper towel.

I flushed the toilet again and opened the cupboard behind the door. There were stacks of pink bath towels, hand towels, and wash-cloths, each stack tied with a white satin ribbon and with a little sachet tucked under each perfectly tied bow. It made me sad to see those white ribbons and sachets, to think of the effort that went into making them look just so. And for what? For whom? I remembered running into Thelma once, not long after I'd come home. One rainy Sunday afternoon I'd bumped into her near the sheets in the Linen Shop at Belk's. She'd been without makeup that day, wearing an old, frumpy corduroy jacket and a scarf over her hair. Without makeup her eyes looked rabbity, and she had a weak chin. Under one arm, she carried two rolls of floral shelf paper. "Such a dreary day," she'd said. "I couldn't stand to be in the house. How about you?" I'd realized then, with a shock, that I'd gone to Belk's for the same reasons as Thelma: to pass the time, to keep from going home. There was nothing I needed there, nothing I even wanted. And now I lifted up a stack of towels and peeked underneath. What was I looking for? Anything. A shaving kit, a razor, something male that would place him with her, in this house. Something, I almost laughed, that would stand up in court.

The shelves above the towels were lined with cosmetics and medicines, half-empty bottles of Moon Drops moisturizer, Pepto-Bismol, aspirin, Dramamine. I flushed the toilet again and stood on tiptoe, then reached behind the clutter of bottles. Every child knows that this is where you find the things the grown-ups want to hide. Confusing, thrilling things whose purpose is both obvious and un-nameable. Zippered bags that open to reveal coiled rubber hoses attached to curved plastic nozzles and folded rubber bags. Flesh-colored rubber rings in plain, beige cases. Tubes of clear jelly rolled neatly from the bottom. I patted around behind the bottles, but I found only the plain, wooden shelf. Not even the flowered shelf paper reached that far. It made me angry and sad because it was the same shelf paper she'd been holding on that Sunday afternoon at the mall, and I wondered if she'd come back that rainy afternoon and worked till dark lining her shelves, but only halfway, with paper. I wondered if it had gotten her through the afternoon. Or if she'd wept. And to whom she could have told her grief about my father.

I thought I heard a sound—a footstep?—whispering on the carpet outside the door, and as I turned I caught a glimpse of myself in the bathroom mirror in my low-cut dress, my face flushed, my eyes wild, hair straggling everywhere, with one hand behind Thelma's towels. I was a sneak like my father had been; I had found him at last.

Matthew used to say that I have never been good at keeping my feelings from showing on my face. Thelma must have seen it when I rushed out of the bathroom and down the hall, grabbing my purse from the wicker table under the ceiling fan that stirred the air in her solarium. "Thank you for the tea and the cookies," I said. "I didn't realize how late it was getting. I've got to get to the reception or Mother'll have a fit. You know Mother."

At last I had gotten to her. She looked down at the floor and said in a small voice. "Yes, I know your mother quite well."

On the front porch she put her hand on my arm. Her eyes had lost their distance. The hanging basket of fuchsias in front of us twirled in the breeze, and as it revolved, Thelma pinched off the brown blooms with one hand and dropped them into her other palm. She squinted out across her lawn as if she suspected that someone was hiding in the shrubbery. "Are you holding up all right?" she asked. "It's terrible to lose your husband and your daddy that way. I know, believe me, I know." She looked at me with that shrewd, appraising look I'd seen her use on Papa's clients sometimes. ("Never underestimate Thelma Radford," Papa always said. "You'll get yourself in big trouble if you do.") She cleared her throat. "You know, ah, when your husband died, it just about broke your daddy's heart."

"What did he do?" I said. I felt tears gathering behind my eyes again. I'd meant it to sound stern, part of this cross-examination I was trying to conduct on Thelma, not the way it had come out: Help me Thelma. He's gone again. I can't find him. I can't find him anywhere.

But I had caught her off-balance. I saw fear in her eyes, and confusion. Then she looked down, folded her arms, began to outline a brick in the porch floor with the toe of one shoe. She took a deep breath and looked directly at me, her eyes unwavering, unafraid. "He couldn't concentrate at work, for one thing," she said. "He lost cases that he never should have lost—easy things, right-of-ways, that sort of thing. I had to follow around behind him correcting his mistakes. He talked all the time, day and night, about going up to Pennsylvania and bringing you home. I don't know how many times a day he picked up the phone. I must have made plane reservations for him half a dozen times. He couldn't stand it that you were so far away with all that had happened to you." Her chin trembled then, her mouth yanked down, and she gave the brown fuchsia blossoms in her hand an underhanded toss. They landed on the perfect, thick green grass of her lawn.

And I felt that purpose again the way I'd felt it with the colonel—a cold, clear, hard space in the center of my brain, a cold, clear question. "You say he talked about me night and day?"

She had been about to go on, I could tell, then her mouth snapped shut and the wariness came back into her eyes. "That's what I said. Night and day," she said.

And yet, he had not called me, he had not come to Pennsylvania. Maybe he had lain in Thelma's bed and talked and talked night and day, and she had listened, as Mother wouldn't have listened, to the gloomy, churning worry that he turned on things. If he had told Mother, she would have looked him up and down. His struggles with decisions made her disdainful, impatient. Then she would have delivered her judgment. "Well, go then," she would have said. "If you feel that strongly about it, just get on the plane and go, John." But she would have missed the point, I thought, as Thelma had not. It was not judgment or even advice that he'd wanted. What he'd wanted was sympathy for the agonies that his innocence and goodness led him into. And Thelma, no doubt, had indulged him in his fretting. It was she who had carried the weight of his character as my mother had refused to do. Because Thelma was a woman who saw life as something to be survived. When she saw her chance, she took it. And now he was gone forever, gone where nobody could claim him. I took Thelma's hand. It was cold and plump. Poor circulation, Papa had said about her: "That girl has the poorest circulation of anybody I've ever known."

"I hope you're holding up all right, too," I said.

On the way to Planter's Landing, the Dodge shimmied badly at sixty, but when the speedometer needle hit seventy, the shimmy disappeared, and the car ran smoothly down the road, though it swayed alarmingly on the curves. But I didn't care. I wanted to take chances. I passed on hills and solid yellow lines, on curves, and in every car that I passed I imagined I saw Thelma, vanishing in the rearview mirror. But in every car I ran up behind, there she was again, and I had to get around her. "Night and day," she'd said. "Night and day." What did my father call what they'd done? An affair? No, that was too worldly. In New York City people had affairs. Down here, people cheated on each other. But my father would never have called it that; he would not have risked a swerve so close to that truth. How about running around? That was it. He was running around on my mother. That's more like it. If he had called what he'd done with Thelma anything, my father would have called it something playful and childlike. He was ruthless that way; he would have done anything, anything at all, to go on believing in his own goodness. He would have destroyed anyone who suggested that it might not be true. I thought of him stretched out on that thick, white carpet at Thelma's, his head in her lap, her small hand stroking the worry from his forehead. At Thelma's, there would have been no sharp rapping of Mother's heels on the hardwood floors to reproach or goad or contradict him, no anger to disturb his rest, only Thelma's softness into which he could sink and come up still clean.

But there was more, I thought, as I drove onto the Southland Timber Company land. The sight of the long, straight rows of pines clipping by made me feel terribly afraid, as if I were going down one of them toward somewhere I dreaded, somewhere I couldn't stop myself from going. *"When your husband died,"* Thelma said. *"When your husband died.''* That was two years ago. Even after she got her money, her house, she and my father didn't stop. How long had it been going on? Ten years? Fifteen? While Davis and I grew up and after we left home. Half of his married life with my mother. While he claimed our loyalties, demanded our allegiance as necessary to his life, then went out and made us a part of the life he looked beyond for happiness and satisfaction. And why? Maybe he didn't know what he wanted, just that this with Thelma felt more like it than what he had. Maybe it was nothing I could bring myself to name. I thought of Thelma's soft, small body, her perfume. I thought of my father with her, closing the door to the bedroom, the yellow satin spread, and I felt as if I stood on the edge of a wilderness with no signs to point me across.

Planter's Landing

A fairyland. That's what Mother had promised she'd turn the Planter's Landing ballroom into in time for Mel's wedding reception. Something extraordinary, she said. Something this town has never seen. The day we'd driven out there a week earlier, only Mother could have believed that it could be done. The room had looked and sounded like a sawmill then. Table saws whined, compressors knocked, workmen called to one another over the rattling heat of their hammering, and the twenty-foot Palladian window leaned against a wall, still in its crate. "Candles here," Mother had shouted to me that day over the whine of the saw as we waded through extension cords, fast-food bags, scraps of lumber, paint cans, and drop cloths. "Bride's table there." This is my mother's genius, her faith, the alchemy of her mind and heart. Looking at the present, she sees a shining future, as if the present were only a window, only the means to a view. And since she sees the future wherever she looks, she never loses hope. There are always plans to make, dates ahead to circle on the calendar of this better time. What would she do, I wondered, if she ran out of beautiful futures to trust?

Fairyland she'd promised and fairyland it had become. I stood at the door and looked in. The ballroom swam with light and smelled of fresh paint and new wood and perfume and flowers. Flowers everywhere, as she'd promised, flowers and greenery on every table and windowsill, lilies and orchids and yellow sweetheart roses and ferns and trailing ivy. Under the enormous chandelier in the center of the room, four long tables had been arranged in a square and covered with white cloths and piled with food. Men and women in tall chef's hats worked the middle of the square. They speared shrimp and dipped up meatballs and, with huge shiny knives, carved at a roast beef the size of a small car. There were three champagne fountains and a bar, and two hundred candles, by Mother's count. Tall, white candles on the windowsills surrounded by magnolia leaves and flowers. Candles on the tables and the bar. Candelabra on either end of the bandstand at the end of the room opposite the window, where a twelve-piece orchestra added a syrup of strings to the mix of light and greenery and perfume.

Candlelight and women dressed in bright silk, whose voices sounded as bright as their dresses, and men in expensive suits standing next to them with glasses in their hands. And all of this swirling toward a table along the wall at the end of the room opposite the window, which held a garden's worth of flowers, a cathedral's share of candles, and a five-tiered wedding cake. Mel and Canady stood in front of this table, surrounded by a crowd of people. Looking into each other's eyes, they raised two golden goblets in a toast while a flashbulb went off. Canady's white linen jacket was unwilted, his sharply creased trousers still perfectly pressed. Mel's train pooled around her feet just so.

Fairyland. Pink, white, gold, and perfumed. Land of happily-ever-after and sweet, faithful love, where Mother was queen. I heard her laugh and then I saw her, hauling her brother, Big Tom, around the dance floor. He looked grateful for the help and followed her dutifully. *Queenie*, Papa had called her, and I saw why. She was a head taller than any other woman in the room. In her green satin sheath with its chiffon overdress swept and caught dramatically on one shoulder by a diamond pin, she looked like a statue of a goddess, the one being lifted from the water. But my father didn't like queens as it turned out, he preferred women who bowed to him as king.

When she saw me standing at the door, she stopped smiling, let go of Big Tom, and came toward me, like a big ship under full sail. "I am absolutely mortified," she said, so loudly that people close to us turned to look. Then she stopped. "What's wrong?"

"I'm fine," I said.

"You don't look fine. Where have you been? You've completely missed the receiving line. Big Tom's already danced with Melody. Your timing is inexcusable. I don't know what you're thinking about. Honestly."

"I got lost," I said, and I laughed. I once was lost but now I'm found. I was blind but now I see. All claims to innocence are forfeited here. "Now let me go speak to Mel and Canady," I said.

"Remember, you congratulate the groom and compliment the bride," she called after me as I walked away.

What foolishness, I thought. Why not congratulate the bride? That one rule contained the germ of everything I found hateful here. You do not congratulate the bride because congratulations belong to victors, and it is not becoming for a woman to be active enough to win anything; she must seem to have gotten it effortlessly. "She chases him until he catches her." That old, sticky deceit. I'll speak to the bride, I thought. I'll say, "Congratulations, Mel, on getting what you wanted. I hope you hold onto it, I hope you go on wanting it for the rest of your life."

Mel held out her arms and pulled me close. "Oh, Annie," she said, "here I am on my wedding day, can you believe it? Isn't it beautiful?" She had flowers in her hair, lilies of the valley—tiny, white bells—and it seemed as though a light were burning just beneath her skin. She bit her lip and looked all around the room. She laid her cheek against Canady's back, which was turned toward her while he talked to another man about the Planter's Landing golf course. What right did I have to question her happiness, to say something mean and small?

"Mel, I wish you all the happiness in the world," I said.

Mel squeezed my hands and looked into my face, her eyes brimming. "Thank you, Annie," she said. "And I just know we're going to be celebrating yours real soon."

"Probably not, Mel," I said, "but that's all right."

"Oh, now," she said, shaking my arm. "Don't be such a pessimist."

Now Canady had turned; he put his arm around Mel's waist and drew her to him. "Ah," he said, "the fair Annie."

"Congratulations, Canady," I said. "You be good to my cousin, now."

"Nothing but the best," he said, nuzzling her neck.

"Canady," Mel said, looking up into his face, "talk to Annie about pessimism, would you please?"

"Lucky me," Canady said. He winked and waited, then he laughed, the way he always did when I didn't wink back.

"If you'll excuse me," I said. "I need some more champagne." Five minutes later, Canady found me. Not that I was hiding from him. In fact, I stood near the champagne fountain in the middle of the floor and watched him walk toward me as if he were browsing, stopping to talk, to touch, to be kissed and hugged, then ambling on, smiling his lazy smile. When he came up to me, he took my hand and looked into my eyes as though he had urgent business there. Not that I withheld my hand, either. In fact, I offered it to him, squeezed his own, and passed my thumb slowly over the new, wide, gold wedding band he wore. I wondered if Canady would appreciate what I'd noticed about men who wore wedding bands. The wider a man's wedding ring, so I've observed, the less seriously he took his marriage. As though a wide and weighty ring were all the proof he needed that he was married; from behind its gold expanse, he could do what he pleased. My supervisor at Westinghouse Learning Systems had worn a ring that had been hammered into facets as though it had been forged from a chunk of pure gold by the Norse god of matrimony. I learned to recognize his footsteps coming toward my cubicle, to step outside into the corridor to talk with him. If he came into my cubicle to check my work, he would put his hands on my shoulders, and once, he slid them down to cover my breasts as he leaned over to look at what I'd written. After Matthew died, he asked me out.

"You like?" Canady said.

"It's big," I said, and I drained my glass and watched him over the rim. This time when he winked, I winked back, and a new light came on in his eyes, the quickening you see in a cat's eyes when it first spots movement in the grass.

"Big enough," he said. Without looking away, he took my champagne glass and held it under the fountain, then handed it back to me with a bow and a smile. *This is outrageous*, some faraway part of my mind said. This is your cousin's husband, her wedding reception. She has been kind to you. What are you doing? But isn't it fascinating what you can do once you've dropped the pretense of innocence? Almost anything, really; you were that free. And what better man than Canady Reeves with whom to celebrate that freedom?

With a dark, insinuating look he reached into the pocket of his jacket and pulled out his cigarettes. He tapped one on a thumbnail, fitted it into the corner of his mouth, and lit it with a silver lighter engraved with his initials (Mel's wedding present to him), never taking his eyes off of my face, as if any minute I might run. But I wasn't going anywhere. "Now," he said, blowing smoke toward the ceiling. "What did my bride send me here to talk to you about?"

I did not like the way he said *bride*, as though it were set off by quotation marks and not to be taken seriously. "Pessimism," I said.

Just then the band began to play "Begin the Beguine," and I laughed at the old-fashioned drama of it. Laughed with my head back and felt my hair, warm on my shoulders, and Canady watching. He held his cigarette behind his back and leaned close to my ear. The smell of his cologne was so strong I felt as though some soft, fragrant net had been thrown over me. "I don't understand," he said as he ran his finger under the strap of my dress, "how a woman who looks as good as you look could be pessimistic. About anything."

"Oh, it's got nothing to do with looks," I said. "But thanks anyway, Canady."

I had made him sad again. He stood back, shaking his head. "Annie," he said. "Annie, Annie, Annie. You're so serious about everything." He made a dragged-down, sorrowful face to show that seriousness was not good for me.

"Well not about *everything*, Canady," I said, and I bumped him with one hip.

He laughed then, showing his teeth, and I saw Mel turn to look back over her shoulder at us as Big Tom led her toward a champagne fountain. Mother also watched, a glass stopped halfway to her mouth, and the band played much too loud. This is all wrong, I thought. Too fast and all wrong. I felt the champagne sour in my stomach, and I remembered I hadn't eaten anything since that morning at breakfast. "I need food," I said. "Don't go away, I'll talk to you later."

"Absolutely," he said, in a voice that mocked seriousness. This was his trick, I knew: to spin the mirror of his attention around so that I saw myself in it the way I appeared to him, foolishly prim. But he didn't follow me. Following was not Canady's style. I felt him watch me walk. He would like high heels, I thought. The lilt they gave to a woman's walk. Waiting was Canady's style. When I was a few yards away, he called after me, "You save a dance for me now, Annie, you hear?" in a voice that practically glowed with sex.

"As many as you want," I said, without looking back at him or at the laughing women and men whose silence began as I walked past them. The women disapproved—I could feel it—but it pleased the men. They smoothed their ties and cleared their throats; they looked down at the floor and smiled to themselves. If my father had been here, had seen this, I thought, he might have looked down at the floor and smiled to himself as they did, remembering.

At the buffet table, I asked the chef to cut me three thick slices of roast beef and I made myself a sandwich on heavy, brown bread. Something warm and heavy, I thought, to soak up the champagne. The last time I'd drunk too much champagne—the day the lake opened—had been the last time I'd seen Legree. The taste and feel of it in my mouth, golden and bristly, with a sweetness that soured before you'd swallowed it, reminded me of him, the door that had closed in his voice that day. "Virgin," he'd said. Far from it, I thought.

Just then Ethel Bowie, the colonel's daughter, came around the end of the table carrying a plate of food in her hand. Ethel was a broad woman with pale-gray hair drawn up into a bun on top of her head, pale eyes that disapproved of champagne, and a heavy face permanently set in an expression of sorrowful suspicion, as if she were used to having her worst fears confirmed. She held a paper plate away from her so that the shrimp she was eating wouldn't drip down her flowered silk dress. It was a relief to see her; I felt as if I'd just came back to earth with a bump. "Ethel," I said, "come here and tell me how the colonel's getting 'long."

When she'd finished chewing, and had scrubbed her mouth with a napkin, she said, "He isn't."

"Oh," I said. "Well, what do the doctors say?"

"They don't say more than we can see with our own eyes," she said, as though I'd asked the world's most ignorant question. "They ought to pay us for doing their work for them. 'He's not expected to improve' is what they say." She sighed and speared a shrimp off her plate, then held it up in the air, studying it. "No," she said, "Papa is gone from us forever. 'Might as well get used to it' is that the doctors all say." And I wanted to ask her, But how do you do that, Ethel? How do you get used to forever? Out of the corner of my eye, I saw Canady dance by with one of Mel's bridesmaids. "We go to see him every Sunday, but it doesn't seem like he knows us half the time." She wiped her eyes one at a time with the paper napkin.

"I'm sorry, Ethel," I said. "I'm sorry for all of us. Every day when I go over there to feed the dogs, I can't believe he's gone." *Hypocrite*, I thought. What right did I have to speak to Ethel that way, I who'd tricked her father, a bewildered old man, into betraying his oldest friend? Who'd driven off a good man and attacked Thelma Radford with smiles and appalling meanness? There were no limits, no boundaries to what I was capable of. I was free of those now, fallen and free. Why don't you say, "I hope he dies soon," Ethel? He *wants* to be dead, I could feel it.

"We're all sorry," she said, moving off now into the crowd, "but that isn't going to change a thing."

After I'd eaten my sandwich I felt better, so I had another glass of champagne. When the orchestra struck up "Moon River" and people began to dance, Canady handed Mel over to his best man. As he came toward me through the crowd, I drank the last of it and set the glass down on the buffet table, and I felt as though I were about to discover something about myself that I'd never known before. We smiled at each other as though we were members of the same tribe who'd been separated for too long. He bowed deeply. "Madam," he said, "would you care to dance?"

"I certainly would," I said. For a moment I imagined Legree's serious, ugly face, the way he demanded substance, wanted depth, as though substance and depth were food and water and oxygen and light. But the thought of Legree and what he'd wanted seemed as oppressive to me then as the dense heat outside this cool, fragrant room, oppressive as the lake. Something to be run from because death was in it, and every possible betrayal and the inevitability of loss that was love's surest end. Why not take this with Canady as far as it would go? If life betrayed you—my father's greatest lesson, his legacy to me—then to what, to whom, did I owe allegiance? Better to live in a place where no promises were made, so none could be broken. Had my father felt this way once, with Thelma? Slipping out, slipping free? Weightless?

Now there was Canady, and I moved toward him. He took my hand and drew me to him, tight against his body. "I want what Canady's got," Mel had said. Now I knew what she'd meant. Tan hands with perfect fingernails and dark eyes and a restless way of never quite bringing his attention to rest on you, which kept you off balance and made you feel that if only you could please him, if only you could only be exciting, giddy, beautiful enough, if only you could attract him strongly enough, he would stop his wandering and stay with you. Keeping him interested would be a lifetime's work, I thought, and somehow I think Mel knew that. But for now (which was all that mattered), how lean his waist was, wrapped in the red cummerbund, how good he smelled, how easily he moved, easily and in control, never doubting that what he wanted would be his.

"Let's dance," I said. He laughed and pressed the small of my back so that my hips came against him, and I did not pull away. I put both arms around his neck, laid my head on his shoulder, and felt his lips brush the back of my neck. All around us, people danced and talked, but when we danced by them they stopped talking and watched. But I kept my eyes closed so I wouldn't have to see them, and Canady hummed and blew gently into my ear and I moved my hands up under his jacket, stroked the smooth, tight muscles under the cool, tight cotton of his shirt. I felt his hands come up under my hair and lift it, let the weight of it spill over his wrists and arms, and I had my hands up under his jacket, tugging his shirttail free. "Oh, lady," he breathed into my ear as though he were in pain. "Lady, lady. I went in the wrong door that night, didn't I?" His hands moved over my bare back, warm hands, and he was saying how smooth my skin was. "So smooth," he whispered, breathing hard.

"You did," I said, "you did."

"Where's your car?"

"In the parking lot," I said. "Under the tree over by the pool." I had to stop and catch my breath.

He didn't speak, his breathing said it all. He knew exactly where I meant. He might have been there a time or two himself. In the dark at the edge of the parking lot, where the branches of a live oak swept low and made a kind of cave. I will have time to clean out the backseat, I thought wildly. How would it be with him? I thought. But even as I asked, I knew it didn't matter. What mattered was that, having screwed my cousin's husband in the back seat of my car during their wedding reception, I could never dare insist that I was innocent again. I would never be like my father.

"Meet me there in five minutes," I said. Our hands were sweaty and peeled apart, and as I turned to go, I bumped into Mel and Canady's best man, who had danced up behind us. He was holding Melody at arm's length, nervously, as though she were something expensive. She shook herself loose from him and stood beside us, and I stepped back from Canady, though he held tightly to my hand. Mel had tiny buttons on the high neck of her dress, on the sleeves, up the bodice—a hundred tiny buttons. I thought of her that morning at Mother's, working the button hook in and out of the loops, watching herself in the mirror until she'd buttoned every one. Desire drained out of me, and for a moment I thought I might throw up. She looked from me to Canady and back again, and I saw the same look on her face that I'd seen the night before at the rehearsal dinner as she'd watched Canady making the rounds from woman to woman, watched him bend to nuzzle someone's neck or graze her earlobes with his lips. All right, her look said, a calm, desolate look that made me feel transparent. What kind of trouble is this, and what do I have to do about it?

I shrugged stupidly. Then she looked at Canady. His mouth drew down at the corners. Mel's face closed into a stubborn frown, and his face tightened, too. It was not so handsome anymore. As he stared over at her, there was something clenched about him, like a fist. He might hit her one of these days, I thought, when she tries to stop him from getting what he wants. He might hit her and she might hit him back. It looked like an old quarrel, an unwanted guest come back in new clothes to spoil things again.

"Hello, darling," he said. "Your cousin and I were just having a little talk."

"So I see," she said. He tried to tuck a strand of hair back behind Mel's ear, but she leaned away from his hand.

"And now," he said, "if you'll excuse us, we'll get back to it." He turned toward me again, and Mel didn't move. She looked at me and kept on looking.

"No, Canady," I said. "We've danced enough already." Through the window I saw the lake. The sun was gone, and the water was dark. I felt like walking straight out into it until the bottom dropped away suddenly, until I sank and drowned. "I'm sorry, Mel," I said, but her expression did not change. I willed myself to walk away slowly until I got through the doors, and then I ran.

In the sky, a bank of clouds glowed pale coral with leftover sun, but the air was a thick and sunless gray. As I crossed the parking lot toward my car (down at the dark end, where I'd promised Canady it would be), the music and the sound of voices from the ballroom dissolved in the warm, thick air, and there was only the pocking of a tennis ball and the call of a bird that never sings at night, the wax and wane of cicadas, and then other footsteps behind me. *It's Canady*, I thought, *Canady coming after me!* and my throat tightened. But it was Mother. I knew it from the way the hair prickled along the back of my neck. If I lived on the moon for decades, a blind hermit in a cave who'd listened to dust and space so long I'd lost even the memory of human sounds, and I heard those footsteps, I would know that it was Mother, coming to warn or question or confirm some rumor that had sifted down through light-years of galactic space and reached her back on Earth.

At the car, I found that my key ring had snagged on a thread in the lining of my tiny satin purse. When I yanked it loose the lining ripped, and as I stared at the shredded cloth, it seemed for a moment that I was about to be given a name for everything that was wrong with me, because somehow it had to do with that stupidly small, stupidly delicate purse and the way I'd just ripped the lining trying to get away from Mother. I rested my head against the top of the car. As I worked to free the keys I watched Mother out of the corner of my eye, and I allowed myself a second's worth of hope. She walked with her head bent, her hands clasped behind her back, studying the ground as though she had a lot on her mind. Maybe she was coming to take me in her arms and tell me it was all right. She'd seen everything, and she loved me. In fact, she loved me more, having looked through my outrageous act and into the trouble that had caused it. Or better yet, she was coming to laugh with me. How would it be, I thought, to laugh with Mother about a man like Canady? It might make him into a different man, funnier than he'd ever seemed to himself, less potent.

Are you crazy, girl? Have you lost your mind? she might say, her eyes shrewd and sharp as a mockingbird's.

Mother, I would say, *I am, I have.*

Me, too, honey, me too.

"Where're you going in such a hurry?" she asked. As soon as she spoke, I knew I had been foolish to hope.

"Home," I said, trying to keep my voice steady. "I'm going

home. I'm not having a good time and I want to go home. I feel sick." The key shook loose from the lining of my purse and I fitted it into the door lock.

She leaned against the car with a swish of taffeta. The orchid on her shoulder had wilted. She stared off toward the lake, where bats tipped and wobbled through the air. "I guess you do," she said.

I took my hand off the key, left it in the lock. "OK, Mother," I said, "I'll say it for you. What I did in there is the lowest thing I've ever done. I hurt Mel, and this is her wedding day. I will not blame her if she never forgives me. Everybody saw it. I know all that, Mother, and I'd rather not hear you say it again. I'd like to go home. I've had too much to drink, I'm ashamed of myself. Good-bye." I turned the key, and she sighed and pushed herself away from the door. The lock sprang open with a deep, satisfying clunk.

And then it seemed a miracle was about to happen. "Oh, Annie, come here to me," she said. She held out her arms, and I moved into them, rested my head on her shoulder while she stroked my hair. Her perfume was the same she'd always worn, and the feel of her neck. Maybe we will cry instead of laugh, I thought, the way we did when we found the dove at the bottom of Papa's freezer— the ones she'd plucked for him when they still loved one another. Crying would be good, I thought, because Papa was dead, and Matthew. And yet, even dead, they were not safe; they went on changing until it seemed that I lost them now, every time I found them again. My father had been married to my mother for thirty-five years, and for at least fifteen of those years he had slept with Thelma Radford and provided for her; he'd arranged to go on providing for her after he was gone. And what would have become of Matthew and me? I could no longer believe in the future we might have found together, or that the way we'd lived was the best life I would ever live. Let's cry, Mother, I thought. Let's wail for all that, and for you, and for how hard you worked all those years to hold onto your dignity.

"Sweetie," she said, patting my back, "we're all in need, I know that. We all have our appetites."

Appetites. I pushed away from her. The word had a fulsome sound, like the name of something damp and rotten that Miss Annie

Vess might find in the cellar on a hot, August night, after tracking an odor down into the darkest corner there. Is that what I had? Appetites? Is that what had made me press my body against Canady's body and want to crawl into the back seat with him, forgetting all I'd ever known about loyalty or love? No. What I'd wanted was to prove that there was no such thing as loyalty or love, to celebrate this discovery with someone. I wanted someone to spend this inheritance with me, someone to give it to, as though it were my virginity I were losing all over again. "I guess it runs in the family," I said.

But she didn't hear. A breeze had come up; it stirred the hot air around us. She lifted her face to the sky and sighed. "If only Papa were here," she said, "or Matthew—"

"Yes," I said, quickly. but not quickly enough to stop her from saying Matthew's name, calling him, and setting him moving toward me across the dark water.

"—this never would have happened."

"Who knows what would have happened, Mother?" I said. "How can either of us say what might have happened?" Then I stopped. What she'd said was not a question, nor an invitation to talk. It was a lesson, taken from the same book of lessons where you found *congratulate the groom and compliment the bride*. Lessons in how to live in a make-believe world of appearances, a world of graciousness and beauty and truth. That's your kind of innocence, Mother, I thought. But not mine, not any longer.

"I want to ask you something, Mother."

"Yes, what is it?" she said, standing tall and regal, hands folded.

"What did Papa do when Matthew died?"

For a moment she looked like someone walking into a dark room, feeling for the light switch. "What do you mean, 'What did he do?' " she asked. Her attention rested on me now, fully, warily.

"Did he talk about coming to Pennsylvania? Did he make lots of mistakes at work?"

She drew herself up. "I don't know what you're talking about, and neither do you. That's utter foolishness. Who told you that?"

"Thelma Radford," I said.

For one glittering, spiraling second, I thought she might hit me. Her face was terrible, her hand was raised to do it as I reached for her and said, "Mother, God, I'm sorry, don't listen to me." Then she held it up to stop me from coming any closer, and just like that, the turbulence was gone. She began to compose herself again as though she'd spilled herself and was picking up now: hands folded, smile back in place, hair tucked up, dress straight. Now Mrs. John Vess of Timmons—Queenie—was back. I have watched this for years, I thought, and I have not known what I was seeing. This slow, sad climb into that formal room where she could go and close the door, where her life became an occasion, and she, the hostess, presiding over it.

"You went to her house?" she said briskly, in the voice I'd heard on the telephone these past few weeks, checking with the florist, checking with the caterer. Just checking.

"Yes," I said, and I looked at the asphalt under my feet; it was soft and my feet stuck to it and came away with a peeling sound.

"What's it like?" Her voice sharp as wire, piercing.

"What?"

"Her house, Annie." She stamped her foot.

"*Mother.*"

"Well," she said, defiant now, "you brought it up."

"That's true." Why not tell her? I thought. For years, without ever stepping through the door, she'd been a guest in Thelma's house. She'd visited every room, sat in every chair; she'd lain in the bed, listening. "The bathroom's pink," I said.

"*Pink?*" A triumphant look, full of malice, flashed across her face.

"Pink."

"Of course," she said, serene in triumph. "It would be." Then she hurried on. "You know, John was over there the night he died. I don't even know what time he came in."

"Mother, how can you say that? How do you know?" I said wildly. The words went around and around in my mind, echoing the question I'd asked her on that dreamlike morning when she'd called and told me he was dead. *He's not moving,* she'd said. *He's not breathing.*

[238]

How can you be sure? I'd asked, trying to make a crack in the wall of dark knowledge that rose over us, a crack through which hope might flood, like light. "How do you know?" I asked now.

"You and your questions," she said, but she might as easily have said, "Pass the mints" or "Today is Saturday." Her eyes were clear and mild again. "When you were little, you just about drove me crazy with your questions. One time I forbade you to ask me 'why' for one whole day."

"No, you didn't," I said quickly. But I felt the sadness coming, settling into me the way the last light was fading into the lake.

"Oh, I always knew when he'd been over there. I could smell it on his clothes," she said. "She'd cook him pork chops and gravy. She gave him cream in his coffee. I know she did. She fed him whatever Dr. Mac said was bad his heart. I guess she thought she was pampering him, but she was killing him. I kept a list of the things he couldn't eat posted on the refrigerator, and we ate according to that list."

"I didn't know, I had no idea, Mother," I said. "I had no idea."

"No, you didn't," she said. "You children were always blind about your father."

"It seems to me that you were the blind one, Mother," I said.

"Does it?" she said, but I had no heart for this, only a long habit of opposition. Talk to me, scream at me, I wanted to say. Scream at *her*. Haul up the worst words you know—whore, cunt, words I would be shocked to learn that you know—and throw them at her. And I will ask you only how you kept from saying them all those years, how you got through those nights.

She checked her watch, held it up to her ear. "Anything else you want to know?" she said, her eyes angry, her mouth grim.

"Yes," I said, and I felt my eyes filling with tears. "Why didn't you divorce him, Mother?"

"*Divorce* him?" she said, as though the words were repugnant to her. At least I've given you something, I said to myself, at least I've given you something to rally around. "I did not *divorce* him because our generation took its marriage vows seriously."

And then I was moving again. My hands were on the keys, the

key in the lock, and anger pushed its way through my veins like thick, black blood. "No, Mother," I said, "you keep that story, don't tell it to me."

"Fine," she said. "Why don't you go home now? You are no longer invited to my party."

And she started back toward the clubhouse, walking fast, her back straight, the chiffon lapping around her. From the clubhouse I heard laughter, then applause, then she disappeared around the corner of the building and I heard her voice, vehement, commanding. "Now where are *you* going?" she said. "No one leaves my party until at least midnight."

I twisted the key so hard I thought it might break off in the ignition switch, and I drove out of the parking lot and onto the road. And then I was winding through the streets of Planter's Landing, past the dark, half-finished houses and onto Longman's Ridge Road, and down the Devil's Backbone Road. The road was deserted, the moon high, and so full, the shadows of trees fell across the road. I didn't realize until a car finally passed in the opposite direction and flashed its lights that I was driving without headlights, driving blind, just the way my mother had said it had always been.

Blind

Midnight, and I was on my way. At Mother's house, I'd gotten restless, I didn't want to be there when she came home. So I'd put the dogs in the car for company and started driving. First, I drove around town, but it made me feel sad to pass the end of Legree's driveway time after time, look down the avenue of magnolias, and find his windows dark. Besides, town was full of lights. Headlights and streetlights and porchlights and lights that still burned in the back rooms of houses, as though someone were expected home. What I wanted was dark and I knew where to find it. I needed no maps to show me the way. Out through the Southland Timber Company land and past White's Mill, where the dry millrace gleamed white as bone. When I came to the sign that read "Givens-Reeves Wedding," and the arrow that pointed down the narrow blacktop road, I cut the headlights and drove by the thin light of the new moon that hung above the pines. All night, the sky had been clearing, as though a broom had swept the clouds away, and now the center line flashed like a series of dashes, and the black pines massed on either side of the road. Then the lake appeared at the end of the road, silver and calm, and the bridal boat that had been brought back across the lake and floated there, its white satin ribbons trailing in the water. When I pulled into the parking lot and switched off the headlights, the muggy dark closed in, and all of a sudden I was very tired again, as though I'd come a long way and could rest now. I closed my eyes and rested my head against the back of the seat, while Napoleon whined and tried to force his head over my shoulder and out of the window to smell the wind in this new place.

Blind, Mother said. We were blind. She said it with malice, triumphantly. Our blindness pleased her, I think—a secret, bitter pleasure that came from watching Davis and me believe in Papa while she knew the truth all those years. From someplace above us all, she must have pitied our ignorance and nursed the cold fire of that superiority until it gave off what felt like warmth. Or maybe superiority was what her hurt turned into, when to go on feeling the hurt might have destroyed her. There is a necessary alchemy to people's lives that will not allow us to see ourselves as small or beaten, that gilds our strategies for survival with brighter names. So Mother's hurt turned to a faith in her own higher integrity, into pity and contempt for my father's bankrupt character and our own blind faith in him. What sad, lonely power it was that required our ignorance to survive. But I was no longer ignorant; I had said Thelma's name and let loose the sorrow again. And now the sadness of my mother's life seemed as wide as this lake I was about to go onto: blind, and wanting to be blinder.

The road I had followed to this place had once been the road to Little Awando. Now it ran into the lake and disappeared. I wanted to follow that road to a place where I would see nothing but night, hear nothing but water, remember no touch, no desire, no hurt or betrayal. Where I would forget the feel of Canady's body, the desolation on Mel's face as she'd looked from Canady to me and back to him. The hurt, vengeful look on my mother's face as she'd raised her hand to slap me when I'd said the name that she'd kept locked up in a black box inside her for so long. Thelma Radford. Where I could be without shame or apologies, the virgin that Legree had named me before he went out through the Steakhouse door and did not come back. My father was wrong to wish that the lake had not come and filled up this place. Water is good, it dissolves things and it washes away sins. You go down into it and come up clean.

The dogs tumbled out of the car, and while they ran around with their noses to the ground, I took off my shoes and waded out toward the boat. The surface felt warm, but just below the surface the cold began, as though the sun had not touched it. I felt water soak into my hem as I waded out, and the bottom of my skirt swirled heavily around my calves. Wading out to the boat was the hard part; the satin came down easily. Mother had sewn and gathered the cloth in long, loping stitches that pulled loose as though they were never meant to hold. I worked my way around the boat, pulling out the threads as sheets of cold satin tumbled into my arms. When I had it all, I waded back to shore and folded and stacked it beside my shoes. Then I unlocked the boat. The cable was looped around a concrete post and locked with a padlock, but I had the key to the lock and the key to the boat. I looked at the keys in my hand. In another life, it seemed, it had been my job to return those keys in the morning to the marina where Mother had rented the boat.

Far away across the water, light spilled from the windows of the ballroom at Planter's Landing, where Mother had gone back to the fairyland she'd made, where Canady was still a faithful husband, where people complimented Mel on her beauty and wished her happiness, and did not congratulate her on her marriage. As I listened, a commotion of horns began. No doubt Mel and Canady were leaving on their honeymoon in Canady's silver Mercedes, tin cans and rubbers tied to the bumpers, while some people threw rice, and other people danced in the ballroom at Mother's command. But I was on the other shore and the boat was what it had always been—an ugly, square, gray boat with a corrugated roof held up by wrought-iron posts.

"Sit," I said to the dogs. Instantly Jo obeyed, but Napoleon grinned and stretched, then looked up at me hopefully. After all these years, you still have to push on his behind to make him sit. When that was done, I waded back out to the boat and lifted the anchor on to the front deck. "All right, dogs," I said, and I clapped my hands. "Come!" The sound was sharp but it disappeared instantly, as though the air had sucked it up. Jo hesitated and then she walked into the water and jumped onto the boat, through the gate I'd opened in the side railing. Napoleon started after her, but at the edge of the water he stopped, whining and shifting his feet nervously, so I waded back for him. But when I grabbed him, he pulled back in a panic. His collar slipped over his head and he took off running across the parking lot toward the picnic shelter, yelping as though he'd been shot.

"Stop that racket, Napoleon!" I yelled. "Come back here!" But he scuttled along with his backside close to the ground and disappeared into the pines beyond the picnic shelter. For awhile I heard him blundering through the woods, and then the yelping and crashing stopped, and it was quiet again; so quiet I heard the small waves wash the shore and slap the boat's pontoons. Then, from back in the woods, Napoleon began to howl. The sound started high then wavered down a minor scale until it bottomed out in a hoarse, round moan and every animal sorrow was in it—something hollow and old and round as the blue earth spinning through the dark blue air. Something human was in it, too, as if he were howling for everything that had ever been lost. "Napoleon," I yelled, and when he kept on howling, I yelled after him: "Stupid fool!"

"Fool," the echo came back. I liked the sound of it so I said it again. "Fool," and I threw his collar up onto the shore and waded back to the boat while Jo watched from the deck, calm and alert. I took her muzzle in my hand and laid my cheek down on it. "You too, Jo," I said. "Me too. We're all fools." I scratched the top of her head. "Let's go."

The engine bubbled deeply when I turned the key, and then it caught and I could not hear Napoleon any longer over the noise. I swung the wheel hard, pointed the boat toward the center of the lake, and pushed the throttle wide open. When I looked back toward shore, I saw my shoes and the pile of satin and Napoleon's collar at the edge of the water, and I had to laugh. What kind of clues would those make? Say the boat sank in deep water, too far from shore for swimming, and then the searchers would come and find the car and the boat cable, and on the boat ramp a dog collar and a pair of high-heeled satin shoes, a pile of white satin and ribbons and old flowers. Mother would come, of course. We'd had an argument, she'd say. Oh, God, why did we argue? And around this pile of discarded things, she might build scene after scene in which I had forgiven her. Why else, she would demand to know, would she have folded all that satin? Why would she do that if she hadn't wanted me to know that she forgave me?

Everytime I looked up I saw the lights at Planter's Landing, and once, when the breeze blew toward the boat from land, I thought I heard music and knew that I had not gone far enough. I needed a cove, some blind corner where there was nothing but night and water, where I was nowhere, and nothing could touch me but the hollow smack of water against the pontoons and the sound of the breeze in the tops of the pines. It was out there, I could feel it, the darkest place on the lake. Jo seemed to smell it, too. Nose in the air, she sniffed the wind. At last I steered the boat into a cove, and Planter's Landing was gone. It was darker here, the dark like a sponge blotting up even the dark of the pines on the shore, as though they were being taken back into the dark from which they came. As though there were no place where they stopped and the darkness began. I cut the engine and let the boat drift. Jo came and rested her chin on my knee. I put my hand on her head, propped my feet up on the boat railing, and spread my wet skirt over my legs. It felt cold and heavy against my skin. "Now, Jo," I said. "Here we are." She lifted her head and looked at me alertly, the old hunting dog waiting for the next command. How many times had I seen her look at my father that way? But I would not think of that now. *Now I am nowhere*, I thought. Out of sight, out of hearing, out of reach. No one on earth knows where I am.

Then I looked up and saw Pegasus rising in the east, clearing the trees on the far shore, and just like that, as though Matthew were riding on the back of that constellation, I remembered the night we met, how Matthew and I had watched that great, winged horse climb the sky. Before it had dissolved into the oncoming morning, we'd claimed it as our own. One summer, when Matthew had gone to Cheraw, I walked outside of our house in Pennsylvania and found Pegasus, flying, and imagined that Matthew might be looking up, too, from the rise just past the pond in the cow pasture. This was the place where he went early and often when he was home, as though from that one place on earth, he could make sense of all others. Now the horse galloped up the eastern sky, beginning its summer transit, and overhead I found the lion, Leo. Before there were maps there were stars, and people steered by them, grouped and named them, like stepping-stones across the wide sky. Out at the Laughing Place, on a summer night just like this one, we had first seen the lion prowl across the top of the sky, past my father's pointing finger. Sickled curve of head and flowing mane and hind-quarters and bright tip of tail. ("There," he'd said. "Follow my fin-ger, look right where I'm pointing.")

I leaned on the wheel and put my hands over my face, and they were cold, startling, as though they belonged to someone else. In the bow, Jo growled then yipped once, a sharp, piercing sound. I took my hands down from my face. "Quiet, Jo," I said. "I told you to hush. Now lie down and hush." But she whined again, and I looked across the lake where she was staring. Way off near the shore, something white moved on the water, like the track of the moon swimming up the lake. Jo yipped and an answer came back—another yip—and I saw that it was Napoleon, out there in all that water, swimming for the boat. "Go back, you imbecile," I yelled to the white swimming head. Any minute now, I thought, he will turn back, and fear kicked at my heart when I saw the distance he was trying to cross. Already he was too far from shore to turn back, too far from the boat to reach it. He would drown before he got here, swimming his stupid head off until his heart quit or his legs gave out and he sank into the cold at the bottom of the lake and turned into one more drifting huddle of bones down there in the dark where the water got into everything. Why not let him die, I thought, an old idiot dog without the sense to stay on shore, who only knew he'd been left behind and started swimming? Let him go under once and for all, and be forgotten.

And then I remembered Napoleon as I'd first seen him: new-born, blind, and wet in the whelping box at the colonel's. Climbing, tunneling, swimming through the other pups, he'd driven into his mother's side and grasped the nipple and pulled so hard she'd closed her eyes and grunted. Papa and the colonel stood over the box with their flashlights trained on Napoleon, while tension collected in the spring air as thick as the bloody-smelling steam that rose from the litter of newborn pups. Snaky body and swampy back, misshapen skull and outsize knee joints and webby feet, the flashlight beam found every flaw.

"Look at that little devil go," Papa said.

"That's not a *dog*," the colonel said. "That's a goddamn salamander."

"Damnedest thing I ever saw," Papa said, reaching for his machete.

I had crouched there beside the newborn pups, afraid to look up into my father's face or the colonel's, breathing in the smell of blood-soaked newspaper, listening to the sound of the bitch's exhausted grunts as the pups kept up their ferocious nursing. I knew the rules. A freak born to a purebred dog must be destroyed before it ruined the bloodline. But it was April. Matthew and I had been married since December, and there was tenderness in me like a new soul, heavy and sweet, that flowed out to every living thing. I had reached in and stroked Napoleon's damp head and tiny, clean ears, and I felt his entire body consumed with sucking, felt the gulps go through him as though his whole body were a throat and the world, milk.

I do not remember why they let him live. Pride, my father said later. Plain old hubris. Or maybe I had claimed him after all, out of the fullness of my love for Matthew, the promise of the life we had started. Whatever it was, their flashlights went out, the tension left their voices. "What the hell," my father said. "We can always sell him to the circus." So Napoleon had eluded them and their plans for perfection, and now he came on through the water. He was not just an old dog; even drowned, he would not be lost. Whenever I looked at the lake, I would remember. Just as when I walked out under the sky, I thought of my father. Or passed a persimmon tree and saw Matthew's smile. Why do the dead go and leave themselves scattered around the world? Why don't they take every memory with them? Why don't they return, full of mercy, while the living sleep and pluck memories one by one from the minds and hearts of those who loved them on earth instead of showing up in the stars and the wind, in the taste of peaches or the look of a back disappearing around a corner? Why doesn't death mean complete silence, utter absence for the living as well as the dead? It seemed a kind of cruelty that nothing on this earth can finally be lost, nor will it rest. It will disperse, dissolve, cling, come back in the stars and weather and seasons and times of day, in gestures and in the slant of light through trees, until the whole world echoes with reminders of the habits and loves and failures of those we have loved.

The motor turned over with a deep blurting bubble, then died. I ran to the stern, to the engine, and heard my footsteps echoing between the pontoons and out across the lake. Napoleon yelped again, a sound as clean and high and joyful as when he was off on one of his idiotic chases. I squeezed the bulb in the gas line hard, twice, and ran back to the wheel and turned the key, turned it again. The motor caught and I swung the bow toward Napoleon's swimming head and shoved the throttle wide open. But this was no speedboat. It sat back deeper in the water and churned along at a maddening pace as I stood on tiptoe behind the wheel, ducking and leaning as if the dark were something I could see around, trying to keep his head in sight. Each time his head went under, my heart stopped and my hands would not unfasten from around the wheel. Each time the boat seemed to slow or stall, and I felt the cold rise from the bottom of the lake, then his head popped back up and the boat moved forward again, while Jo leaned out through the front railing and whined. Then I could see him plainly. He swam with his head high and the whites of his eyes showing, his legs churning the water as though he were trying to climb out of it up a ladder.

I'd meant to cut the engine and turn the wheel so that the boat drifted close to him slowly and I could reach out and snag him. But I misjudged, and when I cut the engine the boat shot by him too fast. As we came alongside him, I opened the gate in the side railing and knelt in the opening; I grabbed for the loose skin of his neck but caught his ear instead, and saw fear in his eyes. As his ear slipped out of my hand, he climbed toward the sky, his legs churning the water to froth. I brought the boat in a wide, slow circle back around toward Napoleon, but as I circled he tried to follow the boat, and then he went under. I headed for the place he'd gone down, kept my eyes on it. I would have jumped after him, but his head broke the surface, he was gasping and wheezing; the boat glided toward him, and then I was down on my hands and knees again. I knelt on my dress and felt the waist rip, and suddenly Napoleon was right beside the boat, clawing at the pontoons, pushing the boat away, the whites of his eyes shining in the dark. I began talking to him as quietly as I could. "Napoleon," I said, "here, now, calm down. It's all right." And I think he heard, because he stopped thrashing, and I reached down and grabbed the loose skin on the back of his neck and held on. He came up swimming, his legs still climbing the air, and I hauled him onto the deck and knelt beside him while he trembled and panted and twisted around to lick my face, making a joyful, whining noise deep in his throat.

"You idiot, you stupid idiot." I spoke to him in the same voice I'd used to quiet him in the water until the trembling stopped. I wrapped my arms around him and held him while the water from his coat soaked through my dress and I felt his foolish dog heart pounding. I laid my cheek down on his back, onto the short, wet coat that I had touched the hour he was born, while Papa was alive and I was married to Matthew, and I cried until it felt as though, for now, I'd emptied myself of sadness. Then I turned the wheel and started for shore.

Scrabble

Friday night was Scrabble night. It was nothing Mother and I had talked about or agreed on; it had just evolved, like so many of our routines. We always played in the dining room and we each had our jobs. Mother's was to fold out the Scrabble board and set it on the lazy Susan in the middle of the table, pour the letter tiles into the top of the Scrabble game box, and turn them all facedown. My job was to fix the drinks. Which is what we were doing when I opened the doors in the sideboard and found the shelves and the drawers empty. The silver tray and tea set that once sat on top of the sideboard under the mirror were gone, and so were the silver candlesticks that had stood to either side of the tea set. Now only the Vesses were left, staring down their long, thin noses out of their dark, cracked portraits, as disappointed as ever in the way things had turned out.

"Where's the jigger?" I asked.

"Up in the attic with everything else that needs polishing," she said, and the Scrabble tiles kept up their steady *click, click, click* as she turned them.

That was the end of *that* conversation. Short and to the point. No feelings wasted. In the week since the wedding, our words to each other had all been like glancing blows: a question, a statement,

and then the skeletal reply. Without the spread of conversation to
cushion the words, you realize how bare a thing human speech can
be.

"I won't be home for supper."

"That's fine."

"I'm going to the store."

"We need milk."

She left every morning before I got up and came back after
supper, and if I'd kept a plate of food warm in the oven for her,
she said she'd already eaten and scraped it into the garbage can.

Late at night, she cleaned. *Uncluttering* she called it, *setting her
house to rights.* She did it with a vengeance, which in most cases is
a figure of speech but in this case describes the pungency of the
force that drove her. Vengeance in the set of her mouth, in her
eyes, as she packed the Vess silver and carried it up to the attic,
still in grandmother Vess's mahogany boxes lined with worn green
velvet slots in the shapes of knives, forks, spoons. "The whole kit
and caboodle," she crowed. Now, what was left in the silverware
drawer was a set of stainless steel and some mismatched silver serving
pieces. Stainless steel got the food to your mouth just fine, she said,
and it never needed polishing. Besides, she was tired of looking at
all those flowery V's on the handles of her knives and forks whenever
she cut her meat or lifted a forkful of rice to her mouth. Everytime
she looked at those initials, she remembered how much better the
Vesses thought they were than anybody else. Well, she was through
with that now, through with *them.* Of course, she means my father,
I thought. She believes she can purge herself of him by putting his
things out of sight. She has forgotten about the inner sight, the
heart's eye, which will go on seeing him everywhere.

I went to the kitchen and mixed the drinks in two jelly-jar
glasses, and when I came back she was standing by the open window,
looking out at the light rain that shushed and pattered down through
the pine needles and oak leaves. "Raining," she said, "why does it
always rain on the weekends?" She folded her arms and looked out
into the gray twilight, the soft rain, the blur of pines behind the
rain. She still wore the black slacks and white blouse with the

floppy bow that were part of the pantsuit she'd worn to work that morning, though she'd taken off the jacket and shoes, put on her pale blue scuffs, and pulled her shirttail out to get comfortable for the game.

Watching her, I imagined that I saw Mother now, in this place, looking out at this night and rain, and Mother a long time ago. I pictured the path that ran between the person she'd been then and the person she'd become, and it was as if I were looking at one of those time-lapse photographs that show a star surrounded by the tracings of its revolutions through space, or a flower unfolding petal by petal from around its center.

On one end was Mrs. John Vess of Timmons with her Joy perfume, her good wool coats and low-heeled pumps and pearls, her volunteer days at the hospital. Her seat on the county historical commission, her seat in the front of the courtroom when Papa argued an important case, her seat at one end of the table in this room, covered with its heavy Vess linen and set with Vess silver, presiding over holiday dinners through all those years of Thelma Radford and my father's innocence. A person of dignity, who had worn no makeup to my father's funeral, who had refused Deke Taylor's arm and led the way toward the bright blue tent, who'd packed up the Vess silver and let her mind and heart go their own way. And as I watched and thought of her walking that long path of years, I got a sense of the will, the strength, and the intelligence it had taken to walk it, the instinct for survival that had brought her all this way. And now, what if what she was doing was not revenge at all, but her own way of letting go, moving on? Because the truth of any life is how it changes. And if that is so, then how frail and transient are the certainties on which we base our lives.

When Mother won twenty-two points by placing the F in her first word, F-A-K-E, on the double-word score star in the middle of the board, she sat back smiling and took a big pull on her drink. Then she spun the lazy Susan so fast I thought the letters might fly off the board. "Your turn," she sang out.

Nothing in the world makes Mother happier than beating me

or Davis at Scrabble. Her eyes brim with happiness, her mouth barely holds back a mocking smile. Her hands snap down the tiles with marvelous precision. Winning seems to prove something to her, something she might forget about herself if beating us at Scrabble didn't constantly remind her. *I never finished college,* she seems to say, *and I can still beat the two of you with one hand tied behind my back!*

I suppose Mother's fierceness came from the days when Davis and I teased her about being from Georgia. Somehow over the years, we had purged ourselves of her Georgia blood, which, like gravity, would have held us close to the ground, and we soared into the pure upper air of South Carolina. Somewhere along the line, we became South Carolinians. Not just by birth—anyone could do that—but by some process like an anointing, we became superior in all ways. Heirs, not just to an old name and good cheekbones, but to heads full of heights from which to look down on the rest of the world. We made fun of Mother's drawl, the way she pronounced certain words as if they were mush in her mouth. "Say *library,* Mother."

"Lie-berry."

"Say *diaper.*"

"Die-a-per."

"Say *nice white rice.*"

"Nas what ras."

Going to school only made us more articulate in our judgments: "Georgia was originally a penal colony," Davis informed us one night at supper when we were discussing Lester Maddox's election as governor of that state. "What do you expect of criminals? Brilliance?"

I added an R to the end of her F-A-K-E. She looked at me scornfully, her bottom lip drooping. "Well," she said. "That was easy."

We played silently for the next few turns. She made R-O-A-M and S-A-C-K, and I made F-O-B and S-T-E-W, and the rain came down steadily and softly outside the window, filling the room with the smell of grass and wet pine needles. When I finally added it up,

Mother was ahead by three points. For her next word, she made M-A-L-E, and when my turn came I used the final E of her word to make my own: M-O-L-E. That struck us both as hilarious, and every time we'd just about laughed ourselves out, one of us would say "male mole" again, fast, running it together, and we'd break out laughing again. And it was after one of those bouts of laughing that she pulled her glasses down onto the end of her nose and keeping her finger on the nosepiece, looked around the room brightly. "Annie," she said, still laughing. "That job's opened back up at Lonnie Graves's office. Where's this morning's paper?"

"In the trash," I said, matching my voice to hers. "Don't distract me remember?" In the course of these Friday night games, we'd added our own rules to the list printed on the inside of the box top, and we kept our own as strictly as if they were official. No talking during the other's turn. Challenge a word and lose, you forfeit two turns, not just one. We'd lived by those rules since I'd come home. Rules and promises and rituals. On Sunday mornings, when she wandered down into the kitchen and back up the stairs to her bedroom as though she couldn't remember why she'd come down, I'd take coffee up to her room and sit on the edge of her bed and look through wallpaper sample books or Sherwin-Williams paint cards with her. Sometimes, during the week, she'd call in the middle of the afternoon from the tax assessor's office to find out what I'd especially like to have for supper. Or she wouldn't call, but she would stop at the fish market on the way home from work on a Tuesday or a Thursday—days when trucks came up from the coast loaded with shrimp, mullet, oysters in season. She'd pick up a pound of fresh shrimp that we'd boil with peppercorns and bay leaves, then dip in horseraddish sauce so pungent the first taste burned all the way up the backs of our noses and brought tears to our eyes.

I took a sip of my drink and set it back down.

Now she reached across the table, moved the glass into the coaster, and wiped away the ring. "I won't distract you," she said. "I just want to know if you saw it."

"I saw it," I said. When I looked up, she was watching me. It seemed like the first time we'd looked each other in the eye since the wedding, and we both seemed startled to see each other, like two people who've rounded the same corner and found themselves suddenly face-to-face.

"Now just look at those words you've made," she said. "*Fob, stew, mole.* Davis would surely find something Froodian there, wouldn't he "

"Look at your own," I said. "*Sack, web, male, roam.* It's pronounced *Froidian,* Mother, by the way," I said, sipping my drink.

"Froodian, Froidian, what's the difference? He didn't know what he was talking about, anyway," she said. "A lot of those psychologists are way off-base, let me tell you."

"There's plenty of difference between Froodian and Froidian," I said. I felt like crying then, I don't know why. A feeling welled up in me that I'd felt all my life, a childish tangle of frustration and rage and sadness at her stubborn pride in her own ignorance.

"Oh, fiddle," she said, waving her hand as though she were waving away smoke.

I studied my letters and considered the drift of this conversation. We were heading someplace familiar and dangerous, I knew that much. We were going there like passengers on a boat in the grip rapids while the sound of the falls grew louder by the minute. Only in this case, the sound was the mounting roar of Mother's plans for me, or worse, her hopes. Another's *plans* for us are practical, brisk, easily thwarted. Their *hopes* are more intimate and sinister, rooted in their imaginings about our inner lives, our longings. To hear someone's hopes for you is to hear their vision of the state of your soul. I had to stop her. Once she'd unfolded her plans, revealed her hopes, I'd have to refuse them because the more I became her project, the less I seemed my own. Then I would be all stubborn resistance again as I'd been as a teenager, buying ugly clothes, slouching around this house, refusing to go to parties that I really wanted to go to, all because she wanted me to dress well and stand up straight and be invited to the right places. I thought of Miss Jenny in her glider, and I felt the first brushings of the wings of panic in my chest, felt my hands grow clammy as the longing rose within me to make myself so small or deformed, I would not fit into any of Mother's plans.

N-E-T won me five points, and I got another four for making

N-O across the O in F-O-B. I took a long gulp of my drink. "N-E-T and N-O. Nine points. Your turn." I heard her sigh but I looked down. "To answer your question, Mother," I said, "I'm not calling Lonnie Graves about that job. In fact, I hope not to speak to Lonnie Graves about anything ever again."

"Well, now, what's wrong with Lonnie Graves, please tell me?" She took off her glasses, folded the stems, and set them down on the table. Then she gave a little cry of pain, as if something had stung her, and covered her face with her hands. I felt the old fury boil up in me at the sound of Mother weeping, as bitterly as if by rejecting Lonnie Graves I'd rejected her too, and broken her heart. Fury at the ease with which she insinuates herself into the world so that I cannot move without betraying her somehow. The old fury. She'd get no sympathy from me for that pain. And then, as though she'd decided something, she took her hands away from her face and picked up her glasses. Just as quickly, the fight went out of me, as suddenly and as physically as if I'd misjudged a step and tumbled off into thin air.

I saw us sitting at this same table, hundreds of Scrabble games along into a future in which our quarrels were no longer separate, hard chips of argument about particular things. Ham or chicken for dinner? Green or blue for the downstairs bathroom? Did Papa win that Loudermilk murder case in 1963 or 1964? What did Thelma Radford do with all that money? Instead those subjects would have all dissolved into the Big Quarrel. It had no subject, it had no end, it had become the atmosphere we lived in, the air we breathed, that circulated around and through every question and charged every word. And nothing would keep this life from being anything more than an accumulation of days and years and quarrels with Mother, anymore than someone was going to stop Miss Jenny Hanks's glider and tell her to stand on her own two feet. I could live here until I died and it would still be Mother's house, Mother's life. And there was no prize, nothing she could give up that would make me any stronger or surer or better. Nothing I could add to myself, because I'd wrestled it out of her hands.

She fiddled with the bow of her blouse and color crept up her neck, but when she spoke her voice sounded tired. "Well, if that doesn't suit you, Mrs. Vanderbilt?" she said. "Mel's going to need someone to help her with that decorating business. Of course, you'd have to get some training or something. I don't think that's something you can just up and do. And, of course, you'd have to make up to her for that business at the wedding." I couldn't let her go on talking like that, with the eager look on her face and the dream in her eyes. Mel and I knee-deep in forgiveness and fabric samples and money, traipsing through the condominiums at Planter's Landing like good fairies, while Canady watched over us and indulged us, granting our wishes as though we were pretty children playing at our lives.

"Mother," I said, "look, I went to see Pug Simmons the other day."

"What about?" she said, without looking up as she picked up one letter tile, then another, and peeked underneath and checked her score.

"I asked him if he'd give me a job on the paper."

"And what did he say?" The tiles moved more slowly now.

"He said yes." And that, incredibly, is just how it had happened. I'd sat in Pug's office and asked him for a job, and without hesitation he'd said, "Can you start Monday?" As I stood outside the *Courier Tribune* office, employed and blinking in the sun, I understood again how easy it must have been for Charles Hartley to tell my father about the lake. Relationships here make certain actions inevitable. Pug's family had known my family for so long, we were almost kin, and when I came to him asking for help, he did for me what one member of a family would do for another: He gave what he had.

"Oh, Lord," she said, looking at me now and shaking her head sadly, mournfully, as if she were *sorry* for me.

And just like that, the old, trapped feeling was back, the same feeling I got whenever I arrived at a place I thought I'd discovered, but found Mother there, waiting. I looked at the Vesses, the wall sconces, and the fans of dingy yellow light they threw. And I knew that the longer I stayed here, the smaller this place would become. I had to make a door, or a tunnel, a window, some way out. "And Mother," I said, "I'm going to look for a place of my own to live."

We stared at each other, mouths open. I couldn't believe what

I'd said. I'd just closed my eyes and jumped. Sometimes, throwing the words ahead of you and then following where they lead is the only way to move. Didn't Matthew and I know all about reckless beginnings? But this was my beginning, without Matthew or Papa or Legree, without anyone to lead the way.

"Oh, for heaven's sake," she said, and she pushed back from the table and fled for the kitchen. I heard her scuffs, muffled on the hall runner, slapping on the kitchen linoleum.

When she came back, her eyes were red but her face was composed. She held her head high, and as she walked back to her seat, she touched the back of each chair at the dining room table, wistfully, the way I'd seen her do in a store: *Can I afford this?* But when she sat down again, she was all business. She handed me a paper towel. "When did this decision come about?" she said in her competent head administrator's voice, her pencil poised over the scorepad where our totals were written.

"I take it back, Mother," I almost said. "I didn't mean it. I'll be Lonnie Graves's gal Friday. I'll get my fresh air every day and join the Jaycettes and dress in primary colors and look stiff as a grenadier—and smile till my face aches. I'll be whatever anyone wants me to be. Just let me stay here with you. We'll mourn our losses and hold on to each other for dear life. We'll talk about Papa and Matthew, make shrines for them with our stories, where they can live safely forever." But it was too late for that. There was Thelma Radford, and I'd told Mother I was going to find myself a place of my own, and now we had nothing to say. Where would we begin? With so many words crowding in, which could you choose, and what would happen if once you began and let them all loose? Who would they hurt as they fell? Where would they settle? They might roll into corners and under tables and spoil there, giving off smells that no one could trace after a while. It was easier for us to talk when my father was alive, when I was married to Matthew, when they were newly dead and still safe in my memory, and I was coming home to Mother's house. Those were surer times, stories we knew, but time rows away, rows away fast from any certainty. I blew my nose, aimed the towel at the garbage can in the corner of the room, and tossed. It bounced off the rim and fell onto the floor.

"How many times have I asked you not to do that?" Mother wiped her eyes and stuffed her paper towel down into her glass.

"At least three thousand."

"Well," she said as she toasted the Vesses with her empty glass, "I'm hereby giving notice that I'm tired of pushing everybody and correcting them and trying to make them do right all the time. You can make your own decisions. I'm thinking about selling this place anyway. Canady's already said that he'd give me a good deal on a condo out at Planter's Landing."

Well, I thought, that seemed right. Let her sell the house, I thought. It's her house to sell. Let her decorate a condo just the way she wants it on the site of my father's betrayal of her. The circle would at last be unbroken. "That's a good idea, Mother," I said. "You'd never be able to do this house like you want it."

"Too many memories," she said, looking around the room.

"That's true."

That said, she looked at me sadly. "Annie," she said, "I do not know what you want, but I genuinely hope you find it."

She said it as though we'd never see each other again, and I had the craziest urge then to tell her what I wanted, what I knew. That life cannot be lived as a series of blows to be avoided, as a self-pitying canceling out of possibilities. That if you make yourself up out of refusals and rebellions, you turn into a ghost, all absence. That grief is the love that persists for what is lost or failed or broken. And I did want something. It occurred to me then what I wanted.

I went back in Papa's study and stood in the middle of the room in the dark. The easy chair was gone, along with the pipestand. The closet was empty, everything sold or gone to goodwill, only coat hangers hanging on the rod. The walls were bare now because I'd taken everything down, the sign from the Laughing Place, the charts. Even Papa's map was gone; it had been his way of making sense of his life, and I did not need that way any longer. I stood there quietly. Now I could hardly feel my father in that room, as if his presence were running like water back from where it came, the way the water had once rolled back from the shore of the ancient eastern ocean and left its mark forever in the rocks and the air and the wind.

When I went to the kitchen to rinse out my glass, my knees felt weak. The bourbon soared to the top of my head and swirled there in an amber galaxy full of stars and lightning. I let the water fill the glass and spill over the sides.

Mother came into the room. "I'm tired," she said, "and you're grown," as though she were getting in the last word in an argument.

I said, "Yes, I'm grown" with my back to her so that she couldn't see my face. Yes, no, it added up. A person chose one thing, refused another; her life took on direction from those choices. Then, once she'd chosen, she stood at the sink and watched the water spin down the drain and wondered what she would do when the last of it had disappeared. I've always believed that mothers possess a set of special senses tuned forever to the world and to their children, made for making one known to the other. That they held a globe in their hands with scenes of life suspended inside. When you came to them, needing to understand, they turned the globe one way to the light and continents came into view, surrounded by their oceans. They turned it another and the mainland appeared, its houses firmly anchored. But Mother was no longer outside holding this globe—no one was outside, ever. We were both inside; she would not lift and turn it until death and life rolled into view, their places revealed, their questions answered.

We went back to the dining room then, and I studied the board again. Q-M-T-P-I-H-O, my letter tiles read. What sort of word could I possibly make with those letters? No word in the English language, and I knew no other.

"So, when are you thinking of running off and leaving me?"

"Oh, Mother, for God's sake. Do you always have to put everything I do in the worst light?" That old tug-of-war. Whatever I said, she had to drag it over onto her territory before she could defeat it.

"I don't know why you have to emphasize everything with swearing," she said. "And with your education, too." The rouge had worn off her cheeks and her lipstick was faded. The bow on her blouse was coming untied. She had bullied me and I had hurt her, things were back to normal. "I wish you wouldn't be so bitter," Mother said. "I don't understand the hopelessness of your generation, you and Davis both." She shuddered, as if she were cold.

"Bitter is not what I am," I said. "Or hopeless, either."

"Oh," she said, and she looked around suddenly at the window, listening, the way she used to listen when Papa's car drove into the yard. Then she sat up again and pushed her glasses back up onto her nose. She looked weary, deflated, and the skin on her face seemed to have sagged till it hung on the bones. "How did you stand it all those years, Mother?" I almost said. "Tell me, and I will tell you about Canady and the lake, how dark it was there, how alone I felt." But we would need a new language to tell each other these things, words darker than the words we've spoken to each other all our lives. A language without words for love or loyalty or vows, a language that spoke of need and fear, of rage and hate and confusion and sorrow.

"Whose turn?" she said listlessly.

"Yours."

"I pass."

"No you don't," I said. "You're only ten points behind, and if you skip this turn I'm going to win for sure."

She sat up straight and tucked the pencil she'd used to keep score behind her ear, then smoothed down the bow on her blouse, brushing at it. "Well, I sure-bud don't want that to happen," she said.

The rain had stopped, though heavy, single drops still spattered onto the ground outside. From the den off the kitchen, Grandaddy Vess's clock struck ten. The wind picked up, clouds broke away in tattered clumps from around the stars, moving across the moon. And then the sky emerged, clear and full of sharp stars. This is the starting point, I thought. From here, the way leads out. I will never live in this house again. I could see a long way into the sky; it was hard to look at, the way it had been when I was a child and first tried to think about the vastness of the universe, a distance that could only be measured by something just as incomprehensible: the speed of light.

Finally she picked up a Scrabble letter and held it between her fingertips as if it were a tidbit of food, before she set it down. She picked up another one and positioned it the same way. Then she tidied the word, pushing it into line with her fingers. "Sometimes," she said, "your simplest words are your best bets," in the brisk voice she'd used when she'd taught me to iron or make beef stew: "Start with the collar first, then do your sleeves. That way, your blouse stays crisp and fresh." Tears came into my eyes. I looked at the board and saw that she'd made the word P-E-A, and because the P landed on a triple-letter square, the word added eleven points to her score. She'd won by a single point. She was humming now, happy. "The smaller the margin, the sweeter the victory," she always said. She won, and I didn't let her win because she is my mother. And there is nothing I can give her that doesn't already belong to her.

A Long Look

Kiawah Island is two islands, really. The first island begins at a gate and a guardhouse, a small, gray-shingled booth. To drive onto this island, you must prove that you belong there to a man who sits in the guardhouse, watching a tiny TV set whose restless blue light flares and subsides. When you stop the car, the man puts on his hat, squares away his gun (because it is, after all, two o'clock in the morning now), and comes out of the booth to lean in the car window. He brings his fleshy face, his narrow blue eyes, his mouth that looks as if he chews his words, too close to yours and asks you to state your business, then feigns surprise when you tell him.

"Now what in the world would you want with those boys back there in the swamp playing nursemaid to turtle eggs this time of night?" he wants to know, studying you, suspicious. I'd left Mother a note: "Gone to Kiawah to find Legree. Be back sometime." To the guard, I did not say I'm going to find the man who fills buckets with hatchling turtles. The man who carries them down the beach, and turns them loose to feel the sand under their bellies, so they will not get lost as they crawl toward the light on the water. I told him that I worked for the *Courier-Tribune* in Timmons, South Carolina, and that I'd been sent here to write a story about the turtle project. "They told me to come at night," 'I said. "Night is when the eggs hatch. Nights with a moon are best." Told him, yes, I believed Timmons had been Triple A state champions once, a few years earlier. Until at last he said, "You just follow this road straight down the island until you come to the end of it." Then he slapped both hands down on the window and, serious all of a sudden, conscious of his authority, stepped back inside the booth and raised the striped arm of the barricade, waving me through.

From there the road runs straight onto this first groomed and trimmed island, which is all palmettos and clipped green fairways and white sand traps, rows of golf carts lined up in a parking lot lit up bright as day, a snowy egret standing motionless in a water hazard. Driveways that curve away into jungle, banks of condominiums snugged in among the palmettos and oleanders. On the other side of the road, facing the ocean, the big houses stand. Some of them are lit up like Christmas, with people moving around inside, and some are built so close together it looks as if they are trying to shoulder each other out of the way. And in the gaps between the houses, through the dunes, you catch glimpses of the ocean at low tide, flat and tin-colored, with small, white waves curling in.

But then, so slowly at first that you don't notice it, the dark returns. Houses appear less frequently, then not at all, the road narrows, the streetlights disappear. The swamp comes up and stands close to the road, a tangle of oak and palmetto, the oaks rounding over the road and draped with moss, so that it feels as if the car's headlights bore a tunnel through the dark. Then suddenly the headlights flash onto a cemetery under the oaks, a half-collapsed iron fence and leaning headstones, a brick sarcophagus with the lid broken in, a tomb like a small Greek temple with the door missing. You know that if you stopped and read the tombstones, the dates there would astonish you. Eighteenth century angels and lambs and weeping willows in relief on the blackening stones. You know you would find the graves of many children, stones with the names and dates effaced, and graves that are nothing more than depressions in the soft, spongy earth. Driving down this road, you remember that somewhere on this island a fisherman in a boat on a marsh creek at low tide found a dugout canoe buried in the mud of a creek bank. A prehistoric canoe, the archaeologists who came to study it said. But when they pulled it from the mud, into the light and air, it crumbled to dust. Driving down this road, it is not hard to imagine that if you traveled far enough it would carry you back to the beginning of the world, to the darkness there, and the silence. And then abruptly the jungle ends and there is a fire, burned down to a bed of red coals, and three tents drawn into a semicircle with their backs to the ocean. The moon is up and heavy in the sky, thowing a long track of light across the water.

I cut the headlights, coasted in, and when the car stopped someone stepped out of a tent and stood in front of the fire pulling on a shirt, his body a shape against the fire's glow. Legree. I felt my throat tighten. I would know his shape in the dark if there were nothing but dark, and Legree a darker shape against it. Or with my hands, if there was no other way. And maybe Mother was right, I thought, to wish me blindness if within that blindness I might have this sight.

I shut off the engine and opened the door. "Legree," I said. "It's me, it's Annie." And the heat closed down like a blanket suddenly thrown over me. It was stifling, one of those nights when the sea breeze stops and the land breeze, too, and nothing moves the heavy air; even a fan only stirs it like thick soup, round and round. I took this heat for a bad sign: the bloated moon, the heavy air, the cemetery I had passed, the dark road down which I would surely be leaving, as soon as Legree said, "Go."

"Well, I'll be damned," he said, in his slow, careful way that makes choosing words sound like serious business. He threw a piece of driftwood onto the fire, and when it blazed up I saw that his skin was brown, warm brown, but his face was haggard. As he watched, he buttoned his white shirt over the cutoff jeans he wore, and I saw that he'd pulled on his workboots without socks, without lacing. There was something frayed and worn about him, and he buttoned his shirt to the top, and stood there, waiting.

"Where are the others?" I said.

"Out on the beach," he said, "checking nests." He waved a

hand toward the ocean. "Listen," he said, "what brings you here, anyway?"

I took a deep breath. "You."

"All right," he said, and he turned away, but not before I saw him smile. "Why don't you stand closer to the fire here? It's hot, but the mosquitoes won't bother you."

He'd said "all right" that way in the cemetery, the day I met him. Standing across the fire from him, it came back to me now what I had liked about that. There was nothing meek or resigned about it. Nothing craven. It was *all right, that's the way it is. All right, now I know. All right.* I looked at him, and he looked back across the fire at me. "You know," I said, "the way you say that is one of the first things I liked about you. I remember you said that the first afternoon we met each other. I told you that my husband was dead and you said, 'All right,' like you were accepting it, and I thought you really were something."

He folded his arms and looked down and traced an arc in the sand with the toe of his boot, then erased it. "But circumstances since have forced you to reevaluate your initial impression, is that what you drove down here in the middle of the night to tell me?"

"No," I said, "they haven't. That's what I'm here to tell you."

"Oh, yeah?" he said, and he laughed, a harsh sound that I'd never heard before. Of course, I thought, of course I'd been wrong about him. When had I not been wrong, inventing another person as someone simple, transparent, entirely good, untouched by hurt and incapable of cruelty? The old, sad lie of innocence that makes betrayal inevitable. "How'd you get past Lurch at the gate there?" he said, more gently, nodding back up the road I'd come down.

"I told him I was doing a story on you-all," I said. "Pug Simmons gave me a job at the paper. I start Monday."

This seemed to give him a private kind of pleasure, the kind that catches his whole face at once. "Nobody ever said you weren't light on your feet."

"That sounds like a eulogy to me."

He looked at me hard, and in the firelight his face looked old and severe. "Come see my turtles," he said.

We walked, not touching, out past the fire and the tents, and followed a path over the dunes. The thick sand there was still warm from the day's sun, and the tide was dead low now, the ocean as flat as a lake. In the soft sand just in front of the dunes, we came to a picket fence that had been squared haphazardly into an enclosure where small squares of stiff wire lay on the sand. Beside each square there was a stake driven into the sand and on these stakes someone had nailed strips of tin covered with numbers: "7/31, 134," one read; "7/23, 56," said another. Legree unhooked a section of fence and stepped inside, then went down on his knees, moving one of the mesh squares. I went in and sat down beside him. "This is it?" I said. He sat back on the sand and he laughed then, with his arms draped across his knees, his head down—laughed until his shoulders shook. "What's so funny?" I said.

He reached out to touch my hair, then let his hand fall on my shoulder the way a brother or a teacher might do. "You," he said. "The expression on your face. What did you expect to see here, anyway?"

I shoved my heels through the sand and thought about that, and the more I thought about it, the funnier it seemed. I'd been building it up in my mind until I'd come to imagine some sort of small industry down there, buildings and gauges, elaborate incubators, something complicated at least, something visible, something tangible. Not these small plots of sand marked with flimsy squares of chicken wire. "Machinery," I guess," I said. "Monuments, I don't know. Something a lot more complicated than this. But I guess for this work you don't need a lot of machinery." I sifted some sand through my fingers. It felt warm and clean, and I thought of the turtle eggs below that sand and the way Legree had squatted there as if he were conscious of his weight on the sand, the fragile eggs below.

"Sorry to disappoint you. No," he said, "for this kind of work you need patience. See those numbers on the markers? The top one is the date the eggs were laid and the bottom one is the number of eggs in that nest."

"My God," I said, "there are thousands here, thousands of turtles." I put my hand down on the sand and I imagined I could almost feel the sand humming with them. I imagined them boiling up out of the sand, and Legree leading them up and over the dunes and down toward the water, the Pied Piper of Turtles.

"Yes," he said, "there are. There are four or five other nesting places as big as this one, but almost none of the turtles from any of them will make it. Maybe twenty or thirty out of this bunch. What the coons don't get before they hatch, the gulls will when they try to make it into the ocean. And what the gulls don't get, the fish do. When we leave the place unattended, people poach the eggs. One morning during nesting season, I found a female turtle dead on the beach. Someone had split her shell open with an ax, then drove a Jeep around and around and around her."

"So why do it then?" I said. "Why keep backing up and running into that same wall? All that work for nothing."

He stood up quickly then and looked at me angrily, as if I'd called him a simpleton, a fool. I stood up, too. "Sorry we can't give you more of a show," he said, and he bowed and backed off and started straightening the stakes. "Maybe if you stuck around, a nest would hatch and make it worth your while. Maybe not."

"Don't be snide, please, Legree," I said. "I never imagined the odds, that's all."

"Odds," he said. "Is that what we're talking about here, odds? Look, do me a favor. Don't try to make this into something that it's not. You can't be sentimental about this work. It's what I know. I don't know anything else. That's why I do it, OK? This isn't a crusade. I'm not your father or your husband."

One is, I guess, never prepared for the possibility of cruelty in a person one has trusted. My face stung as though he'd slapped it. "You've waited a long time to say that, haven't you?" I didn't bother with the path through the dunes; I walked straight over them, sea oats slapping against my legs. "Don't walk on those dunes, Annie, goddamn it," Legree called after me. "That's a very fragile area."

"Where are the signs that say that?" I yelled back. "I don't see any." If everything fragile were marked with a sign, the world would be nothing but signs. *Warning: Fragile. Needs Tenderness, Care, and Peace to Survive.* Now it was time to leave this place where things were too fragile to survive. The car. That was where I needed to be, not in this wilderness where Legree had led me and left me stranded. This is it, then, I thought, as I walked. Just take all those things you've discovered that you love about him, bundle them all up now, and leave. You'll have plenty of time to take them out and cry over them later. I had the car door open when he caught up with me. He slammed it and pinned my arms down at my sides. He came so close he frightened me, the fierce look in his eyes, the strength in his hands. "I'm sorry," he said. "That was a shitty thing to say. But this is what you do, isn't it? Just turn your back and walk away and trample on things while you're at it? Now, didn't you come here to tell me something, or did I hear you wrong?"

"Let me go," I said.

He released me instantly and shoved his hands into his pockets, breathing harshly through his nose. All around us there was silence, silence and the low crackling of the fire and the electricity of the cicadas back in the palmetto grove. And I knew that if I did not speak, the silence would just keep getting deeper and deeper, until nothing would break it. But I could not find the words; I should have rehearsed them after all. And Legree waited—not patiently, not impatiently either. He waited as he must have waited for the turtle eggs to hatch, to see which ones lived and which ones died, waited to be there for the living and to accept the dead.

Remind me to tell you sometime, Legree, I said to myself, if I ever have a chance to say it, how the set of your jaw is as hard and righteous as those Baptist preachers you think you've left so far behind.

"I don't know what to say," I said. We both looked down at the sand at the same time. "I came down here to tell you something, I know that much, Legree. All the way down I kept thinking how I had this big important thing to tell you, some big statement that would wipe away the hurt I've done to you, some grand scheme to make it right, to make sure you wouldn't ever leave me. But I don't." He listened fiercely as though he were taking my words into his body. I said it again, because it felt good to say it. "I don't." I took his face in both of my hands and I kissed his mouth, his eyes,

I kissed every error of his face, and he sighed and moved his head under my hands. And when I was done I said, "But I do have something to tell you, Legree. I don't want what I had with Matthew. I don't want what I could have or might have had. I don't even believe my life with him was the best life I could have had anymore. It's you I want, and this. I want us to go on." And I want, I said to myself, to lay down the grand gesture, the summing up. I want to take up patience. I want eyes to see, ears to hear, a heart to love the smallest sign of life. In these there is no betrayal, because there are no promises, only the moment-by-moment willingness to believe.

"All right," he said. "I've never believed much in proof myself." And then it was my turn to rest myself against his hand as it followed the line of my cheek and my throat and my breasts. "All right," he said. "I want you to come with me."

He ducked into his tent and came back with a blanket, a flashlight, and a can of insect repellent. Then we started for the palmetto jungle behind the dunes. Inside the palmettos it was utterly dark. Legree switched on the flashlight and I followed him down the narrow sand path, the flashlight swinging and silvering the tangle of undergrowth on either side. Once, I turned and looked back. The path was as dark as if someone had shut a door behind us. "Legree," I said, and he must have heard the fear in my voice because he said, "Not much further now." Soon there was light ahead of us, then a shining length of river and the marshes beyond the river, and on this side of the river the dark shape of a house surrounded by a chain-link fence. It was a bare-fronted house set up on high, brick footings, the windows all shuttered, the roof beam sagging, a place with a feeling of abandonment about it. As though no one had lived there for so many years, it had ceased to be a human dwelling place and become something else thrown up by the river, or something that had grown there and was now crumbling, going back.

Legree unlocked the padlock on the gate of the fence that surrounded the house, and as he closed it behind us, I moved closer to him. "What is this place, Legree?" I asked. I pressed myself against his back and wrapped my arms around his waist. He had slung the blanket over his shoulder and I pressed my cheek against its scratchy folds.

"The last of the original houses on the island," he said. He let the lock fall back against the pole. "You wouldn't believe what they're doing to it. They're numbering everything inside—banisters, floorboards—everything has a number now. There's even a section of wall where a Union army regiment signed their names. That may be gone by now, though. They've been working like ants, you wouldn't believe it, carrying things away. They're going to set it up again and restore it on the grounds of the Charleston Museum. I hope the floor is still there."

We walked toward the house and climbed the broad, brick steps onto the stoop. The front door stood ajar and the house breathed out its strangeness, a moldy smell of age and water. Beside the house, the palmettos rustled, their shadows shifting across the shuttered windows. "Should we be here?" I said.

"No," he said, and he pressed me to him, "but we are." We wrapped our arms around each other and I tried to touch every part of him with every part of me. It seemed like a definite thing to want, this pleasure that I felt as our bodies touched. As we held each other, an angry local wind came up and rattled the palmettos that stood on either side of the stoop. They scratched against the house. "I read somewhere that a wind like that is the sound of ghosts warning you off their territory."

"Is that right?" he said, his voice all thick and smoky. "Do you think we ought to listen to them, then?" Without looking around, he shoved the door open wider with his foot. Over his shoulder I saw the dark come out, then smelled it, thick and musty. The walls just inside had been torn away down to the uprights.

"No," I said. "No ghosts tonight."

He let the blanket slide off his arm and onto the porch. "Goddamn," he said. And then his hands were working the buttons of my blouse and moving slow and warm on my breasts, and my hands were up under his shirt, feeling his ribs with my palms, the strength of his back. "What kind of story did you say you meant to do?" he said as he stripped off my blouse. The breeze was all over my skin and his thumbs were on my nipples, then his mouth. "About you,' I said, "about you and me." I held him by the hips and pressed against him, moved against him.

"And what will you say?" he asked, rubbing his cheek against my nipples as I held his face against my breast.

"I don't know yet," I said. "I don't know." There was salt in the hollow of his throat when I kissed him there, salt in my mouth. I found his belt buckle, the snap on his jeans. "But I know how it starts."

In his tent later, I couldn't sleep. Morning was on the way. If I slept, I might miss something. The tide was coming in now and the breeze had returned. The tent lifted and fell as though it were breathing. Once, I heard an old man from Kentucky tell the story of the New Madrid earthquake. He told how the earth had split and cracked and buckled, and how the Mississippi River had looped back on itself, so violent was the upheaval of its riverbed. He told of the year after the earthquake, when aftershocks walked the land, and people fled to the woods and lived in shelters woven of light branches that would not crush them if they fell. And it seemed to me that on this night, we rested as lightly on the earth as any other refugees.

Just as it was getting light, I touched his face, which in sleep looked like a map of error and sweetness. "Come live with me," I said. "I'm moving out of Mother's house."

I thought he was asleep, but he opened his eyes and stroked my cheek. "We'll see," he said. "I've just signed a six-month lease on a house down here, but we'll see."

"Six months?"

"What's six months?" he said. "We'll see." He moved my hair, kissed me, pulled me down and snugged my head against his chest, and I heard his heart beat slow and steady, heard his breathing slow and deepen and carry him back to sleep.

We'll see. There was a vista in those words, a long look. I lay on my stomach and watched the morning come. Big waves reared and crashed onto the beach, and where they drew back, sandpipers appeared, running along the tide line on legs that seemed to twinkle. A thin line of pink was laid along the horizon and then the spreading light began. There were shrimp boats far out against the light, trolling slowly with lowered nets. Wreathed in gulls, they rocked patiently, patiently on the water. "We'll see," he'd said. It was enough.

Out Bean Blossom Road

Early in September, once I was settled, I invited Mother over for supper at my house. A sign of peace, an offer of reconciliation. "Come to my house," I said. "I'll feed you." My house, my own, bought with the money my father left me. My house and twenty acres seven miles out of town on the Bean Blossom Road, down a long, sandy driveway that runs between tumbling hedges of Cherokee rose and ends in a hickory grove. The house in the hickory grove, the one where the wood has weathered a beautiful, silvery gray—the color of cold weather. The two-story house with a long brow of tin roof pulled low over the porch, and tall, green shutters on all the windows, is mine.

When I'd told Mother about the house, you'd have thought I was moving to Alaska. We were sitting back on her patio in the cool of early evening, drinking white wine and shelling snap beans. The fountain splashed, the moonflower vines sagged with seed pods, but the impatiens and hostas still bloomed in neat, curved beds around the fountain. It was hard to remember the latticework porch with its clutter of dog-food sacks and tools, and the long, precarious wooden steps that used to lead into the backyard. They were part of a world that had ended long ago.

Mother snapped off the ends of the beans, stripped the strings, and threw them into the colander in her lap in three quick, sure motions. "The woman down at the market tells me this is about the last of the string beans," she said.

"We could can some," I said.

"And get myself all worn out in a hot kitchen all day? No thank you," she slapped at her calf where a mosquito had been feeding.

"You've got central air, Mother," I said. "It's fall."

"Even so, canning is for young people." Her bottom lip had started to poke out; soon, I knew, it would be hopeless to talk to her about anything.

"Well, I've been thinking," I said. "You know that house I've been interested in?"

She didn't look up. "The one way out there by the chain-gang camp?"

"That one," I said, "I think I'm going to buy it."

Now her bean stringing became more precise. Each bean required total concentration. "How's that old car of yours holding up these days?"

"Well enough."

"That's good. I wouldn't want you to have a breakdown on that road late some night."

"No."

She took a deep breath then and drew a Kleenex out of her skirt pocket, dabbed at her upper lip, her forehead, up under her hair. She set the colander down on the wrought-iron bench, stood up, and smoothed down her skirt. She walked to the corner of the house, turned on the spigot, and picked up the hose. Then she wrenched the nozzle open, and a fine bell of spray came out that she trained onto the nearest clump of impatiens. She stood there for a long time, watering.

"You're going to drown those plants if you don't watch out," I said.

"I don't see why you have to move so far away all by yourself," she said.

"I'm not going to be all by myself," I said.

"I don't see why you don't go on and marry that boy," she said, not moving the hose an inch to the right or left.

"Maybe I will, Mother," I said. "And I hope you'll do the flowers."

"No," she said in a discouraged voice. "You'll probably just elope. "Or go down to city hall and see a judge. I know you."

No, you don't, I almost said. *You don't know a thing.* Instead I kept quiet, and she watered her flowers, and below that silence like the sound of a river heard from far away, it seemed that I heard the murmur of this conversation that we will never have: "You are leaving me, again," it goes.

"Yes, Mother, again and always."

"But why?"

"Because I have to leave you, again, in order, to live. The way I first left you when I'd grown too big for the place where you'd held me and given me life."

"But why?"

"In order that we both may live." But I wish someone would tell me in what book of laws it is written that leaving your mother may only be accomplished through pain: pain given, pain given back?

Promptly at 6:30, the Oldsmobile pulled up in front of the house and Mother stepped out, waving as though I were the first relative she'd spotted on the pier after a long ocean crossing. "You certainly live a long way from anywhere," she said. "I thought I'd never get here." She wore a brand-new yellow slack set and pearls. On her head was her old tan poplin rain hat, and not a cloud in the sky. At the sound of her car coming down the drive, Napoleon and Josephine had crawled out from under the front porch where they'd taken up residence. Now Napoleon raced to her and jumped, planting his paws in the middle of her jacket. "Down, dog," she commanded in a withering voice, shoving him away, but Napoleon would not be pushed away that easily from someone he adored. He jumped again and knocked her backward, and when her hat fell off he grabbed it in his teeth and ran around the corner of the house, shaking it. "My hat!" she cried as she felt the top of her head. "Don't let it get away." So I chased him down and caught him, and hit him hard because Mother was watching, so hard he yelped and looked back over his shoulder reproachfully as he slunk back under the porch.

"Thank you, Annie," she said imperiously when I handed her the hat. She squashed it on her head and brushed angrily at her jacket. "That dog never had a lick of sense and never will."

"Probably not," I said. My mother is getting attached to that hat, I thought. She is turning into an old person, and soon she will need more love than I can give her. I felt the future rolling toward me, a scene just like this one. Mother and me inching along. Mother clinging to my hand, her precious hat on her head, as necessary to any outing as a child's special blanket or stuffed bear. Mother growing as helpless as I had once been with her, an astonishing circle if we both lived long enough to close it. And she would be difficult in decline; she would not go gently. Like Grandmother Vess at the end of her life, who insisted that my father hire round-the-clock help to care for her in her own home, then drove them off within a week with outrageous demands and accusations of theft and cruelty.

"Come on in, Mother," I said. "Watch your step." I held out my hand, but she waved it away and climbed the two stone-slab steps up to the porch. She frowned at the sign from the Laughing Place that I'd hung under the eaves. "I wondered where that old thing got to," she said, then she stopped in astonishment to size me up. "Why, Annie," she said, "I've never seen you in an apron before. It's very becoming," and she laughed in a way that made my stomach lurch. She's gloating, I thought. As if she'd waited years, years, biding her time, to say those words and win. Then she turned her cheek, thick with sweet powder, to be kissed, and I did, and that was the end of that brief flight of goodwill. This is what my father lived with, I thought: the rage kept banked but fanned, the grievances pushing up underneath her words, warping and blistering them so that as they touched you, they burned—you couldn't say just how.

I took off the apron and hung it on the screen-door handle. "Let's go for a walk," I said.

She sighed and retrieved a pair of glasses from her purse, and slipped them on. The lenses began to darken, and as they darkened she played the boards on the porch floor with the toe of one low-heeled bone-leather pump, as if my porch were a keyboard and she were picking out the notes to a melancholy song. While I waited, I felt that foolish hope entirely fade that had preceded her coming, the hope that had sent me flying through the house washing windows, mopping floors, pulling down cobwebs, unpacking boxes, bringing in bouquets of autumn grasses and flowers. The stubborn and willful hope that when Mother saw where I lived now, she would say, "You are my child. I see who you are and it is good."

"You are my mother," I would answer. "You have brought me to a place where I can do what makes me glad." In another world, maybe. A world where peace between people came easily and my father had not betrayed anyone, where Matthew had lived and there were no lights to confuse Legree's turtles as they crawled into the ocean. A world where every one survived and I had walked away from Canady at the first wink. Why had it taken me so long to figure out that our dreams only move us along to the next place where we're going to have to learn to live? That the world in which I lived now was not the world my father promised it would be. It was smaller than that, less exalted, and it was not the world that Matthew and I hoped to find. It was plainer, less ornate, but richer and stranger. How do I live here? I asked myself. What do I do now?

When Mother's glasses had darkened completely, she sighed and picked up a walking stick that Legree had propped against the side of the house near the door. It was a good, sturdy hickory stick, stripped of its bark, with a crook at the top that made a natural handle. "Now where?" she said.

"Let's go see the spring, as long as we're out here," I said, though I felt my enthusiasm darken like her glasses.

As we picked our way through the fallen limbs and high grass beside the house, she swept the cane from side to side as though she were blind. "Snakes, go away," she said in a loud voice.

I felt my shoulders hunch and round as though I were folding around something in myself, hiding it from her. In between sweeps of the stick, she disapproved. "Uhn, uhn, uhn," she said, "haven't you got your work cut out for you?" as though the condition of the trees, the yard, and the house were all symptoms of the defects of my soul: a tolerance for unruliness, stubborn downfall, and debris.

By the time we got to the spring, I felt as gray as her glasses. "There," I said, pointing to the small pool of clear water that bubbled up at the foot of a tall sycamore tree. The pool was lined and edged with stones that had been chosen so carefully and fitted so tightly, the surface of the wall looked smooth. How many hours I'd already spent there, admiring the fit of the rocks, the grace of the sycamore.

"Springs are such pretty places, aren't they?" she said, musing up into the sycamore. "I always think of that verse in the Bible about living water when I see a spring."

"You do?"

"Don't you make fun of me about this, Annie. I can't stand it," she said, and I was startled to see tears standing in her eyes.

"I'm not, Mother," I said. "I'm just surprised, that's all. I just don't think of you as someone who knows her way around the Bible that well. I didn't mean to hurt your feelings."

"There's a lot you don't know about me," she said, squinting off into the distance as though she were watching the approach of an enemy.

"I'm sure," I said. "Want to try some of the water?" I'd bought a blue tin cup and had hung it on a hook that Legree had made out of a length of coat-hanger wire, embedded between two stones at the head of the spring. The water tasted clean and sweet with an undertone of rock and iron to it.

"Lord, no," she said, backing off. "I haven't had a typhoid shot."

So much for living water. We walked back toward the house. I did not show her the cemetery I'd found on the rise behind the house. Up a path that leads out through some old, collapsed outbuildings, on top of a small hill, there is a clearing, and in this clearing there is a cemetery with half a dozen headstones standing in a line, their old-fashioned names barely visible: Addie Louise

Blake. Herschel Charles Blackmore. Among these graves pine seedlings have begun to grow, as though the last people who'd lived
here kept it cleared, and now the pines, given their chance, were
returning. And somehow, what is important about that cemetery
and why I go back there often has to do with the way the pines
have come and stood among the graves. What a wonderful thing, a
cemetery on your own land, a growing-over cemetery and a spring,
the whole round. But I did not tell Mother that. I would not show
her that place; I would keep it for my own, a point on the compass
of this world where I have come to live.

Inside the house again, Mother popped her head around doorjambs
and whipped open closet doors as though she expected to surprise
someone zipping up his pants there. She found no man (Legree had
left that morning for Kiawah), but there was plenty to be disappointed in without finding a man actually *hiding* in my house. She
picked up a pair of Legree's socks, and a belt from the dresser in
the downstairs bedroom, and carried them with her from room to
room, like evidence. As I sang the praises of the wide, pine floors,
she sniffed the air in shallow breaths as if she might breathe in
spores if she inhaled too deeply. In every room, she sang a chorus
of advice: "Coat of paint will fix this wall right up/put smoke alarms
on your list/this old place is nothing but kindling/it would go up
like a tinderbox/these floors will have to be refinished/call Orkin
about these suspicious-looking holes in the hall floor."
     Up the plain, steep staircase to the second floor, we climbed
together, up to the two big rooms under the slope of the tin roof.
At the top we both stopped. I had forgotten about the mattress.
Legree and I had dragged it up there because it was raining hard
one night, and we wanted to sleep under the tin roof in a drumming
rain. It lay in the middle of the floor, the sheets bunched, the
pillows mashed together, and Mother stood at the top of the stairs
with her hand on the railing and stared at it. I walked over quickly
and straightened the sheet, but that only made it worse. "I'm going
to put a bed up here for guests and whatever," I said.
     "I wish you and this *guest* would make yourselves legitimate,"
she said, starting down the stairs again.

"Yes'm," I said, and I began to wish I had never asked her here, had never let her in the door with her load of shame.

Downstairs again, I walked into the largest room and yanked the shades up: one, two, three, four, so that the light poured in. "This is going to be the living room," I said. "I'm going to take these windows out and put in bigger ones."

"You need some furniture," she said.

"Just look at the light, Mother," I said, and at the same moment, she said, "I hope you're going to put up some drapes in here. Anybody prowling around outside could look right in." And then we both stopped talking. We'd each had our say and now we stared across the empty room at each other. I felt the jut of her jaw in my own, and I knew that there would be no converts in this house, not to the Church of the South-Facing Windows or the Church of the Fear of Prowlers in-the-Night. And I will never tell her that some days, just watching the light move from room to room—a slow progress that leaves no room untouched—I feel that if I could learn the patience of light, I might know how to live on this earth as though I belong here.

At last, we made it to the back of the house, to the kitchen As she washed her hands, then washed them again, she examined the shallow, pock-marked sink, the arthritic-looking faucet. Well, the house was just more *primitive* than she'd imagined, that was all she said. Primitive, yes, that would do, I thought. Close to things Then: "Whose business has Pug Simmons got you poking your nose into these days?" she asked. She sat at the table, put her hat in front of her.

"The dead," I said, and laughed to see the blank look on her face. Pug had hired me on the spot, it's true, but when I went to work, I started where everyone else started, writing obituary notices. ("I want you to know this work from the ground up," he said, "*literally*.") "I call the funeral homes every Monday and Wednesday morning, and they read me the list."

"How morbid," she said, shuddering, spinning her hat in front of her on the table.

"It's not so bad," I said. "I do the police and fire reports, too, and the public records, marriage licenses, divorce decrees, land transfers. He said we'd go from there. He'll send me out to do a story soon."

She made a disapproving sound in her throat and got up again. Mother can never sit still for long. Standing to one side of a cabinet, she inched the door open, then peeked around it, as if she expected something to jump out at her.

When we were kids, Davis loved practical jokes, and I was his accomplice. He kept a stash of hand buzzers and whoopee cushions, rubber vomit, red-hot chewing gum, and dribble glasses hidden behind the *World Book Encyclopedia* in his room, and he brought them out on special occasions—when we had guests, or on holidays—when the embarrassment they caused would be more acute. On certain Wednesdays it was my job to sneak Mother's cigarettes out of her purse and help load them with little sticks that exploded when she lit up at bridge club. We gave her presents, cans marked "Peanut Brittle," that she always exclaimed over and opened eagerly, only to have a cloth snake spring out at her. And then she would make this peculiar sound, "Oooooh," and sit there with the empty can in her lap and this funny look on her face, anger and dismay and fear. *Tricked again.* No wonder she stood aside when she opened a cabinet door in my kitchen. She was the one on whom we'd always sprung things, who existed for us to test ourselves against—sturdy, like one of those workbenches made for pounding with small tools, made for small fingers to use roughly. Watching her peek around my cabinet doors, I wished that I could tell her these things, tell her that I understood something of her wariness, tell her that I knew she was the one on whom we tested our force, who would not strike back, against whom we pushed, on whom we tested the give of the world. No wonder she acted as though our *lives* were about to give her some sort of bad scare. Her history with me was as confusing and heavy with hurt, as mine was with her.

By then she'd found my spice cabinet and started making noises in her throat, high, disapproving sounds accompanied by more rummaging. Finally, I couldn't stand it anymore. "What are you looking for, Mother?" I said.

She turned, a bottle of oregano gripped in her hand like a club, and she shook it at me. "Nothing but some old Worcestershire sauce," she said, color crawling up her neck. "How do you find anything in this mess?"

I stuck the tip of the knife into the cutting board and leaned on the handle. "I know exactly where it is," I said. "And if you'll stand aside, I'll find it for you. I organize things by similarities of taste, if you want to know," I said. She stood to the side of the cabinet with a receiving-line smile on her face while I reached right in behind the cinnamon and the gumbo file, pulled out the bottle of Worcestershire sauce, and put it into her hands. "Worcestershire sauce," I said.

"Oh," she said, and she turned the bottle and studied the label, frowning, as though she expected this to be a trick. "That doesn't make a dab of sense to me," she said.

"It doesn't have to," I said. "This is my house." And I turned back to the slaw. I cut the cabbage into fine shreds, then I got out a sharper knife and cut them even finer.

"I do my cole slaw in the food processor," she said.

"I know, and it comes out soggy. I use a knife."

"Oh," she said. "Well, all right, then," but she looked subdued, and you might think I took great pleasure in that, but you would be wrong. What pleasure is there in having to subdue someone in order to make them be gentle with you? No pleasure at all. Only sadness. I felt it where I'd always felt sadness: in my bones, as though they were growing heavy inside my skin. And when she disappeared into the living room with a can of Endust and a rag, her chin high, humming, as if to say "Try and stop me," I kept my attention anchored to the chopping block and the cabbage and the knife, the task right in front of my eyes.

The cole slaw turned out tasteless and dry, and I burned the hamburgers. We ate in the twilight in the kitchen, on the dishes I'd unpacked that afternoon especially for this supper. Mother ate her hamburger, one small bite at a time. "It's good," she said, choking down the meat, smiling. She was doing it for me. I felt like weeping; I'd wanted to do it for her. Here we were, again. As a teenager, I used to lie on my bed watching the wisteria vine strangle

the pine, indulging myself in an agony of absolutes: *She is the vine
and I am the tree. Soon I will be out of this house forever and I will
never look back.* Now, of course, I see that it is much more complicated than that, it always is. We're both vines, both trees and roots,
grown together in a tangle that can never be untangled.

While she wandered around the house, I willed myself to be
calm, and then I heard her come back and sensed her standing in
the door. When I turned around, I found her staring down at the
dust rag in her hand, folding and unfolding it.

"Mother?" I said. "Are you all right?"

"Oh, sure," she said. Then she leaned toward me. "Tell me
something," she said in a low, confidential voice. "You just aren't
very domestically oriented, are you?"

For once, there was no challenge in her question. "No, ma'am,"
I said, "I guess not." And for once, there was no sarcasm in my
answer. I saw the tenderness in her eyes and felt it in my own.
Then she nodded crisply. "That's what I thought," she said. "I'd say
I'm a pretty good judge of character, wouldn't you?"

"Yes, ma'am," I said again. "You are."

Christmas Gifts

Beyond the woods, on the south slope of the hill, Legree and I found the remains of an orchard one weekend late in October. A few old, dark apple trees, fractured and split by the weight of their own limbs, and four peach trees, shapeless with neglect, smothered in brown mats of kudzu vine. But we tore the vines away and saw that the trees were still alive. They were young trees, really. Amber sap oozed from the joints of their branches, and under the kudzu we discovered a few small, hard peaches. How they'd grown there I cannot imagine, but their skins were pallid, the insides withered, tasteless, dry. The moment I tasted one, I knew that I wanted to feel in my palm the warm plumpness of a peach from my own tree, that I wanted to bring back their inside juices. Legree said forget it, it'll never happen. Peach trees aren't that hardy or long-lived, he said. That's why a big peach farmer is always planting new trees. It's not like an apple orchard, he said, which is not to say he won't give it a try. Mother wondered, Why not start over with new trees, for goodness' sake? She brought me catalogs from Stark Brothers' Nurseries, with the corners folded down on the pages where the dwarf fruit trees were listed. I wasn't opposed to it, but as long as the old trees were still alive, why not try and keep them that way? I said. If they die, I will take what I have learned and start again.

Trees need to be pruned when they are dormant, and so in December, on the first clear day after days of low skies and sharp, cold rain, Legree and I went out carrying ladders, pruning shears, a limb saw, and wound dressing. He chose an apple tree and I took a peach; we climbed up into our trees and set to work pruning the dead limbs and cutting off the suckers that robbed the live limbs of nourishment. That morning, in his sure and careful way, Legree gathered small sticks and fallen branches, brushed away leaves and built a fire. All day he fed it steadily with dead limbs, and all day we climbed down from our ladders to warm our hands there.

All morning I watched as Legree worked on his apple tree. He'd saw off a limb, climb down from his ladder, and stand back to see what that cut had done to the shape of the tree. Then he'd climb back up to cut another limb, as though he were working his way patiently around a problem. And once, I turned and found him leaning on his ladder and watching me as though he liked what he saw. And it seemed to me that this is how our lives went now; it seemed that we were messengers, passing in and out, over and through each other's days and nights, carrying news from one place to another.

That day, I worked on past Legree. I worked until the light began to fade and my hands got too chilled and clumsy to guide the shears. Then I smothered what was left of the fire with dirt and took the path up and over the hill and through the cemetery, heading home. The sun was coming low through the pines in thick, yellow slabs, and the headstones threw their shadows a long way across the soft pine needles, like arrows all in flight toward the same target. And something made me stop and look at the slant of the headstones' shadows again, and that's when I saw that every one of those graves faced east. And the moment I knew that, the people buried there became real to me, and those who'd loved and buried them, and what they'd hoped for and what they'd believed. As I came back into the yard, the house had never looked so good, with Legree's Mustang pulled in under the hickories and the smoke going up from the chimney to show that he was inside. I stood there and I looked and looked. I could not get enough of the dull gleam of the roof tin, the light winding like a river through the crowns of the hickories around the house. And it occurred to me that home is where you are when you know what you see when you look at a house, or a history, or into another person's eyes. And if that is true, then I am home.

At Christmastime that year, Legree and I took Brother to the State Hospital in Columbia. In October he'd begun starting fires: in the field next to the house, in the road in front of the house, in the yard. Once his fire was burning, he guarded it. No one could pass on the road or coax him back into the house until his fire had burned to white ash, and if someone touched him before the fire died down, he hit at them. Legree and his mother talked every night on the telephone. "He doesn't mean any harm," she said. "He's like a little child, you know that. We just have to keep the matches away from him."

"Little children hurt themselves and other people sometimes, Mama," Legree told me he said to her. "You need to be smart about this, now. What does Daddy say?"

"He says I should do what I think is best."

"She's lived with him so long, and she still thinks of him as a child going through a phase," Legree said once after he'd finished talking with his mother. He hit the kitchen table hard with his fist. "All he has to do is light one fire inside and the house'd go up like that. And my father's oxygen tanks, my God! They'd never get out."

The Monday before Christmas, Brother piled up sticks and dry leaves on the back porch and lit the pile.

"It just charred the wood on the porch and a little under the eaves is all, son," his mother said. "No need for you to come all the way up here. We don't know where he keeps finding those matches."

Two days before Christmas, early in the morning, Brother stripped the quilts and sheets from his bed and piled them in the center of his bedroom. He was working at the matches when Legree's mother found him. When she took them away from him, Brother pushed her down and ran out of the house. The sheriff's deputies searched for him all day, but it was a neighbor who found him hiding in the wood lot on his land, brought Brother home, and stayed with the family until we got there around midnight.

On Christmas Eve day, we took him to Columbia. Legree's mother walked Brother out to the car with her arm around his waist, and Legree carried the square, brown suitcase covered with stickers from Mackinac Island, Michigan, and Laramie, Wyoming, that Legree had bought at a secondhand store for him before we'd left Timmons. "Brother, you be good," his mother said, when Brother was settled in the back seat next to Legree. I was behind the wheel with the engine started. She reached in to touch Brother's shoulder, but his face was already straining forward eagerly, as if the car were moving and he had to look where it was going. On the way to Columbia, Legree and Brother opened the presents that Legree's mother had wrapped for him. Socks and pajamas. A flannel shirt and Donald Duck comic books. They opened them slowly, one present every twenty miles or so. While Legree read Donald Duck to him, Brother rested his head on Legree's shoulder and laughed continuously, and I drove and passed coffee, sandwiches, and Christmas cookies back to them. Legree's mother had made them, too. She'd gotten up at five and wrapped Brother's presents and packed a tin with his favorite cookies—fat sugar cookies in the shape of Christmas trees and decorated with red and green sugar and little silver balls.

The administration building where we'd been directed to come was at the top of a steep range of granite steps. On the doors were two enormous wreaths decorated with bells and red bows. While Legree buttoned him into his heavy plaid jacket, pulled the flaps of his cap over his ears, and wiped the crumbs off of his face, Brother laughed and pointed to the decorations. When he laughed, he looked as though he were in pain. His caved-in face seemed to fall back into itself. When he was dressed, he shook hands with me. "Hello," he said solemnly.

"Hello, yourself, Brother," I said, and I held his hand and looked into his eyes. They were an odd shade of golden brown that seemed to reflect light from a faraway source, like Legree's eyes with the intelligence missing. Small eyes set too close together in a face creased in perpetual worry, and a soft, wet mouth. He looked like a man who had lived in a maze so long he could only think as far as the next turning. Beneath his white skin, his beard looked blue, and there was a fleck of shaving cream under one ear. I wiped it away and he touched the spot in surprise, looked at his hand, and stuck it into his pocket as though he were hiding something. Then he grunted and started across the road toward the steps.

"I'll go," Legree said. "I want to take him in myself."

"I'll wait right here," I said. "I'll watch for you."

I kissed Legree and he held me close. I could feel his heart beating, hard, underneath his jacket. Then he turned the collar of his jacket up and ran after Brother, who was halfway up the steps, climbing and pointing at the wreaths and laughing.

The sky was clear blue and so hard it looked as though it would shatter if you struck it. Legree held Brother's hand and carried his suitcase. Just before they went through the doors, Legree turned around, and I stood up and waved until the doors had closed behind them. And I thought I understood then why Legree's mother had stood in the cold that morning with her sweater pulled tight around her and waved, and kept waving, as we drove away. Before the road curved and the house dropped from sight, I had looked in the rear-view mirror, and I said, "Legree, your mother's waving. Let Brother see." And Legree had turned Brother around so that he could see her, too, standing in the yard waving as though she wanted Brother to remember that the last time he'd seen her, she was thinking of him, wishing him well as he rode away. As if she wanted him to carry that sight away with him like a promise: I am still here; I have not forgotten you.

A low stone wall bordered the administration building parking lot, and a line of immense, warty magnolias grew behind the wall. As I waited for Legree, I walked up and down under the magnolias, collecting cones from the ground. Only the most shapely cones would do, those stuffed with seeds so red and shiny they looked lacquered. I collected one armful, then another, and spread them along the top of the wall. Still, Legree did not come back. So I began to harvest the slick, red seeds from the cones, pushing each one out of its pocket with my thumb until I'd made a small mountain of seeds at my feet. But the doors stayed closed, the ribbons on the Christmas wreathes fluttering in the breeze. When finally the door opened and Legree stepped through, he hesitated, shading his eyes with both hands as he looked out at the parking lot. I climbed up on the wall and waved. "Here," I said. "I'm here."

Up close his face was all bony misery, slack and sad, his eyes red-rimmed. "He won't be walking out of there anytime soon," he said. "I have just taken him to the end of the line." There were iron cots, he said, a long line of them in a big white room. And a smell, a sickening blend of disinfectant and old animal hides. A heavy, metal door that closed with a sound that killed hope.

Back in Honea Path, we ate supper without speaking: baked hen and dressing, green beans, pecan pie with ice cream. Legree ate three helpings of everything, as though he were starving. Then we went into the living room and his mother switched on the silver metal tree on top of the enormous old TV set. It was decorated entirely with red lights and tinsel. We sat with our coffee and opened our gifts. For us, she had made a quilt out of Legree's old shirts and scraps of material she'd brought home from the mill over the years. It was done in a pattern called Churn Dash and sewn with fine, even stitches. The fabrics she'd chosen were nothing by themselves, but together, the way she'd placed them next to one another, they'd come alive: reds and browns and blues and golds joined and spun across the quilt. The longer I looked at it, the more intricate it seemed. Legree stood up and shook it out. I said, "I haven't see anything that beautiful in a long, long time." And she had given it to us, there was no mistaking that. "To Annie and Legree," the card on the package had read. "Warm thoughts from Mother B."

"I started on it last spring after you-all were here," she said. "Brother sat with me while I pieced it. I'd say, 'Brother, now hand me a dark piece. Now hand me a light piece.' He could do that, you know." She passed her hand lightly over the quilt, and then she stood up. "Y'all excuse me," she said, and walked into the kitchen. Legree followed, carrying the quilt, and they talked for a long time in low voices, and I heard Brother's name come around again and again.

For his father, we'd bought a radio so he could listen to football in the fall and baseball in the spring. The radio had been my idea, and Legree had found for him a small, glass globe with blades inside—one dark, one light—that turned on solar energy in a sunny window. For his mother, we'd picked out a set of sharp knives and a thick, pink bathrobe. She put it on over her dress and wore it until we left, while his father sat in his wheelchair and studied the radio, fiddled with the dials, and dozed, still smiling.

While the winter twilight dropped and settled, I drove us home to Timmons, past houses outlined with lights and dark houses and houses where Christmas trees shone in the windows. Legree sat on the other side of the car, wrapped in the quilt his mother had given us, staring out of the window. Every time I looked at it, I saw new intricacies there. Once, Legree closed his eyes and rested his head against the window, but almost immediately he startled and woke. "Goddamn," he said, and he wiped his whole face with one hand, then shook his head. "I keep seeing him on that bed, just sitting there where I put him. He wouldn't let go of his suitcase so I left him there holding it, and a nurse was talking to him. I told them they'd better let me stay and help get the suitcase away from him, because if they tried to do it, I knew there'd be trouble. But she told me to go on, she'd handle it. So I went to the office and filled out the papers, and then I went back and looked in through the window in that door and he was still sitting there. They'd gotten his suitcase away from him, but there were all these doped-up old guys in their slippers and droopy pants with their shirttails hanging out, standing around his bed staring at him. What will he do? How will he survive in there? He doesn't have a clue. I wish I'd never gone back and seen him sitting there like that. I wish I'd left him at the office like they said I could do. But, no. Mama asked me to take him and settle him in and that's what I did. She kept asking me this morning, 'What are we going to do now? What are we going to do now?' I'm going to tell her that the first thing we should do is tear down Brother's pigeon cages so that we don't have to think about him every time we walk past them. Tear them down and throw out his geraniums, burn his clothes."

"You could do all that," I said, "and it would help, because you have to let go. But when the grass comes up greener where the pigeon coops were, you'll remember him. Listen," I said, "you can't outrun them, and you can't forget. You have to learn to live with them gone the same way you lived with them being here. And you will, I know you will."

"You talk like you know," he said. "I guess I'd better listen. I guess I'm pretty glad to be driving down this road with you tonight. I wouldn't want to be anyplace else."

"Neither would I," I said.

There were Christmas carols on the radio, and as we drove we listened, and sometimes we sang along. I had never heard Legree sing before. He had a good voice, warm and plain, and he knew verses I had never heard. "O little town of Bethlehem, how still we see thee lie./Above thy deep and dreamless sleep, the silent stars go by," we sang. On the road that night, it wasn't hard to feel what the writer of those words must have felt. They were about a mystery and a vision. Wide heaven and tender, sleeping earth, and the winter silence of the dreamless sleepers rising to meet an answering silence in the stars. And they were about a moment of peace, a place of rest, where all were taken in and no one was left outside, wanting, for the duration of the song.

The next day we made Christmas dinner at my house. At the last minute, Mel and Canady went to Baton Rouge to spend Christmas with his mother. Mel had been pregnant and sick since September, throwing up every day. Some of his mother's cooking would fix her right up, Canady said. Davis came, too, with a woman named Carrie. They stayed in a motel in town—Davis had to keep his distance—but they came. I had imagined a cool, carved brunette with perfect clothes and expensive jewelry who endured her time with us for Davis's sake. But Carrie wasn't that way at all. She was a little overweight, she had frizzy hair fixed in no special way, and she wore corduroy jeans and oversize sweaters. And she fed Davis things at the table, and tickled him until he squirmed in spite of himself and his face turned red.

On Christmas Day, Mother arrived at noon carrying a suitcase. It was so heavy she had to drag and push it up the front walk, and as I watched Legree go out to help her, I let myself imagine that she'd come to stay. I'd been up since six baking and basting and cleaning. The house was full of the rich smell of bread and turkey and pine. Pine garlands draped over every door and picture frame. A tree cut from the cemetery. She could be part of this, I thought. There was enough richness to go around. We'd put her in the sunny back bedroom nearest the kitchen, give her a garden spot to tend. When the children came, she would care for them.

What she had in the suitcase was the Vess silver—every last pickle fork and ice-tea spoon—all freshly polished and wrapped in soft, red velvet wraps tied with velvet ribbons. And the good linen tablecloth, the one with the big V's stitched into all four corners. Also, the heavy Vess candlesticks and two long, white candles of pure beeswax. And when we had them all spread out on the dining room table and she'd called Davis into the room, she put an arm around Davis's waist and an arm around mine and she said, "These are you-all's things now. Merry Christmas. Divvy them up as you want to."

"Don't you want them?" I said.

"No," she said. "They're yours. They're Vess things."

"Your name isn't Vess?" Davis said.

"I'm through laying up treasures, Davis." And the way she said it, I wondered if she believed that she could give my father away, and that once she was rid of him, she could start again and see how she turned out this time.

"Where'd you learn your way around the Bible?" Davis asked, but she wouldn't be drawn into a fight.

"Everybody should know the Bible," she said.

And there was a moment, after everyone was seated and the plates were all served, when nobody spoke, as if we were waiting for someone to speak. Mother's eyes were closed, her head was raised as though she were facing into a storm. Davis stared at his plate.

Legree had folded his hands and rested his forehead on them. The candle flames fanned slowly. We might have been waiting for Papa to tell his story where each of us mattered and found a place. But Papa was not here, and nobody else, it seemed, knew that story anymore, or else we were all telling our own versions.

I brought one of Legree's hands down and held it, rough and warm, against my leg, and as we sat there quietly I imagined that I felt a powerful force eddying like water around the table legs, pulling at our chairs the way the flood used to move across the land between the rivers where the Laughing Place had stood. An undertow that would sweep us away into a place where our failings and betrayals roared so loud, they overpowered any other sound. What kept us here? I wondered. What kept us from being swept away? Was it forgiveness? And what is forgiveness but the constant giving up of innocence, a widening to allow for more of the world's possibilities? When we had sat there in silence for a long time, Legree said, "Amen," and everyone laughed.

That night in bed, Legree said, "I want to tell you something. It's been on my mind, and you deserve to know it. The day I took your father's photograph, the woman you've told me about was with him. She had on a black fur coat and I thought it was his wife at first, the way she fussed at him and looked at her watch and said she had to go. Then I realized she couldn't be his wife because he was showing her around, telling her about the history of the place. It doesn't seem right that I'm the only one who knows after what you've been through about your father."

"Thelma Radford," I said. "I'm not surprised. Nothing you or anyone else could tell me about them would surprise me now." No matter how deep you think the past has sunk beneath the surface of your life, another piece always breaks loose and floats to the surface.

I sat up in bed and hugged my knees, but he pulled me back down and held me close. "Look here," he said, "what would you say if after the nesting season is over in a couple of months, I moved up here?"

"I'd say yes."

"I wanted to hear you say it," he said. "I wanted to hear it come from you."

Later Legree slept, sprawled out as if he'd fallen from a high place and onto this bed. I looked at his body, thin and strong, his face in its sweetness and sadness, his arms and legs flung wide. How could he sleep so deeply, as if no harm could come to him?

The moon was full and silver, rising into the clear winter sky, and as its light came into the room, the room grew colder. Even under the quilt, lying close to Legree's body, I could not get warm. Whenever I closed my eyes, I saw that photograph of my father on the bare banks of the Keowee River near the Laughing Place on the day they came to bulldoze it down. Saw his hands—fists—jammed into the pockets of his hunting jacket, the dark and angry lines of his face, the trees piled up in smoking heaps all around him. While outside the frame of the photograph, his human life waited to take him back, wrapped in a black fur coat that he had given her. Thelma Radford. I'd told Legree that nothing about the two of them could surprise me anymore, but that wasn't true. The feeling of it had ambushed me again, and now it sat in my chest, cold and bitter, crowding against my heart.

And it seemed that I needed to talk to my father. The urgency of it sent me into my bathrobe and downstairs, where the smells of the day hung suspended in the cold air. Turkey and yeast and pine and fire. The floors ran with currents of cold air and it seemed I was wading through them. In the living room the Christmas tree was a dark, pointed shape against the window, its ornaments flashing in the moonlight. On the floor below the tree were the gifts that we'd given one another. The running-horse weather vane from Legree. A set of pearls from Mother. On the mantle piece there, I saw what I had come for: a photograph that my mother had given me that morning. In that cold room, the silver frame was cold, and I carried it close to the window where it was bright enough to see. It was a picture I had never seen before that morning when I'd lifted it out of its layers of green and red tissue paper, a photograph of my father holding me on the front porch of our house (though it was his mother's house then), surrounded by clouds of wisteria and jasmine. "Annie's christening, April 20, 1948," Mother had written on the mat.

In the daylight on Christmas morning, when I'd looked at that picture, I'd seen my father standing proudly in the dress uniform that he wore on special occasions for years after the war, his captain's bars, the Purple Heart, and the crossed rifles of his combat infantryman's badge pinned on his chest. Within the circle of his arms, I am asleep, an infant in a long, creamy gown that spills over his arms and ends in a deep, scalloped hem, a fancy cap shadowing my stubborn, frowning face. Now I saw he was not smiling, saw the steel-rimmed glasses, the gauntness of his face and its shadows, the pride and stiff resolve of his body. There was something possessive about the way he held me and stared at the camera, as if he were about to turn away. And something frightened, too, as if he knew what lay beyond the camera, and he wanted to hold me forever and not let go. As though this holding on was what he knew of love. Looking at that picture, I thought that maybe my father had left me something after all. Perhaps, in coming to know his life, I saw the world in a wider way, and not so much a wilderness. It was a gift of great value, and I wanted to tell him that. He had raised me; I wanted him to see how I had grown up into a person who had lost one kind of faith—that people are whole and undivided—and found another: that this universe of broken and divided beings is the only world we have in which to live as best we can. What is wasteful is to live as if it were otherwise. I stood there in the cold wanting to tell him that.

Saved

Spring is the minister's favorite season. In spring every pulpit and sanctuary rings with the promise of resurrection, and for a few months the world can be trusted not to talk back, but to harmonize and confirm. In the midst of death we are in life. Believe them, the irises, the daffodils, the lilies of the valley say, shooting toward the light out of the winter darkness of their bulbs and roots. Believe them, the courthouse oaks join in, sprouting catkins along their ancient branches. On Easter Sunday morning, Mother and I went to services at All Saints Episcopal Church. There was a chorus of lilies on risers around the pulpit. Reverend Reid spoke of victory, we sang halle-lujahs and hymns to light and joy, though Mother, who prayed with her eyes shut tight and her hands knotted, made prayer look like hard labor. I sat behind my hymnal and wished for another kind of celebration. The kind my mother might lead. Because I've come to believe that Reverend Reid and the ministers are mis-taken in trying to make spring all flowers and victory and hymns to light. What comes around in spring is life, it's true, but life undomesticated, making its unpredictable swerves and dips and plunges. And it seems to me that it is this strangeness that we should celebrate, how spring will not be put to our use, how it exists beyond us, incapable of promise or betrayal. What would such a celebration be? I ask myself. A dance or a solemn procession?

In spring yellow pollen sifts down from the pines and c ts the roofs and hoods of cars; it drifts through screens and into houses and covers windowsills, tables, mirrors, with a layer of fine yellow dust. That year, when the pine pollen stopped falling, it was time for kitchen cleaning day at Mother's house. Even though I'd moved away, there was no question that I would help as I have helped since I was ten, the year we moved into this house. On that first cleaning day, Mother had been determined to wash all traces of Grandmother Vess out of her kitchen. Over the years, as Grandmother Vess disappeared entirely, cleaning day developed trappings, pace, directions of its own. Every spring we carry furniture out into the yard. We *wash* the kitchen. Furniture and baseboards, woodwork and windowsills, stove hood and exhaust fan, light fixtures, cabinets and drawers, inside and out. At the end of the day, we sit in the kitchen and breathe in the wide, white smell of cleanliness, a smell that collects in a place high up in your nose, and we go to bed, aching and satisfied.

Hands and knees work first—the baseboards. I have always enjoyed scrubbing baseboards. The rhythm of it is soothing—scrub and rinse, scrub and rinse. And the tools—a stiff scrub brush, a bucket of warm, soapy water sharpened with bleach—pleasing to use. A year's worth of dirt breaks up in front of my brush, dissolves, and rinses away as the water in the bucket turns slowly brown.

On kitchen cleaning day, the coffeepot stays warm; the windows are opened wide and a spring breeze blows through; my father's big band tapes play on the cassette player. But on this day a tape of gospel music played: swells of lush and holy sound made by a hundred-voice choir. As she scrubbed, Mother hummed along, and sometimes words broke through. By the time the water in my bucket was black, the first side of the tape was finished. When I came back into the house from emptying my bucket, the other side of the tape had started.

"Aren't you ready for another tape?" I said. "How about some Benny Goodman?"

"I want to listen to this one all the way through," she said. "I'm waiting for a particular song." *Swish, swish, swish,* went her brush. And then a bass note so deep it made the speakers hum came out of the tape player. "Were you there?" the choir intoned, "when they crucified my Lord?"

Mother scrubbed and listened, and when the hymn was over, she threw her brush into her bucket of water. She sat back on her heels, peeled off her yellow rubber gloves, and brushed hair off of her face with the back of her wrist. "Annie," she said, in an elaborately casual voice, "I have something to tell you." Her tone spoke of long thought, the weighing and measuring of words, of decisions reached after long thought. A man, I thought. She's met a man and she's getting married. And just that quickly, I tried to imagine what I would say. "Good for you, Mother," I would say. "No one expects you to live alone for the rest of your life. You go right ahead, you deserve to be happy."

I dropped my brush into my bucket and sat back, too, and faced her. "I'm listening," I said.

"You remember I told you I've been going to these Full-Gospel Businessmen's Fellowship meetings now and then, just to, you know, meet some new people and get out of the house and keep busy?"

I nodded, and felt the smile going stiff on my face, felt the bones of my knees press against the hard floor.

She took a deep breath. "Oh, why mince words? Last night at one of the meetings, I accepted Jesus Christ as my personal savior. I've been saved, Annie. Saved and baptized in the Holy Spirit, all in one fell swoop." *So there,* she nodded, and climbed to her feet.

"Are you serious? You're not serious," I said, and I stood up, too. She looked at me tenderly. *Don't do that!* I wanted to shout. *Fight with me so I'll know you're still you.* But she just stood there, smiling, forgiving. "What exactly is it that you've been saved from?" I asked.

She looked up at the ceiling with exaggerated patience, the way she used to do when we'd pestered her with the same childish question for the hundredth time. "My own sinfulness and error, of course," she said. I might have known that she would have all the answers.

They had this speaker, Mother said, quickly, before I could

stop her, a man who'd spent ten years in prison for stabbing another man to death in a barroom fight. He'd been a violent man before he came to the Lord and realized that his violence, his rage, were symptoms of an inner emptiness, a void waiting to be filled. He was a big man, she said, half Cherokee Indian, with tattoos on the backs of both hands, and his message was this: God did not intend for us to be lonely or lost. "He had a beautiful way of speaking, Annie," she said. "He was so gentle and kind." He said that God could lift the loneliness and pain from our lives in the twinkling of an eye if we would only let Him in. If He loved us enough to send His only Son into the world to die for our sins, surely He could do something as simple as take away loneliness and pain. The longer this man spoke, the more she'd felt this powerful urge to *talk* more with him. She didn't know what she wanted to say exactly, but afterward, she'd waited until everyone else was gone, and then she went up and she told him that. One thing led to another. Before long, with his help, she'd realized *who* had spoken to her through him, who it was that had really called her. And right then and there she knelt down on the carpet with him and accepted Jesus Christ as her personal savior and received the baptism of the Holy Spirit. Right there in the backroom of the Steakhouse. Imagine. "And now here I am," she said, spreading her arms in surrender, "a new creation."

There was something eager in her voice, something relieved and trusting. Where had I heard that tone before? Had she once spoken about my father this way, as though he'd lifted her out of danger, as though she were grateful to him for rescuing her? Yes, gratitude is what I remember in the story she once told me. The shy girl from a respectable Georgia family—fatherless, though, and shaved thin by poverty—persuaded by her girlfriends at the last minute to go to a dance at Camp Wheeler, where she meets the handsome lieutenant from a fine, old South Carolina family. Or maybe what I was hearing was myself talking about Matthew to my friends at college, talking into the night, planning the happiness of the rest of our lives, talking and talking.

"How exactly did he do it, Mother?" I said. "Did he lay hands on you?"

She bit her lip, wiped her palms down her skirt, stared at the floor. I might as well be Papa, I thought, interrogating her this way, as though he knew more about her than she knew about herself. "Forget I asked that," I said. "But you'll forgive me for being shocked, Mother. Stunned, actually."

"Of course I forgive you," she said. "But look here, there's nothing ignoble in what I've done, now, is there?"

It was a challenge, not a question. Ignoble? Mean or petty or low? "No, Mother, of course there isn't."

Her cheeks burned as though she'd been out in the cold too long. "Well, why don't you let me go my way then, without being caustic and snide?"

"Yes," I said, "you go your way and I'll go mine, is it a deal?"

A cloud of doubt crossed her face. If there's one thing Christians can't tolerate, it's tolerance. There was nothing new about Mother's evangelizing spirit. She'd been out to save the world all her life, I think, and in her eyes, I certainly needed saving from one mistaken way of life or another. But this, I knew, would be more urgent. The stakes now were not dating the right people or getting invitations, but my immortal soul. I felt us settling in for a long season of struggle.

Now, it is said that Jesus' serene and loving nature was clouded by one passion, and that was revulsion to the point of nausea at the thought of Christians so lukewarm in their faith, they lacked the courage to speak up for Him and carry His word to the fallen world. And if the opposite is also true—that He loved best His loudest and most impulsive warriors, then Mother must surely be one of God's great beloved. Mother went right to work. By the end of the month she'd converted her boss, Grady Sims, the county tax assessor. "Oh, Grady," she said, "he's so pitiful, but he surely loves the Lord." Soon, on any given morning—if I went down early to the courthouse to check the public records or check out a story—I knew I would find her in the back hallway at the tax assessor's office where the old maps and files are stored, praying with Grady. Eyes closed, their hands lifted in praise, they whispered Jesus' name and smiled. Any evening, I could find her out at the Victory Fellowship Church on Stamp Creek Road. Mondays for praising the Lord through song, Tuesdays for a healing service, Wednesdays for Bible Study, Thursdays for choir practice, Fridays as a chaperone for the teenagers, Saturdays for typing at the church office. Sundays for worship—twice.

"Full Gospel!" the words proclaimed in red letters at the top of the masthead on the Victory Fellowship weekly bulletin. "Where the worship is free, signs and wonders follow, the Holy Spirit abounds, and Jesus is Lord!" A place where the Holy Spirit regularly descends, bringing spiritual gifts to the congregation. To one, He gives the gift of prophecy; to another the gift of interpreting prophecy; to another the gift of tongues, or healing, or discernment. By the end of April she'd gotten herself elected president of the local chapter of Women Aglow, where she immediately began to mastermind JESUS! '81, a gathering of spirit-filled women from all over the Southeast to be held in the fall at the Omni International down in Atlanta. She seemed happier than I can ever remember, and though some people began to cross the street to avoid her, most of her old friends stayed true.

Of course, nobody here is a stranger to religious feeling, especially not her women friends. This town, this state, the *South*, is full of widows like my mother. Perfectly groomed in their soft sweaters and bright scarves and polished, low-heeled pumps, they emerge in surprising ways after their husbands die. I see them on the way to work in the morning walking around the mile track at the city recreation center in their coordinated sweat suits, talking to one another as they go. They turn out to support the new arts center or they join Great Books discussion groups at the library, where they become serious and thoughtful readers. Sometimes they remarry retired textile mill executives, who move them to Greenville to columned mansions overlooking perfect lawns that slope down to azalea-bordered ponds, who treat them like queens for the rest of their lives.

The ones who stay in Timmons and do not remarry attend the Episcopal or the Presbyterian church every Sunday morning, dressed smartly in their ultrasuede suits or silk dresses. They volunteer through their churches to push the book cart around at the hospital or they tape books for the blind. Their deepening faith is expressed by the extra care they take cross-stitching the Paschal Lamb onto the altar cloths at the Episcopal church. They do not kneel in front of ex-convicts in the back room at the Steakhouse and accept Jesus Christ as their personal Savior. They keep their hands folded, their eyes down as they pray, quietly to themselves. They do not pray with their palms upraised, laughing, crying, clapping, their faces wet with tears of love, as people pray at Victory Fellowship Church. They do not talk about the end of the world as though it were already marked on the calendar, or stack their nightstands with books whose titles shout *Countdown to Armageddon!* or *The Late, Great Planet Earth!* from behind a fence of exclamation points. They do not talk about Jesus as though He lived next door or were the hero of some romance novel. In fact, they do not *speak* about God any more than they talked with one another about their private lives. Their relationship with Jesus (though they would never call it that) is entirely private and sacred, the way their relationship with their husbands had once been.

My Mother, however, claps, cries, talks about Jesus to anyone who will listen and yet they have not given up on her. Mother says "Girls, Jesus was a man like us in all ways but sin. That's why I can have such a close personal relationship with Him." I heard her say those exact words this one afternoon to her bridge club when I stopped by one afternoon to pick up some things I'd left in my closet. I looked into the living room where the card table was set up. There they sat, holding their cards, picking pastel mints out of a cut-crystal dish. "Is that right, Louise?" one of them answered. "Well, isn't that wonderful for you?" And why not? They're used to having their hearts broken, their lives twisted into painful knots by alcoholic husbands or by children who seem intent on smashing their own lives into rubble. All this they have borne in the privacy of their own homes and hearts. What's a little religious fanaticism after that? Something else to be gotten through graciously, like a lady.

Mother, on the other hand, no longer believed in graciousness, if she ever did, really. She believed in getting on with the plan, leading God's Army into battle. Late in April Mel invited me and Mother over for a Saturday brunch. I made a mistake and came early. By the time I realized that Mother's car was not in the driveway, the doorbell had finished its tune and I heard footsteps inside. Then Mel swung the door open, looking stunned. "Annie," she said, grabbing me by both hands and pulling me inside, "come in. You have to see my house, right now."

"I'm dying to," I said. And so, to keep busy until Mother came, to avoid sitting down across from each other or looking each other in the eye, we set out on a tour of the house. That is how it had been since the wedding: Mel had hardly spoken to me, and I didn't know what to say that wouldn't make it worse. "I'm sorry," would not cover it. So I'd said nothing and Mel had said nothing and Mother had said nothing, and now the silence had gone on for so long I would have to explain and apologize for my silence before I could even *begin* to apologize for the wedding. It had all gotten so complicated, I didn't know where to start. So we toured the house instead.

That day, Mel was eight months' pregnant and she was wearing a bright yellow dotted Swiss maternity shirt with a big, white linen collar edged in lace. In spite of her bulk she walked fast, flinging open doors with a flourish like a Realtor, ushering me into rooms. "As you can see, the foyer floor is real marble." A white staircase curved gracefully toward the second floor, its railing made of smooth, oiled cherry. From the king-size sleigh bed in the center of the master bedroom Mel and Canady could look out over the lake. The nursery down the hall was smothered in eyelet, papered in frolicking lambs. At the other end of the hushed and carpeted hallway, behind double doors, Canady's audio entertainment room waited, its walnut shelves stacked high with speakers and turntables, and lined with Mel's pageant photographs and trophies, as though *he'd* won them.

We were down in the basement, admiring the power and efficiency of the central vacuum system, when we heard Mother's car crunch over the gravel and stop outside, "Oh, Lord," Mel said, "my croissants," and she flew up the steps, belly and all. There were giant red poppies on the wallpaper in her kitchen, and a black-and-white tile floor. Mel had just slipped the fat, red, quilted stove mitt over her hand and was taking the croissants out of the oven when Mother popped her head around the door. "Hello, girls," she sang out. "Jesus is coming soon!" which had become her way of saying hello, but Mel didn't know that.

Mel jumped, then she dropped the tray of croissants on the stovetop and covered her eyes with the stove mitt. "Oh, Aunt Louise," she said, "not until my baby gets here." Then she rushed through the swinging doors out of the kitchen, and a door slammed in the back of the house.

"What's got into her?" Mother said. She dropped a package on the table; it was wrapped in fancy paper decorated with lambs and clouds, and tied with stretchy gold cord. "I brought her a few little diaper shirts."

"Well, Mother," I said, "you scared her."

"Oh, fiddle," she said. "It's her hormones, that's all."

When Mel came back, she acted like nothing had happened, of course. Her hair was combed and she'd put on fresh lipstick. As she came through the door, she smiled at both of us, her famous beauty-queen smile. What else could she do, being Mel? She comes from that same long line of women as Mother's friends, for whom the ability to carry on cheerfully and graciously in the face of insult or outrageous lunacy is an inheritance as precious as the family silver. She poured coffee into our cups and put the croissants in a basket covered with a red napkin the exact shade of one of the paisleys on the place mats, then set it in the middle of the table. "Here we go, ladies," she said, and Mother reached over and patted Mel's round, hard belly.

"Annie, when are you going to have you one of these?" Mother asked.

I tried to smile back at her mysteriously, as though I knew the answer. "One of these days," I said. "Who knows? It may even be soon."

Mother sat up as though she'd heard a crash. Her eyes narrowed and she twisted her rings, the heavy lozenge of a Vess diamond Papa her given her, and the slender wedding band. She would take it off, she said, but her knuckles were too swollen. "Well, Lord, let's please get you married first," she said, watching me, tapping her fingers on the tabletop. When I didn't answer, she looked down at her lap, and her lips moved. She was praying again.

"That's another story," I said, sullenly, and I looked down at the coffee in the fine, white cup with the thin, gold rim. I don't know why I said those things. I might marry Legree someday, and if I did I would marry him gladly and fully, and soberly, too, celebrating all the way. But in order to deny Mother the satisfaction of thinking she had made me do something, I would deny myself almost anything. Sometimes it felt like a hopeless, dangerous struggle, like trying to swim through weeds, wrapping, entangling yourself tighter with every move you made to free yourself.

"Oh, Lord," Mother said, and she rested her forehead heavily on her hand, as though she were checking her temperature.

"How about another croissant, Aunt Louise?" Mel asked, "How about you, Annie?" she asked me firmly.

Mother raised her head like an old war-horse sniffing battle smoke. She seemed to have come to a decision, and she sighed heavily and set down her cup. Clink! Her face looked heavy and old, her neck heavily creased, as though the love of God were a hard yoke to shoulder, a heavy plow to haul. "Annie," she said momentously, "I have been carrying a burden on my heart for you."

Clink. I set my own cup down on its saucer. "Well, I wish you'd put it down, Mother, before you break your back," I said. The sound of my voice startled us both. She looked at me. I looked at her. It was one of those times when you feel a door nudged open that has been shut and sealed for a long time. And you know that if that door ever opens, all sorts of trash and dust and rot will blow out. That day, it stayed closed, but Mother went on anyway. She was going to have her say.

She had been down on her knees in the pine straw one day last week, checking the azaleas for leaf rot, when she heard a sound. Gong! It went gong as though the sky were one of those big Chinese what-you-call-'ems and someone had just struck it. And she felt so dizzy, as if the earth were spinning faster and faster, out of control. She'd closed her eyes, and that's when she saw the Lord, the Lion of Judah in His crown, reared up on his back legs, and Satan, an ugly, gray snake, like a gigantic cottonmouth water moccasin, locked in a struggle over the hands of a clock that were about to meet at twelve midnight. God reared back and pulled right; Satan tightened his coils and hauled left, and at the peak—the fever pitch of this fight—with dust rolling up all around them and Satan's ugly head striking and striking, and God's back feet ripping up the ground, God looked at her with His great sorrowful eyes and He said, just as plain, "Help me, Louise."

"And that's just what I plan to do from now on, starting right here," she said. "And the Lord said something else to me," she continued.

"You all had a regular heart-to-heart," I said, and felt that door nudged open again.

Her face blotched with color, but she went on. "When I was kneeling there last night, the Lord spoke to my heart and you know what He said?"

Mel sighed, leaned her cheek on one hand, and began to pick up crumbs with the tip of one finger. "What, Mother?" I said.

"He told me, 'Annie's saved.' " She looked so hopeful, and to say what was on my mind to say would have been cruel.

"I don't think so, Mother," I said. "But I think you need to go let Doctor Mac give you a complete physical."

She waved that idea away as though it were a swarm of gnats. "Well, why would He tell me that if it's not true? Is the Lord a liar?"

The idea was hilarious. The Lord as a kind of snake-oil salesman or gigolo, smooth and handsome like Canady, lying his way into the lives of lonely women. At the same time it made me want to weep. I could have made a joke of it; Papa would have. Flower arranging or china painting—Papa called any passion of Mother's a tangent, meaning, of course, that he knew the straight line off of which this angle had bounced so comically. But I couldn't do that, not anymore. Mother has never been halfhearted or tangential about anything. She learned the language, she bought all the supplies, she went into it wholeheartedly. "At least not in the way you mean, Mother," I said. "I just want a way to be that I find for myself, that no one gives to me." She made a scornful noise, opened her mouth to speak. "Look, Mother," I said. "Live and let live, remember?"

"Well, think about it," she said, and she got up suddenly and began to clear the table.

"I've thought about it," I said.

Saying those words, I felt an old, cloudy, smothering fear rise up in me. Matthew and I had spoken those same words to one another the winter before he died, when he'd started going to a Sufi group, pressuring me to go. Once I went, for his sake, to this group of gentle, smiling men and women who sat in a circle and talked about their God. But as they spoke, I felt smothered in goodness, as though something thick and soft were closing over my head, as though I were drowning in it. When the women spoke, they sounded as if they'd just woken up, murmuring gentle words. Gentleness, in fact, seemed to be the first commandment, but I felt the law behind it, like iron. And I knew I would not fit in, even as I watched Matthew spread like butter in the sun in the presence of these women, with their soft eyes and gentle touches. That first time, we chanted and danced in a circle, then we sat for a long time in silence and I watched Matthew's face ease and grow radiant, as though a light were shining up from someplace inside him. But I could not go where they went. I could not keep my eyes closed, or quiet my mind. When I tried to meditate, my thoughts came to life; they had barbs on them, poison-tipped needles. I was a whirling thornbush of angry thoughts and crimes against gentleness. But Matthew was hungry for it; he went twice, then three, four times a week.

Soon he was talking about going to live in the Sufi community in upstate New York. About *our* going to live there. "What would I do there?" I asked, meaning, of course, Who would I be there? I saw myself sweeping floors, baking bread, sewing long skirts out of India print bedspreads, and I felt that smothering sensation again.

We had fights about this—terrible, ungentle fights in which glasses got broken and books got knocked from shelves, followed by cold silences that lasted for days because I said I could not, *would* not go. Not even for him, not this time. And for the first time since we'd been together, I thought he might leave me. All that winter, fear had stayed wedged in the top of my chest, a square, unyielding block of fear that never softened or went away.

The morning he left for Cheraw, he put a hand on my shoulder, looked into my eyes. "Think about it," he said. "Will you do that much for me?"

"I've thought about it," I said, turning my shoulder out from under his hand. Those were the last words I ever spoke to him. Much later, I found in the pocket of the pants I'd been wearing that day a list I'd made of points to argue with Matthew when he came back home. And now my mother was slipping away, too, going where true believers go, away from the old life that seemed so shabby and mistaken and into the new promised land.

After that day at Mel's house, I started to think about Matthew again, how he might have been saved, too, if he had lived, and where he would have gone to find his promised land. I began to wonder what had become of the place where Matthew had died. Had his parents let it lie fallow and go back to blackberry and kudzu vine and jasmine and Virginia creeper, or had they kept it plowed and tended and growing? I wanted to see it, I wanted to take his ashes back and leave them on the farm there, in the places where he had been most at peace: near the pond and under the muscadine vines that grew in the trees at the edge of the woods on the border of the lower new ground. In the woods beside the spring that bubbled up at the foot of a small ridge. Especially there. Boots unlaced, shirt unbuttoned, he would drink cup after cup of water from the spring, as if he had a thirst in every part of him that only this water could satisfy.

One Sunday morning in late April, I called Mama Settles in Cheraw, and when we'd said all we could about the weather and the season, I said, "I called to ask you, Mama Settles. I was thinking of bringing Matthew's ashes back there. I want to scatter them on the farm. I think he would have wanted me to do that. Will you let me?"

I heard a quick breath on the other end of the line, then silence with turmoil behind it. "Well, come on, then," she said finally, in a thin voice. "We get back from church around noon. I have to go now." When I pulled into the driveway beside the house, I saw Papa Settles sitting under the pin oak that shaded the screen porch, with his tackle box open on a card table in front of him, the reel broken down into a hundred intricate wheels and gears. It was the same way I'd seen him when Matthew had first brought me here. Only now, the tree had grown, and he looked smaller under it. I had never realized that it was a young tree all those years until I went away from it and came back and saw how tall and wide it had spread above him.

Then Matthew's mother came out of the house with her apron on. She walked up and looked once at the box on the seat beside me, then stood there with her hands wrapped in her apron, waiting. Papa Settles came up and stood behind her. "How are you, Mama Settles?" I said as I got out of the car.

"Tolerably well, Annie," she said, holding out her hand. "You?" I had forgotten that about the Settleses: They did not kiss; they shook hands.

"Doing well," I said as I shook her hand, then Papa's. His shoulders were stooped, his blue eyes were bleary. He looked caved in in the middle, his belt drawn tight, and a few wisps of hair, each one made separate and shiny with hair tonic, combed over the bald spot on the crown of his head. I saw there was no welcome in their eyes. Maybe they believe I should not be doing so well, I thought. They were stern, moral, upright people doing their duty for their son's widow, the way they had done their duty and let him be cremated as I had wished, because I was his wife. In their eyes, Matthew and I had been one flesh.

"Will you have dinner with us?" Mama Settles asked.

"Just some tea, thanks," I said. "I ate on the way."

She brought the tea, and we sat on the screen porch for awhile and talked about the weather and the bees. Back near the bright, spring-green woods stood a row of white beehives. A hand-lettered sign out by the road read, "Honey for Sale." They'd been keeping them for the last year, they said. Mama did most of the work with them. Papa Settles was afraid of them, and the bees knew it. "They sting the fire out of him," she said. "But they make the sweetest honey."

"They do that, all right," Papa Settles said.

And then, as we'd done so many afternoons when Matthew was alive, we were quiet together. We drank our ice tea and watched the bees fly in and out of the sunlight and listened to the frogs in the stock pond and the cows tearing grass in the pasture next to the house.

When Mama Settles spoke, her voice was sharp. "You know who would have had a fit over those bees?" she said.

"Who?" I said, quickly. I thought of the box on the front seat of the car, and it felt as though someone had suddenly blown up a big balloon in my chest and squeezed out the air.

"Bud," she said, settling her look on me like a dark cloud, lowering. "Now, he wouldn't have needed to read a book or anything like I've had to do. Bud would have studied their ways until he'd come to his own understanding of them," she said.

"Yes," I said, "that's just what he would have done." I felt my heart beat faster, the way it does when I'm afraid. I'd forgotten that they called him Bud. Because things slip away, you cannot hold on; it is life that gives weight to a nickname or a quirk, that fills in the outline of another's joy.

She bowed her head and looked at the concrete porch floor. She'd aged, Mama Settles, in the two years since Matthew died. Her hair was now almost completely white. When I'd seen her last, her face had been lined with pain and grief, as though her tears were caustic and had left marks where they ran down. Now the pain had retreated, disappeared below the surface again. It had turned into sadness that lived in her eyes like a pool of darker color below the usual brown. It was a color I had seen in my own eyes lately, as though sadness had become a part of me too.

"I think I'd better go," I said. "I want to do what I said I was going to do and get home before too late."

She stood up instantly and her eyes widened, as though she

were afraid. Papa Settles stood too, and shook my hand. "We miss you, Annie," he said, struggling with the words. "In fact, we miss you a lot."

"I miss you, too," I said. "I miss you both."

"You won't mind if I don't walk you to the car," Mama Settles said, opening the screen door so that I could pass through it ahead of her.

"I won't mind," I said. I walked to the car alone and got in. I started the engine, and then I saw Mama Settles walking down the path toward the beehives, hugging herself, looking around at the trees and the cows as though she were interested in them. But what she was really doing was crying. I'd seen her walk like that just after Matthew and I had told them that we wouldn't be coming there to take over the farm, the way they'd always planned. I remembered how Matthew had run after her that day.

"We thought you-all might be ready to come and make your home here," his father had said one afternoon just after we were married. And Matthew and I looked at each other, and then Matthew said, "No, thank you, Papa, but we won't be doing that." We were ready for this moment; we'd talked it over, it was decided. Matthew did not want to disappear into the farm the way he'd seen his grandfather and his father disappear. It seemed to him that those men did not lead or seek; instead they followed a track that had been laid down before they were born, until they reached the places in life that had been prepared for them. Year after year, the way Matthew saw it, as they walked behind the mules that turned the cane press, swatting the animals' bony rumps with leafy branches torn from the nearest saplings, as they planted and sprayed and harvested, tended the chickens, pruned the grapevines and the peach trees, hunted in winter and fished in summer, Matthew said they faded and blurred and merged with their work, until they became as necessary and unremarkable an accompaniment to work as the slap of reins on a mule's back or the ring of metal against metal in the tractor shed before daybreak. He'd watched his grandfather turn into an old man who dozed in front of the fire with a mended mule harness draped across his lap. He saw him in his coffin, an old man with his Bible resting on his chest and his sewing awl clasped in his folded hands, its handle worn silver-shiny with use. But Matthew was destined for more than that. He wasn't born to follow anything.

I looked at the box of Matthew's ashes that rested on the seat beside me and at Matthew's mother, walking away, hugging herself and crying. Matthew was no longer my husband, I thought, but he was still their son. He was their son, forever. A marriage can end and death will finish it, but death cannot change a child into a stranger. I have no right, I thought, to leave his ashes for the wind to scatter, for the rain to wash away. Matthew did not want to disappear, and there were people here who remembered how they loved him, who loved him still.

Matthew had run after his mother once before, but this time it was I who was going, walking fast down the white sand track, the box of Matthew's ashes in my hands. "Mama Settles," I called. Seeing the box, she walked faster. "Ruth," I called. She stopped and turned, I held it out to her. The hum of the bees was constant here; it sounded the way I imagine the earth would sound if we could hear it working. "I want you to have this," I said. "Please."

As she reached for the box, pain rose to the surface of her face again I heard Papa Settles coming, shuffling through the sand. "Bless you," he said as I ran past him toward the car. Then Mama Settles began to cry. The last sound I heard was the sound of their voices, speaking low to one another.

When Matthew had first brought me here, the field they called the lower new ground had been full of broom sedge and pine seedlings. Now it was fenced and planted in long, straight rows of soybeans. Seeing that, I realized I had been dreading this moment all day, the moment when I saw that the field had been abandoned, gone wild as grief, unrecovered. But I should have know the Settleses were not people who would abandon a field or give over a life to grieving, even for their only son. I stepped on the bottom strand of barbed wire and ducked through the fence, then I started across the field in the sun, stepping carefully down the long rows of young plants. It had been a dry spring, and with every step, I broke through a crust on top of the ground. Back toward the woods, the field became sandy, the soybean rows thinned, and I saw the stump of the tree that Matthew must have hit with the bush hog that day. It had been pulled halfway out of the ground and burned, and yet it seemed as firmly rooted as it must have been when it was alive. Someone tried to pull it up, I thought, and failing at that, had set it on fire— and failing at that, had gone away and planted the field in soybeans. Then panic flared up in me, like fire suddenly burning. "This is the place where Matthew died," I thought, and I covered my face with my hands. It seemed to me a terrible injustice, to be able to stand at the small and definite place where something as wide as a life had ended. And I felt the sadness rise in me then, not just for Matthew's death, but for the person he might have become and how our children might have been born to us, each one as bright and filled with light as the new green leaves on the trees in the woods beyond this field. But it was only sadness, and just that. There was no menace in it. This was not the field where Matthew had died; it was another place now, just as I was not the person I had been when I lost him. And as I stood there, it occurred to me that maybe, after all, there would have been no future for us. Sooner or later, we would have left one another, pulled apart by the opposing forces our desires had become: Matthew, gone to live with the Sufis; me to God knows where. Maybe it would have happened when he came back from Cheraw and found me awake and unyielding, while he went on dreaming about the next promised land toward which we must travel. Yes, I thought, it would have happened then. I felt lighter, somehow, for knowing that, as though I'd fitted a piece back into myself and plugged up a hole. The sunlight felt warm on the top of my head, like a hand placed there gently. Matthew was beyond the reach of salvation or rescue now, but I had finished the journey for him and brought him home.

Jason Tull Reeves

The hospital called at four in the morning to say that Mel was in labor and asking for me. When the phone rang beside the bed, I woke in a panic, as if I were rushing toward a white wall too fast, out of control, about to crash. Who was calling? It had to be Mother. Mother was calling and someone was dead. Maybe Legree was dead. Yes, that was it. But how would they know to call Mother?

"Who?" I said.

"Mr. Reeves had to leave," the official voice said. "Mrs. Reeves asked us to call you."

Outside, the moon had set but the light had not yet risen. It was the time of absolute stillness, of deepest dark. Even the cicadas and the crickets were silent, the world seemed poised, as though something were finished, something else not yet begun. A pause, like a breath drawn in. The breath let out would be morning. It was cool and I smelled rain on the breeze that ruffled the tops of the hickory trees around the house. I stood there for awhile breathing it in, listening, and it seemed that if I turned, I might find my father standing next to me, looking up at the Cherokee stars, here on the shore of the ancient eastern ocean with morning coming on. His world was the same, but he was no longer in it. The dogs crawled out from under the porch and sniffed the air, then Napoleon walked over and nudged his lumpy head up under my hand. I picked up one of his ears and let it fall. I bent down and laid my cheek against the top of his head for a moment, and in that moment, it was as if what I missed about my father was no longer a way of talking or any particular habit of his mind or heart. What I missed about him was everything, all at once, pouring over me like the air on this chilly morning. What I missed was his presence on earth, and I knew I would miss him this way for the rest of my life.

Just before I pulled out of my driveway and onto the Bean Blossom Road, I looked back at the house in the rearview mirror. It looked small and faraway, dark against the trees with the porch light burning, as if I'd started on a long journey and left the lights of home far behind.

At the hospital the dark had been chased out of the halls, which were brightly lit as ice, and into the rooms that lined the halls, their doors half open, from which came moans and snores and other whispered and sighed-out secrets of pain. The labor room was all sterile efficiency, too: stainless steel and more bright lights and trays of instruments, tightly sealed. There were three beds in the room. Two of them were covered with stiff, white sheets, and Mel lay in the one next to the far wall with her eyes closed. Her hands rested on two wide straps stretched across her belly that were connected to a machine with a screen where green waves moved steadily. There was a needle in her hand, connected to a bottle of clear liquid that hung on an IV stand beside the bed. In her wrinkled, stained hospital gown, there was something crumpled and abandoned about her, like a tissue that's been wadded up and tossed aside. A tall, skinny nurse stood next to the bed, and an older nurse who wore a happy-face pin on her uniform lapel sat on the side of Mel's bed and patted her knee in time to a tune she was humming. But Mel did not seem to notice. She lay there breathing as if breathing required all of her concentration and will.

"Are you the cousin she was asking for?" the tall one asked. She had sober, gray eyes and lank hair pulled back with a ribbon, and she carried a basin against her hip. "Her husband had to go," she said, smiling. "That happens with some of them."

"Yes," I said. But Mel did not move or open her eyes. She seemed involved in some inner work that took all her energy and made her frown. No one would look at her now and call her beautiful. Is that why Canady had left? I remembered sitting beside him at the Miss South Carolina Pageant while Mel sang "What's It All About, Alfie?" As she'd moved around the stage, the spotlight had followed her, touched her golden hair, exploded off the sequins on her tight, blue dress. And Canady had followed her with his eyes, hunched forward on the edge of his seat with his elbows on his knees, his mouth open, as if he couldn't believe what he saw. Now it seemed she had climbed down off of that stage and into this bed, there was a baby coming, and he had gone. I felt ashamed all over again for seeking him out, for almost agreeing to turn myself into a dot on his map of the known world of pleasure though which he moved.

"Is that Annie?" Mel called in a sharp, brittle voice. She struggled up onto her elbows, her eyes wild and dazed. Just then, the waves on the screen of the machine to which the straps across her belly were attached began to develop peaks. Mel gasped, fell back onto the pillow and gritted her teeth. The older nurse stood up from the bed and took Mel's hand. "Relax your jaw, Mrs. Reeves," she said. "Let's pant and blow now, shall we?"

Mel jerked her hand away, gripped the edges of the bed as though she were holding onto a small boat in a heavy sea. As the peaks on the waves crossing the screen sharpened, her features seemed to grow smaller, to disappear behind a veil of pain. She panted like a dog, with her tongue out, and once, she groaned, a deep, gut sound that made the hair stand up on my neck. I thought it was the sound the earth might make, if the earth had a voice, as it split to let a plant push through. How alone she was, far out on the edge of this pain. "This is an emergency," I thought. "Why is no one doing anything?" The older nurse stood beside the bed, watching the jagged crests of the waves on the screen and breathing along with Mel, and the tall one stood beside the bed, holding the basin against her hip. And then it was over. The crests subsided into waves, then turned into a green line that undulated across the screen. Mel leaned over the edge of the bed and vomited into the basin that the tall nurse held for her. When she was done, the tall nurse carried the basin into the bathroom.

"That was a good, strong one, hon'," the older nurse said cheerfully, as she wiped Mel's mouth. "Keep that up and your baby'll be here in no time."

Mel pushed her hand away and looked at her with pure hatred. "Give me the goddamn epidural," she said. The tall nurse, who had just come back from the bathroom, stepped to the side of the bed, bent over, and spoke loudly, close to Mel's face. "It's too late for that now, Mrs. Reeves," she said, slowly, pronouncing her words with exaggerated care. "You're nine centimeters already. We can't give you the epidural when you're almost fully dilated. A few more contractions and you'll be ready to push that baby out for us."

"Fine," Mel said, as she collapsed back onto the pillow. "I hope somebody ties you down and sticks knives in your stomach someday, too." Then she began to cry, with her hands over her face.

"What can I do?" I asked the tall nurse.

"Do you know anything about Lamaze?"

"I know it's about breathing." The two nurses looked at one another and smiled. Then the tall one shrugged. "I guess you'll have to sit this one out," she said.

I stood beside the bed, feeling helpless. What was I doing here? Why had she called me? I didn't know any breathing patterns to talk her through. What could I do to relieve this pain that seemed like no pain I had ever seen before. All pain is private; it takes you where no one can follow. But this pain seemed willful and full of intention. It had seized her and shaken her, and there was no way to pull her free of it; the pain had to finish with her. Maybe, after all, I thought, Canady had left not because Mel was no longer beautiful but because he could not afford to feel this helpless and insignificant, or to be in a world where he had no power. But what could I do? There were beads of sweat on her upper lip and her forehead. I will wipe them away, I thought, and went into the bathroom for a washcloth. That is what I can do. Something simple and physical, to show her that her body can be comforted and soothed, that it can feel something other than this pain.

"Mel," I said, as I moved toward the bed, "it's Annie. Let me wipe your face for you. Would that feel good?"

But she knocked my hand aside as she had the nurse's hand, and looked at me with the same hatred and despair. "Don't you come *near* me, Annie," she said through clenched teeth. "Don't you touch me, you or Canady, either one."

I stepped back, away from the look in her eyes. "Canady's gone," I said, "You *asked* me to come, Mel."

The older nurse got up from the bed and motioned for me to follow her into the hall. "She's just in transition, honey," she said. "She doesn't mean it. A lot of them act like this, cussing out their husbands, hitting at us. I mean to tell you, you never heard such talk. In the old days we just knocked them out, and when they woke up, they had themselves a baby. Now they have to suffer through every minute of it." She shook her head and walked off down the hall.

"Oh, she does mean it," I said to myself. "She absolutely means it." No doubt that look of pure hatred had been there since the wedding, buried under many cool layers of politeness. But what was happening to her now had stripped away all those layers and left the hurt and anger exposed. It was real. The only thing to do was to stand in the face of that hurt and call it by its right name.

I went back into the room and sat in a chair near the door. "I won't come near you," I said. "I'll wait. But I'm not going anywhere." I was ashamed of myself for ever thinking of her as a frivolous person. Just then, another contraction began. The waves built to sharp and terrible peaks, higher than any I'd seen. Mel panted fiercely, her breath caught in her throat. "It *hurts*," she shouted, whipping her head from side to side on the pillow. "*It hurts!*"

"Breathe, Mrs. Reeves," the older nurse said, as she watched the monitor and held Mel's hand. "Breathe. Your baby's on the way." Then she turned and spoke to me over her shoulder: "You'd better put on a gown and a mask and wash up if you're going down to delivery with us."

The older nurse pushed the gurney and the tall nurse pushed the IV stand. As we rolled down the hall toward the delivery room, Mel cried quietly to herself. She'd been crying since the tall nurse had reached up inside her with a steel hook and broken her water so that it flooded out and soaked the bed. The room had filled up with the lush smell of a tidal marsh, and she'd begun to cry, the exhausted, sad crying of someone who's lost a long fight. When we were almost to the delivery room doors, Mel grabbed my hand. "Don't leave," she said. "Don't go, Annie, come with me."

"I'm right here, Mel," I said.

She sniffed and pulled strands of hair out of the corner of one eye with her free hand. Her face was very pale and the bones started up through the skin. As the bottom of the bed bumped against the swinging metal doors, she closed her eyes again. "You look like Old Mother Hubbard in that gown," she said.

"Thank you."

As they were fitting her feet up into the stirrups on the table in the delivery room, Mel groaned and bore down hard. Her face looked like an angry balloon, purple and swollen so alarmingly, I thought she might explode. "Help her," I said. "She needs some help."

"Hold on, Mrs. Reeves," the tall nurse said as she rolled a mirror on a stand into place between Mel's legs. "Hold on, don't push now, breathe. Don't push," she yelled, as though she were yelling to make herself heard in a high wind. Just then the doctor sailed in, pulling up his face mask as he came. I had a glimpse of bright, quick eyes between his cap and mask. He wore running shoes. "Where's the husband?" he asked over his shoulder, as he scrubbed his hands and wrists and forearms at the sink in the corner. I looked at Mel, took her hand. It was cool and clammy. "He couldn't stay," I said.

Mel groaned, and the groan spiraled into a scream. She bore down and squeezed my hand so hard I thought the bones would break. "It's killing me," she said.

"Hold on there, Mom," the doctor said as he flipped the sheet back from Mel's knees. "Whoa," he said, and there in the mirror I saw the top of the baby's head, wet and dark. "Mel, look!" I said. "Look in the mirror. Here's the baby's head. Look!"

She shook her head and squeezed my hand. "I can't help it," she said. "I'm sorry," and her face turned purple again. Then she began to push.

"Scissors," the doctor snapped. A nurse slapped them into his hand, and I looked away as he dove down between her legs. I heard a sickening, liquid crunch. He flung the scissors into a basin on a small steel table beside him and rolled up between her legs on his stool. In the mirror, I saw the blood start. Blood on the gauze pad that the nurse pressed to the cut, blood on the baby's head. Too much blood. "This is death, and they know it," I thought. "That's why they're so quiet; that's why the doctor is frowning."

"Now give me a big push," the doctor said. I felt Mel gather herself and bear down, and the doctor kicked the stool back and crouched like a quarterback between Mel's wide-open knees. "Atta girl," he said. "You're doing great, Melody. One more big push for me now, Mom. We're almost there." Mel did what he asked. "All right," he said. "There's the head." The doctor turned it gently and held it in his palm. He stroked the cheek of the baby's sleeping face. "You want to see now, Mel?" I brushed back the hair that had stuck to her eyelids and forehead. She shook her head, then she groaned and pushed, and with a sucking, liquid sound the baby slithered out, trailing the opalescent cord. The doctor held him, head down, and the nurses moved in with measuring tape and gauze. "All right, now, Mom," he said "You've got a big, handsome boy here."

Mel struggled onto her elbows. Resting in the doctor's hands, the baby had a stubborn, beaked look on his face. His fists were clenched around his head, as though to avoid a blow, and his hair was black and wavy, his wrinkled skin pale blue. Then his mouth stretched and gaped, he drew a deep, rattling breath and began to cry, and a pink flush spread over his body. There was outrage in the sound of his crying, and there was grief, too, as if something had been taken from him and he knew it. Mel lay back on the pillow with one arm flung across her eyes, listening. We all stood still for a moment and listened quietly, as though we were listening to some-one who spoke the truth so clearly it could not be denied.

"Good lungs," the doctor said. The baby opened his eyes then and the pain left his face. They were dark as the clear night sky, lustrous and calm.

"Give me my baby," Mel said as she lifted herself onto her elbows again. One of the nurses cut the cord and swabbed it. She wrapped him in a blanket and put a knit cap on his head, then placed the baby in Mel's arms. "Just for a minute," she said. "We have to do his Apgar scores again." While the doctor worked down between her legs, the tall nurse stood beside him, handing him gauze. They'd turned the mirror away now. Mel flipped the blanket back, uncurled each fist, held each wrinkled, red foot against her palm, and stroked the tiny toes. She examined the baby's penis and his swollen purple testicles. "My little boy," she said, "my son, my baby." He turned toward the sound of her voice, and his mouth opened.

"Are you nursing, Mrs. Reeves, are will he be going on a bottle?" the older nurse asked.

"No," Mel said. "No, I don't think so. We decided to go with the formula," and she looked around the room, as though she were expecting somebody to come and put his hand on her shoulder and say, "Yes, that's what we decided. He's going on a bottle so that you can go back to work, remember?" Then her shoulders collapsed. She held the baby close, rocking him. "I want my mother," she said.

"Now, now," said the older nurse. "Now, now. It's your hormones, honey, that's all. You need to keep still until the doctor's finished."

Mel's crying ended as quickly as it had begun. She kissed the baby on his head and rested her cheek on top of it. "Let's have him back now," one of the nurses said.

"Annie," Mel said, "would you call Canady and tell him it's a boy? Tell him he can come back now," she said, and her mouth made a small, bitter crimp.

"Let me hold the baby first."

They named the baby Jason. Jason Tull Reeves. Tull had been Mel's mother's maiden name, and she insisted. Canady fought her about the first name, though. He gave her hell. They fought about it right there in Mel's room. Mother said she'd never heard such carrying on. She'd come to the hospital to bring flowers, a basket of fruit, a furry lamb for the baby, and she said you could hear them shouting at each other clear down the hall. *"Jason?"* Mother heard Canady shout. "What kind of a trashy name is that?" Canady had decided that his son would be named Walter. Walter Canady Reeves III, after his own father and himself, Walter Canady II. But Mel stuck to her guns. Mother stood outside the door and heard Canady tell Mel how boys in his family were always named after their fathers, and *his* son would be no exception. She heard Mel tell him that *she* had a family, too. Tull was her family name and Jason was a new name, a fine name, a name she'd chosen. She said she wouldn't want him to grow up into a *Walter.*

That's when Mother stepped in and tried to help them reach a compromise. She suggested to Canady that Mel's hormones were making her act this way. (That, I told her, was her first mistake.) Then she suggested that they might name the baby Walter Jason or even Jason Walter Tull Reeves. Lots of children around here had four names, she said. That way, nobody got left out. And that's when Mel told my mother—my *mother*, who had treated her like a daughter, who had planned every detail of her wedding—to shut up. "Oh, just be quiet, Aunt Louise," Mother said that Mel snapped at her. "Whose side are you on, anyway?"

Mother went to the snack bar then, and when she came back, Canady was gone and the baby was named Jason. Jason, Mel said, because she wanted to name him something strong.

On a Friday night late in August, I woke up to Josephine's furious barking, as the headlights of a car swung across the bedroom ceiling and lit up the trunk of the shagbark hickory outside the bedroom window. A radio played, then footsteps crossed the porch, someone knocked, and I felt Legree wake up and lie there listening. Without speaking, we went to the front door together, and there was the silver Mercedes in the yard and on the porch was Melody, with Jason asleep on one shoulder. She had on a Carolina Gamecock sweatshirt, a pair of jeans so tight they looked pasted onto her, and the expensive, red Tony Lama boots that Canady had given her for

Christmas. She might have been on her way to a party, except that it was the middle of the night and the blanket she'd wrapped around Jason trailed on the floor. Diapers spilled out of every pocket of the diaper bag that hung from her shoulder.

When I snapped on the porchlight and opened the door, she looked scared for a second before she composed her face. "Surprise," she said, as the door swung open.

"Mel, come in, come inside," I said, and Legree reached out and slid the diaper bag off her shoulder.

She stepped inside the door. "Actually," she said, "I can't stay." She stooped to look in the mirror beside the door, and with her free hand she tucked a strand of hair back up into the knot of hair on top of her head. She talked as if we'd bumped into each other out at the mall, as if it weren't three o'clock in the morning and she'd just stopped by with the baby. "I'm going over to Columbia to visit Sarah and some of the other girls. I wonder if you'd mind keeping Jason over the weekend. Canady is just being *impossible*," she said, and she laughed and rolled her eyes to show, I think, that this was only a temporary impossibility in which she'd agreed to indulge him. To show that she had even this under control. Only her eyes gave her away. They darted around like something in a cage. And I noticed then how thin she was. She's always been thin, and she'd only gained twenty pounds while she was pregnant. Then, a few weeks after Jason was born, she started having trouble swallowing, and in two months she lost thirty pounds. Mother took her to every doctor in town. It's nothing physical, they said. Now she was more beautiful than ever. She laughed a lot about her new diet, and she was all eyes, the thinner her face got—all eyes and cheekbones.

"Sure, Mel," I said, and I lifted Jason off her shoulder and draped him over my own. He startled, then settled down again, and I felt his breath against my neck. "We'll take good care of him," I said. "You don't need to worry about that. But don't you want to stay over till morning? I won't tell anybody where you've gone." She looked at me gratefully and shook her head.

"That road's tricky at night," Legree said. "If you wait an hour or so, it'll be getting light. It'd be better to drive it in the daylight." She gave him a desperate look, as though she'd been ambushed by the kindness in his voice, then shook her head and looked at the floor. "I want to get going," she said. "I'll be all right. Really."

Before she left I tried to hold her, but she flinched and patted me nervously on the back, and laughed as if to say, "What are you doing that for? Do I look like I want to be held?" I let her go then, because sometimes, to love someone means to let them keep what they need to believe about themselves, since it is the only protection they have. All right, I said. Let her keep it.

Mother said that I was going to end up with that baby. She predicted that Melody was going to light out of here like a jackrabbit one of these days, and when she did, she wasn't going to be weighed down by any little baby. "She's going to leave that baby with you," Mother said. "Mark my words."

"I mark them," I said. I guess that would be fine with me. Because the truth is that I would take Jason in a minute. We had an understanding, Jason and I, the kind you reach with an infant by looking into his eyes long enough to almost get where he lives, which is a little like finding yourself in a deep, blue canyon filled with light, a place where anything is possible.

We set up Mel's portable crib beside the bed, and Legree and I took turns sitting up with him the rest of the night until the light turned pale gray and the birds began to stir in the hickory tree outside the bedroom window. He smelled sweet, like grain, and he wasn't fussy, but he wouldn't sleep either. He just lay there, running through his repertoire of expressions. Sometimes his mouth would reach and suck, or an expression of intense concentration would seize his face. He'd knit his fingers, fill his diaper. Sometimes he would yawn or smile dreamily. I offered my finger, and he grasped it and brought it toward his mouth. As I watched, I got the idea that I was watching his life taking shape. Before my eyes he was evolving, coming up like a prehistoric creature surfacing through layers of stone-dim water. Moment by moment he was getting stronger, practicing his moves. Suck and grimace, grasp and pull, smile.

•   •   •

The next morning early, Legree went back to Kiawah. Out in the driveway, we kissed for a long time, while Jason slept on my shoulder, and the sun came down through the hickories and touched my face. Back in the kitchen I ate a bowl of fruit while Jason sat in his baby seat on the table, fat and imperious as a small sultan, studying my face, entirely absorbed. I thought I saw how a woman could sink into life with a child, down and down until she came to the bottom where time moved thick and slow, where things ripened in their own time, where everything was one thing, and that was *life*, pure life. You held it in your arms close to your body, felt its compact wholeness, smelled its neck and hair, looked into its eyes.

It was midmorning when Canady came. Still in my bathrobe, I was crossing the hall when I heard footsteps on the porch. Then I saw Canady looking in through the window beside the door. Of course, I thought, as I walked toward the door with Jason draped over one shoulder, Canady would feel he had the right to come onto my porch and look through the windows. I thought of the cat in that Rudyard Kipling story, the one who went where he pleased, who belonged to no one: "I am the cat who walks by himself, and all places are alike to me." Only in Canady's case, it would have to be "all places are *open* to me."

"Did you knock?" I said as I opened the door. "I didn't hear you."

"Must be telepathy," he said. He winked and grinned, but he looked like a man who's been partying all night and stopped to clean up in a gas station restroom. His hair was damp and the collar of his blue oxford cloth shirt was wilted. He wasn't wearing socks with his deck shoes. The backseat of his Audi was piled with suitcases and clothes.

"Where are you off to?" I asked, and I held Jason closer.

"The wild blue yonder," he grinned, rocking back on his heels. "She left me the piece of shit car, but I think I can handle it." At the sound of his father's voice, Jason began to struggle to turn around, so I turned him to face Canady, and he smiled and cooed urgently. Canady reached over and jiggled one of Jason's fingers, and the baby held on. "Hey there, sport," he said, and though the

suave mask of his face didn't change or betray him, his eyes looked
sad. "I can't stay long," he said. "I've just come for my boy and I'm
gone."

"How did you know he was here?"

He shrugged. "She told me."

"Come in, then," I said. Of course, she'd told him. Had I
forgotten how it is to be married? Each marriage is like a foreign
country with its own economy and language and currency. Once
inside its borders, promises and secrets made in other countries get
converted into the coin of the realm, to be spent on necessities like
hurt and revenge. This would have been her heaviest coin, pure
gold. ("Well, I'm not leaving him here with you. I'll take him to
Annie's where someone will look after him.")

He followed us down the hall—me and Jason—because I hadn't
offered, and Canady hadn't asked, to hold his son. Listening to his
footsteps behind me, I held Jason tighter. What must it be like, I
thought, to feel your own child threatened, if I'm feeling this protec-
tive of my cousin's baby? And yet I had no claim to Jason, except
that Mel had left him with me, that Legree and I had spent the
night sitting beside him, watching.

At the kitchen door Canady stopped. He leaned against the
doorjamb with his hands in his pockets. He looked like a crow, a
raven; he looked like Matthew, like a wing, ready to fly. From his
shirt pocket he took out a pack of Lucky Strikes. He pulled one
cigarette free and tapped it on his thumbnail before he stuck it in
the corner of his mouth and lit it with the silver lighter Mel had
given him as a wedding present—all in one smooth motion. Canady
would never ask if he could smoke in your house, anymore than he
would think not to spy through your window. Wherever he was
belonged to him. He could do as he pleased there. "You know," he
said, blowing smoke toward the ceiling. "You are probably one of
the only ladies on earth who looks good in a goddamn bathrobe."
It was the voice that had whispered in my ear at the wedding reception, that slow, stroking touch of a voice.

"What about your wife?" I said quickly. "I'd think she looks
pretty good in a bathrobe."

He shrugged. "When she wants to," he said, with his sulky, pirate's look.

"I want you to smoke outside," I said.

"Right," he said, and he stepped to the sink. He dowsed the cigarette under the tap and threw it into the garbage.

"Come here, you little stinker," he said, and lifted Jason off of my shoulder In his father's arms, Jason became Canady's baby again, not mine. He even looked like Canady, same slope to the eyes, same pouting mouth. Canady handled him easily, held him and roughed his cheek against the baby's hair while Jason reached out with his fat hands and grabbed Canady's nose. "Honk!" Canady said, "honk, honk!" It had not occurred to me until then that Canady had played with his son, had felt tender toward him. To allow him that was to allow him a reality that made him dangerous again. "Well," he said. "She's not going to offer us coffee, so we're out of here, buddy." And he started back down the hall toward the front door, holding Jason on his shoulder.

"I promised Mel I'd keep him until she came back," I said as I followed. The baby watched me soberly.

Canady laughed. "Well, tell her that in the big, bad world, promises get broken sometimes. She'll understand that."

"Maybe she will," I said, "but I don't. Wouldn't it be easier to leave him here?" It was the wrong approach, I knew: an appeal to reasonableness. The only way to get Canady was to play on his vanity.

When we got to his car, Canady handed Jason back to me as he reached into his pocket for his keys. And when I looked at the inside of the car, I almost laughed out loud. "But Canady," I said, "where's the car seat?" His face looked blank. "You can't take a baby anywhere without a car seat, it's not safe. It's against the law. Besides, how would you drive? He can't really sit up very well by himself." Canady made a big show of leaning in the window, and looked around the car's interior, moved a few bags, as though he expected to find an answer hiding beneath one of them.

"Did you bring a sweater?" I said.

"Sweater?" He said the word as though he'd just learned it.

"It's cool in the mornings now," I said. "Babies need to be kept warm."

He held up one finger and tested the wind. "All right, OK," he said. "So I'll stop and buy him one, first place I pass that has a big sign outside that says *Baby Sweaters*, OK?"

"Where are you going, by the way?" I said.

"To Charlotte, for a seminar on golf course maintenance."

"Well, let me ask you this," I said. "Who's going to watch Jason while you're in class?"

He frowned and scratched at something on the roof of the car. I stepped closer. "Do you know what he eats? Did you bring any diapers or bottles?"

He laughed, threw his arms up over his head like a person being pelted with rocks, and then he slipped his arms over me and pulled me close, bent down, and nuzzled my neck roughly. Between us, Jason began to fuss and squirm. "Hey," he said into my hair, "where's your car parked today?" The sheer obviousness of it was astonishing. Since the day of his wedding when I'd behaved so shamefully, his son had been born, his wife had temporarily walked out on him, and Legree had moved in with me. And yet here he was, blind to everything except his own vanity, his own desire. Even time, it seemed, was measured only by how long it took him to get what he wanted. What he'd just done was pathetic, and pathetic, I thought, was one thing that Canady could never afford to be. I pushed myself away from him. He released me instantly and stood back with his arms spread. "Hey, no problem," he said. "I wouldn't have gone with you, anyway. Besides," he said, "you're a better mommy than I am. You keep him until she gets back. But don't say I didn't give you a chance."

"Canady," I said, "only a fool would take your chances, and I'm no fool. And neither is your wife, by the way."

"Ouch," he said, wincing in mock pain. But it was a joke, it was all for show. I saw what a long road Mel was looking down, if she stayed with him. He'd keep his looks long after he'd exhausted the few possibilities of his character. He would stay in shape and flirt and party and sleep around and excuse himself to Mel when he got caught, by saying that the woman he'd slept with had meant nothing to him. He might turn into a high-class drifter who ended up down at Hilton Head, playing golf and selling a little cocaine to rich people's kids, pulling off shady real estate deals. And he would never see the sadness in what he did; he would never stop long enough to let it catch up with him.

"See you, buddy," he said. He offered his finger, and Jason's hand closed around it. Then he shook his finger loose—Jason's grip was strong—got into the Audi, and scratched off down the driveway, fishtailing in the sand.

Jason and I sat on the front stoop for awhile, and I thought about how I couldn't blame Canady for coming to get Jason, for seeing the two of them on the road together, father and son, beyond the need for sweaters and caps and bottles and car seats, riding the edge of a dream. I know what it's like to love a dream, to love a destination and not think about the road that will carry you there. Because we dream of wholes, of pure, polished shapes, but we live by fractions and moments.

After we were dressed, I put Jason in the stroller and loaded a bag of fertilizer in the wire basket underneath his seat. I pushed the stroller up the hill and through the cemetery and down the other side of the hill to the orchard, where I parked the baby under the peach tree there. The winter wheat in the field at the foot of the hill had ripened now, yellow and dry. When the wind swept through it, it hissed and swayed. While I worked fertilizer around the roots of the apple trees and the one surviving peach, Jason watched the wind move the wheat. He followed with his eyes a flock of black birds that wheeled over the field. He made long, bubbling strings of sound and soaked the bib of his overalls with drool, as if he were giving everything he saw a new name.

The Laughing Place

Mel came back from Columbia, but when Canady left, he stayed gone for almost a month. After he finished his golf course seminar in Charlotte, he decided to drive over to Raleigh and visit an old fraternity brother who'd just gotten divorced. They went down to Ocean Drive together to have some fun the way they used to do in the old days. Sometimes I get very afraid for Mel. It seems that she and Canady and Jason are being slung around so fast that it's just a matter of time before the centrifugal force shakes somebody loose and smashes them against the edge. And, of course, I think, it would be Mel who got smashed. Or Jason. They are the most vulnerable because they have trusted, by choice or simply by being born.

As nice as that house is, as hard as Mel's worked on it, it looks like somebody's camping out over there now. The two-story Palladian window on the front of the house looks out onto patchy grass and eroded gullies and hay bales thrown into the gullies to keep the dirt from washing down into the lake. Furniture has been delivered and sits in the middle of rooms, still wrapped in plastic. The tables and chairs are covered with laundry that hasn't been folded, and toys and half-finished bottles of milk and juice. If an archaeologist were to come to Mel's house, he might date the beginning of the decline of this civilization from August 28, 1981, the earliest date on the postmarks of the unopened letters and bills piled on the dining room table.

Mel and Jason stay over at Mother's house most of the time now, and Mel goes to church with Mother two or three times a week. After Jason goes to bed, they read the Bible together. Early in September, Jason was consecrated to the Lord out at Victory Fellowship. It is only a matter of time, I think, before Mel finds Jesus and turns her life over to him.

"Come live with us," I said to Mel once, and I meant it, too. What a funny family we would make: Legree and Mel and Jason and me. Patched up and patched together for sure, but sewed with strong stitches.

"Oh, but it's such a long drive out there," Mel said. "I'd have to start in to work at six o'clock in the morning." But she's just being polite, saying "no" that way, when I believe it's Jesus she's really thinking about moving in with. The way Mel must see it, Jesus' promises are more potent than any promises a patched-together family could ever make, or hope to keep. When your life gets too heavy, Mother says, that's when you lay it down and He takes it up, and then it's no longer yours, so it feels lighter. He takes away your pain, He heals your wounds and failures, and bears you up lest you dash your foot against a stone. When Mother talks this way, Mel always looks surprised, then she cries, as if Mother had found the words to name Mel's deepest sorrows. This, it seems, is Mother's gift from the Holy Spirit: the gift of speaking plainly, directly, to people's hearts. She is in demand now in Full Gospel tabernacles all over the state. She has a way of repeating Jesus' words to people so that it seems they've been spoken by someone just like them. And I say, fine. Let Mel find Jesus, this husband-god who will cherish and protect her and lighten her load. Mel has dashed her foot long enough; she's stumbled across a whole desert of rocks.

Once in a while I go with Mother to her Tuesday night prayer circle, because she is my mother and I don't want her to be ashamed, and also, if I go, she stops calling me every week to tell me about a special program out at the church for widows or singles or career women that I mustn't miss. If I go with her now and then, she waits, in faith, for the Holy Spirit to pick me up and carry me to church, the way she's prayed and prayed it will come to pass. A group of women gather in one of the Christian Education classrooms at the church, a small room with folding chairs and crank-out windows, the walls covered with children's crayon drawings of Noah's Ark, or Pharaoh's green army drowning in a magenta sea, and Christ on the cross bleeding purple streams. Christ, in red and purple flames, rising from the dead. One woman is a Realtor, a black woman in a crisp linen suit. One is a schoolteacher, a white woman with a sweet, soft face. One is young; one is old and black, and her granddaughter comes with her. One is my mother. They draw the chairs into a circle and sing hymns. None of them can carry a tune, but they sing anyway, and sometimes if they wander completely away from the melody, if they falter and stop in the middle of a song, they look to Mother and she reminds them that the Lord doesn't give a hoot whether they can sing or not. "Don't you worry," Mother says. "The Lord knows our frames, He remembers that we are dust. And He knows our hearts, too, ladies," she says. "To Him they always sing right on key." And they finish out the song, and sometimes I sing, too, if the hymn is one I know, and Mother beams at me and trades excited, secretive looks with the others in the circle, as though my singing were a moment they'd all been waiting for.

Then one by one, as if they are falling asleep, they close their eyes, lift their hands, and a few begin to wave their arms slowly, as if they were drifting far out at sea in small boats, signaling the shore. Then the whispering begins, so quietly at first it might be the sound of the breeze ruffling the leaves on the sycamore tree outside the window, and then, out of this whispering, the name of Jesus begins to rise. "Praise you, Jesus," the schoolteacher whispers. "Thank you, Jesus," the Realtor answers. "Oh, praise you, Lord, thank you," the old, black woman says now, in a stern, clear voice. "Oh, Jesus," the granddaughter answers, lifting her hands, her voice fluttery, jiggling her legs as though she cannot sit still much longer. "Jesus, Jesus." Louder this time. Now, they are in pain; they are in love.

Meanwhile, Mavis, the schoolteacher with thick calves, a rosy, Irish face, and a pink, flowered scarf knotted around her neck, has begun to moan and whisper, a sound that makes the hair stand up on the back of my neck. And someone calls *Jesus*, sharply, and the language of tongues breaks out among them like spreading fire, a language without words, urgent syllables of desire.

Only Mother does not cry out. Not while I am there. She doesn't wave her arms or speak, though her lips move and her brow furrows with intensity. And then she sits up straight, braces her hands on her knees, raises her chin. As she sits, her face grows stiller than still, as though the flesh were settling on the bones. And with her knees spread, the Bible resting on them, her face going from deep to deeper sadness, she eddies down, down. Then her face is as still and stern and smooth as a rock headland over whose surface has passed the slow tide of wind and time and lives—carving, shaping, stripping, exposing the sadness beneath the expressions that she turns to the world. She looks as stern as a judge hearing a case, and I see in that face with what will and what grief she has claimed her life. And I know that this is the face I have seen in my dreams, the face of the mother who comes to me in a black dress with her hands hidden in the folds, who will not touch me but stands over me, looking down. And I know there are tears for this, down where I have never touched them. I feel grief rising in me, like a prayer that must be spoken and cannot be spoken in any language that I know.

When the fire of tongues has burned down, they pray in a silence that seems to be laid layer upon layer in the room. So I close my eyes, and there is silence there, too, with something moving under it, like wind moving underwater, the way the river used to sound from the back steps of the Laughing Place. And suddenly I have such a clear sense of where I am, it frightens me. I am in a chair, in a room, in a town, a country, on a planet seen from far out in space; a very small thing in the middle of that room in the middle of the earth that is so round and covered with oceans and night and stars. I think that I would call any name, believe anything in order not to feel so alone and so small, lost in this silence like a swimmer far from shore.

And then, inside the silence, the faces of the people I love come back to me. Once, it was Matthew's face. The sad Matthew, the beautiful Matthew of the end of his life, when he was beginning to believe his life, our life together, had failed him somehow. He would shake me awake at four in the morning. "I have to talk with you," he'd say.

"Go put on the coffee and I'll get up," I'd answer, buying myself a few more minutes of sleep. As we sat at the kitchen table together, I'd take his hands. What was it? What was wrong? What? Together, I knew, we would find his trouble and heal it. I would reach into him somehow, find the person I saw there, and coax him out. I'd talk and talk, and he'd touch my hair, smile, as if I were a sad abstraction, a shadow. We were so proud of our suffering then. And I felt that I must speak to him; words I never spoke to him while he was alive. I said 'it was innocence, Matthew, the oldest, deadliest pride, in which we tried to live, in which you died, and left me to grope my way toward the light. Because while we lived in the infancy of our pride, I lived blind. And Matthew, my love for you reaches this far into the darkness where you have gone: I believe you would have grown into the kind of man who could choose the difficult, the fallen, the rooted thing, and there I must leave you, with what you might have become but did not while I knew you, while you lived.'

Another time, it was Legree's face that I saw, rutted as an old road. He stood on a little patch of beach sand as if he'd been standing there forever, and he held an egg in his hand. Inside the egg, something stirred, shifted, a dark spot pressed out against the shell. And once, I saw my father in exile, out beside the Keowee, the smoking heaps of trees behind him, with his fists shoved into his pockets, his anger like iron, and Thelma waiting. And it is the faces and the voices and the lives of those I love that come to me in their sorrow and in their beauty. It is those faces that I remember and cling to at the bottom of this place called prayer. Mother and her grave faith; Legree; the truth of Matthew's life; and Papa, the sad, hard ring to his voice at the end of his life that hammered the joy out of everything. I gather it all, let it come over me, and I bless the dangers and failures and the sadness. I give thanks for their mortal faces and for their fragile lives.

Last week, after prayer service, Mother and I went to Wendy's for a Frostie. Out on the Stamp Creek Road, just after we left the church, we passed a dog, somebody's hound, lying dead across the centerline of the highway. "That's the fifth dead dog I've seen this week, driving out here," Mother said.

I gritted my teeth, nodded. Like all our conversations, this one had only one destination. "Really?" I said. Her books tell her that an increase in the number of dead animals on the road is a sign that the end of the world is near. Almost everything that happens now is a sign. The number of male children born last year who will grow, in twenty years, to fill the world's armies. Unrest in the Middle East. Changes in the world banking system. The steady advance of a credit-card economy. The skyrocketing crime rate. The breakdown of the family. All signs that the world is hurtling toward its end.

Christians have to be prepared, Mother said that night. The Realtor's husband, for instance, was going to open a guard dog training school with a Christian emphasis. "A lot of people's houses out at the lake are being burglarized lately," she said. "They think it's professionals out of Columbia, judging by what they steal. When things get really bad, you'll see more and more of this sort of thing. People are going to need guard dogs," she said ominously, nodding to herself.

By the time we passed Pineshadows Mall and turned onto the bypass, I couldn't help myself. "Tell me, Mother," I said, "do these guard dogs have to accept Jesus Christ as their Lord and Savior?"

She reached all the way across the front seat and slapped my arm, slapped it hard, too, a blow that made me want to hit back at her. "We're not morons, you know," she said. "The *business* is run according to Christian principles. 'Unless the Lord builds the house, the laborers labor in vain.' "

I could not resist. "Unless the Lord holds the leash," I said and I smiled at her, but she looked so hurt I felt ashamed. "Sorry," I said, "that was a mean thing to say."

"Yes, it was," she said, sniffing. "But it's not me you need to apologize to." And we continued on our way toward town in bleak and dispiriting silence. To cheer myself up, I imagined Jesus walking a pair of attack-trained Dobermans on short, thick, leather leashes. Hideous, liver-colored dogs with blond, pointed eyebrows. Jesus and his Dobermans patroling the back alleys, up against the murderers and thieves and junkies of this world. But when the showdown comes, Jesus can't bring himself to unsnap the leash and give the attack command; He is stymied by his own commandment: Love one another.

At Wendy's, we sat at our usual table near the front window that looks out onto the bypass and the Holiday Inn across the road. Mother trailed her finger along the plastic-bead curtain there and sighed. In all of our mutual life, Mother's and mine, I had never felt so bewildered, so far from her.

"Do you know who I prayed for tonight?" she said, sadly, watching the cars travel along the bypass outside the window.

I felt myself tense, I braced myself. I knew whom she *usually* prays for. "Who, Mother?" I said around my straw.

Big sigh. "The Lord just put it in my heart to pray for Thelma Radford," she said. "I saw her the other day out at the mall. She looks like such a lonely person."

Something landed in my stomach then in a cold, sickening way, as if the Frostie had settled there in a lump, and I said, "Mother, you don't have to tell me that. You don't even have to pray for her, as far as I'm concerned." And I thought of Thelma, gliding through town in her butter-colored Cadillac with the magnetic sign on the driver's door. RADFORD PROPERTIES, LTD. Thelma is a real estate broker now, in cahoots with Canady. She sells the big houses out at Planter's Landing, the ones in the upper 300s. And glides into the parking lot at the *Courier-Tribune* every Monday morning, bringing her ads for the Wednesday paper. Her perfume comes through the door before her, and everytime I smell it, anger spurts up in me like a jet of something thick and black shooting up from my heart. Leaning on the front counter, she toodles her fingers at me and I nod, go on typing, while she hands over her ads to the classifieds person. Sometimes, as she turns to go, she winks at me, as though

we're conspirators. Sometimes I wink back, just to keep her guess-
ing. "Enter the great room and bask in the light from the majestic
Palladian window offering a sweeping vista of Lake Charles B.
Hartley, Jr.," one of her ads reads. She composes them herself,
she tells the whole office, proudly. Thelma loves adjectives and
vistas and majesty. That, it occurs to me, is what they had in
common, Thelma and my father.

"Well, that's the difference between you and me," Mother said,
as she stirred her Frostie and frowned down into the cup. "As far
as I'm concerned, I do have to pray for her."

I closed my mouth then, and I kept it closed about Thelma.
Once Mother set out to keep the commandments, she had to keep
them all. You have to admire her for that, for her loyalty and her
seriousness. Once she's found the plan, she has to work it all the
way. I saw a note on her refrigerator recently, written on a page
from one of those "Things to Do Today" tablets and held up by a
Holy Spirit magnet: "Pray without ceasing," it says, in Mother's
handwriting. To me, that note sums up a lot of what can be said
about Mother's faith, the practicality of it, the thoroughness. Of
course she has to pray for Thelma.

But then she started in about Jesus again, and I tried to stay
calm and open-minded and reasonable. When she paused and looked
at me meaningfully, I told her that I liked Jesus just fine. "It's not
Jesus I have the problem with," I said. What problem could you
have with someone who showed us that life shelters within every
death? Who showed us that the divine, the possible, is smuggled
into this world through the small, the dying, the broken? Who bid
us be still, and love one another? As I talked, she chewed her
bottom lip and leaned forward eagerly, her eyes skeptical but daring
to hope for a miracle.

"Honey," she said, "Brother Grice is giving a three-part series
of sermons about just that theme, 'Jesus' Greatest Teachings.' You've
missed the first one, but the next two should be just as good."

At the bottom of my cup, the Frostie looked like chocolate
mud. "But, Mother," I said, cautious now, picking my way from
word to word, "Brother Grice is part of the problem, not the answer,

don't you see?" She sat back, exasperated, the color climbing up her neck. And then, as usual, as always, I went on, I said too much. But every time I think about Brother Grice and his smiling face, his silver helmet of hair and his expensive three-piece suits, his Holy Spirit watch-fob and the love he so tenderly nurtures for the sound of his own voice, the way he seems to swell when he talks, his face staring out from every page of the church newsletter, I know there is nothing he can tell me about God or how to love the world. "My God, Mother!" I said, "When he talks about 'the Lord,' I suspect that he means *himself.*"

But I'd lost her again; she stared out the window, humming to herself, waiting for me to finish. Brother Grice probably teaches them how to tune out the unbelievers, to save their strength for the final battle. What about the 20 percent tithe he exorts them to give, and give freely, in order that God may bless them? I asked. "What's he doing with all that money?"

"Oh, he has plans," she said, mysteriously. "Big plans." Building that cathedral, for starters. In the architect's drawing posted on the wall outside the Christian Education classroom, it looks like an ordinary church that got dangerously overinflated. A cathedral? Did she say they were going to call it a *cathedral?* The cathedrals led your eyes and lifted your soul up to God. They didn't stand over you and boast about how rich and powerful they were. "Mother," I said, "if you give him all your money, what will you live on?"

She smiled at me bleakly. "The Lord fills up what we empty for him. It's a spiritual principle," she said. "You wouldn't understand that."

"Brother Grice explains that, too, I'll bet," I said. He preaches obedience, submission to spiritual authority—his—as the way to grace and abundance. He exhorts wives to submit to their husbands, husbands to submit to the word of God, as revealed through Brother Grice.

"Think what you like," she said, and we both slumped back in our chairs, miserable again, giving up on each other. Looking back on that night, I see that my mistake, of course, was to tell her these things. I should learn from Legree to choose my battles and let the others slide, but I couldn't do that. I told her exactly how I felt about Brother Grice and I went on from there. "Mother," I said, "you're a smart person. Don't you ever feel uncomfortable being force-fed this stuff and handing over your money to that holier-than-thou Phil Donahue?"

"Now, what's wrong with Phil Donahue?" she said, rolling her eyes.

"Nothing," I said. "But he sure doesn't hold the keys to any kingdom I want to live in."

And then we'd gone too far to stop; we were over the edge. "You don't know what you're talking about," she said, raising her voice, finding the current of outrage, going with it. "You're the only holier-than-thou person *I* know. The Enemy must be very pleased with you."

"The Enemy," I said. *"The Enemy?"* Our voices spiraled louder and louder, above the Muzak, and one by one, conversations at the other tables died out and I heard myself shouting again, like one of those monsters of righteousness I have accused and accused her of handing her life over to. Shouting and adding my own righteous noise to the torrent that already roars so loudly through the world you can't hear yourself think any longer.

The manager came out from behind the counter then and walked toward our table, wiping his hands nervously on a towel. "Honestly," Mother got in the last word, a hissing whisper, "you just *have* to take everything to its most absurd extreme, don't you? Just like your father."

"Everything all right here, ladies?" the manager asked, warily polite. A nervous-looking black man with a thin, stiff mustache, speaking to two bickering white women, one of them my mother.

"We're fine," I said. "Sorry for the disturbance." Mother rummaged in her purse for a handkerchief, balled it up, pressed it to her upper lip, her forehead, like someone with a fever. And there we were. Again. We looked out the window and drank the last of our Frosties while the Muzak played and the manager went back behind the counter, watching us as he shook the basket of potatoes in the deep-fat fryer, and the Enemy, the father of lies, the prince of the power of the air, circled the room above our heads, laughing.

As Mother drove me home I asked myself Is this what God wants? Does he want us shouting at each other at Wendy's? Does he want us hurt, distant, alienated from one another? Who is this God who sorts and excludes?

"Want to come in?" I asked when we got to my house.

Legree's truck was parked in the driveway, and she frowned at it. "No, thank you." (From this, I am to understand that she will not forgive me anytime soon.) She braced her arms against the steering wheel and stared straight ahead. "I don't want to be out too late by myself on that long stretch of road."

"I'll follow you back home, Mother, if you want me to."

"Oh, no, don't bother, I'll be fine."

"Well, call when you get there," I said.

"If I remember."

"Fine." I slammed the door; she scratched off. Amen and amen. I watched until the taillights disappeared down the Bean Blossom Road, then I went inside, to the bedroom where Legree sat propped up in bed, a bunch of papers spread around him. I sat down on the edge of the bed, with my arms folded. "Let's move," I said.

"Where?" he said, still reading.

"Someplace where we don't know anybody."

He looked up. "Well, we wouldn't be able to stay there long, you know. We'd have to keep moving before we got to know anyone."

"Maybe we'd get lucky and the world would end before we made any friends." I fingered the quilt that his mother made for us, followed out the pattern that grows more complex as one square connects to another. "Do you think the world is going to end soon?" I asked.

"Is that what your mother had to say tonight?"

"Among other things."

He moved the papers out of the way, gathered me in. "Well if it does, let's go together," he said and he rubbed his cheek, which was warm and scratchy, against mine.

"Let's," I said. I got up and undressed right there and left my clothes in a pile on the floor next to the bed and crawled in next to him. He held me, I held him, and slowly, slowly, as I touched him and felt his skin against mine, felt his heart beating against my chest, the slopes and hollows, the bones and flesh of his body, I started to feel grateful again, the way I'd felt when I'd prayed with Mother and her prayer circle. I began to feel as though I belonged here among my own kind, anchored to earth and to each other, body and soul.

Just this morning I got up at dawn. A dream woke me and I found myself fitted against Legree, my knees folded into the crook of his knees, my breasts against his warm back, my arm flung over his waist. But even awake, feeling his body, I couldn't forget the dream. So I kissed his shoulder, and I got up and pulled on my clothes in the thin light that sieved through the window. It would be hot today, I thought. Already the air felt thick and cloudy, and there was a pearly cast to the light. My clothes were damp and they clung, and while I pulled on my jeans and buttoned my shirt, I felt uneasy, as though someone were watching me. Then I remembered the dream. A giant, baleful eye staring back at me wherever I turned. An eye like the eye in an Egyptian hieroglyphic. Like the eye on the bumpersticker on Mother's car, the one that floats above the words "IN THE TWINKLING OF AN EYE!" In the dream this eye looked up at me from the flesh of a pear I'd sliced open in the dream. It appeared on the back of a dream door I'd closed and locked. It was alive and it moved, as though it were watching something. Its color was arctic blue. In the dream, I was running, but there was no place to go.

I stepped out onto the back porch into the gray light and shook myself. On a late summer morning this house rides like a tall ship on an ocean of noise. Leaf noise and bird noise, the deep, plucked-string noise of bullfrogs, the wax and wane of cicadas, the chant of the whippoorwill, and now and then, the far-off booming of a great horned owl. I picked up one of Legree's walking sticks, stepped off the porch, and started up the path that leads to the cemetery and down to the peach tree and the field. The dogs crawled out from under the back porch and started after me. I felt Napoleon's cold nose touch my hand, Josephine brushed by me, and then Napoleon bumbled ahead of me up the path, like an old chair trying to run on rickety legs.

Mother says that the bumper sticker is about the end of the world, the Second Coming and the Rapture, and how it will happen for believers. In the twinkling of an eye, she says, Jesus will call the elect off of this ruined, rotten earth to join Him before the final and terrible battle of Armageddon begins. And when the summons comes, the believers will be snatched away from whatever terrible or mundane trouble they find themselves in. About to be murdered or stuck in traffic, they will simply disappear. They will be spared the sight of the wicked being purged from the earth, the horror of that final battle in which good and evil will be revealed to the skeptics, the unbelievers, in its cruel and final simplicity, and no one on earth will be spared. And then, when it's quiet again, and the world has been cleansed of evil and error, the believers will return, clean and whole, untouched and unbroken, to reign with Jesus for a thousand years of peace.

How can you live without assurances? Mother's voice follows me through the pines and past the headstones in the cemetery on top of the hill. *How can you live with them?* my own voice answers, as I walk through the pines and past the old graves. And then the peach tree is there, a dark, full shape against the spreading light. The other peach trees died, but this one survived and it is developing a spread now, a shapely squatness—low to the ground and full—that in a peach tree is a sign of health. When the sun hits it at just the right angle, the trunk looks glazed with silver.

Napoleon and Josephine have reached the field that lies beyond the slope. Napoleon runs in a crazy zigzag with his nose to the ground and his tongue hanging out, while Jo works more methodically, back and forth, back and forth. The hay in the field has been cut and baled, and mist rises from the ground. The air above the field is alive with birds. Red-winged blackbirds. They cling to the standing stalks and flash the red bars on their wings, sending their liquid notes across the field. It is still and gray, and over to the east there is a thinning, a loosening of the dark, and the moon hangs on in the sky, beautiful and cold as a fine, curved blade. Then a pale blue begins to the east, like a light shining up from below the horizon. It spreads over the field, and with it comes a breeze that also moves across the field and into the orchard, roughing up the leaves of the peach tree.

As I stand there watching, it comes to me that if the world were to disappear in the twinkling of an eye, this is the place I would want to be when it happened. And I start to number what I would want to see and touch and taste and hear in those last moments. The light coming low, spreading over the field like a river. The smell of water in the air. The errors of Legree's face, softened with pleasure. The silver shine in the trunk of the peach tree, and the tiny, sweet peaches rounding in their own time within the leaves. Those last sights would be enough to send me singing out of this world. Though I would not want to leave such a world, not for any paradise. I would not even want this place perfected and restored to the beauty of anyone's dreams. I would not ask for Papa returned, or Matthew risen, whole and clean and healed. I do not want to live in paradise, this world is enough, so broken and so full of promise.